WAKE US TOMORROW

By the same author

Cross Cut

ISBN 978-0-9557928-0-9

Out of Time

ISBN 978-0-9557928-1-6

WAKE US TOMORROW

Lee Ellis

Time Link

First published 2011 by Time Link Publications
12 Warneford Gardens, Exmouth. EX8 4EN
timelink@btinternet.com

ISBN 978-0-9557928-3-0

A CIP catalogue record for this book is available from the British Library.

Cover design based on an original painting by Carole Ellis

Prepared and printed by:
York Publishing Services Ltd
64 Hallfield Road
Layerthorpe
York YO31 7ZQ

Tel: 01904 431213

Website: www.yps-publishing.co.uk

Author's Note

The Great Revolt is a seminal landmark in the English people's struggle for representation and justice. The events in Hertfordshire during June and July 1381 form the historical background to 'Wake us Tomorrow.' For this I have drawn on the Historia Anglicana by Thomas Walsingham. As a contemporary monk of St.Albans Abbey he may have been an eye witness to many of those events though his account is distinctly partisan. Otherwise, 'Wake Us Tomorrow' is a work of fiction. Any similarity to real persons, living or dead is entirely coincidental except for the historical 14th century figures ie. William Grindcobb, William Cadindon, Robert Tresilian, William at Lee, John Ball.

"Wake up the dead, for the living sleep"

Giacomo Leopardi

1

'IT seems the controversy over the Smithfield Memorial won't die down. Just when it was finally agreed, after a long and bitter struggle to erect a permanent commemoration to the Peasants' Revolt, stories are emerging of baffling incidents at the site. At nearby Barts Hospital a young nurse now admits that for some time she had been seeing a ghostly figure in medieval dress. When pressed neither she nor a psychic associate would deny that on the exact anniversary of the famous confrontation they actually witnessed the climactic events in 1381 'as if they were actually there. '

Warren shoves the crumpled newspaper cutting from nearly a year ago back into his pocket. The fascination never wanes even after reading it for probably the hundredth time, but his wife will be angry if she sees it.

"I've seen him again," he says as he comes in.

Kathleen says nothing at first. What can she say? She's heard this for weeks now. He sits in his chair, staring through the window at what little light remains.

"You work too hard," she says, "All this studying the past, it's..."

"I've always studied the past."

"Not like you have these past weeks, working on that book even after you've sent a copy to the screenwriter working on that film."

"Yes, but it's only the first draft. It might need a little tweaking…"

"Then let it wait for her to comment. Spend some time on other things. You'll see, these…things…they'll pass."

He gets up and shrugs.

"Yes, you're right. It's become too easy to imagine what isn't there. A good night's sleep, a day on other things, by this time tomorrow I'll feel quite different."

But the next evening is the same. As Kathleen advised, he spends the day doing other things. It's hard, but he perseveres. The problem is that while you can *do* other things, it's more difficult to *think* other things. His mind keeps drifting. Best not to think of them. It works for a time, but all day they come back. *Doing* other things seems to be making him *think* even more!

He goes out for his customary walk about the usual time. It's a warm, clear evening and there are plenty of people on the common, walking dogs or simply strolling. He feels more settled than he has for days and with increasing relaxation soon forgets his promise to Kathleen. Trying not to think during the day has put him under intense stress and now he feels relieved. She's right to worry, but it's not necessary. Despite finding it difficult, the 'day off' has done him good. He goes over the latest work, not just the book, but also the campaign. It relaxes him even more and he quickens his pace, walking faster and further from the town.

That's how he's been spending his time – studying for his book and opposing the Waintree Development, delving and campaigning, two aspects of struggle, one in the past and one in the present. He sees them as two sides of the same activity, though in that he's alone. The goodly opponents of the desecration of the country – as they see it – have nothing in common with those that rummage through the relics of the past. Only he has a foot in such dissimilar camps. Those that burrow through 14th century conflicts studiously avoid far lesser ones in the 21st. Conveniently sanitised by time, it's easier to face the stark struggles of the past than wrestle with those of the present.

The actions of long ago have no relevance today. Seen through the prism of the present, long dead events become unreal, no more alive than last summer's leaves. At first he put down what he sees as just imagination. Working so intensely on the book those events would still be vivid in his mind hours afterwards. Studying local history has led him many times to challenge explanations, interpretations, wondering what is real, what is unreal? But what if it's not just a mere memory of what he's just been studying? What if what he sees is *too* real? Deep down, despite what he said to Kathleen, he's come to realise it's got nothing to do with his studies.

For years Warren has struggled with the moving boundaries between what's real and what's not real. Six hundred years is a long time. What's dead is done. Nothing new can be learnt from there. But that means ignoring the land, the real connection. Have the people of this county really lost touch with their own past? But then they've not seen what Warren has seen, what he sees now as he stares down into the town

Many people, walking, running, shouting. By their clothes he knows they are the people who broke down the enclosures surrounding the abbot's woods. Then only one man, running very fast, occasionally stopping to look at Warren as if to speak. Then he's gone.

Though they've never met, Warren has known this man all his adult life. He's always spoken to him even though he's been dead for six hundred years. For Warren knows the man he sees is the leader of the revolt in St. Albans in 1381, William Grindcobb. And now he's sure. It's not just that he's studied so much and therefore knows and understands. He not only sees him, but feels him. Feels as he feels, not just in his head, but in his whole being. It's as if he *is* Grindcobb.

It's been the same for months, ever since the traumatic events a year ago. Gradually her strength returned, but she had to stop working for a time. Only recently has she felt confident to take on a few cases. Not working hasn't stopped potential clients pestering her for help. At one stage she disconnected the phone. It was the only way to get the peace she so desperately needs.

Reaching her early fifties, when it's not unusual to question just about everything previously taken for granted, the months of near exhaustion have taken their toll. Ettie Rodway should be hardened by now. Exploiting those rare gifts she's had from youth, hers has never been an easy path, but what happened in London was different from anything she'd known before. Now she has to live with the fallout. After returning home she felt every life force had been drained and she slept at least fourteen hours a day, often more. Even in the weeks that followed she had little energy. It was like running a car with a perpetually failing battery. Charge it up every night to find it still only running an hour or so the next day before conking out again. That phase slowly passed until sleep was normalised and she could concentrate for more than short periods though they were still interrupted by sudden, uncontrollable flashes from the past, her past, *the* past, but at least from then she could manage visitors.

She's up in London to meet her young friend Vicky. They've been seeing each other fairly regularly for the last year. It's been a month since their last meeting and over several glasses of wine they exchange essential updating, a necessary part of the rehabilitative process. Vicky comments on the positive aspects of Ettie's recovery.

"You're not so tired, though I suppose..."

"I keep getting flashbacks."

"So do I."

"It will...recede."

"Not go away?" Vicky says apprehensively.

"I doubt if it will ever go away, at least not completely. What we've seen and heard, no, it's not possible."

"Sometimes it's as if it never happened...what we...you know. All those people we met. It's like a dream, though I sometimes wonder what became of them."

"So do I."

"It is over, isn't it?"

Ettie opens her palms and grimaces slightly.

"Nothing ever repeats itself exactly."

4

Vicky isn't reassured.

"But it is *resolved*, those things are settled? It's not about how things *might* have been, only how they were, isn't that right?"

Ettie hesitates. Vicky carries on.

"We passed through, that's what you said, Ettie. We *passed through*, that's right isn't it?"

"Yes, we passed through," Ettie says, remembering.

A sudden strange yearning for land and sky and open space persists in her mind. Vicky seems reassured now.

"What about yourself?" she says, "Have you started working again?"

"Not much. I've agreed to a few consultations, but mostly I've been avoiding people. Linking with the past is my work, I can't just switch it off...it stays..."

"Has Chris Pleasant approached you?"

"I'm calling in at the film studio later today on my way home."

"When he came to see me last year I was so afraid, but he only wanted to talk about his film. It was all very innocent, but I was so wound up."

"You were at the height of the crisis. It was understandable."

"I misunderstood his motives. He needed our help. With all the publicity, it was only to be expected, but once I calmed down it was good to talk. He treated me like an expert!"

Vicky laughs. She must be recovering well. Only a few weeks before she wouldn't have been able to laugh.

"You didn't find it upsetting?" Ettie says.

"A little at first, but then it was good to get it out."

"You didn't tell him everything...not about...the others?" Ettie says anxiously.

"No, no...only filling in what was in the newspapers."

Ettie sighs with relief.

"You'll have to remember to do the same," Vicky says.

"Yes, I know. How did he take it...I mean what does he think *really* happened?"

Vicky laughs.

"I think he's swallowed the haunted hospital story."

5

"He didn't want to know more?"

"It's the detail he's into, clothes and houses, all for his film I suppose. There was so much coverage, I'm surprised you've not been contacted by other people."

"Oh I have, but I've managed to keep them at bay. One man has left several messages. Somebody called Warren Grover."

Warren's walk on the common, like his day of 'rest' has neither calmed nor stopped him thinking. He's almost home. He's seen the people again, though not the man, but Warren knows he's still here. For tonight he looked at the people through *his* eyes, saw them as *he* saw them and saw something new, even more alarming. These visions are getting more frequent and it frightens him, this unnerving sense of possession within someone else, of being someone else. *It's all leading to some unknown crisis.*

The thought, once voiced within cannot be dismissed and reverberates all the way to his front door. A crisis for *him*, for Grindcobb and if it's for Grindcobb then it must also be for Warren. Something will happen...to Grindcobb...soon. The expectation, the apprehension, the fear, the unwavering path that must be taken...he feels as *he* feels and can't escape as *he* can't escape. Yet Warren also knows as Grindcobb cannot know for Grindcobb's present is Warren's past and he has studied it so well. He knows and it frightens him. So he feels as Grindocbb feels, but also as he feels himself.

He perused the reports of last year's strange happenings with more than the usual interest of most readers. Ordinarily the unexplained wraithlike sightings wouldn't have got in the national papers, let alone captured the headlines. Nor even that it was close to the site of the great revolt 600 years earlier in Smithfield, but it coincided with puzzling incidents surrounding a major campaign for a permanent memorial to those times. The result was a few weeks of sensationalism and a lot of chatter and hype. Then the press and public moved on, but not Warren. With it all happening on the exact anniversary, 15th June, of 1381 he reached his own conclusions on its real significance. Could the two women's baffling experiences last year be connected to his own disturbances now? Had they unwittingly *released* what he now sees, hears and feels? One of them is reputed to have psychic skills and he's tried to contact her, so far without success. He stops at the gate, hesitating, almost afraid to take his desperate thoughts into the house. He needs help, an explanation, guidance. He must ring Ettie Rodway again. First thing in the morning before she goes out or switches on the ansafone.

"Feeling better?" Kathleen says as he goes in.

He grunts and shrugs as he takes off his shoes. She picks them up.

"All this mud. How did they get so dirty?"

"I strayed off the path."

"Wandering around again, what were you looking for this time?"

He grimaces silently, goes into the lounge and slumps into a chair. She follows.

"Well? What have you been looking for?"

He turns slowly and answers quietly, but determinedly.

"More what's been looking for me."

She sighs and sits in the opposite chair.

"The people, you've seen the people?"

"Yes."

"And the man, you've seen the man again?"

"Sort of."

"Warren you're still working too hard. This has to stop. You've got to ease up. If you carry on like this you'll be in 1381 yourself!"

He shudders. If only she realises how apposite are her words. Dare he tell her more, that he no longer sees, but *feels* Grindcobb? Staggering enough, but what of that newer, startling vision he saw tonight? How would he begin to tell of the gibbet and the line of hanging men?

Ettie and Vicky agreed boundaries around what they'd seen and heard. To say more might lead to misunderstandings, so to most enquiries they kept their accounts fairly vague. That way, the press soon wearied and even if they suspected they weren't getting the full story, soon moved on to other, more current, potentially juicier items. Chris Pleasant was the exception. His interest was more worthwhile, so they opened up with more detail. And detail was what he wanted. How did the people speak, what did they eat, how were they dressed, what did it really sound and smell like, just how many people were really in the city? And many more questions no books or research could ever really answer. The sort of questions that can only be answered by people who have been there!

Anxious to lap up anything for his historical drama Chris was very patient and talking about his film project was almost rehabilitative to Vicky. Gradually recounting those strange, amazing days in a 'safe' environment, her earlier fears seemed unfounded, though she didn't tell everything. The main events had already attracted a lot of media interest, but he took her additional material at face value, never once doubting its authenticity, just as she never doubted his sincerity in making the film.

Now it's Ettie's turn. Chris has been anxious to seek her help and is very pleased when she agrees to meet him. He quickly comes to the film studio entrance. She's a little nervous, but he soon puts her at ease and explains his 'project' of bringing the 'Great Revolt' to the screen.

"It's been a long held ambition, something I've wanted to do for years, ever since I was young. A story that's long been waiting to be told. I only hope I'm doing it justice. It's one of those slices of history that come up regularly in movie people's conversations only to be quickly forgotten. Everybody recognises the potential of the subject, sighs reverently and then moves on to something else. The sheer immensity of such a venture frightens them off. The subject's spectacular, but also too big, too daunting, even frightening."

"And you're going to change all that?"

"Of course," he says with a wide grin, spreading out his hands in purposeful confidence, "We're in the final stages, but I wanted to get your impressions before we stopped shooting. *Hurling Time* will be the ultimate medieval epic!"

He chatters effusively in a mixture of bold statements, verbal flourishes, rhetorical questions interlaced with real ones, giving her the opportunity to respond. It's an exhilarating potion and talking through her experiences proves as cathartic as it was with Vicky. For while Vicky's fragility requires more obvious attention, Ettie's debility is no less serious. Reliving those explosive days, albeit in a truncated, slightly sanitised form, she finds oddly energising, as if a stiff walk leaves her with more energy than when she set out. Perhaps like Vicky she needs to get it all out to kick-start the recovery process. Chris scribbles away feverishly.

"This is fantastic stuff for my writers, incredible, absolutely incredible."

The graphic detail fascinates him and with his film maker's eye for colour and composition, she struggles to recall everything he wants to know. Just what were the designs of the shop banners on London Bridge? The royal barge on the river, how many oarsmen were there? How many storeys did the Savoy Palace have?

Then his questions become less frequent, as if he's learnt enough or it might be because Ettie deflects his questions about how they gained their knowledge. Trade secrets you might say or just a gut feeling to be wary of paddling in dangerous waters.

"Odd title, *time link consultant*," he says, "but I suppose very apt in the context of what happened to you both?"

"It means helping people to make contacts over time."

"In this case over a very long time?"

She doesn't encourage this line of conversation and he has to accept it.

"If it's alright I'd like to talk to you again," he says as he escorts her back to the entrance.

"Yes, if you think it will help," she says, hoping he won't make contact too soon.

"Having said that," he says, almost reading her thoughts, "I've got enough to start shooting immediately."

She gets home late and is very tired. A few weeks of comparative inactivity will be welcome, but it's not to be. She's interrupted the following morning by a telephone call. He says he's completing research on a book and would value Ettie's expertise. She explains she's no historian, but he knows that. The bare *facts* of history he can handle himself, it's the feel for the period he needs.

"I've read about the London events. Your...experiences... put you in a unique position to assist me."

She's reluctant.

"Well, Mr..."

"Grover, Warren Grover."

She really doesn't want to see him at all, but he gets so agitated when she tries to put him off, eventually conceding, "Monday really is the earliest I can manage, it's only a few days."

"I can't wait until Monday. I need to see you now."

"I'm sure a few days won't make that much difference. If I..."

"By then it could be too late...the events in London, I'm sure it's not all true, but..."

"There's been some frightful exaggeration..."

"Of course, but if half of it is accurate, you are the person to help me."

"I've not undertaken much work in the last year."

"But this is urgent. I really do have to see you."

"Well, there is..."

"It's absolutely essential. I am desperate."

"Very well..."

"As soon as possible. I could come tonight."

"I'm afraid..."

"First thing in the morning."

"Monday."

"You couldn't make it earlier?"

"Definitely not."

"Okay, Monday it is. I shall be early."

She didn't ask what he meant by 'feel.' Perhaps she should have done. He was so insistent. And desperate. She sensed the desperation in his voice. But then, so many of them *sound* desperate. To each, their problem is *the* problem that only she can resolve. She should be flattered, but she'd outgrown that long ago. Few cases are really that interesting, but with this one...no, it can wait till Monday. Perhaps she should have been more resistant, but she gets so tired. She needs recuperation. She glances out the window. It's warm and bright. She'll take a stroll round the park. It'll clear her head and afterwards she can rest.

Warren Grover is quite unlike Ettie expects. Disembodied voices on telephones are frequently misleading. His somewhat high pitched voice, but mainly his tense, insistent nervousness, bordering on the neurotic created a mental picture of a small, twitchy, wimpish man. What she finds on opening the door is a tall, dark, well built figure with deep set eyes, strong eyebrows, high cheekbones, a firm jaw and a crushing handshake. He sits straight in his chair, with his palms resting on his thighs like a retired army officer, ready to slap them firmly and recount his most famous campaigns with gusto. His eyes move slowly, deliberately taking in everything in the room with the measured sweep of a canny observer. He takes his tea with a slight curling, not unappealing smile at the edges of his mouth and then gulps it down in one, happily taking a second cup, which is dispatched almost as quickly. There's no indication of reticence, hesitation or apprehension except for an occasional fingering the side of the chair. Apparently secure and confident, he's quick to come to the point without any prompting. What can such a man have to fear?

"I read of your experiences last year with particular interest. You said the accounts were exaggerated, but surely the essential facts are genuine?"

"Yes, but you shouldn't read too much into them" Ettie says guardedly, fearing his question means he's investing her in the familiar and unwelcome guise of guardian angel, "I've been involved in many other similar incidents, there's nothing really special about what happened..."

"Ah, but that's very much the point, Miss Rodway, your experience and your...involvement...in 1381 is really special to me."

"It's not necessarily relevant to..."

"Relevant! Yes precisely, its *relevance* is most important. You see, I believe I may be experiencing something very similar."

"You are conscious of a connection with the past?"

"Precisely."

Ettie groans inwardly. It's as she suspected. The usual vagueness puffed up to sound more important. Better dealt

11

with by more mainstream assistance. How can she let him down lightly?

"Such things are not as rare as many people think," she begins, searching for the right words, "I don't want to deprecate what you may have been feeling, but sometimes the more...shall we say...dramatic incidents don't necessarily mean all instances are the same. As you've read, my work was involved with particular historical events surrounding the..."

"Peasants Revolt of 1381! That's precisely why I've come to see you. Mine is not some ill defined need to communicate and, if you'll forgive me, a gullible predilection for the more sophisticated end of table turning, not even because of your involvement in similar matters, but because of your experience with that particular event. I should explain. My interest in the period extends well over twenty years. In my younger days I was into amateur dramatics. In 1981, the six hundredth anniversary of the Peasants' Revolt, I felt we ought to appropriately mark the occasion. So a group of friends at school staged a re-enactment of the original events in St. Albans. We called our company 'The Great Society.'

'Once I got the bug it was impossible to shake it off. We were young and excited. It was incredibly invigorating. Though we were playing parts, at times it seemed as if... well, anyway, I was so inspired I've been hooked ever since. Our little presentation was soon forgotten, but I carried on studying. Yet the more I did the less I seemed to know. The subject seemed to get bigger and bigger at a rate accelerating faster than I was learning! I studied the whole period of course, including the more well known events in London, but always I was drawn back to the local area. The spin off was an interest in local history and that led to involvement in community affairs generally. In all these things I constantly strive for accuracy and authenticity. Yet the more I study, the less satisfied I am. My standards keep moving upwards and no matter how much I improve I never get there."

Towards the end of this monologue, he averts his eyes from Ettie and looks down, while clasping his hands and flexing his fingers with the nervousness she'd heard on the phone. He looks up, smiles, though its now less relaxed. He pulls his hands apart as if unclasping them might free him from his concerns.

"I've completed a book on the revolt in Hertfordshire. Something I've wanted to do for years. I call it *A Little Liberty*. That has a certain local resonance," he pauses and then, "I'm sorry, I do tend to go on a bit."

"It's okay," she says, "but I don't see how..."

"How you can help? It'll become clear, but I need you to understand the background. It might sound like my feet are perpetually off the ground or my mind is always wandering around in the past, but despite appearances I'm really quite practical and realistic. I'm not easily fazed, but there are some things I find difficult to comprehend."

He pauses again

"With events so far in the past, you're reliant on the interpretations of those at the time. There's nothing magical in the written word. Someone writes hundreds of years ago, purporting to be the truth, but you have to understand where the writer is coming from, not just obvious axes he may be grinding, but how he sees the world. Six hundred years ago they saw it in very different ways to now. Trying to explain the past that's understandable in the present, means constantly keeping a grip on reality."

He pauses again. Ettie is patient, but he's still skating around. She'll have to prod.

"What do you mean, keeping a grip on reality?"

He stares apprehensively. Did he really say that? He's unprepared. She stares back. He needs more time to gather his thoughts, find the best way to say things. If he tells her *everything*, she will help him?

"As I said the events of 1381 have obsessed me since my youth, but then things started happening."

He stops again. She waits. It will come now. He tells of the people, the man, the hanging men.

"How long has this been going on?"

"On and off since last year, getting stronger all the time until the last couple of months definitely more on than off."

"How long do the visions last?"

13

"In the beginning only seconds and even now most of them are quite short, but occasionally longer, perhaps a couple of minutes."

"And you believe these appearances are connected to your studies?"

"Yes, but not in the way you mean!" he says vehemently, "These are not concoctions from my imagination, they're not continuations from my work."

"I didn't say they were. What about this man, do you know who he is, someone familiar to you?"

"I know what I would like to believe."

"Sometimes the dead are more real to us than the living," Ettie says knowingly.

"That's why I've come to you. When I read how you and your friend experienced direct contact with the past, not just with the events, but also the people of the revolt, I knew you'd understand what I've been feeling."

"What do you want me to do?"

"I have to be sure. People will say I'm mad. Come to Hertfordshire so I can show you the places where I've felt these things, seen the people."

"You want me to corroborate your story?"

"Don't fob me off with comforting platitudes. Come and see for yourself!"

Ettie is thoughtful. Her silence agitates him.

"Please come, time is running out. The people of the past are on the march for a purpose. When you see them, you'll be able to advise me what to do. Then there's him. He's trying to talk to me. I'm sure of it."

Ettie is unwilling to commit herself. Sensing her reluctance his pleading becomes more strident and emphatic, but she's not easily swayed and agrees only to give it 'serious and sympathetic consideration,' though partly relents, accepting his deadline of no more than a week before reaching a decision. This perks him up and some of his earlier solidity and apparent calm returns. He pulls a thick file from his bag.

"The first draft of my book," he says, handing over the file, "Once you've read it and mulled over all I've said, you'll see what a unique opportunity this presents for your own activities."

"I'm not sure I'll have the time," she says, gently pushing the file back to him.

"I quite understand," he says, equally gently, but firmly pressing it back into her hand, "You have other priorities, but you don't have to read everything. I've marked the most important sections at the front."

"You'll need it for your work…"

He laughs.

"I have a house full of files. In any case, I can collect it when next I see you."

It's a clever move, guaranteeing more than a polite phone call in response. She hesitates. Their eyes meet and she sees his desperation. She takes the file.

"I look forward to hearing from you very soon," he says at the door.

She watches him until he reaches the corner. If she doesn't contact him he'll contact her and she suspects he'll not wait a week before doing so.

Despite his apparent confidence as he leaves, Warren's foreboding quickly descends and the return journey seems interminable. He avoids the motorways, which is probably a mistake. Driving cross country he gets snarled up in the Oxford ring road rush hour and later still there's a long hold up around Hemel Hempstead. Shut up in his metal box, he feels terrifyingly alone as he ponders on their conversation and reflects on his troubles. He oscillates between the fragile hope Ettie will agree to come to his aid and withering despair that she won't. There's no chance things will get better. A crisis looms and facing it without someone who understands fills him with a soul sucking terror.

Had he been too insistent? He should have presented his fears as an interesting puzzle, a fascinating aside in her vast corpus of the extraordinary, with a matter of fact approach she'd be more likely to respond in a businesslike way. Yes, that's how he should have handled it. A consultation. After all, she is a time link *consultant*. But she would have seen through it immediately and he'd probably have broken down, gibbering out his story in incoherent dribbles. He can't hide the emotion. This is no pseudo scientific investigation to be conducted in laboratory conditions. For a quarter century he's lived and breathed the events of that fateful year, frequently taxing his intellect. Until now he's remained rational. But now he's disturbed. He needs her help and he needs it fast. She has to accept what he says in the way he's said it or not accept it all.

For the rest of the day Ettie gives Warren's troubles, genuine or imagined, little thought, but in the evening they return as she sits in the garden. Warren's obsession with the Peasants' Revolt of 1381 stirs up recent experiences in London and resurrects her discussions with Vicky. Then there's Warren's book, resonating with Chris's film – something they'd both 'wanted to do for years.' The two do not entirely coincide. Chris inclines towards events in London, while Warren prefers his native Hertfordshire, but this is a minor distinction, both are obsessed with the drama of 1381. Then there's Warren's mysterious man, trying to communicate. It reminds her of that other man she'd briefly met in the London of the past. He also came from St. Albans. Could it be the same man?

She'd rather not think about such links and casts them aside before going inside. That night she sleeps better than she has for weeks and wakes feeling refreshed. It's a bright, warm day. She'll go out. That way she won't be tempted to answer the phone and get tied down with wretched people wanting 'help.' She walks across the park and out of town, making for one of her favourite spots, a cool seat underneath a clump of trees beside the river and away from people. She sits, closes her eyes and empties her mind, allowing only the wafting breeze, the rippling water on the stones and the distant noise of the ducks to intrude. But the conversation with Warren returns. She promised him an answer. His story is no different to that of many others. Vague impressions of the past, spruced up with local colour, in his case reinforced by his studies and the inevitable allusion to a particular individual as a proto-contact. She's heard it many times before, what makes this so different? She doesn't know, except a nagging suspicion that it is.

Her unsettlement increases. Yet as she returns home and despite the long walk, she feels none of the weariness of the past weeks, but stronger and livelier, as if a burden has been lifted. It's a good sign, concentrating on such problems, even almost working again, but she's not sure it's wise to take on a new case yet. She picks up Warren's file, first skimming desultorily and then perusing in greater detail. An hour later she's still reading and looks up with a start as the hall clock strikes. She puts it down. This is not a decision she can make alone and there are only two people she can realistically consult.

Almost on cue the phone rings. She's tempted to let it ring, but she's expecting Vicky to call or it could be Chris Pleasant. She picks it up.

"Ettie? I'm so glad I've caught you. I was afraid you might be out."

Jessica.

"Well, I was just..."

"Naturally I don't want to interrupt anything, but I'm in the area, as it were and felt I really must come and see you. I'm in Cheltenham, just down the road so to speak. In fact I've left Cheltenham, I'm in a layby near...er, where is it...well anyway I can be with you in less than half an hour."

"I'll have to..."

"Excellent! As long as I'm not getting in the way, as it were, see you soon!"

Jessica Tennant, Oxford academic, 14th century historian and expert on the Peasants' Revolt, flounces into the house and conducts her usual conversation, ostensibly with Ettie, but really with herself or some ethereal audience which never tires of listening. She's been continuing the work she started a year ago, following up the discovery of a previously unknown rhyme used during the Revolt.

"Obviously, that seventh rhyme we discovered is only the beginning. Other aspects of the Revolt have hardly been touched on. Work still remains for us all!"

"For us all?"

"I can only hypothesise, you understand, it's not for me to encroach on your area of expertise...we believed the outstanding issues from the 14th century had been finally resolved by the rhyme's revelation, then..."

Jessica pauses, a mischievous twinkle in her eyes before continuing.

"...you remember telling me all time periods are really simultaneous rather than consecutive, that the distinctions between past, present and future are like the walls between rooms in the same house...? (Ettie nods absently) Then there may be more to resolve. I just thought you ought to know."

Jessica claps her hands together smartly, pours more tea and glances across questioningly. To her surprise and some chagrin, Ettie doesn't respond. Jessica's academic news doesn't touch her. Whether it's fatigue, uninterest or irritation, she isn't comfortable talking about long lost rhymes. Jessica persists for a little longer until even she tires of the one sided conversation, then watches Ettie for a few moments, suddenly aware she's been pressing the wrong buttons.

"And what have you been up to?" she says.

At first Ettie skirts around vaguely about helping Chris Pleasant, but Jessica's nose is too sharp. She persists and Ettie eventually mentions Warren, saying she's been asked to undertake some 'real work' without going into details. Jessica gently probes.

"If you need more recovery time you might want to wait till you feel stronger..."

She pauses, noticing Ettie doesn't immediately agree.

"I suppose other similar opportunities *might* arise..."

Ettie shakes her head slightly with a 'maybe, maybe not' expression, which Jessica takes as a signal to be more decisive.

"Work is the best tonic in your situation. It's always been for me. You can rest too much you know, Ettie. It's like lying in bed too long on Saturday morning, you can end up even more tired than you were on Friday night! Naturally I'm speaking very broadly. It depends on the particular project. Is it something with which you're familiar?"

Ettie hesitates. Should she say more? Jessica's advice could be useful, but she's reluctant to talk about it.

"Yes, it is something I could handle."

"There you are then..."

"It's just I'm not sure yet whether..."

Now Jessica pushes the best button, reminds Ettie what Warren Grover said.

"The more we know, it seems the less we know."

"...the subject seemed to get bigger and bigger...faster than I was learning..."

"Do you ever study events outside London?" Ettie says tentatively,

"Naturally," Jessica says, sensing a successful pull on her bait, "Any particular area in mind?"

"I was thinking of Hertfordshire. I've read a little, but ..."

"A Hertfordshire contingent in London attended the Mile End meeting with the king They obtained their own charter. Theirs was a mixed urban and rural revolt, mainly directed against the power and wealth of the great monastery at St. Albans. There was no bloodshed, though plenty of noise and activity. For a time the citizens and the peasants were very successful in wringing major concessions out of the abbot, but after the defeats in London they backtracked and reached an accommodation."

"So there was a peaceful resolution?"

"Not exactly. The king arrived later and the ringleaders were quickly tried and executed."

"Executed? But you said there was no bloodshed?"

"There wasn't, but then neither had John Ball, the people's priest, engaged in any violence either, but he too died at St. Albans."

"So Hertfordshire was repressed just as much as the other areas?"

"There were no pitched battles, but otherwise, yes it was."

Ettie is visibly shocked. She's not read everything in Warren's file. Jessica's suspicions are aroused.

"Has this got anything to do with this new case you mentioned?"

"I've had an approach from someone who's written a book on the local story...he wants my help...just one of many approaches I've had since the events in London became so well known."

"And this time you feel able to get involved?"

"I'm not sure..."

"But you must. If this is the sort of task that really excites you then it's the best thing to lift the sprits."

"I'm still not sure."

"Is it only an advisory capacity, a bit like helping that film director you were telling me about?"

"Yes, that sort of thing."

"Nothing more...interventionist?"

"It seems not."

Ettie stops short of further details, afraid Jessica might not be so supportive if she knows more of Warren Grover's pleading.

"He's very keen to get it right," she says guardedly, "has a thing about accuracy."

"And you're concerned you might not be up to his standards?"

This jolts Ettie, which is Jessica's intention, but she doesn't immediately bite and tries to laugh it off.

"I'm only an adviser."

"But what are you advising him about?"

"I've told you, he's writing...I'm unsure whether to embark on another venture which might lead me back into that tempestuous period."

She stops suddenly. It's too late, she's said too much. Now Jessica understands.

"It's up to you how you feel, but remember you answered Vicky when she was crying out for help."

Jessica's response surprises her. It seems the self centred academic really is sensitive to the feelings of others.

"You think this man is in need of my help?"

"Only you can judge that."

They pass a pleasant couple of hours talking of other things until Jessica remembers all the places 'she ought to have been' and all the people 'she should have seen.' After she's gone, Ettie can rest at last and doesn't wake until ten in the evening, in time to go to bed! Even then she sleeps on and lingers in the garden over a late breakfast, giving her time to think, rested and refreshed. Jessica is right. She will go to Hertfordshire and help Warren Grover as much as she can. She rings his number and gets no answer.

Warren walks at a faster pace towards the common. He takes his usual route and has told Kathleen he'll be back at his usual time, but this is not a usual evening. Tonight he has an appointment though what has to be said won't take long. He'd rather it wasn't necessary at all, but such things have to be faced. He exchanges pleasantries with familiar figures, strollers and dog walkers about the weather and the country. He knows them and they know him, but in reality they don't *know* each other at all. He knows none of their names and doubts if they know his even though his name is well enough known in the community. Out here in the openness everyone is *un*known, where names and faces never match. Known, yet not known, where the uncluttered land has been meeting the unencumbered sky for hundreds of years, each free from the incursions of people. Here people hold no more sway than the rabbits and the gorse, here everything and everyone is free.

He slows down, anxious not to arrive too early, not to be alone. It's a light evening, but already shadows from the trees slink along the ground and enfold the bushes. Perhaps the appointment should have been earlier, but if he'd deviated from his normal routine Kathleen would have wanted to know why and he'd rather she knows nothing yet. He can handle it. He approaches Lock's Spinney and pauses. He's not been for some time. It still invokes the past, the decades pulled back as if with each pace the ground peels away the years. He's young again with his friends in this, their special place. Was it right what he saw last night, will he see it again? Perhaps, but not here, this is not the place. He turns and that time is gone, the intervening years piled on as swiftly as they were cast aside.

Then he sees the people trudging across the horizon. What is it they carry? He can't make it out, but they walk slowly, deliberately. It must be heavy. More appear with further loads. He looks away instinctively. He's an interloper. He shouldn't be here, it's not right he should see these things. But he is here. If it's meant, he must witness. He turns back. The people are gone and the dull horizon, lit by the feeble glinting in the west, is empty. A new shape shimmers and as it clears he sees again the grisly form of the gibbet, but it too is empty. No one hangs. The solitary man stands beside it. He beckons and despite his fear Warren moves forward. As he gets nearer he can see the clothes of the past and the face clearly. Then the gibbet is gone and the man moves away, still beckoning Warren to follow. They go a short way and the man stops. He waits until Warren is very close, then turns and points a little further. Warren stands awestruck and silent. This is what he is meant to see and he cannot go until it is finished. Only then does the man leave him. Now Warren understands and must keep his appointment.

It's a pleasant if circuitous drive, meandering along the country, cutting through the Chilterns. With the sun at her rear, casting glint lined shadows into the road she feels a gentle mellowness. This case will get her back into her stride, pick up her spirits. She crosses the county boundary with a momentary, inexplicable shudder. It passes immediately, but feeling it at all is worrying. Is she catching Warren's trembling edginess as she gets nearer? She kept calm when Jessica went on about the revolt in Hertfordshire, but now a figure from the past flits and flickers. Not one of the recorded names of the St. Albans chronicle, so familiar to Warren, someone known to her only fleetingly, one of the contingent Jessica mentioned travelling to London to get their charter from the king. His name, Thomas, comes to mind like a persistent ghost, echoing down the centuries.

This too passes and she feels better as she nears St. Albans. She takes the road north a few miles towards Welstead, nearest town to Warren's home. She comes to wide, open commonland, stretching far into the north and east. There are a few houses, set back on her left, shielded by trees, but otherwise the rolling country stretches undisturbed as it's probably been for longer than anyone cares to remember.

She slows and winds down the window, gulping in the warm, grassy air. She feels tranquil again. The common narrows, there are more houses on her left and some in the distance to her right. She comes to the town centre proper where the open grassland stops at a sharp apex

It's early evening, that intermediate time between most of the shops shutting and the pubs not yet fully limbered up. There's an ambling, relaxed atmosphere of a town contented with itself so long as it doesn't have to pay too much attention to what's been happening elsewhere. Like the common, a natural unchanging sanctuary, it's probably been like this for centuries. Or so it seems. About half way down the high street she passes a small green to her left with a wall memorial. Opposite the green and set slightly back is the parish church with its 14th century tower. Further along the high street are a few shops and an older building, perhaps two hundred years old. The Old Fox Hotel is squat and hunched close to the road. A little further is an alleyway under an arch of the hotel and a sign for parking. Ettie will try it.

The reception gives onto a lounge. A few people are at the bar, but the hotel seems quiet. She glances into the neat and tidy dining room. It looks okay. Ettie says she'll stay two nights initially, but it might be three. Her room is small with a low ceiling, but comfortable. It's at the back, facing the car park and therefore quieter than the rooms on the front facing the main road. She can see the church tower. The clock strikes the hour.

Ettie rings Warren's number again. There's still no answer. This time she waits until the ansafone kicks on. It's a woman's voice on the recording, probably his wife. After explaining who she is, Ettie hesitates. The problem with leaving a message is she can't be certain who will hear it. She doesn't know how much Warren has told his wife and whatever Ettie says might be misunderstood, even alarm her. She says it's a message for Warren. She's just arrived in Welstead and will be in touch tomorrow. That's enough.

After dinner she studies Warren's *A Little Liberty* more closely. It sketches out the main events in June and July 1381 in St. Albans and the surrounding country. This gives her a good grounding in the causes of the local revolt, the main characters and how the action was played out. There are many marginal annotations to books, articles and historical records, much of it in abbreviated form, which to the uninitiated makes little sense. The 'notes' vary between long passages and mere bullet points with every variety in between. The differing quality probably indicates Warren's preferences for the subject matter. There's a particular emphasis on the action at the end of the disturbances, the arrival of the king, the trials and the retribution. Even in its sparse form, the passion and pathos Warren feels for these events leap powerfully from the page. It evokes mixed feelings. She's drawn to the people and the drama, linking to Warren's compelling identification with the times, but also feels the apprehension of someone standing close to some fascinating, but dangerous occurrence. Keep close, but keep away.

Yet the late night reading settles her mind and no longer doubting the case she sleeps soundly. Next morning she decides to make an early start and call on Warren. In the dining room a couple are talking to the waitress. At first Ettie takes no notice. The couple finishes breakfast, but linger. Ostensibly the waitress is clearing the table, but is actually engaging in one of those muffled conversations, whose quietness from a distance always gives away its intensity. She leans towards them at one end of the table while they lean towards her, the woman nodding knowingly, the man cupping his ear. Ettie glances across and the conversational volume drops into a slightly conspiratorial rumble. All Ettie can pick up are a succession of 'I knows' and 'never.' Then the waitress leans away with her pile of plates and announces very clearly 'they know who it is' before returning to the kitchen.

"Did you know him?" the woman says when she returns.

"Not myself, but everyone's heard of him. It's all over the town. Everybody's talking about Warren Grover."

The couple leaves. The waitress comes over to Ettie.

"More coffee, madam?"

"Yes, thank you. Tell me, I couldn't help overhearing, were you talking about Warren Grover?"

"Yes, that's right. Do you know him?"

"Well, yes, I do, slightly."

"And you haven't heard?"

"Heard what?"

"Why, he's dead, been murdered."

2

CHRIS is impatient to get started. He's conceded this scene under pressure and is determined not to give way again. Then, except for a few scenes set aside out of sequence the film can be wrapped up. That would be gratifying, not just the usual feeling of accomplishment, but intense, glorious relief. So he should be happy or at least contented, but he's not. A nagging doubt persists. He's like a man on a precipice. He knows he shouldn't get too close, but he has to get nearer even though it must inevitably mean he'll fall. This won't be the end. There will be other scenes – scenes he doesn't want to shoot, but which he'll be pressured to do. He must resist. This movie has to be finished!

"Almost ready!" someone shouts.

Chris looks up. The set is complete. The dismal grey stone and bare floor of a large medieval hall make him shiver even though it's warm in the studio. It may be June, even July in the script, but there's a coldness to the wooden walls. He feels the stone without touching it as if he's not in the studio at all, but in a real 14th century room. Some of the extras of the vast crowd are already forming up.

"Back, back," he shouts, "get back against the walls, we've got to get a lot more in here yet."

The extras crunch together as more enter from the sides. Chris barks further instructions. Someone shouts they're getting crushed.

26

"You're supposed to be!" Chris shouts, "This is 1381 remember. Every man in the county between fifteen and sixty is supposed to be here."

More extras file in, but Chris isn't satisfied. He won't start shooting until he can *feel* their discomfort just as he feels the coldness of the walls. At last, with dozens of extras squeezed and pressed so hard the wooden walls may soon buckle under the strain, he's ready and the main players take their places. Jeremy Lowther, the young man with the baby face is more nervous than usual today. He's older than the fourteen year old he plays, but retains a teenage innocence which gives him a reticence out of keeping with how Chris envisages King Richard II.

"Buck up, Jeremy," Chris calls, "This is your big day, remember. You've summoned them all here to pledge allegiance and swear their loyalty. None of that can be taken for granted. This is your opportunity for a show of strength. If they don't toe the line in future they're going to be in deep shit. Look as though you mean it!"

Jeremy attempts a nervous smile.

"Okay," Chris barks, "everyone in their places. We'll go to the king's entry. Action!"

The cameras roll. The extras rumble and shuffle. Jeremy and his entourage enter from the left along with Lawrence Bullock, playing the abbot. Chris waves his outstretched arms slowly down to the crowd on either side of the hall and the noise quickly subsides. Jeremy walks to the dais with appropriate dignity and regal aloofness, but a little too slowly. Chris now waves to him with upturned arms in a rapid circular motion. Seeing this in the corner of his vision, Jeremy quickens a little, but his upper lip flickers anxiously. Fortunately he has his back to the camera and by the time he turns he appears more composed. Chris watches him uneasily, pushing his hands up in front of his face encouraging him to speak up. Jeremy stares back, waiting a few moments for the whole party to assemble. Chris waits as he waits. There must be absolute silence before he speaks and Chris is willing every mouth to close, every loose foot to be still, every fidgeting finger to close. The hush comes and Jeremy gets up.

"Know that we are assembled here in front of this great gathering..."

He speaks with strident deliberation, his words reverberating forcefully. Chris is pleased. Jeremy seems to have lost his earlier trepidation.

"...and those that have fled must soon return on pain of..."

There's a slight flurry in the crowd at these words. Chris turns and glares, cursing inwardly. It's going to ruin the scene. It subsides. He looks back to Jeremy apprehensively, but the young man seems undeterred.

"...pledge your allegiance to remain loyal to me and never again rise up against my peace..."

Jeremy's voice trails slightly with the last words. Chris flicks his hands upwards vigorously. If Jeremy doesn't pick up his voice quickly the scene will have to begin again...come on...just in time Jeremy's voice rises.

"...sooner die than obey troublemakers..."

Good, that's better, it's going to be okay!

"...to the best of their ability apprehend..."

Another stirring in the crowd and Jeremy glances across. It subsides again, but Jeremy's attention is distracted and he continues to stare into the crowd.

"...carry out their work and customary service faithfully..."

Jeremy's voice trails again. It's no good, this won't do. Reluctantly, Chris will have to..."

"No, no!" Jeremy suddenly shouts, but these words are not in the script!

"Cut! Cut!"

Jeremy still stares into the crowd. The rumble of voices returns. Chris walks over angrily.

"Sorry, sorry," Jeremy says limply.

"That was absolutely bloody awful, Jeremy. Where was your voice, lost in the damned crowd? You started out well and then you lost it. For God's sake, you're the king. You might only be a boy, but you're the king. You've got to speak like one. And what the hell was that at the end – No, no – where's that in the script?"

Jeremy stares in the resigned hopelessness of someone reprimanded for something he knows he did or didn't do, but can't explain. He opens his mouth to speak, but seeing Chris's aggressive stare he realises he'll probably only make things worse and immediately shuts it again. Lawrence Bullock, the actor playing the abbot, comes to his rescue.

"Don't be too hard on him, Chris, he was distracted by the crowd."

Chris looks at the extras blankly and shakes his head.

"Then he'll have to get used to them," he says, "He's a king!"

Lawrence speaks quietly to Jeremy.

"What's the problem?"

Jeremy cocks his head to one side of the set, beyond the end of the 'wall' and behind the cameras.

"Some of the crowd were looking over there too," he says.

"Over where?"

Jeremy motions his head again and rolls his eyes.

"Some of them felt it."

"What?"

"Don't know, but there's something there."

"Course there is, you stupid sod, the studio's full of people."

"Yes I know, but…"

"Have you sorted him out yet, Lawrence?" Chris bawls.

"Yes, yes, he's okay, Chris," Lawrence shouts and then turns back to Jeremy, "It's alright, but get a grip. It's just nerves."

"It wasn't nerves when we did the Smithfield scenes. I was alright then, but this is different…"

"Sure it is. This is new material. You're getting like me, getting tired of this picture and Chris is…"

Jeremy breaks off as he starts, shuddering and staring at the back of the studio. Lawrence glances in the same direction, but seeing nothing, grabs Jeremy's arm.

"Stiffen up. Concentrate on your lines and get them out!"

Chris is pacing impatiently. Jeremy turns back.

"Alright now?" Lawrence says.

Jeremy nods, adjusts his deep sleeves and gets comfortable in the chair

"Okay, okay, everybody," Chris shouts, "Into position, we'll take it again from the beginning of the king's speech. Alright Jeremy? Quiet, everybody. Now, action!"

At first Jeremy launches into his speech with gusto and gravitas, but gradually subsides as his attention wavers again. Lawrence, glancing to Chris and reading his growing irritation, encourages Jeremy with an obsequious and conspicuous grin, not inconsistent with the script, but to no avail. Reaching the more authoritative sentences at the end of his declaration, Jeremy's voice trembles and dwindles so much Chris has to intervene.

"Cut! Cut! I don't know what it is, Jeremy. Whether it's the rats under the floor or the bats in the roof, but whatever it is you've gotta get it out of your bloody system. Alright, alright everybody, we'll take ten and then go for it again. In the meantime Jeremy get yourself sorted out!"

To Jeremy's surprise Chris walks away, stopping only to speak to Lawrence, who again reassures the director 'that the boy's okay, just be patient,' before disappearing into his room. Jeremy grabs a huge mug of coffee, which he gulps quickly and then sinks into a chair, still shaking slightly. He pulls his hands through his hair and sits up, shivering. Lawrence tells him to take deep breaths and try to calm down.

"Just close your eyes and think of...think of...well anything pleasant, it usually works."

He squeezes his shoulder and moves on. Despite what he says Lawrence is worried about Jeremy and as he ambles around the set his concerns grow. The young actor is not alone. Perhaps because he's a shade older and more experienced, Lawrence acts as an emotional magnet for many of the others and they are anxious to tell him their misgivings. When the set was utterly quiet, they'd heard things during Jeremy's speech. A few had also seen things. None can say what they'd seen or what they'd heard, but all are adamant. It was if someone had been creeping about the studio.

"Maybe someone was," Lawrence says, "it's not unknown."

His disarming smile is met with determined frowns and shaking heads. No one they knew was creeping about. Nor was it someone who would normally do so. This was something *different*. They'd all felt the same 'drawing' of their energy. They ask if he felt something, they're sure Jeremy did.

"Nothing," Lawrence says, "Didn't feel a thing. I don't take any notice of studio superstitions, been in the game too long."

But his bluff geniality is challenged by Lucy and Steve, like him two more experienced actors. They too 'felt' things.

"This was no superstition," Steve says.

"Poor Jeremy was well shaken up," Lucy says, "and with good reason. Chris ought to pack it in for today. Everybody's too rattled."

"Somebody should tell him," Steve says, staring pointedly.

Lawrence dutifully takes the hint and goes to the director's room. Chris sits hunched in the corner, examining the screenplay. He looks up when Lawrence enters and nods silently. He seems calmer. In any case, Lawrence always feels the direct approach is usually the most effective, if not the most pleasant.

"You can't ignore the feelings of the cast."

Chris sighs and looks at Lawrence coldly. His lips set firmly, he could be about to put him down so Lawrence goes on, quickly recounting the collective concerns, giving Chris no opportunity to interrupt. Chris mulls it over for a few moments after he finishes. He respects Lawrence's view.

"What do you think I should do, organise a search, pull the studio down?"

"Stop shooting for today."

Chris considers it for a moment and then Charley Kennet, the chief screenwriter comes in. She's around the same age as Chris and Lawrence, in her early forties, slim with short hair and darting eyes and filled with curiosity and new ideas. They are not always to Chris's taste, but he perseveres for the sake of the few that are brilliant. She understands film instinctively, making the director's job much easier and is willing to make changes, which she works up very fast.

But there's been tension between them lately and he's not welcomed her presence on the set, something that's never bothered him before. She carries a sheaf of papers under her arm and has a small book in her hand. Ignoring Lawrence as if he's not there, she walks jauntily across the room, with some pressing idea on her mind, which won't wait.

"This scene isn't right as it is."

"It certainly isn't," Chris agrees.

"I mentioned it to Desmond and he agreed I should talk to you."

Desmond Manners, another screenwriter enters behind her. He's older, in his fifties and though able, rarely has an original idea of his own, taking his cue from the director or chief writer. Always in their shadow, he stands sheepishly at the door, which slightly amuses Chris. If Charley is about to embark on the presentation of a major change she doesn't need reinforcements. She sits down opposite Chris. Sensing a coming confrontation in which he has no wish to participate, Lawrence moves to the door and slips out with a short wave of his hand. Slowly, Desmond sidles over to join Charley.

"If we have the fealty scene, we have to have the others," Charley says.

She looks to Chris, but he says nothing, continuing to stare at the ground.

"What other scenes?" Desmond says, "I thought it was to be the end of the film."

"The gatherings in the town, the clashes with the abbot, the disturbances, the arrest and trial of the leaders and..."

"It was meant to be the end of the film," Chris says, still looking at the ground.

"It can't be," she says, "It won't make sense on its own. We have to cover the trials of the local leaders a well as John Ball and..."

"But we've already shot the end, so that's it."

"But Chris, it can't stand alone. It'll be like watching the last two minutes of the cup final without the other eighty eight minutes."

"This isn't a football match."

Desmond titters. Charley glares at him and tries again.

"The fight then in the last scene of Hamlet without all the intrigue, the soliloquy and ..."

"This is not what was agreed."

"What was agreed?"

"This would be an end to it."

"But not on its own! We have to have the other scenes."

"That's not what you said!"

"But you must have understood we couldn't shoot the fealty scene in isolation. What's the point of the king receiving the forced allegiance of the whole county if we don't show why it's necessary for them to be forced!"

Chris turns to her for the first time, his face compounded of frustration and sufferance.

"I agreed, not without considerable qualms, to shoot this scene, but no more. An end to it."

His wide angry eyes continue to look intently. She stares back, equally adamant. Desmond is unsure whether he should defuse the atmosphere by saying something or laughing. Before he can decide Charley persists.

"It's not enough to cover the events in London. The film has to broaden out to take in more of the St. Albans action. It'll be unfinished if we don't include the wider story. After all, here we are in a studio in Hertfordshire, it wouldn't be..."

"You're letting your fancies run away with you, Charley. Just because the studio is in the area it doesn't mean we have to pander to its 14th century history."

"We wouldn't be pandering and even if we were, why not? We've already started the fealty scene – the end without a beginning and a middle, it doesn't get to the core of what the revolt in Hertfordshire was all about."

"And what about the budget, I'll have to talk to the producers..."

"Don't blame the producers. This isn't big bucks, Chris and you know it!"

Chris holds his head in his hands and shakes it, emitting a long and deep sigh.

"I accept we have to put the dramatic events in London into context. That's why I agreed to additional scenes dealing with the aftermath of the revolt."

"Including the repression."

"Yes, yes, okay, dealing with the repression, but we've done enough for that. Up to a point I've taken on board we have to reflect the significance of these wider events, but..."

"Without them we're in danger of turning it into all action, daring do and no more."

Chris smarts at this.

"That's ridiculous. This is a deep and sensitive picture. All action daring do! It's a bit bloody late now to denigrate what we've spent months shooting. After all, you wrote most of it!"

"Okay, but there has to be a contrast. We have to bring out the tragic side of the revolt. That's why these extra scenes are so important, they'll reveal the essential tragedy."

"And the failure," he says slowly, quietly.

"Depends how you define failure."

A long charged silence follows, in which they both avoid the other's stare. Then the door bursts open and Jeremy charges in. Shaking violently, he slumps into a chair.

"You've got to do something, Chris, I can't go on as it is!"

"Not again. Listen, Jeremy, you've got..."

"It's not just me. Everybody feels it."

"Not everybody, why..."

"Yes it is! Talk to Lawrence."

"Lawrence is level headed, he's not felt anything."

"But he's spoken to the whole cast. I know he has. He came in to see you, didn't he? What did he say? He said everybody was upset, that we couldn't go on, didn't he?"

Chris says nothing.

"Didn't he?" Jeremy screams.

"He said there'd been some problems," Chris concedes quietly.

"You see, you see!"

Jeremy turns to Charley and then to Desmond, seeking their support. Charley watches incredulously. Desmond's mouth twitches in an attempted smile, but he's embarrassed and leaves.

"What have you seen?" Charley says.

"Nothing, he's seen nothing," Chris says, "just like all the others, it's all vague, hearing things, he's not seen anything."

"I have!I have!"

Jeremy shakes even more, continuing to say 'I have' over and over. He gradually gets quieter, eventually stopping when he realises Chris and Charley are listening intently, waiting for him to go on.

"I've seen a man."

"Where?" Charley says.

"On the set, near the wall, at the end of the crowd."

"What," Chris says, "One man amongst all those extras?"

"He wasn't an extra, he was standing apart from them."

"Was he dressed differently?"

"No," Jeremy concedes, "but he wasn't one of them, he spoke."

"When was this?

"After Lawrence came in to see you."

"What did he say?" Charley asks.

"He said got to get it right...or will be getting it right...or maybe should get it right...yes that's it...have to get it right."

"Get what right?"

"Don't know, but he meant what we were doing. I'm sure of it. He didn't like what we were shooting."

"Where is he now?" she says.

"He's gone. Don't know where, just sort of disappeared. When I looked up he'd gone."

"This is ridiculous!" Chris explodes, "Jeremy, if it wasn't that we've got a schedule to keep, I'd tell you to go away and get yourself sorted out. As it is you've ruined any work for today. But you can't go on like this, at best propped up by Lawrence, Steve and Lucy. If you don't..."

"It's not just me. Speak to the others, you know there've been disturbances for weeks. Ever since we restarted shooting after the new scenes were put in."

Jeremy glances sternly at Charley.

"That's got nothing to do with it," Chris says, "You're an actor, you play whatever scene you're asked to do."

"Yes and every scene we try to do there's a problem. You've said it yourself. It's as if there's some outside interference,

35

checking us, judging us, never satisfied. I won't be able to do this scene unless something is done. I can't work like this!"

"I've had it up to the back teeth with your bloody tantrums, Jeremy. Now get away, get a good rest and be back on the set first thing in the morning ready for work!"

Jeremy glares defiantly for a few seconds, but he can't take Chris's steely stare and leaves. Chris turns to Charley.

"He's right, at least in part. Nothing's been right since we started these new scenes."

"Just because he says so doesn't make a connection."

God, she's cheeky, Chris thinks as he looks down again at the screenplay, a sure signal that as far as he's concerned the conversation is over, but she won't be put down so easily.

"What about these other scenes?"

"You heard what Jeremy said."

"Stupid boy!"

"Stupid or not, there'll be no more shooting today."

"Which gives us plenty of time..."

Chris puts the script down and leaps up aggressively.

"Who's directing this picture? You're very impudent. I'm not having the tail wagging the dog."

"I was only..."

"Don't interrupt," he barks, "I'm surprised at you, Charley. You're a good writer, efficient, timely, practical, but this approach is self indulgent and naive. You make no allowance for the huge personal commitment I've put into the project. I've worked long and hard for many years. You talk of additional scenes as if they can be tacked on willy nilly. This is a major historical film. It's got to be seen as a whole, not a jumbled collection of separate bits, glued together as we go along. Then there are the finances. I know it's not something you pure artistic people like talking about, but it must be faced. I've only just got a sound financial package with reliable backers. I can't jeopardise that now."

"But don't you see, I agree with you," she pleads, hoping he won't jump down her throat, "Seeing it as a whole is precisely my point."

"You don't understand how precarious, even perilous it was to embark on this subject. I've always wanted to do it, but I was aware of the difficulties. This isn't the first time someone's attempted to bring the Peasants' Revolt to the screen, but no one's succeeded before. We can't start chopping and changing now, messing it up when we're so close. It's the realisation of a dream. I won't undermine it by being too ambitious."

Charley tries to intervene again, but he puts up his hand and continues.

"I've studied the wreckage of my predecessors. You talk about broadening it out, but broaden it out and you make it thin, you make it weak. Make it broad and you'll lose it."

"Alright, maybe not *everything*, but take the scene at Mile End we've already filmed. We know they were there in their thousands..."

"Which we've shown very well..."

"Yes, but we make no reference to any peasants outside Kent and Essex. We don't show the men from Hertfordshire even though we know they must have been present. That's a distortion."

"We can't put in everything, this is a picture, not a historical tract. We have to concentrate on the film potential."

"Precisely and yet we don't include important characters from Hertfordshire, William Cadindon and WG."

"WG?"

"William Grindcobb, the leader in St. Albans. It's all here in the book."

She waves a copy of *A Little Liberty*, sent her by Warren.

"You showed it me the other day," he says dismissively.

"There's a wealth of action and drama," she says, waving the book again, "plenty of material to work up into scenes with major potential. If we take..."

"No, no, no!" he shouts, cutting his outstretched arm through the air so close and quick, she has to duck to avoid him clipping her head.

He looms over her, anger and frustration in his eyes, his mouth set firm and resolute. She leans back, but won't give up and glares back defiantly. He sits down.

"No. I respect your views, but I won't shoot any more scenes. The picture is..."

37

A sudden loud crash followed by a long drawn out boom. They rush onto the set. One side of the 'hall' has fallen down and there are cries from people pinned underneath. Around a dozen have grabbed the edges of the wooden structure, but are pulling and jerking in opposite directions.

"Everybody round this side," Chris shouts, "quickly!"

They bunch up at one edge and on his command lift simultaneously. Three people have been trapped, but they shout more in shock than pain and are quickly dragged clear before the structure is allowed to fall back. It bounces noisily and sends up a huge cloud of dust. Despite being almost totally covered by the large, heavy boards no one is badly injured. They limp away with minor cuts and bruises, but are badly shaken.

"Get them to the hospital to get checked out," Chris shouts, "They look okay, but we don't want to take any chances."

The bigger problem is how the 'wall' came down in the first place. No one has a rational explanation.

"...it just trembled...sort of shook, then seemed to move... it just came down, there was no warning..."

The bolts holding the frame have sheared away. These are quickly repaired and the set re-erected. The foreman carpenter is rigorously quizzed by Chris, but is adamant the scenery was put together correctly and can find no reason for the accident. Chris walks back to his room grumpily. Charley follows. She's not yet given up and opens up once more about the additional scenes. Chris only half listens. His mind is still fixed on the accident and how it might have been much worse. Jeremy's concerns and Lawrence's advice reverberate.

"At least include the St.Albans men marching on London," Charley says, "it will be a good contrast to the scenes with Jack Straw."

"Jack Straw?" Chris mumbles.

"When he made his so – called confession we could flashback to him meeting the Hertfordshire men at Highbury on their way to London. We'd have to insert some connecting shots between the men on the march and the discussions with the abbot. I thought perhaps..."

"Yes, yes, alright," Chris says, but Charley doesn't hear him and continues.

"...this would tie in well with the scene at Mile End. I know you don't want to make it too complicated and there's the budget...but if we're really canny we wouldn't need to re-shoot everything. We could make them meet the king quite easily and then I could work up the discussion between WG and the others..."

"WG?"

"William Grindcobb. I said before he was the leader of..."

"Oh, yes, okay then."

Charley stops at last.

"You agree?"

"Yes, but this has to be an end. I want no more."

He speaks without looking at her, quietly, resigned, keen for her to leave.

"A scene at Highbury and new material for Mile End?"

"Yes, yes, but it has to be done quickly. You'll have to get these new scenes written toute suite. I want no delay."

"Of course, of course...how soon?"

"Tomorrow."

"Tomorrow?"

"I want it here in the morning. This WG, what d'you call him, Grinding...?"

"Grindcobb."

"We'll need somebody good to play him, somebody who can step in quickly. I have John Thurley in mind, I only hope he's available. The other one, what was his name?"

"William Cadindon."

"We'll get some somebody who's standing in, I'll look into that...well, what are you waiting for, you've got a lot to do. Take your little book and get started!"

He waves his hands towards her and she scuttles out. He watches her go with mild satisfaction. Getting the new material prepared by the morning will teach her to be so presumptuous and bloody cheeky! Telling him what to include and what not to include, patronising him with remarks about not having to re-shoot everything! We could flashback this, we could insert connecting shots, we don't need to make it too complicated! God, who the hell's the bloody director! Now she's been punished he starts feeling better and walks onto the set with a spring in his step, though it quickly abates as he realises what he's agreed. New material, new scenes, more rehearsals and more sets to be designed. He's not just punishing her, he's punishing himself!

The 'wall' has been successfully repositioned and the carpenters are putting the finishing touches to the set. Chris calls over the designer and explains the new requirements. She looks askance, but Chris is insistent. She must produce workable designs before she leaves today. Then he goes over to the foreman carpenter.

"Will that be okay for tomorrow?" he says, pointing to the set.

"No problem," the foreman says with a self satisfied wave of his arm.

"Good, then you can all get cracking on something new, just a few things I want you to knock me up."

The foreman is no more pleased than the set designer especially within the same tight schedule, but promises to work all night if necessary. Chris makes it all sound so simple. The blank sets can be constructed from easily calculated specifications while the designs are completed. Then they can be put together in the early morning at the latest. The foreman is sceptical, but he's worked with Chris many times and the director has an uncanny knack at getting everybody to achieve the impossible. He agrees and then spends most of the night regretting he has! Chris's spirits lift again. That'll show her. She'll appear in the morning with a half finished script full of errors and impracticalities because she's had to rush it. Meanwhile, Chris will have all the sets ready for shooting, actors in position, everybody ready and waiting and she'll be holding them up!

Actors! Chris suddenly remembers he has to get actors to play Grindcobb and Cadindon. How can they be ready so quickly, even if he can find them? No matter, they have to be lined up, script or not. Cadindon is the easier one. Mark Vane, one of the stand-ins looks promising.

"I want you here bright and early in the morning," he tells the young actor, " it could be a great opportunity."

Mark Vane is excited, but curious and asks about the part.

"All in good time," Chris says, brushing him aside with a regal sweep of his arm, "Just be here and you won't be disappointed."

Chris rings John Thurley, the actor he wants to play Grindcobb, but gets no reply. It's disappointing, but it's still early. He'll try later. Having got Charley and the set design and construction arrangements underway, there's not much more for him to do at the studio. With temperamental and excitable actors and a bolshie screenwriter it's been a fraught day. Added to this, the magnitude of embarking on an ambitious schedule of new shooting is only now sinking in. He was utterly opposed to Charley's proposals, so how did he get to this position? She'd persistently manoeuvred his own anger against him! When will he learn? He shouldn't have relented. Time to go. He can ring Thurley from home.

The large village of Hempston lies where the north – south road crosses the east – west river valley. It was once a sleepy place. The noisiest sound was the trains chugging along the branch railway line that followed the course of the river – apart from the clangorous bells of the parish church on a Sunday morning. The railway went forty years ago while newer noises compete with the bells. For weeks diggers, excavators, cement mixers, concrete makers, carriers of hods and timber, clerks of works, architects, planners, developers, have been busy in long days, every day. The battle for the west fields was lost months ago. It divided the village between those believing it would bring long needed expansion, those believing such expansion ought to be curtailed for ever, those believing it would 'open up' the village and those believing it would destroy it. Such entrenched positions seemed unbridgeable, but old battles quickly lose their adherents if the reasons for the fight become irrelevant and the irrelevance of those earlier conflicts was obvious once the smoke cleared and the 'openers up' emerged victorious. Now the old battles are only re-fought as mild entertainment in saloon bar wrangles.

The development is in three parts. Whether to leave the opposition peacefully nursing their wounds or for other reasons, the west fields as the most controversial aspect have been put temporarily in abeyance. The area has been fenced off, but otherwise left untouched. This has slightly strengthened the pro camp, stimulating a myopic tendency amongst the uncommitted. If you don't see it, maybe it won't happen. There are suddenly many more ostriches in the village, only too keen to bury their heads. You see, the supporters say, it's nowhere near as bad as they said it would be. There was a lot of scare mongering about encroaching on the green belt and now we can see that was unfounded. Most of them are unconvinced, still issuing dire warnings and muttering about the continuing need to be vigilant, but at least for a time their influence has been curtailed.

The second aspect, a 'brown field' development on the site of the old railway station has gone ahead. The new houses and apartments are not to everyone's taste, but at least it's merely 'filling in' and in itself doesn't threaten either the integrity of the surrounding countryside or the village itself. Only the ultra alert or the ultra obsessive realised the significance of the original land purchase, but their warnings of further encroachment went unheeded. Not all of the new properties have owner occupiers. Some remain empty and some have been let. There's a rumour one of the houses has been purchased, but for some mysterious reason never occupied. The owner is never seen. Not all the land was previously railway property. Some has been taken from what was originally part of the back garden of an old house that fronts onto the main street. Some of the opposition noted this, with appropriately dolorous implications, but by then the overall fight was just about lost and few took their grim prognosis seriously.

This meant the third aspect went largely unnoticed because there was no obvious connection to the others and it was not even part of the original proposals. Tonight, all that will change. For the developers purchased the whole property as a single plot, including the rest of the garden and the house. It's a very old house and has been a landmark in the village for centuries, the last remaining example of its medieval heart. Dark brown timber beams protrude from its white walls, the upper floor slightly overhanging the ground.

The pavement is narrower here, remnant of an age before motor cars. The windows have been replaced many times, but retain something of their original character while the stout oak front door is as old as the beams.

Built around 1320, the house has been continuously occupied for most of its nearly seven centuries. In living memory it's been various shops, a solicitor's office, and more recently an estate agent. It's been empty for a few months. It's last occupier, a fancy goods shop, closed when the proprietor retired. Yet for most of its existence the building has been a private house and in the 14th century would have been occupied by at least two and up to four or five families.

The fading evening sun glints through the windows as several men climb the stairs, which groan under their weight, the boards creaking, the old beams wheezing as they tramp around the rooms. These are not inquisitive visitors intent on possible purchase or lease, but have a more explicit and immediate motive for their examination. In their dusty working clothes and heavy boots they could be part of the construction team, but they are separate specialists. One prods the wall indiscriminately with a crowbar while the other kicks the skirting with his boot, as if they are probing the resistance of the building. It doesn't reply. It can't, but that doesn't mean it can't feel.

"I'll be glad to be out of here," the man with the crowbar says, "I've had enough of this place."

The other laughs.

"Don't tell me you believe all the rumours."

His companion doesn't reply, but walks into another room with his crowbar. He feels safer with it in his hand. He starts his prodding again. Some plaster falls from the wall. He keeps prodding and scraping until the brick is exposed. The other man comes in.

"You're hitting that wall so hard, anybody'd think you were trying to find something in it."

"Got to test it," the first man says, pulling back the crowbar, "Any case it's not just rumour. Some of the men have felt things."

"You'll be telling me next you've felt something yourself."

43

The other turns to him, but says nothing.

"God, you have haven't you?"

"Maybe."

"All these old places creak and heave, it don't mean nothing."

The first man shrugs.

"Let's just say I wouldn't want to be in this house at night."

The second man is about to laugh, then seeing the stern, determined, but fearful expression he says nothing and looks round with a shudder.

"Shut up, man, you're giving me the creeps!"

"It's not just our guys, some of the locals have felt things near this place. Ever since we came on the site."

"Well, it won't be for much longer," the other says, looking out the rear window, "We were told not to start until the end of the day. We can do most of it from the back."

"We'll still have to fence off the pavement."

"There won't be much light soon. Are we ready?"

The first man looks around and then nods.

"I'm ready. Let's get out of here."

Chris sits alone in his large lounge staring into the twilit garden. With no lights he finds the dark, shadowy room peaceful. An ebullient blackbird allows not one silent second to elapse before the end of the day, working against time, getting every note out before darkness descends. But it will end as suddenly and abruptly as his brilliance began. Wise bird, he knows precisely when to stop. If he sings beyond his time, the night will eclipse his exuberance. No one listens to a blackbird at night and he knows it. If only Chris had half that bird's wisdom he wouldn't have set in motion such an ill judged process at the studio.

In the tranquillity of the fading light, his earlier vigour ebbs away, replaced by trickling doubt like water escaping from a leaky pond. How can a set be so quickly designed and constructed? It usually takes weeks, if not months, not a night and a morning. He's set Charley an absurd deadline and his anger has elbowed out common sense. Even if she produces the new material it's bound to be rushed and superficial and John Thurley will need a proper script to study. Maybe he should ring him and apologise. He got carried away. It was her fault for going on about it so long and so forcefully. If she'd been a little less...determined...yes, that's it. He'll give her more time and then he can reconsider the whole project, perhaps even break it off. He feels better. It's good to think things through in a calm, relaxed mood, rather than fly off at the deep end on the spur of the moment, coming up with ridiculous ideas. He'll never learn.

But these are purely cinematic technicalities. A director of his experience and verve can overcome them and as for the team – sheer force of personality will carry him through. Under pressure people can achieve a great deal more than they think they're capable. They'll get it done. We'll do it. There are plenty of examples of filmmakers completing new scenes, in fact knocking off completely new films by cleverly reusing existing sets. Didn't Hammer make two films of Edgar Allan Poe stories from a single set back in the sixties? What were they called? He still nurses the embers of resentment against Charley. It wouldn't take much for those embers to be fanned into flame.

"Jumped up, arrogant know all," he says quietly to himself, "who does she think she is?"

Of course, he knows the answer to his own question. Charlotte Kennet is one of those people utterly comfortable with who they are and where they are from, all their life has been mapped out from an early age. Not that she's not good. Her abilities make it even more infuriating, but it doesn't mean he has to like her. He'll never like anyone of her *type*. He's not like anyone of her type and never will be. So many people in this business have the right background, usually through family connections, veritable dynasties, sons and daughters of actors and writers and directors and cinematographers and designers. Not Chris. His was from a humble...no, that's the wrong word...an obscure...no, still not right...an *unconnected* background. So many are connected. Charley must have been connected. If he ferrets about he'll find out and then...what does it matter? Chris wasn't connected. It was a struggle, breaking in from the outside. Not many do it. He should be proud of his achievement. Yet has he ever really been accepted, will he ever be *connected*? He shouldn't complain. He's privileged to be doing what he's always wanted to do. Few can do that. How many of those he'd known at school followed their chosen path, let alone achieved their full potential? He can think of only one, maybe two, for the rest, the mindless grind of earning a living. But there's been the inevitable downside. Two wives, five children. He's lost them all. Was it his 'art' that chased them away or was it him? Too late now to repair broken fences.

His mind returns to the film. He'll ring Thurley. An uncompleted script can only mean an incomplete proposition, but it may be enough to get him to the studio.

"You know I've been working on *Hurling Time*," Chris begins.

"I'd heard it was finished," Thurley says.

"Yes...well...it is...almost...or was going to be...what I mean is we, that is I have decided to extend the movie..."

"Extend?"

"New material...it's exciting stuff...expanding the scope of the picture to take in...the broader perspective...there's an important new character, Grindcobb the leader of the revolt in Hertfordshire. I need somebody really good for this part, someone quintessentially blending vigour and dignity, courage and inspiration. Naturally you immediately came to mind."

"I'm flattered. You have a script?"

"Ah, now as you know I've always believed in including everybody in the team when making a picture..."

"The team?" John says sceptically.

"...so I want to involve you before the script is finalised especially in relation to the character."

"I see."

"If you can spare the time of course."

Slightly bemused, but curiously excited, John agrees. He'll be on the set in the morning. With that hurdle successfully scaled Chris settles back and pours himself a large cognac. It's dark now and he switches on the small lamp beside his chair.

46

It casts wide shadows. He stares at his own exaggerated head on the opposite wall for a few moments, glowing inwardly until it's suddenly banished by an alarming thought. Quite apart from it's effect on the overall structure of the film (something he'd given only passing consideration) all this additional material has financial implications. His earlier doubts return. That 'unartistic' objection he'd levelled at Charley looms up. What if they should run out of funds? The possibility arose before when they were shooting some of the longer London scenes and Chris nervously approached the producer only to be told in his inimitable cavalier fashion to 'keep shooting.' What will he say now?

Most of the time the producer is like an absent friend that can be safely ignored. Until times like now. That very semi-detachment makes it even more difficult to face contact when it becomes unavoidable. Like his audience, a disembodied essence with which he has even less contact. That's the nature of film, unlike the theatre, no immediate audience. All the effort and angst to an empty auditorium. No reaction, no relationship, every decision made on the basis of what we *think* the audience will appreciate, like, dislike, are moved or repelled by. Success or failure consigned to a potentially empty cinema or one filled with the bored, the fidgety, the cynical and all in far away places we've never heard of and will never visit. It reminds him of examinations at school. Entering the room, as prepared as you're likely to be, belting all you've got onto the paper in a couple of hours and then leaving, to have your efforts picked over by an unseen stranger who finally passes judgement on what your whole future depends. A nervy and scary experience most of us will then avoid for the rest of our lives. Yet here we are, doing it over and over again. Okay we have the reception of the last film to guide us, but if that wasn't so good, whither now? His last film wasn't badly received so he shouldn't be fearful. But this is like nothing he's ever done before. How will it be received by the couple on the back row in Lower Bored Drip Under Slime craving stimulation and entertainment?

Then other misgivings bubble up as his mind returns to the studio. The problems with Jeremy, the crash of scenery, the conversation with Lawrence, all jingle jangling in his troubled brain. He's been too soft and given in to Charley, while being too hard with these other matters. The harassed parent with two unruly children, too soft with the one and too hard with the other, publicly embarrassed in front of a crowd of people. Brushed them aside, played them down, ignored the warning signals, now more serious than he thought. Already it may be too late. Too late to stop Charley's disastrous expansion, forcing him to neither wholly approve nor wholly obstruct, either way losing control of his own film! Too late to get a grip on the growing debilitation of the cast from these strange happenings, real or imaginary, threatening the viability of the picture!

When Grindcobb and the others left Mile End they had every expectation that what they had achieved, confirmed in the charters they carried in their hands, was nothing less than the dawning of a new age. Excited at the prospect of their next meeting with the abbot, many times on the long twenty mile trek back to St. Albans they must have relished the thought of his face when he saw the papers bearing the unwelcome message of their freedom. For no matter how much he resented it, he could not gainsay a charter sealed in the king's name. He was bound to stare dumbfounded at the unbelievable words, at a stroke liberating an entire people. Those men on the road must have kept telling themselves this was no dream, no foolish jest at the alehouse or a fantastic reverie of a summer day. Then, so soon, so suddenly, so unexpectedly that freedom was to be snatched from them by events over which they had no control and little influence. Even as they successfully negotiated with the abbot, the winds of Wat Tyler's defeat at Smithfield were blowing northwards to undermine them.

Charley puts down *A Little Liberty*. She's already made good progress. Closely relying on Warren Grover's account, the existing scenes at the Mile End conference between the king and the peasant representatives have been rewritten. A whole new section has been inserted covering his meeting with Grindcobb and the Hertfordshire contingent. She reads on, fascinated and inspired. She already knows the subsequent events, but Warren's enthusiasm and passion for the subject is infectious and she's keen to get a feel for the dramatic potential and lift the story beyond the bare outlines. The next section covers the period between mid June and late July. The mass swearing of allegiance they've just been shooting, known as the 'fealty' scene is in late July while the additional scenes Chris has agreed – Highbury and Mile End – are in mid June. It's a big gap and ought to be bridged, but beyond her remit. The concession for additional scenes squeezed out of Chris on the grounds that without them the film will be unbalanced may actually make the situation worse. The Mile End and Highbury scenes already exist. Effectively they are now tacking on a Hertfordshire element out of context, excluding the separate drama in the county itself. She puts the book down and goes over her notes.

Revolt begins in Essex, quickly spreading to Kent. John Ball preaches to the masses at Blackheath before they march on London. They occupy the Tower and attack the Savoy Palace. Meeting with the king at Mile End where they obtain charters abolishing serfdom. Final meeting at Smithfield – their leader, Wat Tyler is killed and the Revolt starts to disintegrate.

Separate developments in St. Albans and surrounding countryside against the Abbot, the largest local landowner. The prior and some monks flee to Tynemouth. Various disturbances in the countryside such as breaking down enclosures. Delegation travels to London, attends Mile End and obtains charter for Hertfordshire. On the way they pass Jack Straw's men at Highbury. On return to St. Albans commence negotiations with the Abbot on rents, common land, pasture, fishery and use of the mill. Following the defeat at Smithfield further negotiations are less vociferous. Some leaders arrested and proceedings are taken to...

She puts the notes down. More pages detail later events leading up to the arrival of the king. She can't possibly use such a mass of material even if Chris agrees to further scenes closing the 'gap' between June and July 1381. Could Chris be right, will 'broadening out' lose the film? Has she created an impossible burden for herself and the whole project? It started out as just another assignment. The subject was interesting, but not one she'd necessarily take to heart with such passion. Now it could be the turning point in her career, plumbing her core beliefs, fundamentally challenging her commitment and integrity. All the more reason to be sure of the path, especially as it seems she's influencing others to follow.

She checks over the revised Mile End scenes against her notes. She's not needed to undertake major research. *A Little Liberty* has appendices almost as long as the main text, setting out the contemporary records. It may only have been intended as a popular adventure story. In his preface Warren says 'I try to bring the people's past alive, so when they walk down their modern street feel the street of their ancestors, even meeting them on the way.' If that objective is judged on how it galvanises and energises her then it's certainly a success. She studies the material on the St. Albans men's arrival at Highbury, imagining the group coming across Jack Straw's Essex contingent busily burning large houses and summoning them to support 'King Richard and the True Commons.' Some snatches of dialogue and shots come to mind and she scribbles these down, but her mind is already drifting. She's like the teacher trying to count children who keep darting around a room, never standing still. Then she returns to *A Little Liberty*, Warren's words inspiring and anchoring her flying thoughts.

...so much had happened in such an incredibly short time many of those traumatised by the repression must have struggled to understand the full significance of what they had lived through...years later perhaps in unexpected moments they might suddenly experience a cascade of memories and the events of ten, twenty years before would flood their consciousness as if they were yesterday...some days in the fields or in the workshop they would look back as if these things had passed as in the wink of an eye, while on other days it would seem it was as if they filled their whole lives and they had known no true existence before or since...

Now she forgets her earlier misgivings, no longer concerned how to tackle the material and whether she'll be smothered in the task. She may not actually be in the past, but *feels* what they felt. She goes back and works on the Highbury scene, amazed how she can hammer it out so quickly. Hardly stopping to think, she's swept along by the events and the movements and words of the men come to her without hesitation. She hardly looks up, though she's tempted because she feels the vision not only in her head, but in the room itself as if she's actually there! It invigorates and sustains, but is also a little scary. The words and directions keep flowing, but overwhelmed by a sudden fear that what she writes is incorrect she stops. She looks up, but keeps her eyes closed, opening them only very slowly, expecting to see a wide expanse of grass, flaming buildings and hundreds of men. The window, chair, carpet, bookcase – it's her room.

It must be right, it must be true!

Who said that? Her own voice in her head or someone else? She pulls out all her books and notes. What she writes must be truthful, has to be authentic! But aren't Warren's words with his comprehensive appendices enough? She spends ten minutes gobbling every word ever written on that brief encounter so long ago on Highbury. It's right, there's nothing to contradict her script. She sighs with relief and goes back, head down to continue writing. Filled with the splurging words like a cup constantly overflowing, she writes rapidly, she must do the past justice, put down everything they want...*what they want*...what's she thinking about...who wants? She stops, but only for a second as the voice in her head speaks again, as if she's taking dictation. Then it stops. She stops writing and stares at the setting sun at the window. The light flickers through the trees and casts a bright glow on the far wall.

She picks up *A Little Liberty* again and flicks though it desultorily, but what she feels doesn't come from its pages. It's something outside paper and ink, outside herself, outside the room. She listens for anything this force may impart, but hears nothing. She turns back to her work and begins again, but the words and images don't rush so furiously. A new affirmation demands her attention. She talked of tragedy while Chris talked of failure. She must offset the 'defeat' at Smithfield with the 'hope' at St. Albans. But as Chris says, wasn't that also failure? So the film would still be finishing downbeat, depressed. No – poignant, sad, but also courageous, inspiring, uplifting – out of apparent tragedy comes determination, continuing the struggle, a fragile but unbroken line to the present day.

The sun is almost down. In the fading light the glow on the wall is gone. She writes again, but with some effort stops. Yet her hand wavers, it wants to continue. She looks down and can't believe the words she's written. This is not Highbury or Mile End. In fact it's no film scene at all.

It is Friday 14th June and we are gathered together in the evening. The prior left the abbey today. They say he has fled north with four monks to the abbey's house at Tynemouth. A sure sign of the rightness of our cause. He is no loss either to the abbey or the town...

Her hand is still now, though the words keep beating in her head. The dismal view from the window dissipates, replaced by an open space in which hundreds of people gather. At first she thinks it Highbury or Mile End, but the action in both places was in the morning when there was plenty of light. This scene, like now is almost night. She blinks. It will go. It remains and then, in response to that inner voice she starts to write again.

Grindcobb and Cadindon have returned from London. Some say they bring great news and will be with us soon. Tonight we will assert our liberties. Tonight we will make free the woods and fields. Tonight they will belong to the people.

She stops writing and looks up. The throng of people is gone. It's very dark, but she can see the street through the window. This is her room in her time. It was a fleeting concoction, fantastic creation of a fevered imagination. She's tired and such things can come from overwork especially when the mind has been submerged in the past all these hours. There's still more to be done, she must work on if the scenes are to be completed by morning. She looks down and writes again, but can't dismiss what she felt. Is it the unseen voice of the past that speaks, guiding her with its unseen hand?

In Hempston all the preparations are completed. The plant is in position at the rear. At the front a few people passing by have wondered why the pavement and part of the road have been fenced off, but otherwise it's hardly been noticed. With most windows facing east there's little light inside from the setting sun. As the last of the men leave the house a dismal, dusty pall descends. No more those unnerving scrapings and scratchings, heavings and bendings. It's eerily quiet, the air dreadfully, heavily still. Yet this is no dead habitation. The spirits of the past know what is to come and seven hundred years of departed occupants vie for supremacy, their hopes and fears oozing from the floors, exhaling from the walls, gasping from the ceilings. The ears of anyone who now chanced to be in the empty house would be overwhelmed by the rush of competing voices in their final expelling of energy. They would be pressing their fingers in their ears to block the fearful cacophony. But no one hears.

Outside they are ready, unaware of the awakening and struggle within the walls. The minutes pass quickly. They are in a hurry. Much must be done tonight. What is left tomorrow must be irreversible. Inside too the minutes pass quickly. More and more spirits expire and are laid to rest. Most will go the way of the house, but not all. After centuries of silence there are those, whose voices and movements have disturbed the invaders of the building, but that was only the beginning. The brief charged minutes close and the struggle ends. Only those that have lain the longest remain. They have been sleeping, but are now awake. Their time has come.

The ball crashes into the wall and the roof collapses. Doors and windows are shattered, floors disintegrate, beams heave for the last time. It strikes again and the fragile structure that has enclosed so much for so long bends and wrenches apart. What took weeks to build and has stood for hundreds of years will be demolished in minutes. But destroying the building will not suppress the past. He has lost forever the home where he has lain undisturbed for over six hundred years, but he is released. From tonight many will feel 'happenings' and his voice will be heard in the wind.

"I am come and I will be avenged."

3

CHARLEY works through the night on Mile End and Highbury. It's not difficult, the material flowing with the ease and accuracy of an eye witness. At first she keeps 'correcting,' but if reality diverges from established accounts how can she repeat such errors? She completes the last of the new scenes by three o'clock and stops to rest, but only briefly. Images of the night of 14th June 1381 return and despite her exhaustion she must write on. Once she does she's like the marathon runner with twenty three miles behind her, tired and ready to give up, suddenly suffused with new, more intense energy. Many times she tells herself she ought to be in bed and all this will wait until morning, but she can't get the congregation in the fields out of her mind and knows it can't wait. With the guiding voices from afar, she keeps writing, first in short, stabbing bursts, then flowing more smoothly, her fingers flying along, as if they're not part of her at all, but cogs in some automatic machine, belting it out, faster, faster, faster. She's with them, marching across the fields, defying the abbot, breaking down the enclosures, smashing the gates to the woods!

She creeps to bed around four thirty, falling asleep almost immediately, yet no undisturbed rest for she dreams constantly. It's the next day, Saturday 15th June. A large crowd gathers. Someone is proclaiming. She can't tell what is said. Then they are on the move to a place a little way out of the town. Grindcobb and Cadindon are there. She knows them instinctively. They discuss their next course of action. Grindcobb puts forward proposals. All must have access to the woods and fields. All remaining gates and enclosures restraining their free movement must be destroyed. The crowd marches back into town in good order to find at least two thousand strong assembled near the monastery. Villagers have come from the surrounding country. The county is aflame!

After perhaps only an hour's real sleep she gets in early at the studio. On the way more images of 15th June flood her mind, but in the cold morning light they now seem just that – insubstantial images, clever fabrications of a vibrant imagination. She even veers towards Chris's apprehensions. Are they taking on things beyond their control, diluting the impact of the movie by 'broadening it out?' The images flitter again. What or *whom* is beyond their control?

She scrurries about, looking at the sets, already well advanced, talking to the designers, scene movers, carpenters, electricians, other technicians, anyone! It stimulates her again and the images return, this time more benign, more exciting. Now all the doubts she'd harboured and then dismissed in the night, only to be resurrected in the morning are thrust aside again! They've all worked so hard it has to be, it can be successful! A group of extras arrive. She prattles to them and then hurries on, seeing some of the cast, but she should see Chris first. He's not in his room. No one has seen him. How dare he be late after prescribing such a tight deadline and making them all come in so early!

She returns to the set. Lawrence is talking to an actor she's not seen before, though he seems familiar.

"...and Chris asked you to come in this morning?"

"Something I might find interesting. I understand he's extending the film, new scenes, completely new characters."

"Yes," Lawrence says guardedly in a long drawl and seeing Charley beckons her over, "This is just the person who might be able to help. Charley, meet John Thurley. Do you know Chris asked him to come in?"

John Thurley is around thirty five with dark, penetrating eyes beneath long eyelashes and bushy eyebrows. A crop of slightly untidy brown hair lollops over his high forehead. She'll have to congratulate Chris on such an appropriate choice to play William Grindcobb, though she needs to hear his voice.

"Did he say what was involved?" she says.

"He was very flattering, said I had all the right attributes to play the leader of the Revolt in Hertfordshire."

His voice is deep and rounded, very impressive, but Charley isn't sure. Grindcobb's authority must come from what he says and how he says it, not from the tone or pitch of his voice. No matter, she's not the director, casting is not part of her remit. Thurley notices the papers under her arm.

"Is that the new script?"

Charley fumbles with the papers, some drop to the floor. Thurley picks them up and starts to read.

"Interesting. Chris didn't say you were so advanced. Are we going to run through it this morning?"

"I don't know, it depends on Chris..."

"Have you seen this, Lawrence?"

"Er no, we didn't...yesterday was..."

"Come on, let's look through it together," Thurley says, grabbing Lawrence's arm, then turning to Charley as he flicks through the papers again, "Can I see the rest of it? There are other copies so we can involve everybody else?"

Later she'll say it was Thurley's insistence that made her hand over all her scripts and readily take him with Lawrence to the rest of the cast. But it was really the same pressure that guided her fingers in the night, now demanding its message brought to life. Technicians and designers are still busily creating and erecting the final backdrops and structures. The cast, including Mark Vane, claiming his role as 'Cadindon,' huddle in one of the few clear corners of the new set, impervious to the banging and crashing, shouting and blathering. Within minutes the words of the new scenes are coursing freely. Their surroundings don't matter. Is Charley alone in feeling transposed to another place, another time? All they need now is the director.

Chris arrives not long after Charley, but he's too tense and wanders the studio, clearing his mind, deliberately avoiding everybody. He's been too accommodating with Charley and yet too dismissive with the fears of the cast. He must quash this nonsense of new scenes before it gets dangerous. He'll study what she's written with apparent seriousness, but put it aside before getting everybody to talk, calm them down, smooth everything out and re-commence where they left off, put the picture to bed. Now he feels better and heads towards the set, passing the work on the new scenery. The designer explains the changes. He keeps walking as she talks, but isn't really listening, answering with dull grunts as she shows her designs. Everything is well advanced, almost finished. As he gets to his room she asks if everything is okay.

"Yes, yes," he says, "just carry on...for now."

She stands, open mouthed and then says, "You did want everything completed for this morning?"

"I did? Oh yes, I did, as I said, carry on."

He goes inside and shuts the door. She walks away and shrugs. If she lives to be a hundred she'll never understand directors. She sees Charley working through the new material with the cast.

"Is this the new script?"she says.

Charley nods silently. Everybody is excited, not just declaiming the words, but moving and gesticulating, skipping into the new roles with surprising polish and understanding.

"All without a director," the designer whispers admiringly, "which reminds me, Chris has arrived."

Her words break the 1381 spell, enlivened from its six hundred year sleep. Charley sees Chris coming towards her.

"All done," she says, triumphantly waving the new script in his face, "Everybody's already read it through."

His mouth is set hard and implacable.

"Have they?" he says crustily, his eyes boring into her mercilessly, "You've shown this to the cast, without first showing me?"

"Well, you weren't here and John Thurley arrived and he..."

"John Thurley?"

"Yes, to play WG, he said you spoke to him last night."

Chris has forgotten about calling in Thurley.

"This is all very presumptuous."

"We didn't mean any harm…"

"Let me see that!"

He grabs the script and strides back to his room with Charley tripping after him. He flicks through most of it on the way, finishing it off silently in his chair while she waits nervously. She starts to speak, attempting to explain particular sections, but each time he puts up his hand for silence. She waits apprehensively, but he says nothing. Despite his irritation, he knows it's good, but not everything is to his liking. He concentrates on Highbury, suggesting amendments to the crowd scenes and ignores the additional material covering the night of 14th June. She listens patiently, but gradually gets more and more annoyed. As he starts to make similar comments to the Mile End scene she can contain herself no longer.

"You're turning the Hertfordshire peasants into an unruly mob!"

"Well, he says, if the cap fits."

"It doesn't fit at all. It's a disgraceful slur!"

Yesterday's anxieties return. He's angry, but also taken aback.

"Don't take it so seriously, Charley. You're romanticising these people too much. Mass movements have an ugly side."

He strikes out several passages and puts in new directions, thrusting the script back at her.

"This is a travesty!" she screams and storms out.

She meets the others on the set, saying with fiery exaggeration, "He wants to change everything," then turns as Chris comes thundering after her, "We can't go ahead with it like this."

"We can and we will," he says, dragooning the cast into position, but forgetting his original intention of dropping the new material in its entirety.

Charley erupts again. Determined to play him at his own game, she too starts revisiting scenes long since completed, demanding major changes. Both raise their voices, the row soon stifling all other sounds in a fierce hurling of insults and condemnations.

Ettie walks along the path beneath the trees, skirting the ponds, the last almost bereft of water in the heat of the summer. After a long and dispiriting walk her mood contrasts with the bright, warm day, the sultry, but not oppressive air, tempered by a slight, refreshing breeze. Plenty of people are on the common and yearning for solitude she cuts along the deserted cricket ground before reaching the road, heading east towards Hempston. She crosses to the other side, but can't get far. There are police cars and a large area has been taped off. Two days after the murder and they are still busily collecting evidence. She turns away and walks slowly back towards the town.

When she rang yesterday, Warren was already dead, killed it seems the evening before. Had his wife got her message? In her distress, Mrs. Grover had probably ignored the ansafone. What was Ettie to do? Go home and forget Warren Grover and his alleged happenings? She couldn't face the long drive to Gloucestershire, yet neither was she sure she wanted to stay. She spent the day wandering the highways and byways of the county, visiting some famous places such as Hatfield House and Bernard Shaw's place at Ayot St. Lawrence, but her mind had been too intent on other things to fully take them in. She got back to the hotel quite late, unwilling to mix with anyone. More frightful news would have only further unbalanced her, ruining any prospect of sleep on her second night.

It's early afternoon. Her appetite dampened as much as her spirits, she's skipped lunch. Still not sure, she won't make a move today and it looks like a third night in the hotel. A few people are in the bar, mostly residents, the only remaining locals being those with no homes or jobs to go to. She sits by the window and picks up today's copy of the 'The Mid Herts Herald,' lying on an adjacent chair. The headline reads 'Local Man Murdered on Common.' The story is written by the editor and takes up the first three pages. She tries to read, but is continually interrupted by the talk from the other end of the room. It's all about the murder.

"They say there's been odd things going on for some time."

The first paragraphs set out the bare facts, when and how the body was discovered and the predictably bland initial statement from the police. Then follows a long section, contrasting the peacefully idyllic location with the hideous event. The named places are unfamiliar, though they probably resonate with locals. It's distinctly atmospheric, even slightly chilling, bringing back the scene from her long walk. Two men are sitting at bar stools.

"Course, all that wild talk doesn't help."

"It's nothing new, been talking like that for years."

"Even so..."

Ettie listens carefully, but can't catch the next slice of conversation as they turn away, almost whispering. She loses the thread of the article and has to go back a couple of paragraphs.

"...people shouldn't say such things at times like this. It's not right."

"...been saying it for years..."

The second and third pages are devoted to the victim and there are some pictures of Warren. In one he's clearly enjoying himself as master of ceremonies at a local carnival, but the other is more recent and he looks older, the broad grin replaced by a worried intensity. The article refers to Warren's plans for the re-enactment, though it's interesting how the editor, prefers to call it a 're-staging.'

"I still say you can't take all that wild talk seriously, especially when you know where it comes from."

"I'm not so sure you can discount anything. There was a time..."

Her concentration disrupted again, Ettie listens carefully, but the two men carry on in low tones. She reads on. Warren was a well known local activist with his community and historical work, who *will be sadly missed by many, even by those who did not always agree with him.* It doesn't enlarge on who these might be, nor on what matters they took issue with him, though there's a later reference to his *'encyclopaedic, some might say fanatical obsession'* with the Peasants Revolt and a further reminder of the 're-staging.'

'His proposal highlighted a frequently forgotten aspect of our local past... based on his penetrating analysis of the times and his eye for detail...his refusal to compromise his integrity justifiably earning him widespread admiration.'

Positive stuff, but a sting in the tail.

'...though while acknowledging the depth of his knowledge, some critics felt he overly simplified the complexities of the period...' and then *'...Warren recently levelled the same criticism at Chris Pleasant, embarked on a similar project with his film 'Hurling Time...'*

With this incongruous ending Warren gets the last word. Or does Warren's unfortunate death give the editor a unique opportunity to lambast Chris's film? She goes to the bar, but the two men have left, so returns to the window and skims the article again. Perhaps she should visit the editor. She asks at reception.

"The newspaper office is very close, just round the corner, near the church."

It's a surprisingly small office, tucked between a tea room and an estate agent. The front window displays pictures from recent editions, though none from the big story. A woman greets her from behind the counter.

"I would like to see the editor," Ettie says.

"Is he expecting you?"

"It's about the Warren Grover story."

With a curt 'wait here, please,' the woman disappears through the back door, but quickly returns.

"Mr. Carter will see you, Ms...?"

"Rodway, Miss Rodway."

"You're lucky to find him in," the woman says, leading Ettie through, "He's due to go out shortly."

She knocks on a door and enters a room, crammed with files on a couple of tables. The strong electric lamps swell the little natural light coming from the small window, beside which a man sits, glaring at a computer screen. He turns as Ettie enters. Early forties, slightly balding at the edges, hair still brown with streaks of grey, eyes are wide and large with uplifted eyebrows giving him a constantly surprised expression, though they rise still further now. He clears files from a table and motions Ettie to a chair opposite. He smiles widely and introduces himself as George Carter, but beneath the affable openness there's care around the eyes and mouth. The face perhaps of a man who's seen much, some at least he'd rather not talk about.

"You wanted to talk about Warren Grover?"

"Your article is very interesting."

"I'm glad you think so. Now, what can you tell...?"

"You intend to follow up the story?"

"It's likely to still be live next week. What do you...?"

"A very tragic event, but your article went beyond the immediate situation, it was very...comprehensive...in the coverage of Warren Grover's work in the community. It was almost...a eulogy...very fine. I wanted to ask you..."

"Excuse me, but you say you wanted to ask me?"

"Yes."

He laughs.

"This is a newspaper. Our business is to collect the news. People usually come in here to tell *us* things."

"Oh yes, of course, I quite understand that, but before I tell you about him, there are a few things I'd like to clear up."

"Your knew Warren Grover?"

"Yes...in a way...did you?"

He hesitates, puckers his lips and inclines his head slightly to one side, unsure whether to continue the conversation in the vein she's successfully set or challenge her. On reflection, he does neither.

"Why do you ask?"

"The article seemed very...personal."

"Not unusual. A crime story needs the background filled out, human interest, bring the victim to life so to speak, if you'll pardon the..."

"I quite understand. You speak from particular experience?"

He nods.

"Even so, the tenor of the article, had to be written by someone who knew him."

"He was a local figure known by repute. We had met."

"Have you been editor very long?"

"A few months. What does...?"

"You've picked up a great deal in such a short time. I must congratulate you. It's very professional."

He half smiles, flattered, but also irritated. So far she's learnt much more about him than he has about her. She beams, her eyes twinkling mischievously.

"You still haven't told me how you know Warren Grover," he says.

"Through his work on the Peasants' Revolt."

"Oh, that."

She's unsure whether his reaction is of disappointment or concern.

"Why didn't he approve of the film being made?"

"It's a travesty. These film people never have any respect for our heritage, they cheapen everything, sensationalising, distorting serious material down to the common denominator of..."

"So this is not so much based on anything Warren said?"

"Warren advised Chris Pleasant on local matteres."

"What did Warren say about him?"

George squirms.

"Nothing as such, but everything Warren Grover stood for was in direct contradiction to those behind this film."

"And you followed this up?"

"We did a feature about the studios a few months back. I spoke to the screenwriter."

"So you've not spoken to Chris Pleasant?"

But George Carter has had enough.

"What is your interest in Warren Grover, Miss Rodway?"

"He came to see me recently."

"In connection with his work on the Peasants' Revolt in this area?"

"Yes."

"What did he tell you?"

"Some matters are confidential," Ettie says defensively, "I've no wish to talk about them so soon after his unfortunate death. Besides, there are issues that need to be...looked into before..."

63

"Ettie Rodway," he turns the name over, "there's something...what business are you in?"

"I undertake...research...usually of a historical nature..."

"And in that connection Warren sought your help?"

"I suppose we had a common interest."

He looks at her carefully. She suspects he now recognises her name.

"An interest in matters that went beyond historical facts, perhaps, what some might call paranormal?"

Ettie is silent. George snaps his fingers.

"That's it, that's why Warren came to see you! What did he tell you?"

"I was hoping you could tell *me*."

"Warren Grover never spoke to me about anything like that," he says sharply, then musing, "Warren Grover getting *vibrations*...I suppose he was that sort of man...but that's not news...even so...he's spoken to you, hasn't he? What did he see, what did he say."

"I don't think now is the right time, it's a little indelicate..."

"Delicate enough to bring you here. Come on, don't hold out on me."

"I understand there are rumours..."

"There are always rumours," George says stiffly, refusing to bite, "That's one reason why this story won't go away, "If we followed up every damned rumour we'd end up with a gossip sheet nobody would believe and nobody would want to buy."

Ettie remains silent. He tries once more, but she prevaricates further and the conversation finally stagnates. As she leaves he makes a vague reference to her talking to Warren's widow, Kathleen.

"Though the police will be seeing her," he says with banal unhelpfulness.

Walking back to the hotel, she feels she may have blown it. Her probing him may have unnecessarily exposed her and irritated George. He's got the scent and is bound to keep trying. He knows more, but won't talk and seems reluctant to use everything he's got. Guarding his sources perhaps or over reliant on unsubstantiated rumour? What does he really feel about Warren? He wants to know what Warren told her, but dismisses Warren's 'vibrations' as '*not* news,' yet skews the conversation towards Chris's film, which is surely as much *non* news? If *Hurling Time* is news, is it really local news? George hasn't been the editor long. Is he a frustrated national journalist who never made it? In any case, she doesn't agree with him. Chris Pleasant is doing his best to produce an *authentic* attempt at reality, not the 'creative' version George whinges about.

She steps into the hotel and is immediately hailed from the bar.

"Ettie! I've been waiting for you," Chris shouts, "Let me get you a drink."

No one else is around. She sits down as he noisily summons assistance from reception.

"I had to see you," he says, returning with the drinks.

"How did you find me?"

"It wasn't difficult, just a couple of phone calls," he says, then mistakenly detecting annoyance, "I hope you don't mind. I need your help."

"Well if I can, but I've told you all I know about..."

"No, not for the film...at least, not for the content...or should I say, not for the basic material...but then that material may have to be ...no, no, there won't be any changes...but if there aren't then..."

"What are you talking about?"

His hand trembles on his glass. He puts it down and draws closer.

"I'm sorry, I'm not making much sense. It is the film. I need your help, but not in the way you've been working so far. It's more of a...professional nature."

He pauses, takes a long swig of his drink, only continuing when he's sure there's no one in or behind the bar.

"I've had problems almost from the start, but it's getting worse. It started nearly a year ago. I put it down to the usual things, but now ...the picture's jinxed. There's no other explanation, but I have to go on, I can't stop despite what they say."

"Who says?"

"Everybody! They're all at it. Every time I try to move the shooting schedule forward there's another hiccup. There's a problem with the scenery, one of the actors is ill or can never get their lines right, the technicians, they never seem to understand…"

"Surely these are normal problems with…"

"That's what I thought, but now…when we're nearing the end…or at least I thought we were…no, no, these things are not normal, that's the whole point. I'm used to temperamental irritations, but this is different. This morning, even after I'd conceded so much, I've even got people saying I should re-shoot the Smithfield scene. We put that to bed weeks ago. I got your advice, we incorporated every nuance, everything was fine, but now people…"

"People?"

"Charley Kennet, the chief screenwriter, giving me all this nonsense about the fealty scene and now the problems with Jeremy and John …it's too much, all this damned interference…"

"From Jeremy and John?"

"No, no, they're just actors, I mean Charley. Her role finishes with the script, the shooting's got nothing to do with her. She shouldn't be opening up a scene after we've finished shooting, she's got enough to do writing new ones."

"But surely the script has already been written?"

"Exactly, just what I said, but she's forever opening it all up again…and again and again and again. I tell you, Ettie it's got to stop. I can't go on. I should sack her."

"Why don't you?"

He drains the dregs from his glass.

"Another drink?"

She nods.

"I sure need another one."

He returns to the bar and shouts to reception.

"Well?" Ettie says as he waits.

"She's a good writer," he says after a long pause, "I don't want to throw the baby out with…ah yes, gin and tonic and a white wine."

66

He returns to the table, putting down Ettie's drink and immediately emptying his own before telling of yesterday's discussions and the row this morning.

"After all that, now she doesn't like the Smithfield scene," he says, banging down his glass, "Says it depicts Wat Tyler as too arrogant. I ask you, too arrogant. Now, Tim Rosser – that's the actor playing Tyler – he chimes in and agrees with her after seeing the rushes. Too arrogant, actors giving opinions *after* shooting, and sceenwriters with their comments..."

"What does she say?"

"She says 'we have to be true to the past, they'll not forgive us if we're not."

"They?" Ettie says quietly.

"Exactly, just what I said, who the hell are *they*? She just repeats 'the past, the past, we have to be true to the past!' Creepy, damned creepy, I call it."

Talk of the past resonates with Ettie, but she remains silent.

"She keeps pressing me. I can't agree. If we start re-shooting the Smithfield scene it'll mess up the schedule even further...just when I thought I'd got it tied up and now I've got this latest business with the fealty scene. It's too much. I tell you, it's jinxed. I really need your help. What do you think I should do? I'm reluctant to agree, but I have this nagging feeling...but she insists...what did she call it...authentic..."

It's so important to be authentic.

Almost Warren's last words to her...reality and unreality... newspapers and films. George unfairly criticised Chris and she doubted him, but the newspaper man ought to be more concerned with reality than the film director. Now it seems their roles are reversed. She must be true to Warren. What would he want?

"You must help me," Chris is saying, "What are your plans? I had no idea you were in the area, but now you are..."

"I wasn't intending to stay."

"You can't go now. I need you to advise me what to do with Charley."

"I really have no reason to stay any longer."

"You came to see Warren Grover?"

"You've heard about him?"

"Who hasn't. He consulted you?"

"Yes, but now..."

She is silent.

"You have other work?" he says.

"It's not that..."

"Ah yes, of course, silly of me, the expenses and your comfort. I fully understand. You can't stay here. Look, my house is very close, up on the west side of the common."

"But I couldn't possibly stay with you, such an imposition."

"It's no imposition. I bought the house last year. Handy for the studios and I needed to get out of London, but with the film...in any case you don't need to stay with me. There's a cottage included in the sale. It's nearby, but quite separate from the house. I haven't had time to decide what to do with it. It's small, but cosy. A nice area, close to the common."

"Close to where Warren was killed."

"Yes...well, not that close...I'll get it sorted immediately. You could move in tomorrow. Look on it as a holiday, if you like. I'm sure you'll be very comfortable."

"But I ought to pay..."

"Never! I won't hear of it. What do you say?"

She hesitates.

"All I ask is your help with my troubles at the studio. You can forget about this business with Warren Grover."

But that's precisely what she can't forget. She's reluctant to leave the area, but doesn't relish remaining at the hotel. Maybe Chris's offer is the answer.

"Please come to the studio tomorrow."

Still she hesitates, but he persists.

"You can move in immediately."

He scribbles on a piece of paper and hands it to her.

"This is the address. Come to the studio tomorrow morning. Bring your things and you can move in immediately afterwards. I'll get it all spruced up this afternoon. Trust me. I really need your help."

She agrees and he goes. Afterwards, sitting alone in the bar, nursing her half finished drink and staring across the street she feels a simultaneous pull and push. She should grasp the opportunity to stay, but is reluctant to get any further involved with the film with its links to the past. Yet she can't resist Warren's connections and that evening walks up the lane on the west side of the common until she reaches Chris's cottage. She peers in the front window. It's well furnished and comfortable. It faces east across the common and as she gazes into the evening dimness an alluring tranquillity confirms her decision.

Now, in the brightness of the morning as she prepares to leave for the studio, she's tremulous and uncertain. Her doubts about Chris return, though they are more about the studio than the cottage. The phone rings. It's not just Chris that's tracked her down to the hotel.

"Ah, I have you! I thought you'd follow up that case and Vicky confirmed it."

Jessica! Of all times this is probably the least convenient.

"Then I heard about this dreadful business with that poor man. Is it true, the same man that came to see you? Yes, of course. It must be unbelievably distressing, but there you are. I said to myself, this is precisely the sort of intricacy Ettie would get herself into. Naturally, I have every confidence and I'm sure there are... fascinations...that are bound to attract, but even so you ought to be careful of..."

Jessica breaks off suddenly. Ettie doesn't respond and with that shrewd sensitivity that occasionally breaks through her egocentric monologues, Jessica picks up on Ettie's apprehension.

"You are staying?"

"I...I've been offered a place,"

"Offered, a place, what do you mean?"

Ettie mentions Chris and the film. A short silence follows, in which the motions of Jessica's whirring brain can be detected.

"I see," she says at last, "that man Chris Pleasant."

'That man' is delivered with a contemptuous, yet slightly fearful, dismissiveness.

"He's very worried about his film," Ettie says.

"*Is* he?"

Ettie recounts the conversation with Chris.

"Well, you know your own mind," Jessica says, "I don't share your generosity of spirit towards Chris Pleasant and his film project."

'Film project' is uttered with the same dismissive contempt. She could be describing someone buying a lottery ticket. She doesn't wait for Ettie to respond.

"I'm no expert in these matters, but I have to say I find his whole approach somewhat vulgar. Serious subjects should not be debased in this way."

"But surely if it's the only way of bringing them to a wider audience," Ettie protests half heartedly.

"Ah, the excuse of vulgarians over the centuries! Such things are invariably the source of all later distortions. Nothing authentic will emerge from Chris Pleasant's contributions to knowledge!"

That word again!

"You seem to be damning him before he's really begun," Ettie says.

"Not damned by me, but by his own efforts. I understand there have been funding problems..."

"Yes, but that's recently been..."

"...and then there've been the change of actors."

"He says he's had some problems..."

"*Some* problems! A great many if the frequency of the changes is any guide. Why, people have been shunting around more like the ups and downs of a soap opera than any seriously intentioned depiction of great historical events."

"You're very well informed."

"One picks up these things from colleagues involved on the fringes of his so called research. I'm surprised you've not heard already. I think you may have compromised yourself far too much already. My advice is to put some distance between you and any further involvement. There's no reason why you shouldn't pursue your...enquiries... without getting too close to Chris Pleasant. After all, only a year ago we were..."

"I'm perfectly aware what we were doing last year!"

"There was then a particular anniversary and there's another one coming up."

"What do you mean?"

"15th June last year in Smithfield, the crucial date in 1381 when..."

"Yes, yes, I know, but what's this other anniversary?"

"15th July 1381 was the culmination of the events in St. Albans and here we are with it only a few weeks off while this unfortunate business with Mr. Grover...Anyway I would find that much more fruitful than dithering around with Chris Pleasant. As you know, it's not often I give advice on these matters..."

"Of course not."

"...but sometimes I make exceptions. This man is a loser and very shallow. I really feel you should have nothing to do with him."

"I'm seeing him this morning at the studio."

"I see."

"I've already committed myself and I never go back on my word."

"No, naturally."

"He's been very kind with the cottage."

"Indeed."

"He needs...reassurance..."

Ettie is tempted to say more. She stops short, but it's enough for Jessica.

"Reassurance in your professional capacity?"

"Yes...in a way, there have been problems...people...actors, they've felt things."

There's a long pause and when it comes Jessica's response is quite unlike what Ettie expects.

"Does that mean he's not certain about some of the scenes."

"There have been concerns."

"It's absolutely vital anything connected with Smithfield is authentic."

Ettie shudders. The word again and applied to the very scene Chris mentioned.

"He's being asked to re-shoot the Smithfield scene."

"He must," Jessica asserts with a demanding, yet also oddly pleading tone, "Tell him he *must* re-shoot Smithfield!"

Ettie wonders how she's supposed to tell this to Chris when she's also being told to have nothing to do with him. Then with a final, insistent warning to 'be careful' Jessica rings off. Ettie can't get the conversation with Chris out of her mind, not helped by Jessica's apparently well informed, though not unbiased comments...*he must re-shoot Smithfield*... Why was she so adamant, especially after so thoroughly castigating him? How can she get so worked up about a damned film? As a historian, she's surely used to the way entertainment plays fast and loose with...*authenticity?* Ettie sometimes wonders which century Jessica really lives in or does she just get them hopelessly mixed up?

...*the film is jinxed...things are not normal*...Chris's problems first began around July last year, when Chris bought his new house...and the cottage where Ettie is moving to...could there be a connection? Why is the screenwriter as concerned as Jessica? ...*we have to be true to the past, they will not forgive us if we are not*... Also important to Warren Grover...*it's so important to be authentic*... No, these things are not connected.

She's downcast on the road to the studio and her thoughts drift back to 1381. This is also the road from London, where the first travellers would have alerted the people of the debacle in Smithfield. This is their country. Their presence remains. She dismisses it, but remains distracted as if something unseen hangs over her, ready to strike. Then like the sudden invasion of forgotten dreams, images of a medieval town and monastery intrude. It has to be St.Albans. She feels trapped, panics and stops the car. Then she realises she's lost. This is not the road to the studio. She'll go back to the hotel, pack her bag and go home – if she can find the right road. But she promised Chris and a promise, however reluctantly is a promise. The sense of foreboding recedes and she drives on into the country. She'll soon find her way. She comes to a built up area, only gradually realising she is re-entering St. Albans. The town and the monastery draw her. By the time she fully understands it's too late to turn back and parks near the abbey.

All thoughts of the studio and Chris are pushed aside. She walks towards the abbey, its imposing Norman tower looming, luring, but she turns away.

'...we are only a few weeks off...the 15th July...'

Jessica and her anniversaries! nearer to...to what? 15th July. Everyone else is going the opposite way towards the abbey, but she is pulled inexorably towards an unknown, unavoidable destination as the date jangles in her head. Then she sees the old gateway, only remaining vestige of the monastery, its reservoir of strength dammed up over the centuries. Higher and wider as she gets closer, what have these ancient stones seen and heard? Her mind empties, ready to welcome emotions, forces, spirits entombed within. A few people pass by. She lingers, receptive, waiting, hoping, until she senses an attraction. She turns, retreats, pausing only once, but its strength endures and she walks back to her car in a haze, aware of her surroundings, but not wholly cognisant of them. Even as she drives away she has an urge to return as if someone voicelessly calls her. Slowly, as she leaves the immediate area of the abbey it recedes, but with the whole being of the town refusing to be shaken off it takes intense will to break free. Eventually she finds the road again and gets to the studio. She arrives during a break in the schedule and finds him alone in his room, staring vacantly.

For a few moments he chats amiably, then says tetchily, "Things are no better."

"There have been more...incidents?" she says guardedly.

"Incidents?" he says, throwing up his hands, "Yes, there have been *incidents!* I'd like you to look at some of the rushes and you'll see what I mean, there are things in them that..."

"That could be very interesting, if I..."

"Not really incidents, just bloody people! People, Ettie, they're the problem. Despite my better judgement, I shall have to re-shoot the Smithfield scenes."

"But I thought you felt..."

"It's no longer important what I feel. We have to have continuity. If we make changes to later scenes, which I'm being forced to do, there's no narrative or linear balance. I shall have to do it again! I only hope it doesn't disrupt even earlier scenes like Ball's speech at Blackheath. I was hoping I wouldn't have to get Darren back just yet, if only..."

"Darren?"

"Darren Slade, the actor playing John Ball, I've let him go..."

"But surely, he must be..."

"Oh God, Charley what is it now?"

Charley comes in.

"I just wanted to," she says, breaking off as she sees Ettie.

Chris introduces them.

"Ettie's been helping me with background material," he says and then adding, to Ettie's annoyance, "She's a kind of expert."

"You're an expert on the Peasants' Revolt?" Charley says enthusiastically.

"Not exactly," Ettie says, with a sideways glare towards Chris, who looks away while Charley stares expectantly.

Ettie stumbles into an explanation.

"My interest is...concerned with the past generally rather than any specific period. You could say..."

"...costume and lifestyle matters," Chris cuts in, suddenly aware of the embarrassing fallout from his silence, but stopping as abruptly and inexplicably as he began.

Charley waits for a few moments and then gives up with a curt "I'll come back later."

"She didn't say what she wanted," Ettie says after she leaves.

"It doesn't matter," he says, "One less thing to worry me with."

"When did you buy your new house?" Ettie says pointedly.

Chris stares back mystified, wondering why she asks.

"Oh, er, 15th July last year?"

"But that was..."

"What?"

"It doesn't matter."

15th July. The date recurs and bounces. What did she nearly say? His puzzled eyes remain on her for some time, expectant, intimidatory. She ought to say something, anything except what's truly in her mind, but she resists and looks away. The silence lingers until he gives up and fills the vacuum.

"At least she's gone. I'm getting to the stage of pre-empting the next scene she or the others want to change. If I keep going like this I'll be screwing up the entire script and everything we've already shot!"

"It's important for Smithfield to be...exact," she says, listening incredulously to her own words, as if someone else utters them. Then she tries to pull back, recover her own voice, "I mean...it's the central...vital event in the whole... series of...the crucial turning point..."

"Yes, yes, but now there are other..."

"The way Wat Tyler is portrayed has to be..."

"Charley and some of the others, they're becoming obsessed with..."

Jessica's words tumble around her mind. *The portrayal of Wat Tyler...has to be...authentic.* A hammer on a wall or the ceaseless, irritating tapping of a child on a radiator, reverberating throughout a house. *Authentic, it has to be authentic.* Warren said it just before he...and Jessica, so adamant about Chris, disparaging his film...yet emphasising the scene in Smithfield. He has to make it authentic even if it means re-shooting...

"...so many new scenes we have to shoot. I might as well tear up the script and begin again. Charley and Jeremy and even Lawrence won't stop talking about it and all these... happenings. I'm not sure I can resist. It means bringing back Darren. What do you think Ettie, what should I do?"

"Do?" Ettie says, suddenly forced back, "Do what?"

Chris sighs deeply.

"These new scenes Charley keeps talking about. I'm so glad you're here today, it helps to keep her at bay and I really value your advice. She wants to extend the film and take in all the events in Hertfordshire. As if we haven't got enough material as it is, why do we need more?"

"I can see..."

"Just what I said to her, we've almost got it put to bed, now's not the time to build in all this...peripheral material... that's what it is, peripheral...I told her. She didn't like that, she didn't like it all."

"So, it's Charley..."

"It's *all* of them. It makes me so...so...so...but...but..."

He stops to catch his breath his face reddening as he splutters angrily. Ettie comes over anxiously as he wheezes perilously for a few moments. He puts up his hand as his breathing gradually subsides.

"It's alright, I'm okay. You see, I've had to agree, but these scenes...taking time out to rehearse something Charley's been working on. Should I allow it to go further? If I don't... with them all behaving so oddly...if I don't let them take in this new material...will I lose what we've already got and jeopardise the whole picture?"

"You have no choice," Ettie says decisively.

Immediately she regrets being so directive and waits for him to explode, but he looks across, staring impassively beyond her, his eyes dull and hazy, fixed dreamily on the far wall.

"Yes," he says after a long pause, "I believe you are right."

Chris's mood is oddly counterpoised. He's concerned by Charley's 'antics,' commandeering the actors in her support, but he's lost his earlier confidence, even this morning's anger and is reluctant to challenge her. He accepts Ettie's surprising recommendation to go along with her resignedly, but with relief. He's been sitting on a very uncomfortable fence and needed unseating. Now he's suddenly brighter, slaps his hands on his thighs and gets up.

"Come on," he says, "we'll go to the set."

Yet Ettie is less sure, unsettled by the 'director' seemingly no longer directing. They reach a new set, put together since this morning, a wide, open space, with a distant town in the background.

"We'll superimpose the country later," Chris says, "This is where there was a big meeting in St. Albans, on the same day as Smithfield..."

"15th June," Ettie says apprehensively.

There's no crowd, no Grindcobb, no Cadindon, just the two of them standing alone in a vast, deserted space. Chris looks around impotently, like a small boy thrust nervously into the room of some awe filling person, who has not yet deigned to appear. This is not the man Vicky has known these last months. After scrutinising every direction he turns to Ettie as if seeking guidance, almost disappointed the set has not yet been taken over by Charley. Then they hear low, rumbling conversation. Some two dozen people are gathered twenty metres away, off the set. Charley is at the centre of the group. A couple of the others are reading aloud from the script. As Chris approaches several look round. Charley glances up and the actors stop reading.

Chris waves his hand and says softly "okay, okay, carry on."

They resume reading. He watches impassively. Two actors stand apart from the rest. Neither they nor anyone near them are in period dress. This puzzles Ettie. Surely if they've just been shooting a particular scene they would still be in 14th century costume? Then she notices a crowd of around fifty people at the outer edge of the group, dressed for the period, but apparently not involved. At least not as actors, for as she turns and takes in the whole studio, Ettie sees no one else, no technicians, or assistants. They are all here, gathered in this unofficial, spontaneous assembly, drawn as if summoned.

"We are reassured and heartened to see you all," John Thurley as Grindcobb says.

"We never expected to see so many of you from all the towns and villages," Mark Vane as Cadindon says.

Thurley stands on what appears to be a wooden box, though as he speaks this like everything else merges into the background of a vast open space.

"Early yesterday morning we were at Mile End fields near London and met with the king..."

A long murmur permeates the crowd, which is now much larger, at least a hundred.

"There I knelt six times before him and obtained this letter."

He waves a paper in his hand and starts to read.

"Richard, by the grace of God king of England and France and lord of Ireland, to all his bailiffs and loyal subjects, to whom these present letters come, greeting..."

The crowd is now absolutely silent. Ettie glances incredibly across the faces. The numbers have increased again to at least two hundred, many beyond the receding trees and fields towards the open sky and none in modern dress. Yet a moment before she'd wondered why no one was in costume and it was definitely an empty, featureless studio on which Chris said the country would be 'superimposed' later.

"...we have manumitted all and every one of our liegemen and subjects and others of the county of Hertford and we have released each and every one from all bondage and we discharge them by these present letters."

A huge roar emits from the company. Now Ettie can't see the edge of the crowd. Thurley raises his hand for quiet and when the noise and excitement subsides he continues, quoting the provision for pardons and removal of sentences for outlawry.

"...witnessed by myself at London on the 14th day of June in the fourth year of our reign."

As he pauses the crowd roars again in a great cheer. Then 'Cadindon' speaks.

"We made out charges against the abbot, the prior and certain monks that you know...(rumbling assent of nodding heads) ...of their unjust tyranny towards their peasants, their oppression of the commons and withholding the pay of poor men and labourers."

"We saw Wat Tyler," Thurley/Grindcobb says, "the leader of all the true commons and he promised, if needed to come to St. Albans and clip the beards of them all! We'll outdo Tyler himself. These pernicious monks will rue the days they've held us in subjection. The wrath of the people will have its day a hundred times over!"

Another thunderous cheer, then Vane/Cadindon speaks.

"All those capable of bearing arms should be here for they may have much work to do. Any not here may answer to us later."

"Are we resolved, brothers and sisters?" Thurley shouts.

"We are!" comes the clamorous reply followed by disparate cries of 'get them...hammer them down as they hammered us down ...spare no one.'

"Then sharpen your sickles and lift up your axes. Today it's more than grass cutting and wood we'll be chopping! We go back to the town to complete what we've started."

What has now become an enormous crowd turns and following Thurley and Vane's lead extraordinarily moves towards the 'horizon' of what should be the later computer generated background. Ettie, Charley and Chris follow. They walk unhindered along a dusty road even though they know they are actually in a very small, enclosed studio. Like the 'background' this doesn't matter. The minutes pass. The crowd marches on. They see Vane and Thurley at its head, but can't see its end behind them. The buildings of a medieval town appear. They walk with the crowd along the streets, unable to resist or challenge, even to each other. People are at the doors and windows. Chris and Charley stare wide eyed and incredulous. Ettie, with her long experience of inexplicable occurrences, watches and wonders with apprehensive detachment, sensing, hoping she'll soon acquire a better understanding. It comes when they turn the next 'corner' of their march.

The crowd stops in front of a wall and a gatehouse. Another swelling group, peasants from all the surrounding villages, now joins the hundreds that gathered in the fields, in total over two thousand people. Ettie immediately recognises the same gatehouse she was at earlier. People, many complete strangers, now join hands, giving and receiving mutual pledges of support. Some approach the monastery gates and demand entry to the prison.

"Set them free " someone shouts from the back of the crowd.

The gatekeeper immediately unbars the prison gates and some of the crowd rush in. Charley grabs Ettie's arm.

"Is this happening?" she says, "Is it...now?".

Ettie squeezes her hand, "Both. It's now *and* then."

But Ettie is uneasy. All is not right. Past and present is not really fused. The prisoners are released. As they stagger out, shielding their hands against the unaccustomed light they are surrounded and asked if they will swear loyalty to the 'commonalty.' They all do and are allowed to depart except for one who is a murderer. The noise from the crowd increases and there is a great deal of confused discussion. Chris stands a little apart, staring unbelievingly at the raucous shouting. Seeing Charley and Ettie he comes over.

"This is not a scene we agreed," he says angrily to Charley.

She stares back at him in utter disbelief. Is he in denial?

"This is no scene in no film," Ettie says through gritted teeth.

"Certainly none I've agreed," he says and walks away.

He stands nonplussed for a few moments, staring into the crowd. People are making speeches, urging a meeting with the abbot and formulating further demands. With so much rumbling and clamouring Ettie can't hear the precise words. Mark Vane talks excitedly to someone. She assumes it's Thurley, but she can't see him. 'Grindcobb' has gone!

"That's enough, everybody back. Cut! Cut! Cut!"

Chris strides over, pushing into the crowd, flailing his arms and barking more ludicrous commands. There are no cameras to stop shooting, nothing filmed to be cut, but still he goes on howling instructions everyone ignores. Yet it seems to have some effect. Some of the crowd stand back, allowing him to pass, while others even walk away. The crowd, though still dense, seems fewer and not all are now in 14th century costume. Ettie senses tension between opposing forces, though as yet unsure of the protagonists. This could be dangerous. Better if Chris kept silent, but tackling him might be counter productive, provoking even greater recklessness.

Chris reaches the front of the crowd. Mark Vane turns to him with wild eyes and a firmly fixed mouth. He's about to speak, but hesitates. Then one of the extras pushes against Chris. He stumbles and staggers. For a moment it looks as if he may fall down and several burly men gather around. He looks at them aggressively and is about to severely reprimand the man who pushed him, but then reconsiders. Even Chris senses these men, this place, this 'acting' isn't 'normal.' Then they too hold back as if also aware something not right. For a moment the men and Chris and Mark Vane stare at each other in a silent, frozen stand off, no one speaking, no one moving.

The crowd is now smaller while the 'background' of the monastery wall and gatehouse is less distinct, almost hazy. Charley stands so close to Ettie she almost knocks her over. Ettie moves away slightly to regain her balance, but Charley edges closer again. They exchange glances. Charley is both frightened and curious. Ettie begins to guess what is happening, but it gives her no comfort. Simultaneous pressures from past and present conflict, while the real past and the 'false' one created by the film makers struggle for mastery.

"Everybody get back to their proper places," Chris suddenly shouts, "We're reverting to the original schedule."

In the middle of a 14th century town it's not clear what the 'proper' places or the 'original' are meant to be. Yet most of the cast draws back, leaving Mark Vane, still dressed as Cadindon, almost alone except for a handful of associates.

"Take that man," he calls, pointing to Chris.

No one moves. Behind Mark there's now no wall, gatehouse, not even as a misty form, just the stark, hard wall of the studio awaiting its scenery, the 'crowd' no more than twenty, none in 14th century dress. Charley stands stupefied, while Chris, seemingly not noticing all the 'changes,' strides towards her, waving his arms and shaking his head.

"It's all your bloody fault. I should never have listened to you."

Then he turns to the cast, lambasting them for 'listening to her' and 'mucking about' with the script. He glares ominously as he turns in a full circle, perhaps trying to find the man that pushed him, though he's not to be seen. Mark Vane sits on the floor by the side of the set. Chris glowers over him.

"And as for you..." he begins and then breaks off.

Mark is looking at the floor, shaking violently.

"I don't know, I don't understand...what happened, what I was doing..."

Chris steadies him by the shoulders and he stops shaking. He shrugs and then walks back towards Charley. Most of the cast scuttle away to whatever convenient corner or fissure will hide them. Now Chris attacks Charley again.

"You're damned interference is the root of all problems on this picture! Getting above yourself. Who's the bloody director? This...this... happening...this obscenity...it's all your doing."

With the studio now as it was, empty, lifeless, devoid of any connection with great events Charley recovers and shouts back.

"This is not my doing. I had nothing to do with it. I don't even know..."

"You wrote this scene with Grindcobb and Cadindon and the men in the field..."

"Well, yes I did write the material..."

"...and then at the monastery..."

"Yes."

"And all this organised behind my back!"

"No, no, no! I've done nothing behind your back. It just sort of...took over..."

"Things don't just get taken over."

"You were here, you saw what happened!"

"It's this guy, Grindcobb you're so obsessed with, he needs to be wrapped up and got out of the way!"

Chris storms off the now almost deserted set. Charley gets to a chair and slumps down in silence, numb and confused, what they've just seen and heard whirling around her mind. Why is he blaming her? Chris saw and heard it too. Ettie is beside her, the eerie quietness of the studio doing nothing to calm her nerves. Then the noises begin. First a scraping sound. Then a shuffling and a dragging as if someone is pulling heavy scenery. Charley looks up and they both listen carefully, but there's no one to be seen. Mark Vane and other cast members look across, seeking explanation, but afraid to ask. The scraping begins again. No one moves, nothing moves. Yet it continues for several moments. Charley shivers.

Mark Vane is ashen white, his eyes bulging in fear. It stops. For several long elongated minutes the silence persists. Then Charley whispers to Ettie.

"It's me, isn't it, I did this, I made this happen by bringing the past alive and now it's come back to..."

"To what?" Ettie says, "if that's what you've done, why should that anger the past and so..."

"Where is he? I'll stop this nonsense immediately! Where is this Grindcobb, where is John Thurley?"

Chris bounds across the set, looking around, accosting everyone, prodding some, demanding to know Thurley's whereabouts. It breaks the charged silence and the rest of the cast and extras appear from their hidey-holes in response to Chris's barracking and bawling. Except Thurley and Ettie remembers she's not seen him since first they 'arrived' outside the monastery gates.

"Thurley!" Chris shouts, "John, where the hell are you?"

A booming, heavy crash makes everyone turn to the back of the set. John Thurley lies at the bottom of the stairs, inert, lifeless.

4

THE drive to Welstead may be short in distance, but to Chief Inspector Jenner this is a much longer journey back in time. In thirty years the centre of town has changed only so much as necessity dictates. New shops, a few discreet housing developments, but strip away the superficial veneer and its amazingly unchanged. After such a long absence he can reconnect familiar landmarks with comparative ease. There's the large oak tree in the thin strip of green separating the upper and lower high roads where they hung around as teenagers. All the pubs have been 'modernised,' but haven't lost their individual character, especially the differentiation of clientele. What had been the haunts of the proletariat still are. What had been the watering holes of the rich, nouveau or more substantially established, still are. Such consistency is very useful for a policeman.

This is a place without great historical events. Nothing ever *happens* here. Yet it's his world. The only place he's ever felt really secure. Not exactly at home, certainly since he left, but nearer to a sense of home in that it belongs to him. Whether he belongs to it is a different matter. He never really feels he belongs anywhere.

His mother now lives in a sheltered development, so when visiting her he's usually avoided the town. That or busying himself on other things he's not noticed some of the changes. As a boy he worked for three newsagents. Only one of them is still a newsagent. Of the others, one is a Chinese take away, the other an estate agent. A message for the times, he wonders. He drives past the common, a huge wedge of peace protruding into the centre of town, an unchanging reminder of all that continues. For hundreds of years the villagers grazed their animals and it was a perennial supply of firewood, warming and protecting them from the harshness of winter. As a youngster it was a vast playground and later an easily accessible haven of tranquillity, a place to chill out, to think, where gorse and grass and sky absorb and reflect without judgement.

He arrives at the police station, anxious to get started. He needs to be busy and London has been getting him down. It may be good for him, out here in the Chiltern force.

"Get back to your roots," Chief Superintendent Atkinson said, "Even when the tree loses its leaves, it keeps its roots."

Roots or not, why the rush? Was there a problem with the local man, Gladden? Jenner has seen the pathologist's report and skimmed the file. Otherwise he'll have to pick it up as he goes along. He's used to getting up to speed as everything accelerates away. As they say, change is as good as a rest, look to your roots. Who are they kidding? They got him out here quickly because it sounded like that sort of case. Atkinson's levity gave it away.

"Some woman claiming it was all down to villains in the past. Just up your street, Derek."

Just up your street! Bloody weird dead end, he'll be thinking. Send Jenner. He's good at *that* sort of thing! However hard he tries Jenner can't shake off being labelled. She probably is just a nutter, but it's convenient to shunt it over to him, After all, he has something of a reputation.

Walking along the corridor he's surprised to see a familiar face.

"Good morning, sir."

"Good God, Jennifer, what are you doing here?"

"Transferred – at *my* request, I might add."

"But whatever for, surely you were doing well in Nottingham?"

"Personal. I had to get away it was...difficult...failed relationship."

"Quite Well, I suppose you could call mine personal too. Temporary secondment, but transferred double quick because...well, never mind, we'll have to have a chat later. Meanwhile, I have to see my new sergeant."

"You're looking at her."

"But..."

"You should have it in..."

She points to the file under his arm. He examines a memo.

"Oh yes, detective sergeant Jennifer Heathcott...quite, as I've always said, make sure of the paperwork. Better come into the office. I'm glad you're on the case, but, it's a bit..."

"Odd?"

"Coincidental."

"Both of us having experience of..."

"...a case with connections to the past. Quite, well down to business. Warren Grover, 45, married, no children, local community activist. Early morning dog walkers found his body near a clump of trees at the south end of Welstead Common, close to the main road and regularly frequented footpaths, but well shaded. Still mainly light at this time of the year, but no one saw anything. Killed by a single blow with a blunt instrument. The murder weapon has not been found. Time of death between nine and eleven the previous evening. According to his wife he left the house about nine. It was not unusual for him to walk on the common on a summer evening and depending on the route he would have arrived at the murder scene between fifteen and forty minutes later. Late enough for most other people to have gone home. Nothing had been taken so robbery was not the motive.

"The killer must have known the area and Warren's usual movements well," Jennifer says, "deliberately choosing this particular place to waylay him."

"What about this damn woman's accusations?"

"It was an extraordinary outburst in the middle of St. Albans. Apparently Margaret Morton is well known in the area. She's done this sort of thing before."

"Made accusations about a murder?"

"No, not murders, but opened her mouth with a load of garbage. I'm told it had to come because she's been quiet for a time."

"Could she just be an attention seeker?"

"I thought she might have a point. Something in Warren's past perhaps. But then she came into the station, demanding we 'take action.' The interview was rather one sided. Maggie – she's always called Maggie – did most of the talking."

"Anything emerge?"

"Disconnected and incoherent references to 'them,' identified as 'from the past.' I tried to pin her down – what past, how far back, Warren Grover's past – but each time she went off on some new tangent, even less rational and unconnected to the one before."

"Hmm. Well, you may be right about the past. Warren Grover and his wife's great passion was the history of the local area, so that'll interest you. Anything from the preliminary enquiries?"

"He had a broad circle of friends and acquaintances. Just about everybody knew him though there's wide variation in attitude, ranging from virtual adoration to outright detestation."

"So there could be a lot of people to see?"

"I wondered whether we ought to see Maggie Morton again."

He glances at the file and peruses the notes of her interview. She can read in his face the garbled interchange flitting through his mind. He grimaces and then flicks it aside.

"Not yet. We'll start with his widow, Kathleen Grover."

They drive through the southern edge of town passing by the house he'd lived until joining the Met. He never returned, his mother abandoning the house after his father died. It's a place he can't go without intruding on strangers. A link with beginnings denied him. It must be wonderful to keep going back to the family home, touch the walls and walk in the garden of youth. But then, it may not feel so good to everyone. Not everyone has good memories. Not everyone wants to be reminded.

Out of town now, skirting the river valley, the road crammed with memories of adventure, crisp spring mornings, long hot summer days, misty autumn afternoons and mysterious winter nights. Glorious if not entirely misspent youth of long bike rides, football in the fields, falling in the river, chasing girls who always lived in out of the way places. The once quiet village Hempston, where he's heard some philistine developers have pulled down a listed 14th century house and got away with what for them is a paltry fine. So much for looking after your heritage. They take the St. Albans road past Southstead Common, more exposed, open and wilder than Welstead Common. There were longer forays here, sometimes in the company of one of those girls he'd managed to find. Over the hill and they turn off the main road. Jenner drives straight through the small hamlet of Dearswell and along a narrow lane.

"Didn't we come the long way round?" Jennifer says.

"Nostalgic detour," he says, "We'll go back beside Welstead Common."

The Grovers' residence is a modest 1930s semi detached bungalow, one of only four at the end of the lane. The garden is neat, but unimpressive, the same as the house. Reasonably well maintained, but slightly old fashioned. Unlike the other three houses, the windows have not been replaced by ubiquitous UPVC double glazing. This house has no extension, conservatory or window in the loft, not even a tasteful porch. Its unrebuilt stubbornness disdains fashion and form as if advertised by a neon-lit hoarding, its dowdiness exuding revulsion for mere 'show.' What lies within is its message.

Kathleen Grover is in her early forties, slim, almost gaunt, though like her tired eyes that might be the effect of her recent loss. She's hardly slept since the murder. After answering the door, she slips quickly into the house, leaving Jenner and Jennifer to find their own way. They follow her into a small room at the rear, facing the garden. She sits in the corner, near the window. They sit on the settee opposite. The room is a slightly higher grade than the exterior, decoration and furniture just about reaching 'ordinary' rather than dull. There's an old television set, like everything else, utilitarian rather than decorative. Unlike in many houses, it doesn't dominate the room and is probably not well used, dwarfed in its inconvenient corner by the well stocked shelves and cupboards on either side. These are crammed with books, box files, papers and pamphlets, evidently much more important than any mere entertainment function. Despite her exhausted pallor and birdlike flitting from the door, Kathleen talks easily. She's almost dismissive of Jenner's apologetic introduction for asking questions at such a sensitive time.

"You have a job to do. I'm anxious to assist as much I can."

"Can you think of anyone who would want to....?" Jenner says.

"Kill Warren? No."

She speaks with quiet, firm deliberation, not shying away from the blunt language of the moment.

"Did he have any enemies?"

She grimaces.

"Warren knew virtually everyone. Inevitably that included people who did not always agree with him."

"Disagreement enough to want to kill him?"

"I can't think of anyone who would feel that strongly."

"In what capacity was he so widely known?"

"He was involved in every major community issue."

"Something of a campaigner?"

The word 'campaigner' unsettles her.

"When circumstances required it."

"Which would not always endear him to everyone."

"You can't please everybody all the time."

"Quite."

She remains unsettled and shuffles uneasily.

"He was an expert in local history, I believe?"

She drops her eyes and speaks in a peculiarly detached tone.

"His researches were well respected."

"Were you also involved in these activities?"

She may have inadvertently given the wrong impression. Her eyes brighten and she responds more quickly.

"Oh yes, we frequently worked together."

Jennifer has been examining the shelves, perusing the books and the labels on the box files. Now she gently probes the subjects. Kathleen talks of her husband's extensive studies, ranging over wide periods, though Jennifer suspects they were not all of equal fascination to Kathleen.

"Did you work together in all these areas?"

Kathleen stares blankly, smiles and then says, "We were both very interested in the history of St. Albans Abbey. Do you know the monastery was founded by King Offa in 793? I found the events leading to the dissolution in 1539 absolutely fascinating, but very sad. Warren's main interest, of course was in the Peasants' Revolt in 1381."

Jenner's flagging interest suddenly picks up. Kathleen continues.

"He got so embroiled, I sometimes wondered if he was really living in the 14th century."

It could have been a joke, but Kathleen doesn't smile and Jenner shudders inwardly.

"I said there were plenty of other things for investigation, but he always returned to the men of the Revolt. It was like a magnet, to which he was constantly drawn."

With her resigned acceptance there's also disapproval, transmuted from his life into his death. Jennifer switches back to their other studies and Kathleen relaxes slightly. Then Jenner resumes his questions about Warren's contacts.

"I've prepared a list, I'm afraid it's rather long."

She takes out a close typed script, running to several pages of names and addresses. Jenner peruses it briefly.

"Very useful, but are there…?"

"No," she says, "I know what you're going to ask and I cannot believe any of those people would want to harm Warren. Many were also his friends and many more relied on him for support. Why would they want to harm him?"

"These people are all active in the community?"

"In one way or another. Very recently Warren was also involved in the campaign to oppose the new development in Hempston."

"Why was he opposed to that?"

"It will spoil the whole area, a blight on the green belt."

"Is this the lot that pulled the old house down in Hempston?"

"They're the ones."

"So the campaign was unsuccessful?"

"You could say so, though it's not over yet. The developers have some powerful supporters like Monica Freeson. She's a local councillor. She's also very much into local cultural affairs. She and Warren often clashed on those matters."

"In what way?"

"Monica didn't support some of Warren's pet projects. For years he's wanted to put on a re-enactment of the 1381 events."

"Like the film they're making?" Jennifer says.

Kathleen grimaces.

"Well...if you like that sort of thing...Anyway Monica opposed his historical work."

"So Warren didn't get on so well with the...shall we say... more influential people?" Jenner says.

"Oh yes, he could do. He was on very good terms with some business people, two in particular, Richard Tranter and Duncan Fuller. Warren approached Mr. Tranter for sponsorship for the re-enactment and he was very sympathetic. Warren had many cultural contacts. He'd also approached the film director, Christopher Pleasant and the actor, Lawrence Bullock. They both live in the area. Warren was good at fundraising, not just for his own projects, but for those of other people too. Phillip Chedwin and James Crawshaw were very appreciative. That's the local history society secretary and the chairman of the music society. People came for his help because he had such wide contacts, and could tap the wealthy very effectively. He was so well respected and..."

Her voice wavers, she breaks up and becomes tearful.

"I'm sorry," she says, wiping her eye, "It's still...still a shock..."

"It's quite alright," Jenner says, "we won't trouble you anymore today."

"What do you make of her?" he says to Jennifer when they are back in the car.

"Seems genuinely upset," Jennifer says blandly.

Jenner grunts noncommittally.

"You don't believe all the community contacts were positive?" she says, "Somebody he wasn't on such good terms with?"

He skims through Kathleen's list.

"As yet we have no motive, but it may be in here."

"It'll be a long job if we have to interview them all."

"Kathleen mentioned eight specific names. We'll have to see this councillor Monica Freeson, but there could be somebody else she's not telling us about. What about all the local history work they did? You know about these things, what do you make of it?"

"She's very knowledgeable, but I'm not sure they shared all the same interests. She didn't seem very keen on his work on the Peasants' Revolt. Maybe we should look into that?"

Jenner hands her the list and then stares pensively through the windscreen.

"Christopher Pleasant could be interesting," Jennifer says, "He's the director making the film about the Peasants' Revolt. According to Kathleen's list Warren advised him on material."

Jenner looks at the address. It's very close, on the west side of Welstead Common.

"We'll go and see him, but later. First I need to get to the common."

Jennifer knows this is more than familiarising himself with the scene of the crime. He'll want to absorb aspects of the immediate environment and won't comfortably commence a full investigation until he's completed this 'sniffing around' and he'll need to do it alone.

"I'll meet you later at Chris Pleasant's place," he says when they get back to the station.

He leaves the main road and takes the parallel, narrow lane that runs for a half mile, screened behind trees and gorse. The west side of the common hasn't changed since he was a boy. Probably hasn't changed much in hundreds of years. He passes a large commercial building, a laboratory and then the lane cuts through the trees. He slows down.

On his right, facing the common is a row of small cottages, about two hundred years old, originally neat two up, two down labourers' dwellings, long since converted to more up market use. They appear unchanged from when he cycled up here to deliver newspapers thirty years ago. He stops the car and scans the whole scene for a few minutes, taking in the wide green expanse to the east. The past wells in his mind with disparate, flickering images, unconnected except for their age. The past lies dormant for decades only to suddenly trespass like wandering kids cheekily invading long deserted woodland, crackling down decades of undisturbed growth.

A woman's face at the window of one of the cottages seems familiar. He looks away and then back, but she's gone. Then another woman comes from another cottage and looks towards him. He eases the car forward and smiles as he passes her. She watches him suspiciously. A little further up the lane, just before it curves back towards the main road, he passes an entrance on the right. It's relatively new and wasn't there in his youth. It has to be the entrance to Chris Pleasant's place. He turns right at the main road, and after a further half mile, pulls onto the verge behind a couple of police vehicles. This is as near as he can get to the crime scene by car. He trudges along the road a few metres and then cuts along a track. At a clump of trees, he turns sharp right into a more thickly wooded area. Though only a short distance from the track and he can still hear the road traffic it's surprisingly remote. A few officers are still scouring the area.

"Found anything?" he says.

They shake their heads. Jenner is sure they'll find nothing. He stands for a moment staring into the slight hollow where Warren Grover's body was found. There's no indication of him being moved, so he must have strayed from the footpath before being killed. He took regular walks across the commons, both Southstead and Welstead. Although separate, the two commons are connected by a footpath between the fields. That's about a quarter mile away with a further half mile across Southstead Common to their house. Three quarters of a mile, easily traversed by a competent walker in fifteen minutes, but he didn't always take the most direct path. Warren was familiar with every track, almost every tree and bush. He may have first taken a circular route around Southstead Common before crossing over to Welstead Common, taking up to forty minutes. That means he was probably killed between nine fifteen and nine forty. Even on a circuitous route, he would only diverge from the track to meet someone at a specific place they both knew. Kathleen had no knowledge of an appointment, so it was someone Warren didn't want her to know about.

Warren was attacked from behind, so the attacker could have been hiding behind the gorse. Warren arrives, but sees no one. The attacker waits until sure they are alone and, still staying hidden calls out. Warren follows the direction of the voice and is taken by surprise.

Jenner returns to the track, continuing a short distance to the end of the trees. He looks north. From here the common drops gently for a mile towards the town, which he can see faintly in the distance. These tracks and footpaths are well used. Even at that time in the evening people could have been walking dogs, but no one has come forward despite several appeals for witnesses. Yet the murderer couldn't have known no one was about. It was risky, but he could have remained concealed in that hollow fairly confident he or she wouldn't be disturbed. The trees meant the spot could not be seen from the road. Definitely a premeditated murder, in which Warren himself had been an unwitting accomplice by not divulging his meeting to Kathleen. Sworn to secrecy by his assailant or perhaps preferring to keep it quiet for his own reasons? If we knew those reasons or knew why someone would want him out of the way...?

The sun is high now and he feels the heat on his back. People take advantage of the warming dryness. The common is coming alive. The green swathe is a natural playground as it was in his childhood. How many miles a day they must have wandered crisscrossing its many paths, dells and copses. The open rolling refuge still draws him, its lungs breathing its heartfelt stability in a fast reshaping world. So who now breaches its security, violently desecrating its peace? He feels the alien infringement as if his own home has been encroached. For this is his country, his preserve he's bound to defend as if the land itself cries for retribution, demanding the apprehension of the assailant. Perhaps the land, in its anger will yield up what it knows, telling its children what it's seen and heard.

It's time to meet Jennifer. He walks back to the car. He shouldn't be so foolish. How can the land really know? It's his edginess with sudden death. He never gets used to it, however many times he's seen it. He retraces his journey and parks opposite the entrance to Chris's house, just along from the row of cottages. Jennifer has already arrived and is waiting for him.

"Looks like a new place," she says, nodding to the drive.

Jenner grunts an acknowledgement, but doesn't immediately look in that direction, instead staring at the row of cottages, thinking about the face he saw at one of the windows.

"Something wrong?" Jennifer says.

"No, nothing, " he says, turning to her and then striding towards the entrance.

The drive is about a hundred metres and curves to the left away from the back gardens of the cottages. The house is a substantial modern residence with a large ground floor and a smaller upper floor within the steep roof. It's no more than a few years old. The high roof, long veranda and large picture windows give it a slightly Scandinavian appearance. Jenner finds it unnecessarily showy. It's good it's set back behind the road and the line of trees, otherwise it would be too obtrusive, its ostentatious modernity interfering with the heritage of the west end of the common, with *his* heritage.

"It doesn't fit," he grumbles.

The door is answered by a middle aged woman who on enquiry, is the cleaner.

"He's out...can't be sure when he'll be back."

Jenner leaves his card with a message, asking Chris to contact him on his return. The cleaner puts it on a table near the door. They go back to the road. A small van has drawn up outside one of the cottages and a man is unloading small items of furniture. Jenner hovers and then sees the same woman he saw earlier emerging from inside. He stares at her. She glances towards him, but then turns away, shielding her eyes from the sun.

"Someone you know?" Jennifer says.

"Could be," he mutters and walks down.

As he nears the cottage, he passes beneath the line of the sun on the roofs and falling into shadow, Ettie recognises him, then sees Jennifer behind him.

"When shall we three meet again?" she says, still in part disbelief.

Jenner laughs.

"Don't say that. The hurly burly's not yet done!"

"Hurly burly at the moment," she says

"Moving in or moving out?"

"Moving in, at least temporarily."

"It's a small van for all your furniture," Jennifer says.

"The place is furnished, but I wanted a few of my own pieces."

The van driver completes his unloading while Jenner and Jennifer settle in Ettie's sitting room.

"My first time inside one of these cottages," he says, "It's an odd feeling."

"I'm sure you'll get used to it," Ettie says, joining them, "Aren't you on home territory?"

"Yes, but my first investigation in the area."

"Are you like me, finding it difficult to adjust after last year?"

"Sort of."

"True for us all, " Jennifer says, remembering the last time the three of them worked together.

"We are working," Jenner says, "but why are you so far from home?"

"I came to see someone and now... I'm as well here as at home."

"No one we know?"

"Warren Grover."

The pervasive silence is louder than any words. Ettie speaks first.

"So you are investigating his murder?"

Jenner nods. Ettie explains her own involvement and how she came to be in the cottage.

"We came to see Christopher Pleasant," Jenner says.

"He's rarely here, so busy with the film. You know it's about the revolt?"

Jenner nods.

"What do you know about it?"

"He's been speaking to Vicky about her experiences. I've also been helping. The film is a long standing ambition. He's already shot much of the London based material in the studio, but he was held up for a time when the money ran out. Now the finance has come through he's started again, which is just as well because he's already committed himself to buying property in the area."

"We've been up to the big house," Jenner says with emphasis on 'big.'

"Oh, it's not just that. He has this cottage, but he's also invested in the new Hempston development."

"Those cowboys who pulled down the medieval house?" Jenner says with bitter disapproval.

"I don't know whether Chris was directly involved in that," Ettie says, genuinely shocked, "I think his main motivation was the house here. The studio is nearby so it's very convenient. Why do you want to talk to him?"

"He knew Warren Grover."

"He never mentioned that to me."

They exchange information about Warren and Maggie.

"So you think Maggie Morton's outburst resulted in your transfer?" she says.

"She probably has nothing to do with the case, but...once you've been involved in...occurrences...related to the past... the most absurd incidents suddenly assume an unwarranted significance."

The boldness of his words isn't matched by the tone of his voice. Ettie wonders whether it's her or Jennifer or himself he's trying to convince.

"Have you seen Maggie?" she says.

"Not yet. What about you? Seen anyone who might assist us?"

"Only the local newspaper editor, George Carter," she laughs, "he doesn't like Chris's film."

"Kathleen Grover doesn't either, though in her case it'll be because it's about the revolt."

"George Carter said Warren would not have approved."

"What can you tell me about Chris Pleasant?"

Ettie explains the difficulties with the film.

"Been there yourself?" Jenner says knowingly.

She gives a cursory, almost matter of fact description of the recent events she witnessed at the studio, but Jenner isn't fooled.

"What about the actor, Thurley?"

"Nothing particularly serious, a broken leg, but it's put him out of action and upset Chris's schedule again."

"How did he fall?"

"He says he slipped."

"No indication of anyone assisting him?" Jenner says dubiously, "and after all these noises and interruptions, no suspicious characters found lurking around?"

"No."

"I suppose you've not come up with any...experiences... that might be relevant to Warren Grover's death?" he says gravely.

"No, but we need to keep in touch and exchange anything that comes to light."

After they leave Ettie is unsettled. Snatches of their conversation recur for several hours as she busies herself getting things together and rearranging the cottage around her own routines. She puts on the radio, but that only works for a short time until the same thoughts dribble into her mind again. They talked of many things. Jenner's whimsical memories of his youth in Welstead, Ettie's other work since London, even briefly Jennifer's failed relationship that drove her to seek 'a change of scene,' but what dominates her thoughts most are Warren Grover's local interests, Maggie Morton's declamation of the past and above all, Chris's film project. They're too reminiscent of their last 'case' in London, inextricably interwoven with the events of 1381.

Jenner and Jennifer make a start on Warren's contacts.

Jennifer takes on the 'culturals,' Phillip Chedwin and James Crawshaw, while Jenner goes for the business pair. It's early afternoon. No one is at Duncan Fuller's large house on the north side of Welstead, though there's a small car outside the garage. Jenner decides to see him later and drives through town, south along the common and into affluent Fulwood Green. He turns into the upper west common lane. The substantial properties all face east with impressive views across the common. Richard Tranter's house is opposite a footpath striking straight across the common and within brisk walking distance of the crime scene.

A tall man in his mid forties answers the door. Tranter shows Jenner into an expansive lounge backing onto the enormous garden. They sit on opposite corners of an opulent suite of settees set out on three sides. This enhances the sense of space and light, mirroring Tranter's own expansiveness as he talks, as much with his large hands as his voice with slow, circulating gestures as if trying to grasp something in the air around him only to immediately let it go. He might be capturing a wild bird, cradling it and then allowing it to peacefully fly away. Tranter is less buoyant when Jenner reminds him of the reason for the visit.

"I was profoundly shocked to hear of Warren's death. Terrible business, terrible, I can't imagine who could do such an awful thing. Such a kind, thoughtful man. I'll be happy to assist in any way to bring the perpetrator to justice."

"You knew him well?"

"Not especially. He came to see me a few times about his dramatic project, what did he call it...yes, the re-enactment. He wanted money, of course," he laughs and smiles indulgently "he was good at that."

"You helped him?"

"Glad to. The sponsorship of such an event, the tax relief, publicity, it was a small price. He was very successful at raising funds for many projects, not just his own. He could be quite persistent. Well known in the business community. I could furnish you with a veritable who's who of industry and commerce known to Warren."

"Were you involved in other cultural activities?"

"Not as such. I have no direct experience of drama or the arts."

"So this proposed re-enactment was your only involvement?"

"No, he came back later with a research project. There were certain expenses, I was happy to help out. He was an interesting man, a delight to listen to. I'm only sad I won't be able to hear him again. He was so enthusiastic about what he called our unknown heritage. As a returning native, it struck a chord with me."

"You're local?"

"Bred and born in this town. I left to go to university. Work and affairs kept me away. Now..."

"...you've made your fortune and can come back to your roots?"

The wide smile returns.

"Something like that. I don't need to spend so much time in the office. I work at least half my time from home. That's why you've found me in. I've only been here a few months and now I wonder what kept me away so long. It's a wonderful place. What are we, twenty, thirty miles from central London and yet it's a haven of peace."

He glances out the window. Jenner nods slowly, recalling his own memories.

"And on the evening in question," he says, "I have to ask, were you at home?"

"No, I was away most of that week in Birmingham. A tricky matter, thankfully now resolved, but demanding my personal attention. When I came back and heard the news...it was a great shock."

He's silent for a moment. Then the smile, less full, returns.

"And you, chief inspector, I detect you're perhaps not unconnected with Hertfordshire yourself?"

"You're very observant," Jenner says, surprised.

"Our generation, perhaps the last to retain a vestige of a local accent."

"Like you," Jenner says, "bred and born and long since departed. Now..."

"...having sorted out all the criminals in the capital you too can return to your roots?"

They laugh and exchange stories of their childhoods, places, and experiences. Moving in different spheres and with Jenner slightly older, their paths never crossed. They knew different people and went to different schools, Tranter to St. Albans, Jenner staying in Welstead.

Afterwards Jenner sits for a few moments in the car. Richard – Rick as he insists on being called – Tranter hasn't advanced the enquiry, but his list of other business contacts could be useful. More lists, more names, more routine slog, but it can't be helped. Tranter's words return, Welstead and its common, a haven of peace. The big lounge seemed like a haven, separated by much more than a hundred metres from a different reality. Jenner has mixed feelings. Not so peaceful for Warren Grover. Yet Tranter mirrors Jenner's own feelings, the fractured peace and unwarranted invasion. He rings the film studio. Chris Pleasant is there, but can't be disturbed.

"I'll bloody disturb him," Jenner mutters.

It's a twelve mile drive to the Cavenham Studios. The gatekeeper lets him in, but insists on issuing a 'day pass.' Jenner stuffs it in his pocket. He'll show it if he has to, but his warrant card should be sufficient. He parks and is escorted by a young woman from reception.

"I'm sure I can find my own way," he says grumpily.

"We need to know exactly where everybody is," she smiles indulgently.

Jenner snorts wordless disapproval. He's not easily indulged. She leaves him, somewhat reluctantly, at the building. Jenner is surprised how large it is. He'd expected something closer to a theatre without an audience, not a small aircraft hangar or a big car showroom. No one takes any notice at first. He stands a little perplexed, trying to get his bearings. With so much activity, it's difficult to see where the real action is taking place. Then he notices the lights at the far end. That must be where they are shooting and where he'll find Chris. He walks or rather meanders across, having to constantly step around equipment and avoid being trampled by hurrying staff. He reaches the set. The backdrop is a medieval room with grey walls, softened by hanging tapestries and a large open window. Through this he can see nothing except a blank wall. He assumes an appropriate scene will be separately filmed and inserted later. There's a large bed and other items of furniture. The whole is brightly lit by strong lights, casting the surrounding areas into an artificial gloom where people are constantly talking, consulting papers and adjusting equipment. So much activity, so much wasted time. This is no theatre. In the theatre when the performance begins it dominates and suppresses a subservient chattering and shuffling audience. The film studio inverts the process. Most of the time the 'stage' is empty and the 'audience' makes most of the noise. It's as if he went to the theatre and spent his whole time watching the audience!

When he asks for Chris he gets shrugs and gestures to a side door with an unhelpful 'over there.' The side door is locked. Then there's a sudden hush and all activity abruptly stops. People are on the set and the cameras are rolling! Chris is sitting close to one of the cameras. As Jenner gets closer, a young woman steps into his path.

"Who are you?"

Jenner waves his warrant card.

"I wish to see Mr. Pleasant."

"It's a little awkward. Can you wait a few moments?"

She goes up to Chris and hovers. One of the actors, a woman elegantly dressed in a long green gown speaks to one of four men, dressed in simple, rough brown shirts. Jenner can't hear distinctly, but it's clear she's muffed her lines. Chris stops the cameras. Now, Jenner can catch him. He gets closer. The young woman whispers to Chris. He shakes his head and then barks instructions to the actors. The young woman comes and stops very conspicuously across Jenner's path.

"Can you wait a little longer? Mr. Pleasant is very anxious to complete this scene. It shouldn't take too long and if there are any interruptions it'll make it even more difficult to pick up again. You know what actors are like?"

Jenner does not. He's about to speak, but then the action begins again and the woman skips back. Jenner waits patiently. There's another 'interruption,' something Chris is unhappy with. Jenner steps forward only to be forestalled by the young woman again. Jenner waits. There's another interruption, another wait, another interruption. Altogether Jenner tries to see Chris five times. Each time he's blocked, but each time he gets a little closer. Having heard the dialogue five times he can almost repeat the lines himself. The woman is a local aristocrat and the men are some of her peasants, rudely accosting her in the manor house. This time they almost get through the scene until the actor speaking to the lady turns too suddenly and knocks over a chair.

"Cut!" Chris shouts.

Now Jenner turns to talk to him.

"Not now," Chris shouts and then with a few pithy instructions gets the scene rolling again.

But Jenner has had enough. It's not just the peasants that will intrude on the lady's chamber! He marches forward, and turns directly in front of the camera, facing Chris. No one else moves.

"Bloody hell!" Chris shouts, "Get out!"

"Mr. Pleasant, I want a word with you!"

"God! Cut! Cut! What do you think you're doing?"

"Conducting a murder investigation in which you are being decidedly uncooperative!"

Jenner stands rigidly in the centre of the 'room,' between the camera and the actors, effectively dominating the action. Everyone remains frozenly incredulously. Chris moves in front of the camera, almost within leaning distance of him. They glare at each other, neither relaxing a muscle for a few seconds, then Chris loosens and with a gruff 'okay, okay, take a break,' waves everybody aside. With many backward glances and incoherent mutterings the actors leave the set. Jenner remains impassive, still staring at Chris, who now dismisses the technicians. He moves forward, smiles and tries to defuse the situation.

"You have a good presence," he jokes, "it's a good pose, properly dressed for the part we might even re-shoot the scene with your entry. Have you ever thought about acting?"

"Not recently," Jenner says grimly, "I'm too busy on other matters."

"I'm sorry you were kept waiting. It was this scene. We've only just...it's out of sync and nobody's...well, anyway it's been a damned problem. You do understand?"

"No, I don't. Is there anywhere we can go?"

Chris laughs nervously and looks around.

"Everybody's scarpered, not wanting to talk to the fuzz, eh?"

He laughs again. Jenner is still not amused.

"We'll go to my room," Chris says.

They sit in opposite chairs. Jenner studies Chris carefully.

"Won't be too long, will we?" Chris says nervously, finding Jenner's continuing stare irritating.

"As long as it takes."

"Yes, of course," Chris says, less confidently and then, trying to take charge, "Not much I can tell you about Warren Grover, I assume that's why you're here. Are you making any progress?"

"I'll ask the questions."

"Yes, of course."

Chris's assertiveness diminishes further as the interview proceeds. His answers become imprecise, interspersing his responses with quips and wholly unnecessary explanations about the film.

"It'll be called 'Hurling Time,' that's what they called the Peasants' Revolt at the...we've shot most of the outside material...this scene is when the peasants' invade the local manor and ..."

But Jenner is not distracted and Chris accedes to questioning. Yet he's evasive and vague about living in Welstead, eventually conceding he's only been there a few months.

"It's useful for the studio. I can get to London whenever I need to and I like the quiet."

"You have no other connection with the area?"

"It's purely a practical arrangement."

"Did you meet Warren Grover?"

"Briefly, just before...I was given his name as someone who had an interest in the period. I like to follow up all possibilities. Sometimes people are retained as advisors. As it happened his specific expertise did not coincide with my priorities."

"Why was that?"

"Purely local, interesting, but of little significance. My film is much more concerned with the national situation."

"I understand Ettie Rodway and Vicky Evelyn have also been advising you?"

"Yes," Chris says guardedly.

"They have particular expertise?"

"They have valuable...experiences...and have been of great help, but their knowledge is directly related to events in London, which is much more relevant to the film."

"Quite."

"You know them?"

"I have met them. I saw Miss Rodway very recently. She was staying at a hotel in the town, the...oh, I forget the name, you may know it..."

"The Old Fox Hotel."

"Yes, interesting place, opposite a well known landmark, she was telling me...where something used to be, what was it...?"

"Probably the blacksmith's shop."

"That's it, yes."

"I've loaned her the use of a cottage close to my house."

"So I understand."

This admission seems to steady Chris. Jenner is a little surprised. He expected Chris to be disconcerted to learn he knew Ettie. Jenner now turns to the night of the murder. Chris's vagueness returns. He has to be reminded of the date several times.

"I will have been at the studio."

"All night?"

"I often work late, there are..."

"There are witnesses to verify this?"

"Well...I er...what was the date again?"

Jenner reminds him for the sixth time.

"Where were you between nine and eleven in the evening?"

After a long, embarrassing pause, Chris says quietly, "At home."

"Anyone with you?"

"No, I was alone."

"All evening?"

"Yes."

"What time did you get in?"

"About seven."

"You seem to have much better recall, are you quite sure?"

"Yes."

"Did you go out?"

"No."

Now Jenner pauses. Chris fidgets in his chair.

"It means I don't have an alibi, doesn't it?"

"Quite."

Jenner terminates the interview, reminding Chris he may wish to talk to him again. After some hesitation Chris calls everybody back to resume shooting.

Jenner turns to go and then as the actors assemble, he says to Chris, "This scene, Mr. Pleasant, isn't it the case that there's no strict historical basis for the confrontation of the queen mother and the peasants in the castle?"

Chris grimaces and then laughs.

"This is a film, chief inspector. It's not always in the best interests of cinematic impact to stick rigidly to absolute accuracy."

"Quite so, sir, I'll remember that."

In the afternoon Ettie sits in the small garden of the cottage, watching the sun gradually slipping towards the horizon. She wants to go inside, get out of the glare, prepare a meal, finish her unpacking, rearrange what's not yet been properly arranged or ought to be arranged again, but somehow she's unable. She gets stiffer on the hard garden bench though the warmth and stillness are mesmerising. A time to let a hundred undeveloped thoughts flicker through a mellow mind. She's too tired for challenging. Better take a brief respite before *developed* thoughts might be unavoidable. She closes her eyes. A restful emptiness enfolds. She can commune with everything and nothing, very oriental, very enlightened, very transitory. But the meditative breakthrough doesn't come. Disparate thoughts assume human shape. Jenner and Jennifer could still be with her. She even glances round to see if they haven't quietly crept into the cottage to stand at the kitchen door. It's not them that intrude on her tranquillity, but their investigation into Warren Grover, not even his death, but his abiding interest in those seismic convulsions six hundred years ago.

The hours pass. The day's brilliance slithers into a coppery glinting evening. She goes inside, but can't face a big meal, satisfied only with a sandwich. The garden still glistens in a soft radiance and she stands for a few moments at the kitchen door, wondering whether to go back with a drink and imbibe the last of the day's glow. But the spell is broken. The intrusions of the past won't go away. She turns back, goes into the front room and stares out the window. The house casts its shadow across the road and the far verge, but the grassy bank beyond, sloping gently to the main road still sparkles in dying embers of sunlight. The common draws. She takes a chair and plants it firmly on the first sun laced patch of grass.

It's still quiet. No one is about and a line of trees shrouds the distant hum of traffic on the main road. A blackbird sings out his evening greeting. He's probably perched on one of the roofs. She stares into the distance, beyond the trees into the wide, deep common, its bright green covering sprinkled by yellow gorse, darkening into a deeper green and reddy yellow, then as night advances to a creeping greyness and ochred brown. Recalling the conversation with Jenner and Jennifer and earlier discussions with Vicky and Jessica jerk the past into life again. Even though the approaching darkness slinks over the land her sense of connection deepens, holding back the night and she sees further, her eyes gouging a tunnel into the country. Distant trees and houses are in close sharpness as if she looks through binoculars. Then she sees hundreds of tramping forms silhouetted with razor edged clarity on the far ridge against the dismal sky. She shuts her eyes, only to see the images even clearer, closer, the people getting nearer, almost near enough to touch! They march with a concentrated determination she's seen before. This is no purposeless gathering, no Saturday night drunken exploit, but a precisely planned exercise. By their clothes they are of that time. 1381. They know where they're going and won't be easily stopped!

She opens her eyes and they are gone, but as soon as she closes them they reappear, marching on the Sandbourn pond, where they spread out along the whole length of the dike. Then as one elongated force they pummel the earth, turf and stones with staves, pitchforks and axes. The dike is breached in several places, the water first oozing, then trickling, finally bursting through and destroying the barrier until the pond is utterly drained.

She opens her eyes. The image is gone. Only the quiet road and the outline of the cottages, draped in hanging greyness, the blurry edges of the trees caught in the faint swarthy strands of the long set sun. There's no sound except the faint hum of the occasional car on the main road, the soft moan of the night in the breeze and the distant call of an owl. She shuts her eyes. They return, darting over the cascading water, running back to the village, shaking their staves and shouting in triumph. She opens her eyes again and they are gone. Each time she closes them they come back. They'll not leave her this night until she's understood. She feels the chill in the air and rubs her arms, but wants to stay. No one is about as she crosses the road. Inside she takes her hat and puts on her coat, but hovers at the door. It's late and there's only a faint light on the common now, yet still she feels its irresistible pull. She brings in the chair and walks up the road, turning left towards the middle of the common.

Her eyes soon adjust to the dark and crossing the main road, strides quickly over the grass, not slowing until she gets far enough to lose the traffic noise. She heads south, away from the town. To her right, on the ridge is a copse, the trees stark against the faint light of the sky, the place where Warren was found, a place of death. She shivers. Such a violent invasion is alien to this peaceful place. She'll not go there. She walks on, further away from the town, houses, traffic, people...no, not people for you cannot escape them and their unfinished business.

Images of the past return. No longer random brush strokes on the empty canvas behind closed eyes, they intrude her peripheral vision. But she *can* and *must* reject them. They don't belong here. Yet the further she walks the more she senses she's not alone and the intrusions on her ears are less easily dismissed as the resurrected visions of an overworked imagination. In dark open country someone may creep up unnoticed, but in the night the ear is less deceived than the eye. At first it's only the soft crunching of a few feet, then the incoherent muttering and the dulled, but distinctive chattering, followed by many feet, magnified in the still air across the valley. And coming closer. She stops in case the soft thump thump of her own feet on the hard ground obscure and distort. It continues. She turns in every direction and listens intently. Still she hears it, but there's no one. Then the shouting and tearing. Something is being destroyed!

The shouting stops, the footsteps recede, no more tramping feet, tearing and writhing, only the soft moaning of the breeze and the rustling leaves. The stillness of the night returns, but Ettie remains unsettled. If this has been 1381 it is no more, but then through the silence she hears a lone voice.

'...all ends and begins just as from the dying trees of winter must come the seeds of spring. But this winter is so very long, without hope the long yearned spring will return. Yet it will, it must. In the darkest days there is still the faintest light. When we are ready, when it is time, when what was left is finished. The end in that terrible day surely sowed the seeds of a terrible beginning. Those that mourn must also avenge. They may repair the dikes, but we shall destroy them again. They may dig up the dead, but the living will return. Can those that fled return? One day when we are finished...'

The voice is stilled. The dark silent night enfolds. But now come the cries of despair, of defiance, cries of warning, cries of destruction. Faintly struggling to get through, they are quiet now, but they have not gone and Ettie has heard them. It's difficult to see and hear in the fog of the past, but even a fog leaves a residue, a clinging moisture. Their faintness was the separation of time, not space. For however faint, they are close and they get closer. Is it another incursion into the peace of the land or does the land itself speak, yielding up messages entrusted to it long ago?

She walks on, but the peace of the country has been compromised. She feels the darkness, not just the night, but of dark spirits that flit and abide on the common, relics of some other faraway darkness, messages of destruction, protest and warning from the dispossessed. Inevitably images of recent experiences in London, recollections of the great revolt flicker across her mind. Yet such messages are dulled and fumbled, indistinct, confused as if they come not from 1381, but later. After the revolt was suppressed, did the unvanquished stir in 1382? Tomorrow she must check.

A cool breeze blows from the west. She pulls up her collar and turns towards the cottage. The dim lights of the town herald people of her own time and a warming uplift that the overlong summer night may soon pass. She thinks no more until she reaches the track for the main road, but as she turns so the lights of the town are no longer to her front and her disquiet returns.

When she gets in there's a message on her mobile from Chris. He apologises for being 'thrown off balance' and is desperate for her to come in tomorrow in case there are 'further developments.' She considers going up to the house, but he probably won't be there. She rings his mobile and getting no answer leaves a message. She'll go in, but not early. If he doesn't like it he'll ring back. She sleeps uneasily, what she felt and heard on the common juxtaposing with her last visit to the studio. Perhaps she should reconsider her involvement with the film. It was probably a mistake getting involved at all. Vicky had been nervous ever since Chris approached her. That tremendous leap into 14th century London a year ago, but she's alright now. Everything was resolved, put back. She remembers it so vividly. The Savoy, Blackheath, Smithfield, all now enlivened in Chris's film, living again in glorious colour...

In the morning she goes over again the unexplained incursions on the film set. Chris can no longer dismiss 'feeling things from the past' as actors' superstitions, but he may be right to resist the film being widened to take in the Hertfordshire events. He might have already stirred up forces not easily controlled. Perhaps he knows and is panicking, trying to close a time door too heavy for him to handle?

She gets to the studio around midday. There's no activity on the set. Chris is in his room, presiding over a large meeting. He waves nonchalantly as she opens the door with something inaudible involving 'later.' She returns to the empty set and tramps around looking for Charley, who was not in the meeting. She finds her in a quiet corner, burrowing into a thick ream of papers, individual pages scattered liberally on the floor. On an adjacent chair *A Little Liberty* lies open.

"Working on more scenes?" Ettie says.

"Yes," Charley says, collecting the papers together on top of the book.

"Do they meet with Chris's approval?" Ettie says guardedly.

"He was opposed at first, but said he'd think about it."

"But you've gone ahead anyway?"

Charley shrugs, shuffles through the papers, handing some to Ettie.

"I've nothing to lose, except...Take a look."

Ettie studies them distractedly, concentrating more on Charley. Despite her enthusiasm there's agitation and nervousness in her eyes.

"You were going to say," Ettie probes.

Charley shakes her head, but under Ettie's piercing gaze, puts her papers down.

"It's just...the other day...I said I made those odd things happen..."

"...and I said you couldn't have done."

"...but I keep wondering if it was connected to what happened to John Thurley."

"He fell down the stairs, didn't he?"

"That's what it seems."

"Has he said anything?"

"Only that just before he fell he felt someone else was on the stairs with him."

"Has he told anyone else?"

"No."

"And was there anyone on the stairs?"

"No one was anywhere near, but I can't help feeling that I..."

"Listen Charley, if forces from the past were involved in Thurley's accident it had nothing to do with you."

"Then they must have been connected to John himself."

She looks to Ettie for confirmation, but Ettie switches tack.

"What's going to happen about the Grindcobb scenes? Will they be delayed until John Thurley has recovered?"

"Don't talk like that," Charley says, suddenly alarmed, "That's why I've been writing some new material involving more crowd scenes. We're safer with them because we can get away with not having WG in the forefront."

"But surely your whole approach is to bring him to prominence. You said he was the leader and had..."

"Yes, of course, but not now! If we have no actor to play WG it gives Chris another excuse to drop all the Hertfordshire material."

"But at some stage you've got to face the issue. John Thurley could be out of action for weeks. After that..."

"Chris hasn't said anything, neither a replacement nor a pulling back. It puts everything in limbo and I'm frightened to say in case it pushes him into the wrong decision."

After a long silence Charley says, "I want your advice on something I've been working on."

"I don't know anything about filmmaking."

"But you do know about the Revolt."

Charley has been working on Saturday 15th June 1381, based on *A Little Liberty*. She flicks through the book, quoting as she talks.

"After the meeting outside the monastery (Ettie shivers, remembering how they'd been swept along by the heaving mass of folk) the crowd got even bigger. People came in from Barnet...*at the third hour of the day (ie. around 9am as we would compute it) Richard of Wallingford, who had specifically stayed behind in London, arrived with the letter from the king to the abbot. He carried before him a standard* with the arms of St. George, just as all the peasants had done in London. The crowd ran out to meet him and after dismounting he fixed the standard and said all should support it as they would do in battle...What a scene Ettie, just imagine it, all those people excitedly congregating around the symbol of their freedom.

'Anyway, Warren goes on...*the leaders consulted on their next steps while the crowd waited at the standard. Richard sent a message to the abbot. At first the abbot was reluctant to meet them, but some monks, probably afraid refusal might lead to further trouble, persuaded him and he came to the church where the local leaders were gathered. Some of these may have been with Richard in London. Then the abbot was...*"

Ettie watches Charley's lips, but hears nothing. Not just Charley's voice, but all the squeaks, rumbles and grunts of the studio are submerged. Then the numbing silence is pierced by a voice, gradually increasing in volume and clarity until synchronising exactly with Charley's lips. She mouths the words, but Ettie only hears this other voice. Charley continues, utterly unaware what Ettie is hearing, perhaps unaware not just her voice, but also her words may have been supplanted. Ettie knows the voice. It's the same voice she heard on the common.

"...*the abbot, stands dazed and tense, without his customary confidence as Richard hands him the royal writ. So long I savoured this moment as I tramped from London, imagining his deadened eyes trying to take in the impossible. He doesn't lift his face from the paper...but he can't deny... how many times must he read it...not wanting to admit...but the words are clear...I know them by heart....*

'...*at the petition of our beloved loyal subjects of the town of St.Albans, we wish and command that you hand over certain charters which are in your possession to the burgesses and good people of the town concerning the common land, pasture and fishery as the law and right require, so they may have no grounds for complaining to us in the future in this matter...*

'At last he looks up and begins his mealy mouthed wheedling.

'...such pleas were terminated in the times of your forefathers, so in accordance with the laws from earlier times you have no right to claim all the demands you are making...

'Curse him! But Richard speaks.

'...We are the lawmakers now! We are not concerned with such laws and will not accept them. Therefore I urge and advise you not to anger the commonalty for it cannot be pacified until all these things have been secured..."

Then Charley's own voice suddenly intervenes as Ettie turns around as if she might see someone running away.

"...but the abbot still refused and put forward other arguments. It was a tense moment, Ettie, but the abbot was wavering and others quickly intervened..."

Now the past supervenes once more with Richard of Wallingford's booming voice hurtling through the centuries.

"The thousands of people at the monastery gates are waiting for a speedy reply. If we delay any longer they will turn their fury on us. They will have their demands at once or overthrow this place!"

Ettie twists and turns, looking for Richard and the owner of the other voice, but there's no one. Charley is speaking and glances bewilderingly at her.

"...so the abbot conceded their demands for new charters of liberties and released the people from the pledges their fathers had made to the monastery."

They are gone now, as quickly as they came. Ettie stares at Charley in disbelief. What right has she to explain for those that *live* the past? Is Ettie suspended between Charley's present and the past of Richard of Wallingford and the mysterious messenger? Messenger. The word unsettles her. She's come across a *messenger* before and the voice is not just what she heard on the common, but of another time perhaps. Is this someone she's met before?

"...so negotiations with the abbot continued throughout the morning and into the afternoon," Charley says, skimming through Warren's book, "Then around three o'clock they entered the cloister and lifted the millstones, which had been laid on the floor by the parlour entrance as...

...a reminder of the monastery's control over the milling of our corn. We carried them away, brought them to the commons and smashed them into small pieces so each man could take a fragment just as the bread is blessed and distributed in church. Such a moment, when we prevailed at last over the oppressive power of the monastery, will live forever..."

The voice – one she still cannot locate – subsides, but the fury, tempered with a defiant remembrance of a fateful day remains.

"Just imagine them lifting those ancient millstones," Charley cries excitedly, "carting them out, smashing them up. What dramatic potential!"

Then Chris suddenly appears. Standing in silent vigil he drives out the last vestiges of the past, dismissing the images as an irate parent might disperse mischievous children. Charley and Ettie sit impassively, silenced by his silence, struck dumb by the contagion. Having thought it over he tells Charley the existing modifications to the original screenplay are onerous enough. There's no need for further scenes. She starts to argue and as before he struggles against her determined promotion of the 'bigger picture.' The same issues are flung around once more then, sensing imminent defeat or perhaps remembering previous happenings on the set, he panics and turns to Ettie.

"Tell her we don't need all this, how dangerous it is to meddle with the past."

Ettie is dumbfounded. She has no wish to be part of this fight, but Chris is desperate.

"You agreed to help me when I told you the picture was bugged..."

"I agreed to come to the studio."

"Anyway...as you said she shouldn't be opening up scenes after we'd finished shooting."

Charley glares at Ettie.

"If I recall," Ettie says firmly, "It was *you* said that. I expressed no opinion."

"Then there's your experience in London. You said that clearly indicates the need to be extremely cautious with these..."

"I've never referred to what happened in London though you've asked about it many times. You've made your own assumptions, believing they're based on things I've said to you, which isn't the case."

"I...I have...well it's no matter...these things..." Chris struggles.

His misleading impression that she's been critical of Charley irritates and surprises Ettie. Her obvious annoyance only strengthens Charley's determination and Chris's grip on the film slips away rapidly. Sensing his weakness, Charley grabs her papers, calls to the cast and hands out various 'parts.' Chris protests and implores Ettie to intervene as a 'specialist adviser,' but she's intransigent.

"It's no good soliciting my help. There can be no harm in at least trying out what Charley has written."

"I can read the script," Chris says dryly.

"But if it's read through it can come alive and that makes all the difference."

Chris no longer has the heart to resist. The forces ranged against him are too powerful to be taken on alone. Only Ettie has the skills and she's siding with Charley. He slinks away, to watch from the sidelines. The 'reading' begins and the events of the afternoon and evening of Saturday 15th June 1381 are enlivened again. Yet Ettie's intervention has surprised her as much as Chris. She hadn't intended to support Charley so vigorously. Sharing with Chris, though for wholly different reasons, a sense of the film slipping away she no longer wants to be here and wishes she'd never come. She ought to have remained strictly neutral during their fight. Her outburst was crucial, yet was it she who really supported Charley or others speaking through her?

Ettie listens, but her mind wanders, the past resurrected not so much by the words and gestures of the actors, but from what she senses from those same forces Chris feels so powerless to resist. Some unseen person is at the edge of the group, weighing the words and meaning with the eyes and ears of one who knows, judging the performance as only one who was *there* can do. Soon, if Chris's fading resistance can be finally overcome, this run through will be converted into film, a magic reel of repeatable if ephemeral reality. The past lives its moment just once and then is gone. But what if the past really is like a film with each recorded moment capable of being endlessly played back?

She finds Chris sulking in his room while the 'reading' continues. He's morose and doesn't respond to her. She persists. Whatever is happening he can't abdicate. He has to resume some degree of *direction* over his own creation. He looks at her with dispirited, resentful eyes.

"You've also betrayed me. Go away and don't come back."

She doesn't go back to the reading. She wants to put herself well away from film studios. She could easily avoid St. Albans. A short hop up the motorway, turn off at Sandbourn and back through Fulwood Green to Welstead. That's her intention, but she keeps recalling her conversation with Charley and the continual incursions of the past. Was she alone, did Charley and the actors feel it too? She also worries about Chris. He saw and heard the same as she and Charley. Does he cry against something he's partly created, playing with forces beyond his control?

Lost in her thoughts she drives automatically and enters St. Albans before realising she's missed the junction for the motorway. It's the last place to lose any residual presences, but she's drawn unresistingly. She'll make the best of it. She doesn't feel like cooking. She'll get a meal before going back to the cottage. Yet she makes no immediate attempt to find a restaurant. Instead she walks around the town, hovering near the 15th century tower before reaching the old gateway, where she stops, agitated, but unwilling to leave. Facing up to your obsessions is the best way to purge them, getting rid of recollections, and forebodings. She feels better and walks back into town, intent on really finding a place to eat and composing her jangled nerves.

She ambles along the main street. The pubs and restaurants are coming alive in the early evening. A small, dark haired woman in her early forties in a flower pink dress emerges from one of the pubs. She stands on the pavement, holding a hat in her hand and stares one way, then another, unsure which way to go. She bumps into a few people, apologises and then tries to engage them in conversation, but they ignore her. Then she steps into the road, turns her back dangerously to the traffic and speaks to whoever passes by.

"No one listens!"

A car stops and toots its horn. She turns and gestures rudely with her fingers. The car reverses and then proceeds around her, the driver responding in similar fashion.

"You have to listen to me," she shouts to anyone who cares to listen, either on the pavement or on the opposite side of the road as she turns towards the traffic, "You can't ignore it, you must listen to Maggie!"

Is this the same Maggie Ettie has heard about? Then Maggie sees her and twirls round to face her.

"You'll understand. They forget their own past in this town. West Hertfordshire is a place inhabited only by the deaf, for no one hears, no one hears..."

"Hear what?" Ettie says.

Maggie looks intently at this one person who's deigned to speak to her. Others also stop now. Seeing Ettie's large black hat and perhaps acknowledging a fellow spirit, Maggie puts on her own hat and rams it down, almost over her eyes.

"The past!" Maggie screams, "No one hears, no one wants to hear, but they've all heard the rumours (she turns from side to side to the small crowd now forming on either side of Ettie) You've all heard you ignore them at your peril! They're not just rumours, I've felt these things, I know!"

Several cars have stopped and a bus waits at the stop even though all passengers are on board. Everyone waits, listening as Maggie twirls again through almost 360 degrees and capers her arms and legs in a little jig of triumph.

"They did it, they got Warren Grover, they killed him."

"Who, who are they?" Ettie says.

"Them...them from the past...they killed him...you can't play with them...they're not toys...you can't make the dead perform...they'll do it their way..."

5

JENNIIFER is out early. Work at the murder scene is almost completed and after checking on progress she walks south across the common, from where she sees the commuters scurrying like animated sticks along the road towards the station. They easily outnumber the few on the common. In a quarter mile she passes only a couple of people, both with dogs until as she almost reaches the road she catches up with a woman walking slowly. Jennifer smiles in acknowledgement as they draw level. The other woman looks puzzled. Jennifer breaks the silence.

"You're some way from home. "

Kathleen Grover stops, but still looks bemused.

"On the common," Jennifer says, "I would have thought Southstead is nearer and what with..."

"The association with Warren, you mean? I suppose that's why you're here."

"Well, I have..."

"I came here *because* of Warren. This morning I felt I had to be...near him...I was going up to where...but I turned back."

"I quite understand."

"I wasn't sure what I'd feel. If I could think about Warren...it might help me to...but I've hardly thought about him at all...it's this place, the common. Once I was up here other things welled up and wouldn't go away and..."

She stops and turns to Jennifer.

"Are you in hurry to be away, sergeant?"

"Not necessarily, if you want to talk…"

"Yes, I think I would. There's a coffee shop at this end of town. It should be open by now. Can we go there?"

Despite her yearning to talk Kathleen sits in the almost empty café spooning her undrunk coffee and starring gloomily out the window.

"You're not from these parts originally, are you?" Kathleen says at last.

"No, I've recently transferred from Nottingham."

"People who don't know it think Welstead is one of those snooty upper crust places, conveniently sited on the railway line, not too far yet not too close for getting to London. It's agreeable lush Home Counties, divertingly anonymous, where nothing too grand or dramatic ever happens or has happened so long as the lawns are mowed and the upper middle classes conform to a respectable predictability. It's a veneer at best. Scratch the surface or bury your preconceptions and you'll find it's not like that at all and as for nothing having happened…that's another story."

"Is that what you were thinking about on the common?"

"I thought about the land that's always been here and always will be irrespective of the petty prejudices of people. That's how Warren would see it. His work on the Peasants' Revolt was very much tied to the land and I kept thinking how much the land had seen…but it was after the revolt I couldn't get out of my mind. Warren always said that was as fascinating as the revolt itself. 'If only we knew more,' he said, 'first the glory then the tragedy. There must have been hundreds of tales in that ruthless suppression, all over this country.' And now he's cut down as they were cut down. Perhaps it was the way he would have wanted to…"

She stops to dab her eyes before continuing.

"…and all over this country, I kept thinking, everywhere in this peaceful, oh so *respectable* country where they ran and hid and were hunted and cut down. Every one of those brash and lavish houses they've built on land grabbed from the country was originally theirs and fertilised with their…blood…and now it's Warren too…they've shed his…"

She stops again, staring forlornly for a time at the window, then turns back, whispering falteringly, "Everywhere."

As the numbness goes, her voice gets stronger and more resolute, the full force of her loss released to sear and stab.

"What would they think, those senseless plutocrats who've bought into that Hempston development if they knew they'd built on the wild land as Warren called it, where our people were suppressed, where those went with nowhere else to go? People like that film director, Christopher Pleasant."

"But isn't his place on the west side of the common, that's nowhere near..."

"Oh yes, his big house, but he also bought a place in Hempston, though I've heard he's never lived in it. Guilty conscience maybe, it ought to be. Warren was against the development."

"Did you take part in the opposition?"

"Not me. Oh I was against it, but these protest movements are a bit like your relatives, you can't get to choose who you work with. Some on your own side are a damned sight worse than those you're up against. I told Warren, I wouldn't take an active part with people like that lunatic Margaret Morton involved. Spouting her mouth off in public about Warren. She's mad that one, you can't take anything she says seriously."

Jenner was assigned to this case largely through Maggie, but despite Jennifer's several reminders he's been putting off his meeting with her, after the latest outburst further prevarication is impossible. Only slightly drunk and presenting no danger except to herself she was arrested in St. Albans, but quickly released and taken home. Ordinarily Jenner wouldn't have been involved, but in the station (where she's well known as a local eccentric) she persisted in her crazy ravings about Warren Grover. After that he had to see her.

"I ask you, villains in the past," the chief superintendent had said, "but her allegations will have to be investigated."

Must they? Jenner thinks. He's used to nutters and intemperate appeals to 'extra normal forces' behind Warren Grover's murder are best avoided. If the police take seriously everything of this kind...

He reaches the house in the small council estate. Maggie answers the door. She's dressed in a floppy sweater and jeans on which she's wiping her wet hands.

"Don't want to see the cops," she says as Jenner shows his card.

"That madam is the unfortunate view of many of your fellow citizens. Likewise, I do not always relish meeting many of them. This is just such an occasion. In that respect we are therefore both unfortunate, but we have no choice. May I come in?"

He steps neatly to her side and before she can object is over the threshold and into the hall. She bangs the door and trips after him.

"Hey, copper, I didn't invite you...I'm in the middle of..."

But Jenner is already seated by the window in her living room.

"Middle of what?" he says as she stands at the door.

"Tea."

"Thank you. Plenty of milk and no sugar."

She leers ominously ready to tell him to 'clear off,' but then goes to the kitchen, muttering about 'tea' being a meal not a drink and she's not in the habit of 'pandering to coppers.' She returns with two very large mugs.

"I don't use cups," she says aggressively.

"Quite so," he says, "I much prefer my tea in reasonable quantities."

"I told everything at the police station. Just because I choose to talk about Warren and the past and...anyway I was released without charge."

"I haven't come about that. I'm interested in anything that might assist my enquiries into Warren Grover's murder."

"Nobody's been interested in what I've said before."

"Have you said much?"

"What I've said is what's been seen for a long time."

"You knew him well?"

"Everybody knew of him, but I'd known him for years, we were at school together."

"It goes back that far?"

"Oh much further back than that, before Warren was born!"

She hunches herself up in her chair, enthused and ready to blast off gleefully into her subject. Jenner doesn't relish it. Events before the victim's birth, even if they are accurate, which he doubts are not relevant. He'll steer her onto more solid territory, but she gets going quickly, hardly drawing a breath and leaving no opportunity for him to interrupt.

"People have been reporting things for hundreds of years. If your mind is closed (she glances at him disparagingly) you'll say the stuff of legends. If your mind is open it's the story of our shared past. Suppression or ridicule can't stop them (another contemptuous glance) for they are buried deep in all our true souls. Over the centuries too many have seen and heard the marching and shouting for them to be discounted. There was..."

"So nothing very specific," he cuts in, "which doesn't..."

"But I've seen and heard these things myself!"

"That may well be so, but how are these...sightings... connected to Warren Grover?"

"I told Warren. He understood. Then he told me the things he'd seen and heard. He wasn't the first, don't you see? Warren was following those that went before. Those in the past..."

"You know who killed Warren Grover?"

"Of course, I keep telling you, those in the past."

"Who?"

She gets up.

"You're mug's empty, let me fill it up."

She returns to the kitchen before he can challenge her again. She's calm now, her mood subsiding as quickly as it erupted and no longer concerned with 'pandering to coppers,' as she calls, "No sugar, wasn't it?"

"Who are these people?" he says, following her to the kitchen.

"Those that leave," she says, handing him the replenished mug.

"What, leave the area?"

"Not of their own accord...not naturally...they disappear."

He sighs in frustration.

"If this has any relevance to…"

"If you dropped something into the old pond in town you had to catch it quick before it was swept down the stream and never seen again. You won't know what I mean, not many know about the old river."

"The pond was outside the old forge and the river ran through the middle of town, then disappeared to emerge at the large ponds at the end of the common."

"Aha, so you are from these parts!"

"I was born in Welstead."

She nods and claps her hands knowingly, seemingly including him in her circumscribed world, not something he's comfortable with.

"You said it," she says.

"What did I say?"

"You said the river disappeared and so have the people. Just like you dropped something into the old river. Nobody questioned it, but they'd gone all the same," she says, pouring more tea for herself with mysterious self satisfaction, "So you see…"

"No I don't see," he says irritably, "Which people disappeared, when, how? I need details."

She looks at him incredulously as if the answers are ludicrously self evident, then shrugs, stirs her tea noisily and says, "Then there was the falling man."

"Falling man? What are you talking about now?"

"I saw a man falling down."

"Where?"

"On the common."

"When?"

She grimaces and moves her fingers slowly.

"A few days."

"Can't you be more precise?"

"No I can't, I don't run my life like a timetable."

"No, I'm sure you don't. Was this before or after Warren Grover's body was found?"

"Before."

"Was it in the same place."

"I told you it was on the common."

"The common is a big place."

"I know every blade of grass, so I don't walk across it with a map, ticking off bits like a kid collecting car numbers. How do I know where it was?"

"Was anyone else about?"

"No...well...I suppose there could have been someone hiding...I wasn't close enough to see."

"And you saw this a few days ago?"

"And before."

"Before?"

"I saw him before."

"The same man?"

"'Course, the same man."

"You saw this same man falling down on other occasions?"

"Oh yes, lots of time."

"How could the same man keep falling down?"

"Because he keeps coming back."

Maggie recounts more sightings of the 'falling man,' her enthusiasm increasing as Jenner's expectation of having found a witness to Warren's murder wanes. He listens inattentively except for a wearying "How long have you been seeing him?"

"Months."

"But how can it...?"

"That's how it is with spirits."

Jenner groans. All he wants to do is terminate the interview and get out as fast as possible.

"Ghosts," he mutters

"Yes, but real ones."

He gets up to leave.

"I don't investigate ghosts, real or imaginary."

"Real," she says, "Not celluloid ones like Chris Pleasant and his film. They only makes things worse."

"Nobody seems to like his film."

"It's provoking the spirits!"

"Maybe, but for the moment I'll confine my activities to flesh and blood suspects."

Ted Skinner's grand, detached house couldn't be more different from Maggie's, all twee windows and ancient ivy, standing in extensive grounds on the better edge of Hempston. Now only working part time as a consultant for his old firm he's free in the afternoons. Jenner is shown into a large, comfortable study at the rear of the house with fine views of the garden. The sun streams through the windows. There are a few well stocked bookshelves and a cupboard for files and papers, but with the television, hi fi and the plush chairs it's more like a lounge. Almost self sufficient, perhaps like the man himself. Skinner, slightly balding, slim and wiry, smiles broadly, but his darting deep set eyes look suspiciously at Jenner. He's more like a shrewd countryman assessing an 'incomer' than a semi retired executive. What you see is definitely not what you get, Jenner thinks. They sit opposite each other, the large space between the chairs emphasising their separation.

"You worked closely with Warren Grover opposing this new development in Hempston?" Jenner says.

"Of course," Skinner says, his jaw set firm, then slightly loosening up with a forced smile, "as would all sane people."

"If you're right and judging by your lack of success, this area must be predominantly populated by the insane."

Skinner laughs.

"Our arguments were always well researched and powerfully marshalled, but the sane are not always in command of the process."

"Sometimes reputations are made or impaired by the company you keep."

Skinner laughs again, but it's clipped, sardonic and he glowers belligerently.

"I think you are ahead of me, chief inspector. Margaret Morton has already rung me."

"I wasn't necessarily referring to her."

"I hope you're not implying Warren or I employed other than wholly legitimate means to further the campaign."

"Why could there possibly be such an implication?"

"No reason," Skinner says uncomfortably, the strained smile returning as he shifts ground, "I don't understand why you went to see her at all."

"I'll see anybody who may be relevant to my enquiries."

"She wasn't even a major player in the campaign."

"She knew Warren."

"Everybody knew Warren. You're surely not going to see them all."

"Not everybody has made allegations about his murderer."

Skinner laughs, this time loud and raucous.

"She means no harm. Maggie always makes bombastic assertions. It doesn't mean anything. I don't think you should be harassing her."

"I'm not harassing anyone," Jenner says stiffly, "and how I conduct my enquiries is not a matter for discussion."

"She's an innocent. By seeing her you assist her attackers."

"I don't assist..."

"Maggie leaves herself wide open. They set her up to knock her down."

"Who?"

"Those supporting the development. While Maggie makes her perhaps extravagant but essentially harmlessly remarks about Warren's murder it diverts attention from other matters."

"Like the campaign against the development?"

"We're not done yet."

"Did Warren have enemies as a result of the campaign."

"It was inevitable."

"Even in the local community not everyone agreed with you."

"There are always some..."

"Like those who found it convenient to use Margaret Morton?"

Skinner hesitates.

"I'm not making any allegations..."

"Quite so."

"...and it's not for me to tell you how to carry out your investigations..."

"...but if you were?"

"I would tell you to go and talk to Monica Freeson. There's also something else you need to know…"

Skinner's support for Maggie seems incongruous. It would be difficult to find two people more unalike. One urbane, patrician, realistic, skilful in public affairs, the other unsophisticated, dreamy, naïve, one comfortably well off, the other struggling. Impressions can be deceptive. Hidden insights might lurk amid the jumbled speeches of confused minds. Perhaps it's not just the promoters of the Hempston development who seek to divert attention. Is defending her his subtle way of distancing himself from what she says? That's a matter for later. Now it's time to see the opposition, but Jenner is curious about the development and only moves his car out of Skinner's drive to park it close to the village centre. From here he can walk to Monica Freeson's house.

He strolls down the main street, past the church and the shops until he reaches the river and where the old railway line once crossed the road. The new houses on the site of the old station are not to his taste, though hardly enough to warrant a major campaign. But it's not for him to get into the minds of aesthetic crusaders and conservation warriors. Though if he did he might better understand the intricate relationships surrounding the murdered man and the motives of potential suspects. He comes to the gaping hole where once stood the 14th century house, destroyed by developmental vandalism. His mood changes. This is no academic question of individual taste. He feels it personally. This was an attack on his world, his heritage, his past. The perpetrators will be prosecuted, the approved plans not extending to the destruction of the building. Jenner wishes the action successful, but no matter what the eventual punishment might be (he suspects something utterly lenient compared to the immense profits) it can't bring back what's been lost. Destroy the past and it can't return. Can it?

Work continues at the rear of the empty site where yet more residences are being constructed, but nothing here at the front. A kind of belated atonement perhaps. A short silence in memoriam. At least until the next shift comes on duty. He walks on, along the footpath behind the new development, through several roads and finally at the end of a small cul de sac to 'Meadowland' home of Monica Freeson. At least a hundred and fifty years older than surrounding properties, it appears less impressive than Skinner's pile, smaller, squatter, less ostentatious, but this is misleading. It's certainly less grandiose, less showy, but the comparatively narrow frontage hides a substantial interior while the spacious grounds enhance the sense of space with views of the rolling country. The smallness of the front is almost like a magical door opening onto a fabulously secret world. Except for those in the know it's not secret. For as local councillor and dignitary with extensive interests across the community, Monica Freeson frequently entertains the great and the good, though this afternoon she expects no one to call, least of all a detective chief inspector.

With her always immaculate yellow hair, high cheekbones and eyes with a perpetually surprised expression she has the polished features of a woman whose attractiveness, like most else about her, needs time to mature. Actually in her mid forties, her age seems indeterminate. At twenty she probably looked old. At sixty she'll probably look young. Never underdressed, even in her own sanctum, she's always coordinated from top to toe, though in a narrow range of colours. Her buff suit and shoes with matching hat and gloves on the hall table show she's not been long in the house. After a slight momentary unease at their meeting, she greets Jenner cordially and confidently. Such social skills come naturally, like breathing. Her face is a practised oval of measured and expressionless detachment.

"What can I tell you?" she says in answer to his general enquiry, "I knew Warren Grover, everybody did."

"You shared an interest in cultural matters. As chair of the Arts and Leisure Committee..."

"I have to balance many conflicting demands for resources and finance. Warren Grover was one of many trying to secure support for his activities. Some we could help him with, some we could not."

"He had a particular interest in the history of the area."

"You mean the wretched Peasants' Revolt!"

"You didn't share his interest?"

"You mean his obsession!"

"I believe he sought funding for a projected re-enactment, which you refused?"

"As I said we have many conflicting applications."

"The project was very important to him. He would have deeply resented your rejection of his application."

She stares open mouthed, unsure what to say and then smiles.

"If our decisions were based solely on possible reactions we'd be unable to make any at all. The man was an obsessive, often out of touch with reality, so wrapped up in his re-enactment he was incapable of taking an objective view."

"I understand he circulated very widely."

"Yes, but within a concentrated milieu. I had to consider the impact on the public at large. His proposal was too restricted. There was no appeal to a wider audience. Besides I wasn't comfortable with the subject matter. It was too...base...too earthy...we couldn't be associated with a celebration of such a violent episode in the county's history. It would project the wrong image, too partisan. Now if he'd come to us with something more like this film that's being made, what's it's name – Hurling Time – that would have been much better."

"So you don't object to the right kind of obsession?"

"It's not the same. I tried with Warren, believe me, it wasn't easy. It's not as if we didn't support some of his other more...accessible proposals."

"You also clashed over the new development. He was active in the opposition campaign while you..."

"Another example of Warren being out of touch with reality He wasn't prepared to consider the economic needs of the area..."

"As you saw it?"

"I wasn't alone."

"Neither was he."

"Ultimately decisions have to be made."

"And you are in an influential position."

"I'm only *one* member of the Planning Committee. "

Both conscious of having slightly raised their voices they are suddenly silent. Jenner has surprised himself. The demolition of the old house has unsettled him more than he realised and he ought not to let it unduly influence his enquiries. It wouldn't be surprising if Monica took exception to his line of questioning, but she says nothing. Her social poise gradually returns and she wonders how best to pull back the conversation to a more even temper, but Jenner is first.

"Such a strong willed character must have made enemies."

Monica leans back in her chair, eyeing him with a dubious smirk.

"No one I know felt strongly enough to kill him."

"Quite."

"Besides, while Warren could be irritating and was annoyingly misguided, at least he was open and direct. One always knew where one stood with him...unlike others."

Jenner knows he's expected to react, but he prefers to wait. If Monica feels strongly enough she'll return to it.

"I've heard he could be decidedly direct at times and not above personal attack."

Now she prefers not to react.

"Is it true he recently made scathing remarks to yourself?"

She laughs and flicks her hands dismissively.

"Nothing serious, the usual cut and thrust one learns to expect in public life."

"He accused you of abusing your position as a councillor in relation to planning matters, of failing to declare an interest in a particular contract and..."

"That was wrong! He was forced to retract that accusation."

"Even so, strong words. You must have been angry?"

"Not really, much of what he said was in a private meeting. Just because Warren and I had certain disagreements doesn't mean I didn't have great respect for the man."

"Yet he didn't seem to have much respect for you?"

She ignores this remark. Jenner's informant is more important to her than the information.

"How did you know this?"

"That's not something I can..."

"You're right I was angry, but not with Warren. He did make some relatively trivial remarks at a public meeting, certainly nothing to cause a major stir, but they were reported wholly out of context."

"Reported?"

"In that scurrilous rag *The Mid Herts Herald*. I was hounded for weeks by the editor."

"The newspaper backed the campaign against the development?"

"No...not...exactly. Carter's too clever for that. He operates on innuendo and vile suggestion. He twisted Warren's rather pathetic remarks out of all proportion, coming close to libelling me and..."

"But not close enough for you to take action?"

"Unfortunately not. Have you seen him?"

"Not yet, he's not part of my enquiries."

"He ought to be. Got his filthy fingers in every nasty pie in the area. Probe him deep enough and you'll be surprised what you'll find."

Ettie spends most of the morning walking. First into town for small items of shopping, then returning the long way onto the common, skirting the ponds and back across to the cottage. It does her good. She needs to breathe plenty of fresh air and feel the warmth of the sun in her face. They might counteract the debilitating effects of the studio and the street in St.Albans, both of which she finds claustrophobic, though that has nothing to do with cramped walls or imposing buildings. The confining is in her mind. Out in the open, on the move, talking to shopkeepers, she holds the sense of restriction at bay, but now in the enclosed garden, despite the peace and warmth, it's impossible to hold back disturbing memories of Maggie.

Maggie kept repeating herself, looking more ridiculous than threatening and more people crowded around. Ettie didn't want to be part of a circus and hurried away, but it wasn't so easy to dismiss her forebodings. Why did Maggie say Ettie would understand and why did Ettie question her? Did they sense fellow feeling in the other? Maggie is well known and news of her eruption has travelled fast, several people mentioning her in the shops this morning. It's not her first outburst nor as one woman said would it be the last. She's 'had treatment' somebody said with a knowing look, though one elderly lady, perhaps wiser than others, just shook her head and said 'the poor woman's her own worst enemy, if she calmed down people might listen to her more.' Maybe Maggie is more than just a gibbering fool and her outbursts should be taken more seriously, but what is it she really has to say? Yet she could be a dangerous force. She's *had treatment*. What if her attacks on Chris's film are more than deranged torment? What if they are the braying of baleful sprits?

"Sneaking a quiet moment?"

Ettie looks up. Her neighbour, a woman in her late sixties leans over the hedge. She's lived alone in the same cottage for many years. Her life revolves around a careful schedule of domestic chores in which "quiet moments' are precisely built in.

They exchange pleasantries, then the woman suddenly says, "Did you see anything unusual out on the common?"

Ettie feels exposed as if someone has been spying on her. What does she mean, what have others seen or heard? Yet how can they know what's in her head or feel what she feels? She stutters incoherently for a few seconds, trying to justify her walks on the common. Fortunately her neighbour doesn't hear.

"Other people have seen the man again."

"The man?" Ettie says, anxiously latching onto anything unconnected with herself, then wondering if 'the man' is someone she knows.

"Usually at the stile where the fields meet the end of the common at the stream."

"I don't usually go that way," Ettie says with some relief.

"Whenever anybody gets close he disappears. It's a ghost, of course."

"A ghost?"

"Has to be."

"Do they know who it is?"

"Nobody has any idea."

"Nothing connected to the place?"

"Not that I know of."

"Then why...?"

"Always in the same place and falling down. Always falling down. Only a ghost would keep repeating itself like that, wouldn't it?"

"I suppose so."

"I don't think he's dangerous because as soon as anybody approaches he's gone."

"How long has this been going on?"

"A few weeks, months maybe, some say they first saw him last year."

It gets colder in the garden. Her neighbour must 'get on' and leaves with the suggestion Ettie should 'should look out for him' next time she's on the common, though that's something she's unlikely to do herself. Ettie is unsettled. A ghost on the common is an unforeseen complication along with all the other 'happenings.' Once suggested it's bound to become embedded until the eyes see what the mind believes. Perhaps her neighbour is right. It's better to keep active, keep the overactive mind and exaggerated memory at bay. She goes to the kitchen, fiddles around, rearranges, takes things out of cupboards, puts others back, wonders what else to...the telephone rings. It's Charley.

"I need your help. Chris no longer opposes shooting additional scenes. It's really exciting. I've started working on the night of the 15th June..."

"You'll have to remind me," Ettie says.

"That afternoon people arrived in St.Albans from outlying villages, demanding free hunting, snaring and fishing rights. The abbot prevaricated, telling them to come back the following Thursday. That night the men gathered in the fields and pulled down the dykes around some of the pools."

"These villages, was one Sandbourn?"

"Yes."

Ettie shivers. What she's seen and heard in the night is about to be dramatised. The past in the present, the film embraces her reality.

"I really need your help to bring it alive."

No, not alive! Some things are better left dead.

"Will Chris be there?"

Charley is silent. Ettie asks again.

"I'm not sure," Charley says at last.

"But he's the director?"

"He's not acting like the director. He's abdicated. There's a production vacuum."

"But surely he has to be there? How can the new scenes go ahead without him?"

"He ought to be...but we can go ahead without him. Everybody feels drawn, it's something we have to do."

Charley's voice rises excitedly. Ettie doesn't share her exhilaration. The filmmaking has acquired a life of its own, independent of its director and despite all Charley's efforts, detached from the script. What she writes is out of her control. Ettie is fearful of being there. She might act as a magnet for other forces and make the situation worse.

"I'm rather busy."

"But Ettie, you *must* help us!"

"Oh, there's someone at the door, I'll have to ring you back."

As Ettie puts the phone down it seems to bang very loudly. Then she hears the knock again. There really is someone at the door! She's not expecting anyone to call. It might be Chris, concerned about Charley. Already she regrets being so openly supportive of her. Another knock. She opens the door.

"I'm so glad I've caught you. I was afraid you might be out."

Damn! The last thing Ettie needs now is a visit from Jessica Tennant.

"Naturally I don't want to interrupt anything, I was just down the road so to speak. As long as I'm not getting in the way, as it were..."

"But..."

They are about the same age, but as she bustles in Jessica has all the vigour Ettie is lacking. No enervating escapade to dampen her energies!

"I'm alright leaving the car outside, aren't I...?" she says, marching in and perching on a chair by the window.

"Yes, it's..."

"Excellent! You can never be sure these days with these wretched residential parking areas and so forth and they cost the earth too."

Ettie sits opposite. Jessica bobs around birdlike, examining every aspect of the room, then looks carefully at Ettie, noticing her pale pallor and tired eyes.

"My God, Ettie, you still look bloody awful!"

"Thank you very much."

"Better than when I last saw you, that must have been, let me see, just after, no I came to see...oh anyway, whenever it was, you've perked up a bit, but I didn't realise how long you'd need to recover. That damned business in London must have left you absolutely shattered. I think we should have tea. No, stay where you are, I'll get it."

With a "Kitchen, this way?" she disappears before Ettie can answer.

Cupboard doors are opened and rapidly closed.

"The tea pot is..." Ettie calls only to be cut short with a brisk "Yes, I see it," followed by clattering cups and saucers. While busy with the tea, Jessica carries on her one sided conversation.

"I had to come because I've made an interesting discovery... now where's the milk...I thought you'd want to know...ah, here it is...naturally, if you're feeling a trifle delicate, I'll shut up...no, well anyway it's sometimes better to face these things squarely, as it were... (kettle whistling) ... not too strong I believe...bit like hair of the dog for a hangover, not that I'm suggesting...now sugar, no you don't...I don't know why I didn't notice it before, but what with student dissertations and the like...anyway, I'm sure of it now..."

During this disjointed barrage Ettie stares impassively out the window, trying to remain calm, making no attempt to interpret what she hears from the kitchen. Jessica returns, deposits the tea, swishing it into two cups and stirring the milk noisily.

"One can be so easily overwhelmed by the immensity of details. Naturally we have to draw out general trends from particular instances, but there's a corresponding danger, as it were, of losing some detail in the process."

Ettie stares absently. Jessica puts down her cup and leans forward to give her next remark added emphasis and ensure Ettie's full attention.

"It was my fault. In my excitement I didn't analyse such an amazing discovery carefully. Wading through so much material from different sources, but even so..."

"I'm sorry, I still don't..."

"The rhyme, Ettie, it's the rhyme "

Jessica sighs, but not from exasperation. She really had underestimated the extent of how those events have frazzled Ettie.

"Your notes, other notes and material, I've been through them all much more thoroughly. I should have done it months ago, anyway I can now see what was blindingly obvious, I really don't know how..."

Ettie keeps staring out the window as Jessica goes on, occasionally glancing back with a raised eyebrow or an affirmative nod, but actually not really listening as her mind drifts, steered and pushed on its course by Jessica's reference to the rhyme. She's back in London, with Vicky as they talked about the past, all Vicky saw, all Vicky heard...

"...after reaching tentative conclusions, I double checked and sure enough..."

...the strange events of that night, precursor of so much that followed. Now she's running after Vicky as she disappeared into the night, into the past...

"...I know this may come as a shock, but it could require a total re-evaluation of..."

...the 14th century London they saw together...

"...has to be interpreted in 14th century terms..."

...six hundred year old faces as familiar still as anyone walking along the street outside...

"...of course, we may never recover the other parts, but even so..."

...the alarm and the terror of being marooned, the possibility of never coming back...

"...naturally I took the elementary precaution of checking with a colleague..."

...but they had come back and everything had been resolved...

"...all our previous assumptions will have to be re-assessed. What do you think? Ettie! What do you think?"

Jessica's voice stabs into her reverie, the teacher prodding the inattentive pupil. Ettie turns, trying to pull back Jessica's last words, rapidly evaporating from her mind. She splutters some meaningless response, which as she'd hoped, forces Jessica to repeat them.

"Our discovery of the lost seventh rhyme of 1381 was a magnificent achievement, filling in the details of what *really* happened in London. Of course we didn't have everything. A great deal had to be pieced together – not least by yourself and I might say to vital historical analysis by myself – but it's more than a vital record of the last days of the revolt. In many ways it was only a beginning..."

"A beginning?" Ettie says dreamily.

"Yes, it was only when I examined the text of the seventh more closely I realised its infernal cleverness and how incredibly stupid I'd been. The Revolt was characterised in the chronicles by references to 'The Great Society,' justifying a medieval conspiracy of the lower orders."

"But you said..."

"Yes, strictly speaking a conspiracy is erroneous. However, if we no longer regard 'The Great Society' as an *organisation* and more in medieval terms as a set of *moral principles* then what we've discovered in the seventh rhyme points the way to the whole programme. It's only one aspect of 'The Great Society.' Those desperate men drew up their rhymes with three key constituents – revelation, revenge and renewal. The first six rhymes are quoted in the chronicles. They reveal the Revolt to come. Now we have the seventh, which records the London events and the possibility of *revenge*."

"You were disappointed an eighth, even a ninth rhyme hadn't been found," Ettie says, but without conviction.

She neither fully understands nor is particularly interested. Jessica showing off her latest theories is an irritatingly mixed blessing with its reminder of the recent past and its jarring resonance with her unsettled present.

"We may never discover the further rhymes," Jessica continues, "In London what they may have contained caused much speculation..."

"...leading to disaster..." Ettie says pointedly.

"...Yes, yes, most unfortunate, but there was an upside..." Jessica pauses, waiting for Ettie's grudging acknowledgement, eventually coming with a slow nod of her head.

"...Anyway, that's gone. I now believe those speculations... by all parties...were rather fanciful and that an eighth or ninth would also deal with revenge, but also with the aftermath and the hope of renewal..."

Renewal? Suddenly Ettie is shaken out of her introspection.

"So you see it's implications for your work...?"

"My work?" Ettie says, "I can understand for you with your studies, but how...?"

"For you? I can only hypothesise, it's not for me to encroach on your area of expertise...but when we thought the issues from the 14th century had been finally resolved by the rhyme's revelation and the pursuit of revenge, then..."

Jessica pauses, a mischievous twinkle in her eyes before continuing.

"...you say all periods are really simultaneous rather than consecutive, that the distinctions between past, present and future are like the walls between rooms in the same house...?"

Ettie nods absently.

"...then renewal may be the continuing element."

Jessica claps her hands together smartly, pours more tea and glances across questioningly. There's already enough for Ettie to think about from the past, but now Jessica introduces the rogue element from the present.

"How are you getting on with Christopher Pleasant?"

"Not very well. The work on the film is stalled."

Ettie expects an inevitable 'I told you so,' but it doesn't come.

"That's a pity," Jessica says.

"I thought you didn't approve."

"I don't, but anything that brings the great Revolt to life is commendable."

*...to life...*is Jessica also suborned by the past?

"Naturally in the hands of a man like Pleasant, it'll be flawed but...the 15th July anniversary approaches, was he intending to include the Hertfordshire events?"

Ettie hesitates.

"It looks unlikely. There've been problems."

"Any in particular?"

"I'm not sure, funding perhaps."

Jessica is unconvinced and eyes Ettie sceptically. Eventually they talk of other things and pass a reasonably agreeable, if slightly tiring hour. Then, remembering the places 'she ought to have been' and the people 'she should have seen' Jessica leaves, reminding Ettie to keep her 'updated on events.'

Ettie is tired, but when she closes her eyes scraps of the conversations intrude and Jessica's words reverberate with those of Charley...*the 15th July anniversary approaches...I need your help to bring it alive...renewal and revenge...* Whose revenge and on whom? Who will be brought back to life? Should she help or hinder before it's too late? Is Charley an innocent channel for others? Is Chris to be pitied or condemned? Is it too late already? Must all this be done by 15th July? The questions whirl and hammer around, seeking answers she can't find. Why won't the hammering stop? Hammering, metal on metal...it's the door...someone else is at the door! She shakes herself free and gets up.

"Thought I was waking the dead!" Jenner says as he walks in.

"I must have dropped off, how is the investigation going?"

"I'm getting plenty of advice," he says grumpily, "How best to conduct the enquiry, suggesting people I ought to be seeing."

"Maybe they're trying to be helpful," she says, slightly amused and recovering some composure.

"Or trying to help themselves. Ted Skinner tells me to see Monica Freeson. Monica Freeson sticks the knife into George Carter. Kathleen Grover tells Jennifer how mad Margaret Morton is, while Ted Skinner takes offence that I have gone to see her."

"You've seen Maggie?"

"Fat lot of good it did me. Talking about people disappearing and then ghosts, a man falling down."

Ettie shudders. Jenner notices.

"Something I've said?"

"Other people have seen the falling man."

"Is it a ghost?"

"It seems so."

"I had to see her. There was a scene in the street in St.Albans."

"I know. I was there."

Now he's more interested.

"I've only got jumbled reports."

"She said who was responsible for Warren Grover's murder – though nobody you could arrest – unnamed forces from the past. What do you make of it?"

"Maggie said nobody listened to her and nobody wants to hear, but coming immediately after I was returning from the film studio, I had to listen."

She tells of the conversation with Charley, the row with Chris and the mysterious 'messenger.'

"So I can no more dismiss Maggie's contacts with the past than those I hear myself, no matter how mad others may think she is."

"She's not mad. I can't wholly dismiss what she says even though it's all so garbled and cracked! She said she'd told Warren and he'd understood. Then he told her what he'd seen and heard."

"What was that?"

"I didn't ask. Maybe I should, though I'm reluctant to get into ghosts and legends despite what Jennifer says."

Ettie looks quizzically. Jenner grimaces.

"Oh, you know her, not here five minutes and already boning up on the local history. Probably talking too much to

Kathleen Grover. I told her none of this has any connection to our enquiries."

"She's not been wrong in the past."

He grunts in reluctant acknowledgement.

"In any case," Ettie says, "there's more."

She describes her nocturnal excursions, the vision of the people breaking the dikes, reclaiming their rights to the land. He listens attentively.

"I'm strongly drawn to the common, but afraid of the land and the secrets it may reveal. Whether its working with the film, I'm finding it increasingly difficult to distinguish between past and present."

"Hardly surprising with these visions in the night."

"It's not just that. At least out there I know it's the past intruding, the people, the voices, but on the set of a film about that same past I'm not so sure. Are they just actors, mouthing their lines, moving as directed, but who directs them? Not Chris Pleasant. According to Charley he's abdicated. I wonder about Charley, obsessed with Warren's book, including events not in the original script. Why is it so important to her? Why do I back her against Chris when he didn't want to include those scenes? Am I also being directed from the past? I watch everybody constantly, wondering if anyone, everyone is from the past. Charley asks for my help. Chris implores me to help. Then I let him down. Now I'm reluctant to help her, afraid what might happen. It's only a film. Yet everything about it is crazy. No director, a screenwriter operating way beyond her remit, actors performing, yet not performing, more like living the reality, but what reality, a past reality we can't possibly know? A film in free fall, unleashing forces we can't understand or control."

She stops, shakes slightly, gradually subsides and then apologises. He waves her apology aside.

"I'm not helping much," she says, "you need something more definite, linked to Warren Grover's murder."

"What did you make of George Carter?"

"He knew Warren and like him was against the film."

"Did he mention the new development in Hempston?"

"Should he have done?"

"According to Monica Freeson he's been a sneaky opponent, backing the anti campaign, but not too openly. I've since discovered a long history of conflict between her and George Carter. She didn't get on well with Warren either, though her attitude is oddly inconsistent. One moment she's dead against him, doesn't know what he's talking about, hare brained schemes like the 1381 re-enactment, the next he's not so bad, his and her words twisted out of context by diabolical George. Unlike Warren and Carter she's all for the film. She was influential in getting the new development going, which puts her on the opposite side to both of them. She was very sensitive about that, playing down Warren's attack on her integrity on planning matters. There's more she's not saying. Jennifer saw Carter, gave her a lot of material about Monica, but all rumour and no substance, plenty of smoke and no obvious fire. He couldn't print it without evidence, but apparently mentioned it to Warren, who used it against Monica. She played it down to me, but it must have hit hard and there was always the risk Warren might open up later with something more dangerous. Then we have Christopher Pleasant. I need to talk to him about his involvement with the new development. He owns property there. He denied any knowledge of Warren Grover, but if he bought into the development at an early stage he must have been aware of the opposition campaign."

"Are you going to see him now?"

"No. He's not been forthcoming about his connection. I need the facts before seeing him. The development is only at its first phase. Much more is planned. Jennifer's been checking. It'll be interesting to see if his finger is even further in the pie. Anybody involved could have a grudge against Warren."

"Why?"

"Because the opposition campaign is not yet over. Monica was keen to talk about the development, but didn't mention the next phases have been put on hold at national level. That may be down to Warren. When I asked about Warren's attack on her planning activities she was very eager to know where I got my information. She'll think it was George Carter rather than Ted Skinner. And it doesn't end there. There could be another link to Christopher Pleasant and his film. Jennifer's checking on the actor, Lawrence Bullock. He was one of the major purchasers in the original land deal."

After he leaves Ettie finds it even more difficult to settle. All the conversations return again – Charley, Jessica, Jenner – in their different ways disturbing and agitating. Charley and Jessica preoccupied with those in the past, Jenner with those in the present. Past and present juxtaposing, interfering with the film. Maybe Chris is right and Charley is wrong. Okay to portray some of the past, but not all.

"...you can't play with...the past...you can't make the past perform...they'll do it their own way..."

How right Maggie is. Take her more seriously. Keep past and present apart. It's not wise for Charley to go ahead with the night of 15th June and the attacks on the dykes. Ettie knows, she's been there. Or rather they came to her, those presences, out on the land.

"...the 15th July anniversary approaches..."

What is it Jessica fears?

"...renewal and revenge ..."

Even Jenner isn't immune to the influences of the past.

"...I can't wholly dismiss...ghosts and legends...Warren understood...what he'd seen and heard..."

Nonsense, she hears him say, mixing it up, misquoting him...*garbled and cracked*...so it may be, but talking it out doesn't work. There are presences and Ettie must face them or give up. The answer is out there and she must go. Hat, coat and away, across the common, into the country.

She feels better in the evening air. Like the morning, she can't be confined and must have space! In the middle of the common she can hear no traffic and can see nothing except grass gorse and trees. She could be in the open country of six hundred years ago. She walks faster, happy in the gathering gloom, for the twilight holds no fears. There must be a place where there is understanding, where all will be revealed. She walks further, moving now in time as well as space...into the past.

She stops and closes her eyes, listening to the silence. If those of the land are minded to reveal they are likely to do it now...the tramping of many feet, the muffled talking of many mouths. She opens her eyes expecting to see at least one lone dog walker she's misinterpreted as an advancing army from the past, but there's no one. The sound remains and gets louder. Now comes the shouting, the tearing, the cascading swoosh of water. The bursting of the dykes! She stands utterly still. All around, the calmness of the evening, the gentle, almost imperceptible moving of the leaves, the untrodden grass, the emptiness of the common, but still the roaring pandemonium of hundreds on their work of liberating destruction! She waits, one presence might transcend all the others, one voice telling what she needs to know. Nothing, only the writhing, ripping, freeing. She closes her eyes, but it continues. She opens them again, but sees nothing untoward. Then the destructive tumult abates. Tramping again, moving on, receding into an unseeable distance. No 'message,' unless it's the message of the masses. We are here...we have been released...

She walks back into the quiet, ominously advancing darkness. The enchantment gone this is suddenly an open, half wild emptiness, a place of recent murder where a lonely woman is extremely vulnerable. Yet she's still in the past and her fear is not of that other time for they have not yet spoken. But the darkness falls fast and she loses her way, walking south, further from the cottage, towards where the common meets the fields. She hears a soft rippling. The stream and there ahead the stile. She shudders, remembering her neighbour's words. A few hours ago, yet now another place, another age.

"...it's usually at the stile where the fields meet the end of the common at the stream..."

She hovers at the stile and waits fearfully near the stream. The damp air cools her arms and shoulders and she draws her coat tighter. It's an oppressive, gloomy place, but she remains a little longer, unsure and edgy, half eager to see the mysterious shade, half anxious to be away before he appears. She looks round continually, piercing the darkness, assessing the shadows and the spiky shapes of the encroaching night. She gets colder and it's not just from the chill in the air.

Is it two, three, five, ten minutes? She walks on, but stops suddenly on reaching the edge of a small copse. Warren's body was discovered near a copse but this place is too far from the road. Even so it makes her nervous.

Then she sees him. A man standing under one of the trees, no more than twenty metres away. He looks towards her and then falls down. Someone could be lurking behind the tree, but heedless of the danger, she runs towards him, reaching the spot in a few seconds, but there's no one. She walks in a wide circle kicking the ground and peering into the bushes, but even in the faint, murky dimness she knows no one is there. He could be injured and crawled away. If so he won't have gone far. She widens the circle of her search, but finds nothing. The falling man has disappeared. Now she too has seen as her neighbour said, as Maggie said. Was he real? A real man she would have found. So this must be the ghost. Nonsense, there are no such things. Yet there are those disconnected from another time. If so, why are they here and from how far have they come?

She leaves the copse and hurries west. Suddenly the common is a place enmeshed with inexplicable strands from the past, no longer a place to contemplate, to understand, to linger. She quickens, running lightly to avoid the uneven ground and the unseen clumps. She stumbles a few times, but carries on without falling. She mustn't fall. Those that fall here do not get up. They disappear! Would that be her fate too, disappearing, but to where, to what, how far into the past?

"...Tyler has been killed...our leader is dead..."

She stops and listens. She's nearer the road now and hears the dull hum of the traffic, but nothing else save a distant owl. The night is quiet.

"...this Sunday morning news came from London..."

"What Sunday, what news?" Ettie calls out.

"...this Sunday, 16th June in the year of our Lord..."

"I know, I know, don't say it," Ettie calls back, terrified she's been answered, but the voice will not be stopped.

"...in the year of our Lord...1381..."

She puts her hands over her ears, but can't stop his voice.

"...one of the king's knights has arrived with a proclamation of peace, saying all loyal subjects of the king, under pain of forfeiture of life and limb..."

"No! No! No! It cannot, it must not be!"

Another voice, another man and someone she may have heard before...then she sees him, ahead, silhouetted against the sky, barring her path, shouting aloud.

"This is false. I don't believe. There are two Englands, this is the wrong one!"

Two Englands! That phrase. Now she knows who bars her way. Then the other voice booms again from behind and the figure also holds his hands to his ears, but Ettie listens.

"Richard, by the grace of God, king of England, to all our lieges and commons of the county of Hertford, we pray, charge and command..."

"No! No!" the man at the path shouts.

"...you should not do any hurt, damage or molestation to the body of our good and beloved abbot of St.Albans or to our monastery in that place or to any of its goods and enclosure or any places belonging to the abbey..."

"It will not be! I will be an outlaw first!" the man on the path cries and strides towards Ettie.

She sees his face briefly. Is it him? She can't be sure, but will take no chances. She turns and runs.

"...then they will make you an outlaw!"

A woman's voice! Ettie runs on as the first voice booms again.

"...take this command of ours to heart for all the love and loyalty you bear towards us..."

Ettie runs faster, but he is also running and then she hears the woman's voice again.

"...they come this morning from all the towns and villages to press for liberties...from Luton, Watford, Barnet, Rickmansworth, Tring...they are demanding the charter from the abbot..."

Ettie sees the lights of cars on the road. She hurries towards them, but hears only the booming voice coming again.

"...given under our great seal in our city of London, the 15th day of June, in the 4th year of our reign..."

"...1381..." Ettie intones as the sound of the traffic hits her ears.

She glances back, but sees no one. She reaches the road and runs across, hardly looking at the traffic, then down the lane, not stopping until she reaches the drive to Chris's house. She's tempted to go and talk to him about the film. There are always two sides to an argument and she may have discounted his too quickly. It might help decide whether she should help Charley. There are no lights in the house. She could walk up and make sure, but the dark path with the overhanging trees puts her off. If Chris is there she'll not see him tonight. She walks towards the cottage. From here the solitary lamp at the bottom is intermittently hidden by another tree as the branches waft around in the breeze, shadows dancing and leaping across the road and the houses. She takes no notice until about half way down she sees two figures standing close to her own cottage. One, a little taller than the other is looking towards her. It nudges its companion, who also looks in her direction. What new confrontation is this, come to deliver a message or antagonise her? She stops. One figure lifts a hand, a challenge, a warning, should she go back or go on? Then the smaller one moves towards her. The other follows. She freezes, unable to move forward or run back. They get closer, their faces obscured in the shadow of the lamp. She feels the coldness in her back, her hands tightening in her pockets. She longs to run, but can't.

"Ettie."

They know her name! A woman's voice. They are almost upon her.

"We thought it was you," says the taller one.

"My God," she says, recognising Jenner and Jennifer, "you frightened me to death. What are you doing here?"

"We came to see Pleasant," Jenner says.

"I couldn't see a light at the house."

"That's because there's no one there," Jennifer says.

"I expect he's at..."

"He's nowhere he should be," Jenner says, "The door was open, the place is empty and most of his clothes have been taken. He's done a bunk."

6

HE hurries. Last night he slept under a hedge on the road near Barnet. Yesterday he had no breakfast and only a little water. Hungry, thirsty and very tired, he kept going until mid afternoon. The hot sun still beat him down, but in a couple of hours it started to cool. After a rest and a meal shared by travellers on the way he made better progress. He'd hoped to get to St. Albans by nightfall, but did not. Already the news was beginning to peter out. People he passed had all asked the same question.

"Is it true?"

Some had wanted to know more, but he'd said little, anxious to keep moving, but also reluctant to go over what he'd seen, reliving what he wished had not happened. It's not so easy to dismiss from his thoughts. In the tramping miles, the dusty road, the wide blue sky, the relentless heat, the interminable fields and hedges, the idle mind constantly jerked like a ball on its string, always pulled back to the cup. His return will be a mixed one. Welcomed by some for his safety, unwelcomed by all for what he must tell. The others, those that left with the charters after Mile End, will have gone back in triumph, feted and applauded, the precious papers passed around like gold, guaranteeing their freedoms, vindicating their determination, justifying their sacrifices, capping the summit of their struggles. Not so the news he will bring. In a few short, pithy, heavy phrases all their efforts could be wrenched from them, the new foundations of their emancipated lives swept away as swiftly as a deft kicking aside of a milkmaid's stool sends her bumping under the cow's feet.

Wat Tyler assassinated. Is it really true? Fast comes redemption, so fast must come retribution. Those that easily give can as rapidly take away. Even now he can hardly believe. It is as a dream. But what is the dream, their erstwhile grab for freedom or the sudden, startling snatching back? Dream, disbelief, but his eyes and ears do not deceive. Never have so many reached so high, then fallen so low in so short a time. For those remaining Smithfield seemed the pinnacle of their high hopes but unexpected and unprepared, the fall came in a few minutes. Stunned into frozen irresolution after their leader was felled their freedoms were cradled in a fragile balance and they lost the momentum of the struggle. But for their enemies it was expected and they were prepared, swiftly turning surprise and immobility to their advantage.

Self preservation overcame faltering delay and slipping apart from others in the confusion, not stopping at St. John's Field where so many were headed, he continued north, away from the city. Now he nears his home, downcast and dispirited on this bright, warm Sunday morning, 16th June 1381.

After the 'visitations' on the common Ettie needs company and welcomes the talk late into the night. Chris's apparent disappearance compounds her concerns and she wonders if he was the mysterious man who accosted her, but was it him now or him in the past?

"Have you any idea where he is?" she asks.

"We've checked all his usual haunts," Jenner says, "some of these showbiz people are like urban gypsies, never in one place more than five minutes, but then a moving target is more difficult to hit. It must be great to have the money and flexibility to flit around like a bloody bee!"

"More likely it shows his serious insecurity," Jennifer says.

"In more ways than one," Ettie says.

They listen sympathetically as falteringly and with many hesitations, she tells of the marching and tearing crowd, the men and the voices. Except for a weary 'bloody hell' from Jenner when she mentions the falling man, they don't interrupt until she finishes.

"You didn't know either of them?" Jennifer says.

"Not the falling man, but the other seemed like... but then, with Chris disappearing."

"You think it was Chris Pleasant?"

"If it was he can't be far," Jenner says.

"Not if..."Ettie begins.

"Don't say it," he says.

He'd rather not face the awful possibility of Ettie's musings and to rebalance her nerves, she prefers to talk of other things, but Jennifer won't let them. She knows a little, but is curious for more.

"You thought he was like someone you'd seen in London?"

It can't be avoided. Reliving a 14th century past in the midst of a modern crisis means stumbling over raw and charged emotions, but talking about last year's strange events is better than analysing present ones. Jenner listens impassively except to occasionally amplify details, but at the end returns to the events of the night.

"You said the woman said he'd been an outlaw?"

"He said *I will be an outlaw first*. Then she said *they will make you an outlaw*."

"What did they mean, why would he be breaking the law?"

"Presumably if he moved against the abbey. That was the centre of the Revolt."

"But that could apply to them all," Jenner muses, "and she seemed to be speaking specifically to him, about something he'd done."

"Or not done."

"Like what?"

"Not swearing his loyalty after the revolt."

Jenner is intrigued.

"Having to run away and so becoming an outlaw?"

"Something like that."

"I'll have to look into outlawry," he says desultorily and then as an afterthought, "Everyone in Smithfield was accounted for, you said yourself..."

"...not everyone was in Smithfield. Some left before the masses gathered, some before the retreat to St. John's Field, there was someone in particular. I met..."

"Who could be involved?" Jenner says, stabbing 'who?' repeatedly.

He doesn't want to speculate about the past, either the 14th century or the more recent experiences of a year ago. His priority is the present. The past is only relevant if it gives some guidance for his enquiries. Even in that context he doesn't really want to believe what she may be saying.

Ettie understands his frustration as she recalls Jessica's words... *"three key constituents – revelation, renewal and revenge..."* while the answer she must give is less satisfying.

"I can't be precise..."

"...but you said some couldn't be accounted for..."

"...no one can be discounted, we would have to consider the involvement of just about everyone."

"Everyone at Smithfield, past and present?"

"Yes."

"Even us?" he says jocularly."

"Even us," is her solemn reply.

Jennifer is mystified and they have to break off to explain the extraordinary events the year before with past and present swept together on the anniversary of the great Revolt's London climax on 15th June.

"So the reports really were the tip of the iceberg?" Jennifer says.

"A few like Warren Grover guessed much of the rest," Ettie says, looking knowingly at Jennifer, "didn't you?"

"It crossed my mind."

"But you didn't want to believe," Jenner says in sympathetic solidarity.

"Was Chris Pleasant involved in London?" Jennifer asks.

"Not at Smithfield."

"Yet you feel he could be the man on the common?"

"I can't trust him not to be involved."

"You're wise to be unsure," Jenner says thoughtfully, "It was around that time Pleasant started making his film and what was his connection to Warren Grover? Now he disappears."

He and Jennifer chew over their enquiries and ideas about Chris and Monica, how they are related to the new development and potential confrontation with Warren Grover and the opposition campaign. Ettie relaxes precariously, her mind drifts back to Smithfield. Was it Thomas she saw in the path or Chris or someone else sprung back in the recoil of time and who was the woman?

"...what do you think, Ettie?" Jenner interrupts, "What do you think of Lawrence Bullock?"

"The actor playing the abbot?"

"He's a local man with contacts like Monica Freeson. He may have known Warren Grover, just about everybody else did."

"He's very supportive of the younger actors on the film set, something of a buffer between Charley and Chris."

"Do they need keeping apart?"

"Most of the time. Why is being local so important?"

"He could also be involved in the new development. Something we need to check in the morning."

"Warren was involved in many campaigns," Ettie says sceptically.

"Maybe, but connections to the development in Hempston is the best line of enquiry we've got."

It's an unspoken criticism of less tangible leads Ettie might want to follow, but she knows him too well. He's not given up on Warren's researches, the problems with the film or her own contacts, but would rather not talk about them. He'll be feeling he's already said too much to Jennifer. It's unavoidable and she can be trusted, but he longs for the investigation to proceed on purely 'conventional' lines. For now he's had enough and suddenly says he and Jennifer have to make an early start to search for Chris. That leaves Ettie to get through the rest of the night with only dubious memories and speculations for company, making rest impossible until she finally falls asleep with the dawn.

Jenner sleeps a little better, but he's restless and gets into the station early. A good time to catch up on paperwork, but not too routine for then he gets unduly bored and the brain starts playing with ideas. He doesn't need play, but resolution with loose ends nicely fastened rather than fraying around indiscriminately. He works with alarming efficiency and it's then the disparate thoughts start flying about, but he's saved by the telephone. It's a familiar voice, but one he's not heard for months. David Farley, always known to Jenner as 'Rusk,' a journalist on the 'Daily Mercury' and a friend from their early days.

"How are you doing out in the sticks?"

"This is not the sticks," Jenner replies with mock seriousness, "It's God's own country."

"It's took me days to track you down, nobody at the Met would talk."

"Nothing unusual in that."

"What can you tell me about Warren Grover?"

Jenner laughs.

"An unimportant murder in a small town *in the sticks*, I'm surprised a national journalist of your stature would be interested. Anyway, are you the crime correspondent now?"

"I'm the correspondent for anything you do," David jokes, "but this particular crime could have other implications."

"That sound more like it."

"Any leads?"

Jenner is very circumspect.

"I'm not being coy. Box full of suspects, but nothing definite. This other implication of yours...?"

"I need some background information on Warren's death."

Jenner runs down the bare facts of the case.

"You're not comfortable," David says, "unseen depths, just like I feel."

"Stop fishing and tell me why you're so interested in Warren Grover."

"Not so much interested in him as what he was into."

"Like what?"

"Like the campaign against the Hempston development."

"Are we talking about the same development that's caused so much fuss round here?"

"We are. My local contact was involved in the campaign opposing the development. That's why I wondered if you'd found the connection."

"What connection?"

"I don't know. He didn't explain. He had to go and I never spoke to him again."

"And this contact of yours was…"

"…Warren Grover."

"So you believe Warren Grover discovered something about the development?"

"Which may be…"

"…connected to his murder."

"Obviously you've thought of it. So I was wondering…"

"Nothing to tell you yet."

"The local campaign may have national repercussions. You know they've announced a planning enquiry."

"But it's already gone ahead. The buggers knocked down a medieval house!"

"Yes I heard about that."

"Not been much publicity."

"Give it time, all grist to the mill. Anyway, the development has only just begun. It's the next phases that will be the subject of the enquiry."

"Who's doing it?"

"A retired judge called David Burton."

"Never heard of him."

"You know what enquiries are like. It may or may not uncover everything. So, if you could keep me informed and in return…"

"You have information relevant to my investigation?"

"Not yet, but if we could exchange what we have."

"Have you any other local contacts?"

"Somebody local has been keeping me up to date, but he's not given me anything I can use."

"Who's that?"

"Ted Skinner."

"I see."

"You know him?"

"We've met. I'm surprised you're not using the editor of the local paper, George Carter."

David is silent.

"You do know him?" Jenner says,

"He doesn't return my calls. He was my original contact. It was him that put Warren Grover onto me."

"So he was supporting Warren's campaign?" Jenner says, remembering Monica's assertions.

"Very much so – at least in private."

"He's not said anything to us."

"He wouldn't."

"This is a murder investigation," Jenner says gruffly, "Has he got anything useful?"

"I don't know, like I said he won't talk to me. He said he had information about alleged financial irregularities, but it was nowhere near strong enough to print. Just tipping me off in case it got bigger. Said he had a contact who knew more. Next thing Warren rang me, the rest you know."

"And now Carter won't talk to you?"

"No. Perhap's he's been frightened off."

"Or he's the one doing the frightening."

Ettie wakes around ten and immediately panics. It's far too late to be up and there are things to be done. Then she remembers it was nearly six before she got to sleep. Unlike her neighbour she doesn't organise her life around a timetable of domestic chores, so there's nothing to get up for, but she's not normally a late riser even when she's not working. Lying in bed when the sun burnishes the wall makes her uncomfortable. She peers out the window. There must have been a heavy dew for light ground mist is rising from the grass on the common. She gets up, but can't focus on any activity, constantly flitting between minor tasks. She could go in the garden, but it's shaded and she doesn't relish an embarrassing dissection of last night's experiences with her neighbour about the ghost.

It's ground she's been over far too much already and even suitably edited, would still be distressing.

She goes out, intending to go into town, but at the pub changes her mind, crosses the main road, strides towards the cricket ground and turns back up the common, keeping close to the road. She walks very fast and deliberate as if late for a specific destination, yet she has all the time she needs. She stops at the south end of the cricket ground and sits on a bench, facing the town. *I really need your help to bring it alive.* Charley wants her at the studio. She shouldn't go. It's not right to encourage her, but if Ettie's not there she won't know what they're doing and with the cat-director conspicuously absent...who knows what the irresponsible mice might try to play. She's reluctant, but staying away will give her no peace. She returns to the cottage and drives to the studio.

It will be a strange meeting. *Everybody feels drawn, it's something we have to do.* Charley is either incredibly gifted or perilously misguided. Yet she's not alone. Ettie is also drawn. She could have taken the road towards the motorway, coming off further south and avoiding St. Albans, but instead drives straight into the town and parks near the Abbey. It's a bright, warm day. There are plenty of people about. She avoids the gateway, scene of so much activity and attack in 1381, and goes into the great church, something she's not done before. *It was founded by King Offa in 793.* Kathleen Grover's words as reported by Jennifer. Will none of them leave her alone?

She walks along the railings beside the outer south side of the nave, containing the remains of the original 14th century cloister, long since demolished. She hovers as if unseen hands hold her back, stopping her leaving. She looks away from the church and images of the old building stab intermittently. The power of the past is strong here, but it is no monk's voice she hears.

"...this is their place, not ours..."

The same woman she heard on the common, but harder, angrier than before.

"...but our time has come and we will have justice..."

Men are hammering and pulling at the floor of the cloister near the entrance to the parlour while powerless monks look on. They are not ordinary floor stones, but millstones, now prised up and carried away amidst much shouting and celebration. As the men leave with their prizes she hears them being smashed followed by jubilant cheering from a large crowd. Feeling the anger and determination of those that watch while the monks run away, she has no wish to be caught between them. Walking quickly away out of that time she reaches the abbey's west front. For a few moments she stares up at the massive Victorian restoration and the carved portrait of St. Matthew above the doors, all very 1870s. Her sense of the past dissolves, replaced by an unsettling numbness. She slips into the Abbey entrance and stands awestruck by the nave's sudden vastness, staring at the distant altar, trying to take in everything simultaneously, looking up to the roof and then down and along the rows of Norman arches. The immanence of the past is immediate like a sudden rush of air from an enclosed room. Those in 1381 are close again. The immensity of size and age overwhelms and as she walks slowly down the centre of the nave the centuries sweep and roll away. The serried ranks of chairs are gone and she hears a monotonous chanting close to the altar, then sees the monks standing with their backs to her. She stops, conscious of the sound of her feet on the flagstones, afraid they'll hear her. No one stirs. No one turns. She freezes, unable to move forward or back and afraid she'll be soon discovered. Then the image fades and the chairs and the people wandering around the church reappear. Yet the chanting incongruously continues for some moments longer, before that too is gone.

She's exposed in the middle of the church and turns to leave, but remembering where the monastery cloister invaded the south wall, knows she'll not escape the incursions of the past outside. Perhaps there's safety in narrower spaces? She turns into the north aisle. In the piers of the north side are the remains of medieval wall paintings, some from the 14th century. Covered in whitewash until their discovery a hundred and fifty years ago, most of the surface colour has gone, but their Biblical scenes are still recognisable. Ettie is fascinated and walks steadily from one to the other. The past she felt outside returns, though now without the sense of being pulled in opposite directions. Here, with the Crucifixion, the life of the Virgin and portraits of the saints, there is only the pull of the people.

She walks further down the aisle and reaching the central crossing stares up into the tower. The arches here are the oldest part of the building, yet the force of the past, though powerful is not as strong as beside the aisle paintings. Here the monks were stronger. The people's pull is weaker. She turns away and walks up the north transept. Now it grows stronger again. She hears many feet, not like the tramping on the common, but the slow shuffling of a long line. She stops by the wall, conscious of being close to an open door, though there isn't one. Then she sees them. A long, undulating string of pilgrims, making its way to the shrine behind the high altar containing the relics of St. Alban. She walks at their sides past the queue of men, women and children in solemn procession. At the chapel pilgrims are kneeling in prayer, others lighting candles. They take no notice of her. To them she is not here. Then they are gone, as quickly as they appeared and she stands beside the modern reconstructed chapel with people of her own time. She turns aside, distressed and confused, unable to look into the eyes of others or risk them looking into hers and walks quickly along the south aisle.

"...*get away while you can, this is no place for free people...*"

The woman's voice again. Now she chases Ettie, propelling her to the west doors. Ettie hurries. It's this place. It was a mistake coming here. If she gets away from the Abbey she'll lose the woman. She'll get back to the car and go on to the studio without further delay. Outside she feels better. The inrush of oxygen as she walks towards the town gives a welcome uplift. Nearer the centre she slows and turns from where her car is parked. She's drawn, this time to the curfew tower, the most conspicuous landmark in town. She stops and looks up. It's open for visitors. She could go in, climb to the top, it's said the view is stupendous. She crosses the street and is about to go in and then...

"...we are not easily frightened, nor will we be cowed by the king's command and charter offered to those who will give up rebellion..."

The voice she heard on the common, the man who blocked her way. The same confident voice spoke to her in the London tavern on the evening before Smithfield. One who knows, one who will act, but for all its incensed aggression the voice is now less sure, less certain what to do. This is the man who's returned from London, getting away after Smithfield, suspecting the awful truth, now hearing it in his own town and refusing to believe it. Wat Tyler is dead. Without the Revolt's great leader it must mean their own rising in St. Albans is fatally compromised, but he can't accept it. Now she hears the crowd, voices too loud, too strident, too desperate to be locals disgorging from the pub. Voices of the past.

She turns from the tower and faces the street, but there are no shops, at least not normal ones with large glass frontages. She looks back to the tower. It's gone! The tower was built around 1410. If it's not there, this must be...1381. Hundreds are gathered. Ettie joins the edge of the crowd. No one notices. Do they see her? They are restless, a muffled grumbling drone diffusing through the host. Then a man in a plain buff shirt gets up and with a raised hand quickly quietens them. Slightly taller than average for these days, brown, longish hair, slightly lifting in the slight breeze, with bright, blue eyes that scan the gathering with a slow, deliberative sweep, but it's his voice, resonant, demanding. Like all the others, it grabs her attention.

"You all know me, Will Grindcobb. They know me in the monastery too and I know them. For I was educated there and understand their ways."

"Tell us, Will," someone cries, "Tell us what we must do."

"See through what we began. We asked for a charter and we will obtain that charter."

"To the abbey!" someone else cries, which is followed by other disparate cries throughout the crowd, though most remain silent.

"We will, we will," Grindcobb cries, then more quietly, just audibly, immediately stilling all chatter as all strain to hear him, "We will go to the abbot in a spirit of goodwill, without commotion, in peace and tranquillity and obtain the charter, which was agreed yesterday."

"What about the old charter," a man says, "the one granted our forefathers by King Offa."

"That too and if it cannot be found (a low groan from the crowd) then the abbot and twelve senior monks will swear upon the eucharist they neither possessed nor knowingly retained amongst them such a charter."

"And what of us?" another cries, "the people of Barnet?"

"And Watford," from yet another.

"And Rickmansworth."

Then more towns and villages are shouted out. Grindcobb raises his hand again and they are quiet.

"Charters for us all, every place where the monastery has jurisdiction. Charters guaranteeing free hunting and fishing and the use of our own mills to grind our corn."

There are a few shouts of 'to the abbey' and 'don't give in,' but most are orderly and relatively quiet. Grindcobb gets down and leads them in disciplined files towards the abbey. Ettie is tempted to follow, but the receding mass shimmers and fades and in a few seconds is gone. The glass fronted shops return, there's the constant rumble of distant traffic and people walk towards her in very modern dress. She looks away though knows even before she has fully turned what she'll see. The tower is back. She goes over and leans against its wall, partly to support and quell her slight shaking, partly to satisfy herself with tactile reassurance it really is there. So much so quickly changing, how can she be sure? Maybe when she turns again she'll be thrown forward another eighty years into the great battle fought through the town in the Wars of the Roses? She tickles the wall, its undulating coldness calming and comforting. She looks back to the street. She's still in the present.

A couple passes. They look at her doubtfully. She steps away from the wall and smiles in embarrassment. She watches them walk on. They turn and look back. She smiles again, wondering if she should have spoken, said something to explain her peculiar behaviour. It would only have made it worse. They turn the corner. She turns back to the tower. Despite being old it's an anchor to the present because it's still not as old as that other age. Perhaps she'll find solace away from the time tossed powers on the ground. She goes inside. It's a long, breathless climb, but the view from the top is magnificent, the whole town, the abbey, the gateway and the Roman remains. She recalls the past again, but now in the 15th century. Picking out the buildings below she imagines the terrible battle fought along the main street. Then she looks further, way way beyond through the rolling country to the north and to the second battle, slugged out at Bernard's Heath near the roads to Hempston and Welstead. But this is only imagining. She sees nothing. Ettie admires the view for a few minutes and then turns to go back down.

"...look to the monastery, we had them there..."

The same soft, quiet female voice, bewitchingly close. Ettie turns, expecting to see its owner standing next to her.

"...in the abbot's chamber our men asked for the charter. They knew what they wanted and dictated their wishes to the abbot's clerk...the abbot agreed to our demands, handed over a written pledge and applied his seal..."

The other visitors are already descending. Ettie is alone at the top of the tower. No one is with her.

"...the charter was taken to the Cross where every one could see it and hear what it said..."

It's an asperous tone. Ettie is afraid and edges to the stairway, glancing around continually. There's no one, but the voice follows, chases her!

"...then came the men from Barnet and Watford and Rickmansworth and they got their charters..."

She reaches the stairs and starts to descend.

"...the Barnet men searched for the book of court rolls for the houses held in Barnet that were unfree..."

The voice, intense and hard, reverberates in the tower as Ettie goes down, trying to escape, but fearful of falling.

"...the abbot agreed to supply the book, but we needed surety...then more charters for more towns and more villages so the work went on into Monday..."

She slides down the stairs faster. She has to get away from the voice. She skips and almost falls headlong before grabbing the wall.

"...*then they broke their promises, but we will seek them out, avenge our people...*"

She leaps the last few steps, reaches the entrance and runs up the street. She doesn't look back, not slowing until she reaches the corner and turns towards where the car is parked. Now walking with a clear direction, she's impatient with others, dawdling, swaying across the pavement, gawping in shop windows. Get out the way!

"...*all towns belonging to the monastery got more charters on Tuesday and everybody determined to do no work or pay the dues...but our time was running away...*"

Get away! She's here, they are here! Got to get away, got to shake off this place.

"...*they come from all towns and villages...*"

No, no, not again, she's already said that! Now another voice, the booming, declamatory one she heard on the common.

"...*you should not do any hurt or damage or molestation...*"

"...*we will not work...*" the woman, angrier, fiercer replies.

"...*I charge and command...*" the booming voice recites.

"...*but we will...*" the woman begins again.

"You have your damned charter!" Ettie calls out.

Some people turn, puzzled, alarmed. Is this another mad woman in their town? Ettie bows her head and hurries on. Why is this woman telling her these things? 16th, 17th, 18th June 1381...as the men pounded at her on the common. She knows! She doesn't need telling. Why hammer over and over the same events? Why keep reminding her? Because *they* need to be reminded. Across the ages, across the centuries. But what has Ettie to do with *them?* Then she realises and runs even faster.

"It's nothing to do with me," she calls out, "I'm not one of *them!*"

If Ellie gets away, she'll go away, won't she? It's the place, this town, the abbey, the gatehouse, the tower and all these...streets...if she can get away from them she'll get away from *her*...from the past. Inside the car, she can be away in seconds. But Ettie knows she can't be away, for her and the past, are not in one place. They are in her mind and how do you run away from that?

Jenner studies Jennifer's enquiries into the Waintree project including the plans for the next two phases. He has to suppress a simmering anger. Everything to do with the Hempston development winds him up and he needs to keep a clear head. Mildly irritated when he saw Monica Freeson, his disquiet has been growing ever since. What he saw in the village makes him sympathetic to Warren's opposition and he understands why the plans have provoked so much hostility. It's not so much the individual houses, but the taking away of the past, which should always be part of the present. Precious things shouldn't be meddled with and their true value is often only appreciated after they have gone. With a gnawing sense of deprivation he feels dispossessed of his birthright and powerless to retain what has been handed down. It's not what he can say, but what he feels and this inability makes him very aware of the frustrations of others.

Passing the Waintree hoarding doesn't make him think of the future. He has no sense of newness, of *regeneration*, that word so beloved of the destroyers. He thinks only of the past, *his* past and it saddens him. The haunts of youth, repositories of personal foundations, unspeaking witnesses to the turning of the boy into the man are special. Damaging them is like wounding a person. It hurts. Taking from such places is like stealing from his life.

"Have you read my report?"

Jennifer is at the door.

"Interesting stuff," he says, "there's no doubt?"

She shakes her head.

"Monica Freeson owns land close to the Waintree development."

"Only close?"

"She holds other land which, if the later phases go ahead, could be of value."

"And of course, when these things were discussed by the Planning Committee she declared an interest and absented herself from the discussion and the decision."

"At the time her interest was technically only peripheral."

"Oldest trick in the book. She primes everybody else on the committee. Probably with promises of support for their own pet projects, meanwhile complying with the local authority's standing orders."

"I've checked the minutes thoroughly. There's nothing we can go for."

"We don't need to. We're not conducting a corruption enquiry. It's enough to establish her interest in a development Warren Grover so fiercely opposed."

"But just because..."

"I know...it doesn't mean she murdered him. For that we need a more substantial connection or forensic evidence."

He sighs resignedly.

"There's more," she says.

"I knew it. Somebody's spoken out of turn at the council. Some honest man or woman..."

"No sir, it's nothing to do with the council or Monica Freeson. I've discovered someone else who's recently bought land, which could be affected if the later development goes ahead."

"Anyone we know?"

"Lawrence Bullock, the actor."

"And a close associate of Christopher Pleasant, the film director. How long has he been involved?"

"He first bought land three years ago, more last year, with a further purchase just two months ago."

"Developing quite an empire, is he?"

"Individually, they're quite small plots."

"They could be totally unrelated to the Waintree development."

"The same could apply to Monica Freeson."

"Indeed it could, sergeant, indeed it could and we might reach Mars next week, indeed anything is possible."

At no time does she ever feel alone. Any moment she expects to hear the booming voice of medieval authority or the hardened vengeance of the man on the common or the reiterating menace of the mysterious woman, but for an hour she's heard nothing. That could be because she's away from St. Albans, epicentre of 1381, though she's now sure there's no physical escape, only a psychological one. If there's one at all. Yet nearing the studio her trepidation increases as she remembers why she's here.

"I...need your help to bring it alive...everybody feels drawn, it's something we have to do..."

Ettie shudders. A film made by actors without a film director, drawn by a screenwriter who talks about the past as if she is really there. This *drawing* is dangerous. Are they drawn to or drawn *from* the past? Does the town bewitch Ettie or does she bewitch the town? Will her presence make matters worse at the studio? Does she draw the past or is it someone else, one of these *drawn* actors or Charley, the above herself screenwriter? If she's not here how will she know what transpires, how can she forestall any complications, block any interference? But if it is *her*, not Charley, then she should go now! She sits in the car, wrestling with her fears and premonitions, unable to move until eventually willing herself to go in.

In the studio all is consternation, overwhelming chaos, however benign or well intentioned. The cast is gathered in several groups, some cavorting outlandishly to no apparent purpose and certainly to no directions. Others mumble together as if reciting prepared lines, though no one holds any script. A third more animated group moves around indiscriminately, getting in the way of the others. A few individuals stand apart, unsure or unconcerned. Among these are Lawrence Bullock and Wesley Greville, who has replaced Thurley as Grindcobb. Inwardly in turmoil but outwardly calm, Ettie slips between them. There's no particular set. Scenery and materials are scattered and disorderly mixed. It's more like a storeroom than an active studio. Whatever is being 'performed' it conforms to no structured plan or design. Whatever his shortcomings, Chris Pleasant's absence is very evident. Charley runs from behind a screen, knocking over several chairs before almost bumping into Ettie.

"You got here! I'm so relieved. I was afraid you wouldn't come."

"I thought it best," Ettie says, making it sound like a chore rather than a pleasure.

"I need to know whether you're happy with the scenes."

"Whether I'm happy, what about Chris?"

"Come! I'll show you,"

Charley leads Ettie to a new group of actors. Ignoring any reference to the absent director, the players have donned their 14th century costume and in their anarchic behaviour insist Ettie does the same. They constantly circulate, forming small groups for a time, which then break up, to be replaced by new ones, composed of different actors, only to split again until the roaming individuals coalesce into fresh clusters. The liquid studio seems in perpetual motion, unfettered, wayless as some primordial glue.

"But how are you putting it together without...?" Ettie begins, unsure exactly what she means to say, even less sure what answer she expects.

"The events guide us," Charley says.

She takes a book from her pocket and waves it as a kind of dramatic talisman. Ettie recognises *A Little Liberty*. Is it Warren or someone closer to the reality of those times transmitting through the ages? Charley herself perhaps?

"Everybody ready?" she says, as if taking on Chris's mantle, but the small group needs no direction. They automatically form into two short lines. When Welsey Greville and Lawrence Bullock come over, respectively joining the two lines, they fan out into two clumps of about a dozen each. No one speaks as they move effortlessly, guided or directed by unseen, unheard conductors. Ettie watches with mixed wonder and alarm. Charley stands slightly apart, her hands rigidly at her sides, intent on the action, but relaxed like a circus ring master, confidently observing the entry of the clowns. As Wesley Greville's company talk among themselves, there's a sudden silence around the rest of the studio with not even a murmur from any of the other groups. Even though she can't hear them, Ettie knows they speak with the authority of the real past. Then they are quiet as Wesley steps forward and faces Lawrence, deliberately accenting each word with commanding severity.

"I asked a question."

"If I find the charter before the feast of the annunciation, I will restore it to you," Lawrence says.

"Lady Day, next spring is a long time to wait."

"But I must search."

"We will have a pledge, say a thousand pounds, confirmed with your seal," Greville says with controlled annoyance.

"But if no charter is found..."

"You and twelve senior monks will swear upon the eucharist that you never possessed such a charter and never knowingly held it from us. The pledge would then be redeemed."

Ettie shudders. This is what the woman said to her in the abbey, on the tower and around the town. She rather than Charley could have written the conversation. Wesley and Lawrence glare at each other, their words emitting such force, they could be their own rather than those of the characters they depict. Competent acting maybe, but this interchange is unrehearsed and undirected. Wesley's grim determination faces Lawrence's intimidating confidence. Do they truly represent the men they play, Will Grindcobb and Abbot de la Mare? Or are they more, real faces of real men? She watches Wesley with mounting fascination. She'd seen Grindcobb near the tower addressing the crowd. Had she been close enough to be sure? The face, strong, open, the features deep, the resolute mouth, the kindly and piercing eyes, all seem familiar, but she'd seen and heard so much. When does the mind go beyond what the eyes see and the ears hear to load the baggage of imagination? Now they part and confer with their associates. Lawrence with actors playing other monks, Wesley with those playing Cadindon and other leaders. Their conversations are muted, but Ettie hears stray phrases.

"Look for the court rolls," someone says to Wesley, "we must destroy those that confirm where our people are unfree."

"...searched for the book of court rolls for the houses... that were unfree..."

The woman's words again!

"We must play for time," Lawrence says to one of the monks, "tell them anything for now until we can get back our authority."

"...they broke their promises..."

"Stop now!"

Charley waves her arms at each group, moving with apparent bravado, but it's really as shallow as her confidence, words and gyrations hiding a deeper fear and anxiety. Ettie senses it immediately, but is Charley fearful of the unknown or anxiously expectant?

Jenner waits in Monica Freesons' lounge with mounting irritation. His distaste for the Waintree development gets stronger and Jennifer's discoveries and Rusk's speculations accentuate his dislike for the woman. He must remain professional, not allow his private views to influence his enquiries. So far Monica has done nothing wrong. In any case he's not investigating financial irregularities, but murder. His only interest is in discovering if differences between her and Warren Grover were strong enough to motivate her towards...

"Sorry to keep you waiting, chief inspector."

She sweeps into the room, her long sprawling dress billowing like a Spanish galleon in full sail, equally as splendid, probably twice as dangerous. He's unimpressed by this display of apparent busyness. Seeing him is more important than any of her other activities even if he has arrived unannounced. She offers him a drink, which he refuses, then tea, which he also refuses. She burbles for a few moments about the weather, the garden, the congestion. Does she seriously think she can deflect him from the real reason for his visit? His irritation is about to erupt, he controls himself, then opens up.

"I imagine with your interest in community and cultural affairs, you were very distressed to learn of the demolition of the medieval house in the village?"

She hesitates, unsure how to respond. It's a question with no comfortable answer.

"Yes," she says, "Most regrettable."

"Especially when it was carried out by an organisation with which you have a connection. I may have missed your public condemnation of their action."

She eyes him carefully. This isn't going to be an easy or congenial conversation. Best to play the innocent at first.

"I'm not quite sure what..."

"You are directly involved in the Waintree development," he says with combative crabbiness.

"Not directly," she says with her best plastic smile, "I have no interest in the development."

"You've sold land to the developers. You also have land, which could be subject to later stages of the proposals."

"*Ideas* at this stage, not yet put forward as firm proposals and as I'm no longer the owner of other land which is the subject of proper planning applications, how can I now have an interest?"

"You benefited financially from your sale."

"*Benefited* is debatable, but even if I did, I was not party to any decisions in the council."

"I understand Warren Grover was aware of all your various interests."

"I wouldn't know, what are you implying?"

"It would establish a source of conflict between the two of you. With his involvement in the campaign..."

"As I believe I made clear at our last discussion, frequent difficult decisions have to be made. They are sometimes bound to cause animosity."

"Aren't you supposed to represent the community, which should mean a *coincidence* rather than a conflict of interest?"

She looks at him aggressively. He immediately regrets the question. It's not relevant and shows his bias. She turns away for a moment and then continues.

"I was going to say that just because people oppose council decisions it doesn't mean they have to be silenced by..."

"You've just told me you weren't a party to the decision on the development."

"No, of course not, but people like Warren..."

"...wouldn't be concerned with the technicalities of council meetings. He'd be more interested..."

"...in needlessly stirring up trouble..."

"...in the real relationships behind official decisions..." he pauses, she glares, "...at least as he saw it."

"I know who's behind this," she thunders, "It's got nothing to do with Warren Grover. It's that damned newspaper editor, George Carter, he's put you up to this."

"Nobody puts me up to anything, madam."

"I warn you, chief inspector, I shan't tolerate this kind of behaviour. If you have an accusation, make it! If you are alleging some kind of financial impropriety on my part you'd better have the evidence. If not, I'm surprised you're allowing yourself to be used by that wretched hack to peddle newsroom tittle tattle and innuendo!"

"I don't peddle and I never mentioned financial impropriety. However, if you..."

"There's a lot about George Carter you don't know! He's not as independent in these matters as he appears. I...I..."

Shaking with rage, she suddenly stops, but Jenner's real interest has been aroused.

"What matters?" he says quietly.

She says nothing, gradually subsiding and then turns to him accusingly.

"Other people have been involved in recent purchases of land."

"Like whom?"

"Like Lawrence Bullock."

"Yes, I'm aware of that."

"But you're probably not aware of his connection to George Carter."

"Connection, what connection?"

"George Carter and Lawrence Bullock and Warren Grover, peas in the same pod. They knew each other very well."

"How well?"

"They were all at school together."

"Now began the transition from redemption to repression. Their brief freedom, so costly bought would be lost and

oppression restored. Events in London, over which the men of Hertfordshire had little influence and no control, now sealed their fate. Some may have witnessed Wat Tyler's murder by the king's henchmen, even bringing the dreadful news themselves to St. Albans..."

Ettie shudders as Charley reads from *A Little Liberty*, almost every line triggering visions – or are they memories – of the past, sent by others...*even bringing the dreadful news themselves*...If only Charley knew how close Ettie has been to such a messenger...but maybe she does know? Is Charley looking at the book or merely pretending to read? Does she speak Warren's words or her own, resurrecting the direct experience of one who's been there?

"...first on 18th June came the king's commission to the mayors, sheriffs and bailiffs, opposing the disturbances with its fateful words..."

"...we enjoin and command you to proclaim and if necessary take such measures with force to ensure resistance to any who rebel against our peace under pain of losing life and limb or all other things which they can forfeit to us..."

Charley stares at Ettie, open mouthed.

"The exact words."

"I...I...er. I must have remembered them," Ettie says.

Charley keeps staring for a few moments, then continues reading.

"Then came the appointment on 22nd June of Sir Robert Tresilian as chief justice of the king's bench..."

Ettie listens, but the words slink over her. She need not think, their meaning is already with her just as her interruption came not from her memory.

"The following day he received his commission to take action against the Hertfordshire rebels."

"...Accursed name, accursed man..."

Ettie turns in the direction of the woman's voice. Surely Charley heard her? But Charley doesn't stir from the book. What Ettie hears is in her head. She's in her head!

"On 2nd July all the hard won liberties were revoked," Charley reads, "The king's letter began...*recently, during the execrable disturbances...we freed and released every one from all bondage and service. Also, we pardoned those same subjects of ours for their rebellion..."*

"...but the said letters were issued irregularly so we have revoked, abolished, invalidated and annulled whatever followed from them..."

Ettie breaks off and smiles nervously at Charley as if inadvertently pre-empting some well known text. But only Ettie knows and only in those few seconds, though she has no idea from where the words came to her mind. Charley looks oddly at her again and then continues.

"I further strictly command..."

But Ettie breaks in again.

"...that every free person and bondsman carry out their tasks, customs and services, which they are bound to do and were accustomed to do before the said trouble..."

"Ettie, what are you doing!"

Charley runs her finger along the relevant lines of Warren's book, checking Ettie's words.

"You are quoting directly from the king's letter of (she looks down and quotes) *on the 2nd July in...*"

"...the fifth year of our reign," Ettie intones.

"But how did...?"

"It has to be 1381, so it must be the fifth year of his reign."

"Even so..."

"I'm sorry. I shouldn't have interrupted. Do you intend to write scenes around these events?"

"I...well...I'm not...no, not these exactly. I was going to move on to the 29th June and the arrival of Walter at Lee."

"Damn him! Damn him!"

The woman's voice again. Inside her head!

"Lee arrived with fifty lances and a large number of archers," Charley reads.

"Is it usual," Ettie interrupts, "to work through scenes without a script with the actors."

"I've explained about..." Charley begins.

"Yes I know, but is it *usual*...?"

"No, it's not usual as such," Charley says, slightly irritated, "but not unknown. There are some directors who kick around ideas with actors before a script is prepared."

"But you're not a director."

"It's the same thing!"

"It's not really *kicking around* though, is it, more like to obey what's bidden?"

"Much like your interruptions?"

Ettie immediately regrets her comment. It's not always wise to say what is felt. It doesn't necessarily come out the way intended. They stare at each other for some moments. Ettie will have to deflect Charley's defiance.

"Who was Walter at Lee?" she says.

"The king was in Essex and determined to exact punishment," Charley reads again, "He was a local knight and sheriff, concerned for local stability. He persuaded the king to appoint him to arrange a peace between the people and the abbot. Many were afraid when they heard he was coming, but Grindcobb..."

Ettie looks across. Wesley Greville stands some way off, but turns as she looks, as if he knows, as if he hears the unspoken voice in her head. Immediately the image of the man in the plain buff shirt comes to mind and as Charley speaks she hears that other voice she heard addressing the crowd near the tower.

"...*Be sensible. We have the help of the surrounding towns and villages. Our allies will come to our aid if we need them. Take courage. Tomorrow morning we meet the knight outside the town and ask him if he comes in peace...*"

"He was met by the peasants and townspeople and led into the town with the usual honour," Charley reads, "He summoned everyone from the nearby towns to appear before him at three o'clock in a field near the Derfold Forest. There he made his proclamation. 'Lords and friends, you are aware how gravely disturbers of the peace...'"

"...*carry out therefore what is right and hand over those responsible for stirring up the troubles...*"

A new voice, shriller, less rustic, speaking without passion in a cold, emphatic deliberation as if like Charley he is reading. Does Walter at Lee speak to Ettie?

"...*villainous deceiver!*"

The woman's voice interjects and then Ettie hears Charley again.

"Many applauded him, saying they would willingly obey his counsel. He summoned a jury of twelve peasants, charging them to return the following day and declare those who were guilty. On Sunday 30th June..."

"...the men came to his chamber and defied him. No one was indicted, for they accused nobody, saying all were good men, loyal to the king..."

The woman again, but now quiet, strong and resolute. Charley has her head in the book and continues.

"He said nothing immediately, but after hearing Mass instructed the jurors to return the charters obtained from the monastery. They promised to return them that afternoon, but..."

"...we would not have it!"

A man's voice now, not Lee, but that same man on the common, yet so familiar, she'd heard him even before that...

"...the charters would not be returned.. In any case those jurors did not know who had them. Lee was angry and now showed his true intentions. He wasn't interested in truth or justice. He held them in the abbot's chamber, refusing to let them leave until the charters were returned. Eventually they were freed and Lee ordered us to meet him at Barnet Wood, but still we defied him. We brought 300 archers from the villages and we were ready to rise up against him. He was afraid and backed away from confrontation. Even those he brought with him might have joined us..."

Charley reads on, but in Ettie's mind the man, the woman, even distant rumblings of others, supersede, constantly interjecting and opening up the energised past. The events of 1381 are no longer raw material for the film. The film has deteriorated to irrelevance. The more Charley quotes and speculates from *A Little Liberty* the more the past takes over. No longer just voices, but fleeting images, people surging and demanding, in the town, in the fields, disturbed, brilliant, passionate. Some shout, some demand, some whisper. Sometimes she understands, often she doesn't, but through the ranging prospect of June 1381 she hears again and again the same man and the same woman, urging, crying, pleading and calling insisting to... someone unknown...could that someone be her?

"...we will be avenged...only then will we be free..."

Then, briefly she returns to the present. Charley reads on, the actors form into groups, they improvise, yet with the confidence of those who know, who are guided. Whenever she sees Lawrence Bullock and Wesley Greville, even if they are not speaking, she sees the abbot and Grindcobb and is suddenly thrust back into that earlier time. The film may be irrelevant, but what of the film*makers*? No longer engaged on making a film, what if they are *making* the past or does the past *make* them? Is the past being invoked, re-enacted more literally than a film scene, or does the past itself interfere, but which past, whose past? Real people of the past influencing 'characters' in the present? Different forces exerting different pressures, best ignore them all and...

...the great meeting in Barnet, hundreds are there, now they are gone...now they assemble again later in the town. More talking, more rumours Where is Lee, what will be his next move? Ettie knows. Nothing can be resolved unless the past is resolved, until violent passions are placated. People are asking. A woman is close to her, talking to her, the same voice, the same woman. She is asking her! What should she say?

"Get out, get away! You do not belong here!"

Visions and voices are gone. She is back in the studio, surrounded by modern actors, but they are shouting at each other! Lucy Seddon, playing Eleanor Draycourt, wife of a prominent local landowner has been encircled by several women 'peasants' and is elbowed aside every time she tries to speak. Charley tries to intervene, but she's shoved away as well.

"But I have to protest," Lucy says, "this is the dispute about the debt owed to my husband."

"Get out, get out!" the women cry, "there's more important business."

Everyone shouts with so much vigour and passion, it's difficult to tell whether the conflict is a performance, a 'real' dispute or an event in which the distinction between 'acting' and 'reality' has ceased to have any meaning. Do they argue in their parts, or about their parts or are there no parts at all? Charley's interventions are ineffectual Even as quasi director and interpreter of the past, wielding her 'little book' like some latter-day cultural revolutionary, she's ignored before being pushed down to the floor. At first this slightly amuses Ettie until she realises the sinister implications and wonders again about the role of the film and the cast. The strongly reiterated demands for revenge may be crucial, but are also unnerving. Does the filmmaking unleash them with unknowable consequences? If the film was itself the catalyst, then stopping it should have suppressed them, but it hasn't. Must they now stop anything connected to past events if the past's takeover is to be averted or is it already too late? Maybe it's not the film or the cast at all. Is she the problem?

"Get out, get out!"

The same phrase, but different voices, different accents, different anger, more desperate, more urgent, more pleading. The past again intrudes, but now sweeping away the studio, the actors, the sets and her world absolutely. The woman is by her side, pulling her along the street.

"They are taken," she says, "Grindcobb, Cadindon, Barbintsor and the others."

"Taken?" Ettie mutters as she looks, bewilderingly around her.

"Arrested, all those that took the millstones from the abbey parlour. That traitor knight, Lee secretly called the bailiffs and constables after our people had dispersed. Our men have been captured and carried off to Hertford. We must free them!"

This is no time arrested island, alternately swinging between past and present. This is the past. The turbulent past of 1381 and Ettie is in the midst of a furious crowd, with no immediate prospect of return.

7

DAVID Farley arrives early for the planning enquiry. He's wise to do so. The room set aside in a local authority building near the centre of town is not very large and is quickly filling. He passes one of those blue plaques on his way in – the sort that begin 'on this site' – but hasn't time to read the rest. He settles into one of only two remaining seats reserved for the press, the others occupied by local journalists. They exchange pleasantries. At the scheduled time the chairman, David Burton, commences the session. He's a burly, tight lipped lawyer and quickly gets through the preliminaries, explaining the terms of reference and how the enquiry will be conducted. He's so punctual some late arrivals are still shuffling in. Burton eyes them aggressively over the rim of his glasses. The few remaining seats are quickly taken and others crowd around at the back.

"That's enough," Burton bellows to the usher, "It's cramped already," then turning to the group hemmed in at the rear wall, "Any noise and you'll have to leave."

As the usher is closing the door a man pushes it aside shouting, "Press" and comes down to the front, mouthing "sorry" to the irritated chairman. He sits beside David. They glance at each other and are about to speak, but the chairman calls the meeting to order and summons the first witness. He represents the developers, a young, smartly dressed company man, full of unctious phrases and benign platitudes, his sentences laced at the ends with a wide, meaningless grin. Burton takes a few minutes of this and then reminds him to 'make only pertinent remarks' and to 'just recount the facts.' So he does, curbing his grins and setting out a brief outline of the various phases of the project. There are a few questions, but the opponents of the development know this is not the main event. There are more interesting performers to come. So far there's been nothing contentious or particularly interesting. David doodles absently. Maybe he should have left it to the second day before coming.

He looks over to his companion. He's not been taking many notes and seems even less interested in the proceedings than David, most of the time looking into the audience rather than the witnesses or representatives. Two women, sitting quite close to each other, but not together, seem to be the main objects of his attention. One is well dressed sitting very upright, thereby enhancing her great shock of hair. She dominates the row. The other, about three seats along is darker, slighter, very casually dressed with short, untidy hair. Most of the time she leans forward, listening, but not looking at the proceedings, making it difficult to see her face. Neither shows any interest in the other. Is the reporter interested in them both or one in particular? Another witness for the developers takes the stand. He's more senior than the other and explains their environmental position, asserting his company's record and their commitment to community involvement.

"What about the house?"

He turns to the audience. It's one of the women, the darker, slighter one.

"I had nothing to do with that," the witness says.

"And neither do we," Burton says, "at least not at the moment. Please continue with your evidence," then turning to the audience, "whilst you, madam will kindly refrain from interrupting. I will not have a free for all in this enquiry."

The woman looks steadfastly at the chairman, but says nothing. The witness continues, stating how the later stages of the development will have no detrimental effect on the environment.

"Lies!" the woman shouts

"It's Maggie," one of the reporters says, "She's at it again."

David's companion is suddenly very interested.

"Oh do shut up, you wretched fool!" the other woman says, leaning across her neighbours, the better to harangue her.

The first woman ignores her and stands up.

"Lies! Lies! Lies! You've been lying from the start and you'll carry on lying until you're stopped!"

Now the second woman stands up.

"This is intolerable. Be quiet!"

"Madam, I've warned you..." the chairman begins, but Maggie ignores him and turns to Monica.

"Don't you tell me to be quiet...you...you...you're up to you're neck with this lot...how much are they paying you, eh, how much?

"Don't be ridiculous!"

"Answer the question. How much?"

Monica turns around and addresses the whole room.

"You all heard that. A disgraceful slander, you're all witnesses. I'll have you Maggie Morton if it's the last thing I..."

"No one is going to have anything except me and I'll have silence!" Burton booms, "Kindly sit down."

Monica does as she's bidden, but Maggie remains standing and now turns her venom on the chairman.

"It's all lies. This pantomime is all part of it. Lies! Lies! Lies!"

"Right, that's it. You will kindly leave the room, madam."

"I'm not going anywhere. Somebody has to challenge this farce. That's what's wrong with this country. Nobody's prepared to stand up and say what's right. Well I'm not afraid to speak!"

"Usher!"

A tall heavy man is coming from the back and already clearing people from the far end of the row to make way.

"I will not be silenced!" Maggie shouts defiantly.

Monica mutters something and Maggie turns on her again.

"You're revelling in this, aren't you?" then back to the chairman, "You're all in it together. You're here to do her bidding. You've been bought, like all the rest."

Burton is calm, but determined.

"Remove her!"

The usher, who could be a night club bouncer in his other job, gets to Maggie and taps her lightly on the shoulder. Again Monica says something that provokes Maggie.

"You're day will come. What you did to Warren, payback time is coming!"

The usher now takes her arm more stiffly. Maggie bristles.

"Get your hands off her!"

The man next to David is on his feet and pushing past people, trying to get closer to Maggie.

"Get back," the chairman calls, "Who are you to interfere?"

"I am George Carter of the Mid Herts Herald."

With things on his mind Jenner called at Ettie's cottage early this morning on his way to the station, knocking a number of times, but getting no answer. Then a curtain twitched in the window next door, a nosy neighbour wondering who was this strange man coming so early. Jenner smiled nervously. The curtain twitched back and he left. He's rung her mobile, but got no answer and also rung her house in Gloucestershire, though she's not mentioned going home. Now he's back at the cottage. The curtain twitches again.

"Have you seen Miss Rodway?" he shouts.

"Not for a couple of days, was it something important?"

"No, it can wait."

He sits in the car for some time, reluctant to immediately return to the station. Earlier he sent Jennifer to see Monica Freeson again, though he didn't expect anything dramatic to emerge. That's the problem with this case. A lot of pushing and poking to little effect, plenty of suspects, none of them definite, much suspicion with no evidence. Hanging over and around it all is the past. With his growing gut feeling of its significance, which he can neither explain nor dismiss, it's not the best time for Ettie to go AWOL. The curtain twitches once more. Lawrence Bullock has some explaining to do. It's a short drive to his house.

"Not at the studio, Mr. Bullock," Jenner says, relieved to find Lawrence at home.

"Nothing much doing today."

"Things not going right with the film? I suppose it's difficult with Chris Pleasant...away."

"Yes," Lawrence says without conviction.

He's still in his dressing gown and hasn't shaved.

"Not so much not going right, but not *going*," he says.

"Well if you have no director..."

"I was uncomfortable before Chris...took off...I'm sure he'll be back...it's nothing to do with him. Peculiar things have been happening on the set."

He pauses. Jenner waits.

"Then John Thurley had his...accident and his replacement came, Wesley Greville. Things got even worse after that."

"What's this Wesley Greville been doing?"

"Well...he...it's more...nothing specific...not something I can easily explain, I just don't feel comfortable around him."

"Maybe it's the clash of the parts."

"I don't see what..."

"You playing the abbot and him being the rebel leader, what's his name?"

"Grindcobb."

"Quite. See what I mean?"

Lawrence is nonplussed, shakes his head and laughs nervously.

"No, it's not that. We are professionals after all."

"But it could be...being professionals...that you've both got truly into your respective parts, become them so to speak."

Lawrence shudders.

"It's cold in here when the sun moves round."

He gets up and closes the French doors to the patio.

"Knew him from some previous engagement, perhaps?" Jenner persists

"Never come across him before."

"You're sure?"

"Yes, perfectly. Why do you ask?"

"It's just you appear to have some difficulty recalling people you've known before."

"What on earth do you mean?"

"I mean Warren Grover. You told me you didn't know him, but that's not true is it? You were at school together. Why didn't you tell me that?"

"You didn't ask."

"I could hardly ask about something I didn't know."

"No...of course not...I meant it never occurred to me to be relevant."

"Let me judge what's relevant."

"It's a long time ago. Can you remember everybody you were at school with?"

"No, but I can remember those I knew well."

Lawrence is about to speak, perhaps to deny being well acquainted with Warren, but he catches Jenner's raised eyebrows and thinks better of it.

"Since you've come back have you seen or even sought out those you knew at school."

"No I haven't, people move away, I moved away...when you asked if I knew Warren Grover I assumed you meant *now*, not twenty odd years ago."

"Quite. You knew George Carter also?"

Lawrence squirms, then forces a smile. Jenner remains impassive.

"I believe we were in the same class together."

"There were others in that class...one Melvyn Strange for example."

"Mel...Melvyn?" Lawrence says slowly, his voice trembling, "I...I've not seen Melvyn."

"No, no one has. He disappeared, didn't he? It must have been very upsetting...to you all?"

"Yes...yes it was."

"Upsetting enough to be remembered right up to the present?"

"What do you mean."

"Was there anything else at that time...anything to do with you and Warren Grover or George Carter?"

"What sort of thing?"

"Anything so upsetting that..."

"...that could have led to Warren Grover's murder?"

Jenner switches to Lawrence's recent land purchases, but he won't be drawn.

"I've come back to my roots. It's good to have a stake in the area and I need some sensible investments. I've never made any money on the stock market. Don't seem to get the timing right. So, heritage and financial security, it all fits together well."

"And nothing to do with the Waintree development?"

"I don't understand..."

"Your property has outline planning permission."

"Yes, of course, but I didn't realise they could be involved. My, my, isn't that interesting?"

Lawrence recovers his verve, casting aside doubts and depression about the film to bat away further questions with a mixture of platitudes, sarcastic surprise and unconvincing innocence. Jenner lets it go for now. When he reminds Lawrence he may be back it doesn't seem to bother him.

Back at the station he sits gloomily waiting for Jennifer. It's not like Ettie to go off without warning. It makes him uneasy. Could it be connected to the odd sensations he's been having lately, resonating with her mysterious communications from the past and the weird film? Experience tells him not to discount such things. Sooner or later they usually become relevant to his investigations. The telephone rings. It's David Farley.

"You weren't at the enquiry today."

"Enquiry?"

"The Waintree Development enquiry. You missed an interesting altercation."

David recounts the confrontation between Maggie, Monica and the chairman. Jenner listens, but his mind is still on Ettie's disappearance while Warren Grover's connection with the far past seems more pertinent than any contemporary machinations.

"I told you before, my enquiries are not concerned with fraud or corruption. I have a murder to investigate."

"But Monica Freeson..."

"It's not going to tell me anything I don't already know."

"Aha! You've found something about her?"

"There's precious little to go on. Monica Freeson wasn't involved in the decision to support the Waintree project."

David snorts derisively.

"Of course she wasn't, but that doesn't mean..."

"Conjecture and innuendo, good enough to imply in your paper, but not for me. I need evidence."

"So Warren Grover's opposition to the development had nothing to do with his murder?"

"I didn't say that."

"So you got nothing new out of Monica?"

Jenner hesitates.

"Not about herself, but she did mention connections between Lawrence Bullock, Warren Grover and George Carter. They were all at school together."

"Were they now."

"We've also discovered Lawrence has been buying land in the area of the Waintree development."

David whistles, "You ought to be there."

Jennifer comes in. Jenner turns to her as David rings off.

"You wouldn't have seen Monica Freeson."

"No, she was at..."

"I know. What about Ted Skinner?"

"I saw them both – Elizabeth Skinner is also part of the opposition campaign – a lot of gossip about the councillors and why they let it get through. They don't like Monica."

"Now why doesn't that surprise me."

"They said no one with half a brain is fooled by her distancing herself from the decisions, owning land contiguous with the proposals, when she's involved, scrupulously declaring an interest..."

"Yes, but anything new, what about the others?"

"George Carter came up. They were ambivalent at first, but then Elizabeth let rip. They grudgingly accept George is probably against the development, but he's not been open enough, never put the paper wholly behind the campaign. They want to preserve their inheritance, the unspoilt country, the pristine green belt that sort of thing..."

"Don't mock, sergeant, these things are important."

"Anyway, they're not convinced. George sees it the same way. Elizabeth said he's too crude. His support is erratic, mere journalistic opportunism, nothing more than juicy pieces for his paper."

"Isn't that the business papers are in?"

"Like David Farley?"

"Just because journalists chase trivia doesn't mean they don't sometimes uncover more substantial matters."

"Maybe not in this case though – at least not as far as the Skinners are concerned. They find George's attacks embarrassing, motivated by personal spite than any desire to get at the truth. He criticises Monica for things unconnected to the development such as her cultural and community work. Warren was aware of it, but wouldn't criticise George because he was giving at least tacit if inconsistent support to the campaign. In the long run though Warren was worried George would go too far and it would backfire. Monica would get public sympathy and the campaign would be undermined."

"He doesn't sound like a very astute newspaper man."

"Whenever they mentioned it, Warren was always going to confront George, have it out with him. If you're really with us, stop messing around, but he never did. Elizabeth wonders if there was more to their relationship than it seemed, something from the past perhaps."

"Not just from George's past, but also Monica's perhaps. What about Lawrence Bullock?"

"Warren knew him and they'd had meetings. Warren said Lawrence was helping the campaign in his own way. When they asked what he meant, he said he needed more information. They believe Warren was on the verge of something big just before he was murdered, but they've no idea what is was."

"Lawrence was evasive and played it down, but finally admitted he'd known Warren from their schooldays. George also knew Warren and Lawrence from way back and he's out to get Monica."

"So we see Lawrence again. What about George, do we see him too?"

"We do, but it won't be easy. He was Rusk's original local contact, but for some reason he's dried up. What exactly was going on between him and Warren?"

"The Skinners may not have it right. George may have been working much more behind the scenes for Warren."

"Or perhaps for Lawrence. He'd known him just as long as he'd known Warren. The oldest loyalties are sometimes the strongest."

"But with Lawrence buying up land in the area wouldn't that put him on the same side as Monica?"

"Quite so, but what is the real issue that divides the sides? Lawrence was evasive about his land deals. Rusk thinks I should go to the enquiry. It might throw some light on Warren's connections."

"There's only one connection that matters."

He curls his lips in disapproval. She glances at the ceiling and sighs.

"I don't believe this," he says, "you don't seriously believe what Ettie says..."

"Warren Grover's interest..."

"He had many interests."

"The one that really counts is his work on the Peasants' Revolt."

"No, sergeant, I'm not going along with this 1381 mumbo jumbo."

"So you discount what Ettie says?"

"I didn't say that."

"If we can find a link between..."

"Alright, that's enough."

Reluctantly, Jennifer has to accept the subject closed...for now. But while he may not want to talk about Ettie, she's not out of his mind. Jennifer wittering on about the past unnerves him and after she's gone he broods disconsolately for some time. Desperate feelings call for desperate measures. Against all his normal prejudices it might even necessitate consulting an academic. He rings Oxford University. Jessica Tennant is as surprised to receive his call as he is in making it.

"This is an unexpected pleasure, chief inspector. Naturally I'm always glad to speak to the forces of law and order. Why, it must be, what nearly a year. We last met in..."

"Smithfield."

"Precisely."

"Have you kept in touch with Ettie Rodway by any chance?"

"As a matter of fact I saw her quite recently. She's in Hertfordshire, you know. Looking distinctly peeky. I was rather concerned. She went to see that unfortunate man who was murdered in the district, what was his name...?"

"Warren Grover."

"Ah, but of course, that's the connection. You must be involved in the investigation. Why, it's getting just like old times, isn't it?"

"I sincerely hope not."

"But you're worried about Ettie."

"She's gone missing. You've not seen her?"

"Not since I called at the cottage in Welstead."

"Was anything particular worrying her?"

"She was very tired. I'm afraid I did most of the talking. Something I'm rather good at."

"What did you talk about?"

"You'll recall the researches on the lost 14th century rhyme?"

"How can I ever forget."

"I won't bore you with the academic details, (Jenner sighs with relief) but any further rhymes might have implications for Ettie's own work. Unfinished business you might say."

"How do they affect what she's doing?"

"Ah, chief inspector, how indeed?"

He waits to be enlightened. It doesn't come and then she's away on another tack.

"Of course it might also be of interest to yourself. With Warren Grover's interest in the Revolt, you see the connection? It's not for me to tell you how to conduct your enquiries..."

"Quite so."

"...but if you can find the common thread linking his work with others, well, there you have it!"

"I do?"

"Then there's the anniversary looming up – 15th July."

"Quite," Jenner says, bemused, "remind me again."

"The suppression of the revolt in St. Albans – very important. Ettie will see the significance. We can discuss it in more detail when I come."

"You're coming to Welstead?"

"Hempston actually. I've been invited. *Everybody* will be there."

"Where exactly?"

"In two days, Monica Freeson's place."

It's a short walk to the house. On an ordinary evening the town should be quiet, but this is no ordinary evening and only those with nothing to talk about are quiet. There are few of those. As Ettie is pulled along the street, the woman exchanges terse words of reproof and encouragement to others they pass.

"...why are you not with us...come quickly...you were not there this afternoon, make up for it tonight...do not be afraid, the people are together..."

The strange narrow street with its overhanging buildings, the people with their drab unfamiliar clothes, the noise from the houses and taverns, all disorientate Ettie so much she allows herself to be dragged uncomplainingly. Then, realising what's happened and recovering some confidence she looks at the woman. She's in her early thirties, short, dark with wide brown eyes and long hair, tied behind her head in a band. She glances quickly at Ettie with a look of sympathetic suspicion, before pulling her again, moving quickly, her free arm splaying wildly as she darts along the pavement. Ettie looks at her clothes and then down at her own to find they are surprisingly similar. Then she stops and wrenches her arm free, slightly tearing her sleeve.

"Leave me," she says, "I'm not to be towed along like some pig to the market!"

Taken aback, the woman steps away, then laughs.

"Who are you, anyway?" Ettie says, smoothing down her sleeve.

"You know who I am," the woman laughs again.

"If I knew who you were I wouldn't be asking!" Ettie snaps.

"I am Martha of course."

"And...you know me?"

"I know of you. When I saw you in the street I knew it could only be you."

"But how...how could you...?"

"Come, there's much to do. We have to tell my husband. He will be pleased to see you."

She turns and walks on, this time making no attempt to take Ettie's hand. After a few paces she stops and looks back. Ettie follows with some trepidation. Husband, someone who knows her? Martha turns into a side alley and then waits at a house door. Sounds of raucous talk come from inside.

"We are here," Martha says as Ettie joins her and then opens the door.

Several men sit around a table at one end of a low beamed room, talking excitedly and so engrossed in their conversation they hardly notice Martha and Ettie enter. Ettie recognises one of the men. She's been right. Thomas, the man she saw in the tavern in London, here, now, in this room. She hangs back near the door. He doesn't notice her.

"Tell me again of yesterday," one man says, "I wish I'd been there. I was delayed, it..."

"No matter," Thomas says, brushing away the other's embarrassment, "You redeemed yourself today. Walter at Lee summoned us all from every town and village to meet him at three o'clock at the Derfold field. He brought many armed men, but we weren't afraid. Didn't we lead him into town yesterday morning with all honours."

"But even so..."

"With the woods behind us, we gathered in the shape of a rainbow and then..."

"He told us why he'd come," a third man says, "How gravely disturbers of the peace have caused offence to the king."

"Sounds ominous," the other says.

"So it was," Thomas continues, standing to mimic the knight, *"It is for this reason the king is carrying out trials in Essex and coming down with a heavy hand on the whole country and its inhabitants. Hearing of the troubles in this town and the monastery..."*

"Now we hear it," a fourth man drones.

"...*He therefore wants those who have committed these crimes to be punished and has decided to come here with a large army!*"

"No, no," the others cry.

Thomas lifts his hand, bends forward, before straightening his back and lifting his head with thrusting jaw in mock imitation of Lee.

"*That army would destroy and trample all the fruit and grain, everything for five miles around where they march,*" he intones and then, stretching out both hands declaims loud and shrill, "*So, concerned such harm would fall on my own district and in compassion to ward this off for my fellow townsmen, I have taken measures to weaken the king's resolve.*"

"Oh how wonderful!" the others shout sarcastically, banging the table.

Thomas lifts his hand again and continues when they quieten.

"*I take this heavy burden on my shoulders on behalf of all those living here, though it's a burden I take up willingly for I hope to serve my county in such circumstances...*"

"Of course! Of course!"

"*...and because of my instant pleading, I was given permission, though this was obtained with some difficulty, to exact justice in my own district on behalf of the king, not outsiders.*"

"Oh that's so much better," one says, "so reassuring to know we may be hanged by our own!"

"*So I will carry out what is right, hand over those responsible for stirring up the troubles and give satisfaction to the abbot.*"

"Aye, give up our friends for that tonsured villain!"

Thomas makes a small bow and sits down. Martha comes over to him.

"Thomas, we need to talk. There is..."

"Yes, yes," he says, waving her aside, "in a moment."

"And did we tell him we'd do his bidding?" the first man says.

Thomas laughs.

"Before we could contradict him a few loudmouthed fools got up, applauded him and said they'd willingly obey his counsel. Some of us tried to speak, but he cleverly manipulated the meeting. *If you support me, then we must act*, he said, immediately summoning and swearing a jury of twelve, directing them to come to him the following day."

"How foolish!" the first man says.

"Perhaps, but not totally," the second says, "For today when those twelve fools returned to his chamber they refused to indict anyone, saying all their neighbours were good men and true!"

"That showed him," his companion says.

"Maybe," Thomas says, "but a sly rogue is our sir knight. He said nothing at first, but after hearing Mass he instructed them to return the charters we'd got from the monastery."

"They didn't give in?"

"No, they promised to bring them to him this afternoon."

"And did they?"

"They should never have returned for it was then Lee showed his real sympathies...*concerned no harm should befall his district* indeed! He was supping with the abbot when they came. He demanded the charters. They said they didn't know where they were. He was angry and called his soldiers to bar the doors, keeping our men in the abbot's chamber against their will. The villain questioned them again. They were afraid of him, but blamed their fear on the community, saying they dared not divulge where the charters were. Lee was unconvinced and swore they'd not leave until the charters were returned. They'd been gone too long and some of us came to the door demanding entry. So now the abbot feared for his own safety and calmed Lee saying he'd try to settle the matter."

"No chance of that, we've heard his promises in the past."

"He thought he could better us," one of the others says, "ordering us to meet at Barnet Wood, but the men of Barnet and Berkhampstead and the villages came to our aid and we arrived with three hundred archers."

"That's the way to deal with knights!" another shouts as they bang the table again.

"He quivered in fear," Thomas says, "He knew if he went ahead with public trials as he wished, we'd rise up against him. Even some of his own soldiers were quaking. They would have abandoned him and joined our cause."

"Thomas!" Martha calls.

"Then we came back to town and celebrated our victory!" one of the others says.

"And after you were carousing and now while you are crowing, the knight has moved against you all!"

They turn as Martha shouts.

"What do you mean?" Thomas says.

"What I've been trying to tell you. Don't you see how cunning he's been? He's only afraid of you when you stand together in strength. Once you disperse as you have tonight, he moves against you quickly with stealth."

"He's safely in his lodgings, he went there after..."

"He may well be, but where is Will Grindcobb, Will Cadindon, Barbintsor? Lee has called out the bailiffs and the constables, telling them in the morning to arrest all the men involved in taking up the millstones from the abbey floor."

"We'll be about in the morning," Thomas says, "That ruffianly knight won't dare move against our people. Don't worry, Martha, Grindcobb and Cadindon and the others are safe in their own houses, I saw them not an hour since."

"I've heard they will be arrested."

"Heard? From whom?"

Martha shakes her head confusedly. Thomas gets up and takes her softly by the shoulders.

"There are many stories in these times, it doesn't mean..."

"Maybe we should go to the knight and find out," one of the others says.

Thomas grimaces.

"Stories, rumours, hard times produce hard tales."

"But we should be sure," another says.

"Alright, alright," Thomas says, "Go get Ned and Wilfred and Alan and Abel and anymore...now...go."

One of the men leaves, glancing at Ettie, who still stands by the door.

"I wouldn't want to miss any more great events," the first man says.

"You won't," Thomas says, "I promise you will see that other England before the new month is out."

The other England...the two Englands...so Thomas said to Ettie in London. Now she can be sure it's him. She looks across, but he has his back to her and doesn't see her. As he speaks to the other men Martha comes over and leads Ettie to the other side of the room.

"Don't be fooled, he hears me best when he appears to hear me least."

Despite his earlier rejection of her, he grabs his coat and goes to the door.

"I'll go myself and roust Dick and Jack. We'll settle this business before the night's too long."

As he goes out the other returns with six men and soon the room is crowded with new arrivals. There are women too and Martha talks with some of them. Thomas returns with more men and the whole company of thirty or more spill into the street. Ettie stays close to Martha. With all the excitement Thomas has still not recognised her and she hangs back, afraid to talk to him. He'll want to know where she's been since Smithfield, but then he must have spoken of her, described her for Martha to know her. She strains to remember what she said to him in London. To him a couple of weeks, to her a whole year, though really some six hundred. Now is not the time to revive such mysteries. Difficult questions incur unpredictable answers.

"Have you seen Will Grindcobb?" Martha says to Thomas.

"No, but he's around."

The party moves off, joined by others from other streets. It's an impressive force, but they have few weapons except for small knives. The whole town is in ferment, people gathering at every tavern and corner. They reach a large house in the centre, the lodging of Walter at Lee. After Thomas raps loudly a servant opens the door. They exchange a few words and then the news passes quickly through the throng. Walter at Lee has left for Hertford.

"See," a man says, "he's running away. The bailiffs will do nothing without him. There'll be no arrests tonight."

Martha is unconvinced.

"But what of the squires in the service of the abbot? They could put pressure on the bailiffs."

"No, no," the man says, "there's nothing to stay for, we can deal with it in the morning."

The men start to disperse.

"Just like this afternoon," Martha mutters, "when we split up they are strong, when we are together we are strong."

When we are together we are strong. Ettie shudders, suddenly remembering she's alone in another time. She stands in shadow and though he looks quizzically, Thomas says nothing, appearing not to recognise her.

"Nothing doing tonight," he says to Martha, "I'm going home."

"I want a word with Jane" she says, nodding to a woman a little way off.

"Don't linger," he says.

Martha watches him until he gets to the corner.

"He doesn't want to believe," she says, "He's not been right since he returned from London. He must have seen more than he tells and what he says is bad enough. Wat Tyler cut down like a rabbit in the field."

"No rabbit," Ettie says, "rabbits run. Wat Tyler didn't run."

"You were there?"

"I...I...I heard from one who was."

"Thomas got away before Tyler was killed, but he had to move quickly. Already the king's soldiers were moving rapidly to block those that hadn't already left Smithfield. He's been secretly hoping we can escape the oppression, but despite his bravado, he has misgivings. If Will Grindcobb and the others are arrested what happened in London could come here. He tries to hide his fears and his troubles, but he's too open a man. I see it in his eyes. The king's letter emboldened the abbot. Grindcobb told us we had to be realistic, more conciliatory. Grindcobb has always stood up for our liberties, bravely expressing our grievances to the abbot and the prior, always daring, never peevish. He won't let us down now so we must protect him as he has protected us."

There are few people left in the street now. Martha seems unconcerned the woman she said she wanted to see has left. Ettie suspects it was an excuse to talk to her alone, but with a shrug Martha follows her husband. They walk silently a few paces. Then another woman turns the corner and almost collides with them. She stops abruptly, recognising Martha.

"Sarah, what are..."

"Martha, Martha, I'm so glad I've..." Sarah blurts out breathlessly, "I've found...found somebody...I need to...to..."

The woman bends down and takes great gulps of air. After a few moments of wheezing and spluttering she comes up, though still a little short of breath.

Jessica was right. Everybody is here, at least, everybody that matters. Having already joined the local history society, Jennifer has secured two invitations, hauling a reluctant Jenner with her.

"I remember the last time you got me to one of these events."

"We might find out something useful."

"That's what you said last time."

Monica has hired the ballroom of a large country hotel about a mile outside Hempston. It's a fine afternoon and many of the guests have retired onto the terrace with their wine and canapes. Jenner studies the opulent spread with disdain, grunting each time the waiter makes a suggestion.

"Remind me again, what exactly this is all about," he asks Jennifer as they move away from the table.

"This is the pre-launch of Monica's exhibition, which opens tomorrow. It's called 'The County's Living Past.'"

"Looking at some of this lot, some of the county hasn't got much of a living present."

"There'll be other events to get it going – musical, dramatic. The idea is to stimulate interest in local history and culture."

"Sounds like you've read the publicity blurb."

"Monica's trying to galvanise the converted to spread the word. That's what we're all here for – though she might not be pleased to see you."

"I'm as cultured as the next man. Surely it's not really *her* exhibition?"

"She's the chair of the organising committee and with her position on the Leisure Committee..."

"Is Ettie Rodway with you?"

Charley Kennet almost bumps into them.

"No. What are you doing here?" Jenner says aggressively.

"I might ask you the same..."

"I suppose it's because of the film," Jennifer intervenes.

"Yes, Chris got the invitation, but he's not around, so I came instead. I thought Ettie might be with you. I really need to talk to her."

"Will you be helping with the exhibition, I believe there's to be a section on 1381?"

"Not directly, though we've loaned some stills for background. They have a separate adviser."

"Who might that be?" Jenner says.

"Doctor Jessica Tennant – from Oxford."

"Quite so," he says, noticing Jessica approaching from the main door.

"There you are, chief inspector. Good to see a familiar face in unfamiliar surroundings."

Charley is fascinated by Jessica's work and Jessica is only too pleased to expound on 'the rhyme,' while also probing about the film. Jennifer listens carefully, but Jenner slopes off, muttering about 'keeping an eye.'

"Are there many scenes remaining to be filmed?"

Charley hesitates.

"It must be difficult to be precise with Mr. Pleasant...er... indisposed."

"He's not indisposed," Charley says indignantly, "he's just not around. There are additional scenes I'm anxious to do, but Chris isn't enthusiastic. You're familiar with the rehangings in St. Albans?"

"Indeed I am. One of the more gruesome aspects of the Revolt."

"Chris is against it, but I feel strongly we should include it in the film. He doesn't think it 'enhances the narrative flow."

"Is he right?"

"It depends. He's right if you interpret the rehangings as a completely separate incident, tacked on after the high point of the executions, but they're central to the core of the rising. They show the people's strength and determination not to be defeated. What do you think?"

"I know nothing about filmmaking, I wouldn't presume..."

"But you know about the Revolt. You've advised on this exhibition."

"I answered a number of questions and referred to the principal sources..."

"But with your researches...you must have a view."

There's an electrifying demand in Charley's voice and an earnestness in her eyes as if someone else is also pleading. With Jessica possibly on the edge of a great discovery, an appeal to her researches is difficult to deny.

"I've been working on documents, contemporary with the Revolt, which have a number of features pointing to this area. I'm absolutely certain there were more than the six rhymes recorded by the chronicles. At least one must have covered the period after the suppression of the Revolt. In other words there's a vast untold story *beginning* when the other accounts finish. Your projected rehanging scene would fit precisely and be very apposite."

Charley's face immediately lights up with relief and enthusiasm.

"Writing the scene is easy. It comes automatically, as if those that were there are dictating to me."

She and Jessica stare into each other's eyes, gripped as their thoughts concentrate on those awful events so long ago. Neither speaks. The chatter and flamboyance of the room fades into a hazy background as the past encroaches, the guests supplanted in their peripheral vision by others, dark, drab, silently watching. Jennifer feels it too, but also hears voices, incoherent, but getting louder. Then just one voice, struggling to be heard. She strains to listen while her eyes remain fixed on Charley and Jessica, who continue to stare into that time vastness, like peering into a bottomless well with only the distant splash of the water of another age to disturb the silence.

"Doctor Tennant!"

It's gone – past voices, past people, another time...while the whirling noise and talk of the present bounces back as Monica, in a long flowing gown swirling around her, glides towards them.

"It is you, isn't it?"

Jessica turns to face her host.

"I'm so glad you could get here. I'm *dying* to hear about your latest work!"

Jessica is whisked aside, plied with drink and food and subjected to a machine gun rendition of Monica's project. Jessica smiles and nods appropriately between gulps and mouthfuls, for once unable to speak. Charley and Jennifer look on, like Jessica slightly dazed.

"Ettie ought to be here," Charley says, "she would understand..."

Jennifer nods. The sensations they both feel, which Ettie might understand are only just fading. After a few minutes, with Jessica suitably fed and watered, Monica gets to the end of her monologue.

"You must tell me about your researches. For those of us in the cut and thrust of the humdrum municipal life, it's so easy to get out of touch with the mainstream academic world."

Monica hangs onto every word as Jessica talks about her work, with an occasional 'really' and 'of course' and 'fascinating.' The mouth moves, but the eyes are static. Jennifer wonders how much is passing beyond the ears into the brain. It's good Jenner isn't within earshot, he might not be able to control his tongue. She looks round, but can't see him, but there's someone else, vaguely familiar at the door, also scanning the group. The woman is appropriately dressed, though not smartly for the occasion, someone unused to such an event. Jennifer knows the face, but struggles to recognise her. She's comes over as Jessica winds up.

"You must be very proud of your local man, all the work he's put in over the years."

"Er...local man?" Monica says.

"Most unfortunate what happened, a real tragedy, not just for his family, but I imagine for the whole community."

"Er...yes, indeed, you mean..."

"Warren Grover."

"Yes of course...as you say, a terrible tragedy. I knew Warren for years and always admired his work. It would have been so wonderful for him to be here today. His gentle wisdom and fine mind are greatly missed. There's so much we owe him. I was only saying the other day..."

"Bloody hypocrite!"

Monica turns to face her accuser, as do most others in the room.

"You hated him in his life, don't insult his memory by pretending you're his friend when he's dead!"

Now Jennifer recognises Maggie, uncharacteristically dressed in a plain blue suit, probably the only one she owns and at close quarters showing the wardrobe creases.

"How the hell did you get in here?" Monica shouts, "Get out!"

"Not before I have my say."

"This reception is by invitation only. You..."

"Lying hypocrite," Maggie shouts, moving closer, "You're not sorry Warren's dead, you probably had something to do with it!"

"Get out before I call the police!"

"They're already here," Maggie shouts, shaking her arm and glancing towards the terrace, from which Jenner has just emerged.

"In that case..." Monica says, turning towards Jenner, who makes no move.

"That's it, call up reinforcements, you never could fight your own battles. Murderer! Murderer!"

"I'll shut your foul mouth for good," Monica shouts, lunging towards Maggie and striking her across the face.

Maggie stumbles and Monica is about to strike her again, but a man's arm is thrust between them and pushes her back.

Martha holds the woman's hands as she gradually calms.

"Sarah, whatever is it? Slow down, catch your breath."

"I had to find somebody....somebody to talk to..."

"Slowly, slowly," Martha says, taking her hands.

"I saw them...didn't know what to do...it was...talking to the bailiffs...saw them myself."

"Who did you see?"

"The squires."

"I knew it! What did I say, the squires could put pressure on the bailiffs. Did you know them, which squires did you see?"

"Richard Perrers, John Chival, Thomas Eydon, William Eccleshall."

"I was right! They are all in the service of the abbot."

"They were talking to the bailiffs, arguing with them. The bailiffs looked unhappy. They were distressed."

"Did you hear what was said?"

"Not much, I had to keep my distance, but I heard one of the squires saying 'you must do it tonight, they must be taken."

"They're going to arrest our men."

"That's what I thought. I came straight away, but I've seen no one till now."

"Where was this?"

"Near the abbey gatehouse."

"Quickly," Martha says, "Get the men, get everyone you can. Go, away, off with you!"

The young woman gulps a few times for she's still not completely caught back her breath and then runs towards the crowd. Ettie moves to follow, but Martha stops her.

"No, not that way," she says and pulls her round, "this way."

"But surely...where are we going?"

"To the abbey gatehouse."

Martha takes Ettie's hand, then releases it, but carries on. Ettie is unsure and nervous of going towards the abbey. A woman on her own in a strange place in another time at night, surrounded by hundreds of potentially hostile people. At least she knows Martha or more correctly Martha knows her. Yet is that good? Alone with the woman who chased her from the tower and harassed her on the common. A favour or a threat, but what choice does she have?

They pass through mainly empty streets, becoming even more deserted the closer they get to the abbey, Ettie's nervousness increasing in the darkness. The noise from the town recedes and for the first time she misses its reassuring din. No dog barks, no cat mews, scratching scurrying rats are silent while in the air no owl breaks the eerie hush. It doesn't feel right, living things have decamped, responding to some unknown, but palpable terror. This is walking wilfully into danger. She came away from here, away from the past, now in the past she's allowing herself to be led into peril. Yet she goes on, dutifully following Martha, who strides ahead with a fatal confidence. They near the gatehouse. She must speak out.

"Is it wise," she says, just loud enough for Martha to hear, afraid to disturb whoever may be listening in the noiseless night, "to come here alone, without the men?"

"Not wise," Martha says, stopping suddenly, "but if we are wise why are we here at all?"

"But if..."

"Quiet!"

Martha pulls Ettie into the nook beside a doorway and then cocks her head like a bird, motionless. Ettie strains to listen.

"Come," Martha says after a few moments, leading Ettie back along the street.

Is she too afraid? Does she hide her fear in activity as her husband hides his in swaggering prattle? They pass the last house and see the gatehouse ahead, but Martha stops. Several armed men bar their way.

"Bailiffs," Martha whispers, then calls to the men, "Why are you standing there?"

"Guarding," one says, peering through the gloom and then seeing the women, "If you know what's good for you you'll go home!"

Ettie pulls at Martha.

"Do as he says, this isn't safe."

"Who is in the gatehouse?" Martha calls.

The man doesn't answer.

"Are you beholden only to the abbot's slime?" she persists.

"Come away," Ettie whispers.

"Those that defied the abbot maybe, Will Grindcobb, Will Cadindon, John Barbintsor?"

Still the man doesn't answer. Then he turns and walks back towards the gatehouse.

"You're holding them there!" Martha screams.

"Go home, woman! Before we arrest you too!"

Their roles reversed, Ettie turns Martha around and drags her quickly back up the street, not even pausing to look behind. Martha doesn't resist and they walk on silently, then hear footsteps and shouting.

"More soldiers?" Martha whispers.

They stop, slink to the side of a house and wait. The footsteps, now running, get louder.

"Might they not go into town?" Ettie says.

"This street only leads to the abbey. There's nowhere else for them to go."

They crouch down, helpless human hedgehogs, instinctively making themselves as small as possible. Like hedgehogs they can't disappear and unlike hedgehogs have no prickly defences. Many feet clatter over the cobbles. They are near. Martha shivers, much more afraid than when she faced the bailiffs, but they were known, this is the unknown. Ettie shivers. It seems darker and colder on this warm summer night. Many voices shouting now, very close. It's hard to make out anything they say through the din, but then Martha turns and steps back into the street.

"It's our people."

Around twenty men and some women swarm into the street, led by Thomas.

"They are taken! You should have waited," he shouts to Martha, his voice quivering with fear for her. "They might have arrested you."

"They threatened to."

"We can't find Will Grindcobb, Cadindon and Barbintsor. Are they locked in the gatehouse?"

"The bailiffs won't say."

"It's the abbot's accursed squires, infernal lackeys of the knight!"

The group carries on towards the gatehouse, but Thomas is nervous and sends Martha back home. She doesn't argue. Ettie steps from the shadows only after he's left, still apprehensive, though sure he's recognised her. Martha says little on the way to the house. They pass many groups discussing the possible arrests. The whole town is fired up though as many disbelieve as believe the conflicting rumours and reports.

"We will deal with it in the morning," a man says, "If they are taken we will get them out."

Others are less sure, their earlier confidence after the meeting with Lee replaced by a brooding melancholy. The house is empty. Martha prepares a simple meal, then sits quietly with Ettie in the rear room. She says nothing directly about the arrests. Her earlier fire now seemingly turned on herself as she frets about Thomas and worries about the uncertain future. Both are tired, but Ettie has to say what's been nagging her since she was thrust into this town a few hours ago.

"How did you know me?"

Martha, nodding gradually into a light sleep, lifts her head at the sound of Ettie's voice.

"I told you, Thomas..."

"But you've never seen me before and he was not with you in the street."

Martha looks at her unbelievingly as if Ettie has just denied knowing an old friend after many years. She shakes her head slowly, but then sees Ettie unmoved.

"I just knew you'd be here...so when I saw you it was obvious."

Ettie could challenge Martha, but how would she cope with her questions?

"What do you want?" she says.

"Your help of course."

"But how can I help you?"

"For the cause."

Ettie stares incredulously into Martha's wide, innocent eyes. Isn't it obvious, isn't it simple?

"You mean...for the people...?" Ettie says, "Tell me, what can I do?"

"No matter..." Martha says, shaking her head, "For you've not been able to see us until now."

Does she mean talking to Ettie on the common, in the tower? Dare Ettie confide in her? Tell her she may need Martha's help as much as she wants it from Ettie? Martha gets up and goes into the back room, leaving Ettie to wonder about her.

Was it Martha that summoned her? If so why *now?* Can she really make others leap across time? She spoke so vigorously on the common and in the town, so why not? Unless it's not her that levers time, but someone else, projecting...pulling...Ettie herself drawing her? Until now she's assumed her powers were merely receptive, at best a conductor, a willing vessel for the past, but what if she's now a magnet that draws and attracts across the centuries? It unnerves her. She's not conscious of any change in her voluntary will. If she's acquired new powers, she's not sought them and doesn't welcome them. Perhaps it really is Martha, devoid of the powers herself, but able to will them on Ettie, clutch a fellow spirit and mould an unknowable future to her needs. But that would need superhuman concentration Ettie doubts she possesses.

She stares searchingly at the plain walls and up to the low ceiling, seeking the explanation for why she's here. To what questions does Martha seek answers across the centuries...if only it had been different, if only this had happened or that hadn't happened? Does she want Ettie to intervene, change things, help her to make or stop events happening? Ettie knows what is to be...what must happen. Martha doesn't know these things, but she's afraid and maybe senses the future as Ettie senses the past. Somehow she's willed and enticed Ettie. It's not Thomas who knows her (didn't he look so blankly) but Martha. *I knew you'd be here.* Apprehensive about Grindcobb, Martha argues against the confidence of the others, as if she senses disaster to come. She mustn't be pressured. She must fight any attempt to influence the past. She cannot help Martha to stop the inevitable unfolding of events, however unpleasant that may be, however sympathetic she may be to her cause.

It's been a long evening. Ettie tires and joining Martha, she settles on the long form in the back room, pulls up the covering, falls into a deep asleep and dreams.

A man sits at a high table, flanked by clerks and soldiers. In front of him a large group of other well dressed men, headed by four squires. Some are armed. At the far side are three plainly dressed men, guarded by soldiers. One of the squires is talking to the man at the table and pointing to the men under guard.

"...and therefore we lay these charges before your lordship and demand justice in accordance with the full rigour of the law!"

One prisoner tries to speak, but a soldier restrains him. The squire repeats his demand.

"We have seen others dealt with. We require the same, *the full rigour of the law.*"

The man sitting in judgement is about to speak.

"Stop!" someone cries and the meeting is suddenly disrupted as another group bursts in from the back. One approaches the table.

"We have an urgent message for the squires...they must read this before you begin...listen to us...listen to us."

Then Ettie hears many voices and hundreds of feet running outside. She turns to look, the images fade, but she still hears the shouting and running. As she turns again she hits her head against the edge of the form and wakes.

She opens her eyes, looks up to the beams and then at the walls. No long table, no assembled men, but a small, sparse, empty room. She closes her eyes. Is this another dream or a vision as she tramps through the dew on the common? She opens her eyes again and looks down at her feet, protruding through the bottom of the blanket. No grass, no dew. Of course not, she's inside! She rubs her eyes and peers around with disbelief. This is no dream, no vision. Memories of yesterday stream into her mind. She must have fallen asleep wondering about her new old future and now a new day, a new month, 1ˢᵗ July 1381. She gets up and rubs her arms and legs, stiff from the night. In the other room she hears Martha's voice above the increasing dirdum from the street. There are two other women's voices. The three turn when she enters.

"I left you to sleep on," Martha says, "There's trouble everywhere. The town is alive with rumours and terrible tales. Thomas was out early when the first news came."

"News?"

"As I feared, we were surprised again. On Lee's orders Grindcobb and the others were taken early from the gatehouse gaol to Hertford."

"Ah...yes."

"You don't seem surprised."

"I...well...it's what you said. Three of them?"

"Yes."

"The men are holding meetings," one of the other women says, " they say they will kill a hundred of their enemies for every one of their neighbours killed."

"They are calling meetings in the fields and woods as well in the town," her companion says, "some want to attack the abbey and..."

The door is thrust open and Thomas enters.

"I must go to Hertford."

"Oh no, we are lost!" Martha says, putting her hands over her face and then going to him, "What can you do?"

"What I should have done last night and listened to you!"

"But that was last night, this morning..."

"...is different? No, no, all is the same. You were right."

"No, I was wrong. You couldn't have stopped it. No more than you can now. This is not Smithfield."

Mention of London pulls him up. He glances across to Ettie with that same look of puzzled recognition, then grabs his coat and goes to the door.

"The burgesses and other powerful men, squirming and creeping in support of the knight, have gone to Hertford, taking a host of armed yeomen along with those accursed squires. Dick says the abbey is undefended and we should attack or besiege it, even set it on fire!"

"No, no, no fighting!" Martha calls, grabbing his arm.

He puts his arm round her and strokes her hair.

"The abbot is scared. He's sent for Draycourt and other gentlemen of the district to protect the monastery."

"God preserve us!"

"Don't be afraid. The abbot has heard his wretched squires have overreached themselves. They are calling for our men to be put to death..."

"No!"

"...but he knows that has incited the town and county, so he's sent messengers with a letter commanding them to return with their captives."

"Then why must you go?"

"There are enough in town to keep the abbot on tenterhooks, but we can't trust those damned squires. We've mustered men to go to Hertford with the messengers and get our people released."

Then he's gone. Martha follows a few paces, tears in her eyes as she watches him strutting down the street, gathering reinforcements from the houses. She waits until he disappears and then, wiping her eyes, turns back to where Ettie stands in the doorway. She goes inside, takes her coat and returns to the street.

"Come, we must go."

"Where?"

"Thomas said some remain to keep the abbot on tenterhooks. I can't trust those men to do the job properly. They'll probably allow the old goat to slip away and gather his league of gentlemen! We'll have to get around and stiffen them up!"

She strides away. Ettie isn't fooled. Martha is frightened and can't remain helplessly in the house. Ettie catches up and they walk on together.

"I might go to my brother's place in Hempston," Martha says, "Though like most of the men in the country he's probably here."

So they spend the morning, witnessing, sometimes participating in the troubles and plots that break out all over St. Albans in meetings and assemblies, talking and arguing with the heady mixture of hope and anxiety. There are those who plan for better times, formulating how a new society might be organised, but most are apprehensive and nervous, knowing it's an uncertain future in which their enemies suddenly seem more powerful. Others still feel the absence of their leader like sheep without their shepherd, children without their teacher. By midday the excitement reaches fever pitch when the squires return from Hertford. Rumours and counter rumours rampage across the town. The squires bring back no prisoners and quickly disappear into the abbey. What has happened to Grindcobb and the others? Gradually people drift to the east end of town where, in the distance a group tramps along the Hertford road. The women are relieved to see all their men returning and in their midst Will Grindcobb, but not Cadindon or Barbintsor. Thomas and Martha embrace and now for the first time he acknowledges Ettie, asking if she'd 'escaped unharmed from Smithfield.'

"I got away," she says enigmatically, but there's no time for enquiry or explanation.

As he tells what happened in Hertford, Ettie listens with increasing uneasiness as images of her dream return.

"We arrived as the four squires, brazen and heartless, were setting out their accusations. *According to the law* they kept saying as if that had anything to do with justice. Some had been in Essex, one in Smithfield. They'd seen the execution of other prisoners and now demanded the same in this county. Walter at Lee sat silent at the high table, surrounded by yeomen and soldiers, with grim expression, hard mouth and cold eyes. It would be like pleading before a devil to extract mercy from such a man even without the denunciations of the odious squires.

'*We demand similar punishment.* The abbot's messengers stood motionless at the side of the room. We knew what was in the letters they carried.

"Stop!" I cried and pushed one of the messengers forward. Everyone turned. Now the messenger ran over, crying "We have an urgent message for the squires." The squires were surprised and on their guard. They could see us at the door and suspected a trick. The messenger reached them, shouting to the knight, "They must read this before you begin." He looked irritated and it seemed he might ignore the interruption.

"Listen to us!" one of our group cried and then again, "Listen to us!"

'One of the squires snatched the letter. The abbot knew. If our men were condemned to death it would unleash a whirlwind. He commanded the squires to return immediately with their prisoners. The squires were annoyed. One screwed up the letter, then thought better of it, smoothing it out before putting it in his pocket.

"We are commanded by the abbot to return," one said to the knight.

"For what reason?" Walter at Lee replied.

"We don't know the reason for the summons," another said, "We are compelled to leave before the conclusion of this business."

"If we'd known," another said, "We would have commenced earlier and seen these men executed already!"

'With that they apologised again to the knight and got ready to leave.

"What about the prisoners?" I cried, "they must be released."

'The squires ignored me and hurried away, jostling past us roughly. The knight was reluctant and maundered on about due processes and cases to be answered.

"You told us to give satisfaction to the abbot, whom you said was a very reasonable, just and holy man," I said, "So why won't you now accede to his wishes and release the prisoners?"

"I told you the king is carrying out trials of many men in Essex," he said, "and I have been entrusted with this commission on the king's behalf."

"Release the prisoners!" we shouted.

'The soldiers surrounded us, but we wouldn't move and shouted all the more seeing our three comrades standing there like common thieves. Some of the burgesses from the town grew restive.

'Sensing this, I said to them, "It goes ill for you all if we return alone."

"Can't we reach an agreement in the spirit of goodwill wherein you came here," one of the townsmen said to the knight, "that would be satisfactory to all."

'Then some of the men started shouting "Grindcobb! Grindcobb! Grindcobb!" It got louder and louder.

"Perhaps Will Grindcobb…" the burgess said.

'At which Walter at Lee stood up, raised his hands and shouted "Enough!"

'Our men stopped shouting.

"I am reluctant to release any prisoners," he said and our men began again, "However, maybe this man Grindcobb," then he turned to the burgesses, "Are you prepared to stand surety for him?"

'The burgesses said it was possible, but were shocked when the knight said he needed three hundred pounds. They shook their heads, but our mood was uglier now and we started shouting again.

"Alright, alright," three of them said, "We agree."

"On a pledge of three hundred pounds, I will hand over Will Grindcobb," Walter at Lee said, "He must be restored to prison next Saturday 6th July unless in the meantime an amicable agreement is reached with the abbot. Otherwise each of you will be liable for the whole sum."

'So now we have returned with Will."

"But what of Cadindon and Barbintsor?" Martha asks.

"They remain in prison in Hertford, but under no immediate threat."

Some townspeople are ready to celebrate. There's even talk of hunting down the squires and 'shaving their beards,' but the mood of most is restrained, even a little melancholy. Two men are still in prison and a heavy threat hangs over the third. A large group gathers around Grindcobb, but on the way from Hertford the three burgesses have been thinking over their commitment and are very nervous.

"How can we be sure of you?" one says to Grindcobb.

"I won't let you down," he says.

"We have no guarantee of that," a second says, "In these troubled times you might run away and then we'll be ruined."

Now the men around Grindcobb get angry, accusing the merchants of breaking their word.

"The knight said you should reach an agreement with the abbot," one says.

"The knight is intent on Will's death," Thomas says angrily.

"Precisely," the burgess says, "So either you give satisfaction to the abbot and return the charters or Grindcobb must return to Hertford for execution."

The whole crowd groans, but then falls silent.

"Well?" the merchant says, "What is your answer, what is it to be?"

No one speaks as the full implications of the ultimatum sink in.

"We will give our answer later," Thomas says.

"No, that's not good enough, we need your answer now or..."

A suppressed rumbling suffuses the crowd, but no one speaks. The merchants grow restless again and in the charged atmosphere are ready to go to the abbot and renounce their pledges. Sensing this some of the people mutter 'things have gone too far' and 'it's time to reach an accommodation to save Will.' It's a pivotal moment in which the breath of freedom is gasping for survival. Ettie looks around her. The 14th century street seems incredulously familiar. She struggles to orientate herself and though none of these building will survive into her own time she realises it's the precise location of the hall where the planning enquiry will be held.

Grindcobb looks from the merchants to his own comrades, studying their faces and reading their minds and hearts. He understands their anger and their fear. They are of him, in him. He is them and they are him. What he feels is as if he only exists because of them. Their spirit is his spirit and so with no independent existence his future merges completely in theirs. He gets up on a low wall. As he turns to speak there's complete silence.

"Men and women of St. Albans, my fellow citizens, whom a little liberty has now relieved from the long years of oppression, stand firm while you can and do not be afraid of my persecution and any punishment I may suffer. If I am to die in the cause of seeking liberty and hard fought freedom then I count myself happy to end my life such a martyr. Therefore, act now as you would have acted as if I had already been executed at Hertford. For nothing could have saved my life if the abbot had not called back his squires in time. They charged me with many offences and they had a judge favourable to their cause and eager to shed my blood."

8

IT'S difficult to know who is the more surprised by Rick Tranter's intervention, Monica or Maggie. As he pulls Monica away Maggie pushes through the guests and runs out the front entrance. Jennifer follows her. Monica sits on the terrace, quivering with shock and burbling with rage. A few concerned guests gather around, but Rick waves them aside.

"It's all over, please go and enjoy yourselves. Monica will be with you shortly."

"You should have let me get at her," Monica mumbles, "How did she get in, she doesn't normally look like that."

"That's how she got in."

"Where is she now?"

"She got away."

"Got away! She should be arrested!"

"On what charge, madam?"

Everyone has gone inside, except Jenner. Monica glares at him, her widening eyes getting larger as if about to swallow him up.

"Assault!" she shrieks and then subsides shaking.

"Don't upset yourself, "Rick says.

"Upset myself! Upset myself!"

"Seems to me the only one threatening assault was yourself," Jenner says.

"I didn't touch her, but by God I should have done. You heard what she said."

"I did indeed."

"Oh no, this is ridiculous, you don't seriously believe...I've already told you where I was the night Warren was killed. I was at a meeting of..."

"*Returning* from a meeting if I remember rightly...and alone."

"This is outrageous!"

"Calm down, Monica," Rick says.

"How can I calm down when the police are siding with that...that... lunatic. He's suggesting I had something to do with Warren's death."

"I'm not suggesting," Jenner says, "merely stating the facts."

"And you," she says, suddenly turning on Rick, "what are you doing defending that damned woman," then rubbing her shoulder, "pulling me away!"

"I only did it for your own good."

"My own good, more likely for hers!"

"Monica, I only..."

"You were very quick to intervene, a lightning reaction," Jenner says, "very protective to Miss Morton."

"What?" Monica splutters.

"No, no, not really...I wanted to avoid any... unpleasantness."

"Very commendable I'm sure."

In the car park Maggie is beginning to calm down, but she's not responding to questions. Jennifer tries again.

"Do you have any reason to substantiate your allegation?"

"Substantiate? No, not *substantiate*, but I *know*. She did it."

"Because of the Waintree development, something Warren knew."

She nods, but then shakes her head.

"Yes...no...yes and no. See, she did it, but not on her own. *They* were behind it."

"Who?"

"Them in the past. Could say she was driven. Course it suited her as well, what with her nefarious double dealing, but they were involved. I feel these things. I keep saying I feel things from the past, but nobody understands. You don't know what I mean."

But Jennifer too feels the presence of the past, though she can't be sure it's the same as Maggie. Someone is trying to get through. Perhaps she should probe Maggie's vibes, find a way through the denseness.

"Making a habit of getting men to come to your rescue!"

Jenner comes up.

"I don't get anybody to do anything," Maggie says, "I didn't know Tranter was going to stop me."

"More like he stopped Monica. You should be careful what you say. Accusing people of murder needs evidence, otherwise..."

"I'm never careful what I say."

"So I've noticed. At the enquiry..."

"You weren't there."

"I heard. Where was your friend George today? I would have thought this was just his sort of occasion."

She shrugs.

"Dunno, he don't tell me what he's gonna be doing. Buggered off as soon as we were out of the enquiry."

"Didn't he take you home?"

"Well yer, but then he buggered off."

"Don't suppose she's...? " he says to Jennifer, who shakes her head.

They take Maggie home and then return to the station. Jenner notices Jennifer's quietness.

"Something on your mind, sergeant?"

"I was wondering about Ettie. It's four days now."

This is only partly true. Her concern isn't just for Ettie's absence and she remains withdrawn. Noticing him looking at her she changes the subject.

"I've been checking the 1981 file on the disappearance of Melvyn Strange. No body was ever found. He was then seventeen. All his school friends and acquaintances were interviewed. One of the girls, Sarah, mentioned Melvyn had been seeing one of her friends called Katie, though she denied it."

"So that didn't lead anywhere – probably this Sarah was jealous or something."

"Not exactly. Sarah also mentioned another boy interested in Katie and said there'd been trouble between the two boys."

"Good God, sergeant, we're not interested in adolescent squabbles."

"Bear with me, sir, this other boy was Lawrence Bullock."

"And what about…what's her name, Katie, did she confirm this?"

"No and neither did Lawrence. Denied having anything to do with Katie. So at the time it was put down to…"

"Adolescent squabbles…this Katie, I don't suppose?"

"Long gone I'm afraid."

."But Lawrence Bullock is still around."

But unfortunately he's not at his house and as he drives to the studio Jenner curses himself for not pursuing the issue when he saw him earlier. Lawrence is evasive, if not deceitful on several fronts. Over twenty five years is a long time. If Melvyn was murdered the chances of finding a body are remote, even if they knew where to look. Yet the unfortunate business with the aptly named Strange and the odd goings on around the Waintree development both point towards Lawrence, who's reluctant to talk about either. Warren knew them both. He may have known something, covered it up, but threatened to reveal it later. Lawrence panics and…but why wait so long? It has to be him or Monica. One has to crack and say what they know.

Jennifer's ferreting is admirable, but her brooding worries him. She behaved oddly with Maggie and was vague when he asked what they talked about while he was with Monica. She keeps going on about the past. She's right to do so, but of twenty five years, not six hundred! It's Ettie's influence. Where is Ettie? As he goes through St. Albans he has the uncanny feeling she's close, almost expecting her to be walking along the street. He slows down. She might shout to him. She could be trying to communicate. Yet she can't. She's close, but not close enough.

When he asks at the studio for the set of *Hurling Time* he's directed to a different area. They must have made a mistake at the gate. The lighting is very dim, enough to make his way, but insufficient for filming. He looks up at the huge lamps, expecting them to be suddenly turned on and illuminate the place in an explosion of light. He wanders about, hoping he might find somebody, but the place is deserted. He sits in a chair beside the wall and stares disconsolately into the gloom. Lawrence isn't here and won't be coming. No one will. No wonder the gateman looked at him dubiously, but he'd insisted on being admitted. It's been a waste of time. He'll go back to the station or make another visit to Lawrence or Ettie's place again. Yet he can't get up. He'll leave in a moment after...he shuts his eyes...memories of the last time he was on a film set flicker. Then images of the investigation, places he's been, people he's seen, jumbled and jangling with that damned film. He opens his eyes. Nothing's changed, yet the images persist. Monica's house, the hotel, the old house that was demolished. He sees it coming down, vivid and immediate, even though he wasn't there. Then it appears again, different...newer, yes brighter, clearer as if it's not so old...but how can that be...newer when it was older because then it hadn't been so long built. He rubs his eyes. It goes. Yet it comes again, quicker, fleeting, days and nights jabbing uncontrollably, time running past him very fast. He looks round. Nothing is happening, nothing is moving, yet still he feels as if on a merry go round, everything rushing past like a flickering film at the wrong speed, going faster, faster, faster...It goes, the movement subsides, though nothing has changed. He shakes himself and gets up to go. Some lights come on. He hears voices. Charley arrives with a few others, starting suddenly as she sees him.

"Mr. Jenner!"

"I'm sorry if I shocked you, Miss Kennet, I'm looking for Mr. Bullock."

"He's not here."

"Do you expect him?"

"I...I'm not sure."

"Are you going to shoot a scene, rehearse perhaps?"

"We...there's nothing scheduled..."

"Of course with Mr. Pleasant away."

"...but we...that is I...felt...compelled, drawn to come in...I rang the others and...they felt the same."

"But you didn't ring Mr. Bullock?"

"I couldn't get an answer."

"Drawn you say?"

"Yes, I don't expect you to understand."

"Try me."

"There's a scene...I was talking to Dr. Tennant and also to your sergeant..."

"Yes she told me."

"Even though Chris didn't really approve..."

"You've heard nothing from him, I take it?"

"No, about this scene..."

"And your colleagues, have they heard from him?"

"No, no they've not, you could ask them."

He goes over and corrals the others. They have no knowledge of Chris Pleasant's whereabouts, nor can they offer any explanation for why he should have taken off in the first place. Charley watches with mounting irritation. She didn't really expect him to actually talk to everybody. It's disrupting her plans and she gets impatient.

"Have you finished? I'd like to carry on."

Jenner waves his arm and the group reassembles.

"I'm sorry, Miss Kennet, but you did say..."

"Yes, but this scene...you see I'm afraid if we don't start soon it'll...I'll lose...it's as if someone's telling me and if I wait too long I'll lose it...I'm sorry this must seem..."

"Why is it so important?"

"It must be filmed, it's an extirpation, a release. I feel so much pain. Maybe filming may erase the pain from collective memories..."

"Perhaps even erase the event itself," Jenner jokes.

"How can you say that? That would be...erasing...the past, stopping what's already happened...or is about to happen."

"But isn't that going way beyond making a film? Placating the past?"

He's only playing, but his words run away. Just as time was running away and as he speaks he loses control. He knows she's getting upset, but can't stop.

"It's not about placating, it's about truth!" she says vehemently.

"Yes, alright.".

"We have to go ahead with the rehanging scene."

"Not if I have anything to do with it!"

Everyone turns. Chris Pleasant is standing behind them.

In the first week of July 1381 St. Albans continues to heave and bubble like a simmering volcano, ready to erupt and explode, threatening to destroy all around it. The abbot in his monastery and the lords on their country manors watch and wait apprehensively, but also with growing confidence. Time is with them. The king has sent messengers to all parts of the south country urging the capture and punishment of 'malefactors.' Walworth, the mayor of London, acting on the king's commission is trying rebels just two days after the defeat at Smithfield and rumours are spreading, as Walter at Lee intimated of the vast army attacking the movement in Essex. As with all such stories, the numbers of soldiers vary. Some say the king has five thousand, some ten thousand, a few twenty thousand, one man even says forty thousand! Martha's mood veers around with the stories. One morning she's depressed. The world is coming to an end just as her grandmother predicted during the great pestilence over thirty years ago. By the afternoon she's recovered. The authorities are putting out these exaggerated tales to terrorise and cower them into submission. The next day some fresh rumour sends her down again, only to come up when she's had time to pick over its absurdity.

A week, is it really that long? Ettie stays with Martha. Her mood also swings violently, frequently despondent, occasionally a resigned placidity, but always restless. She's unsure of Martha. Though Ettie doesn't challenge and Martha says nothing directly, she must be the woman who spoke to her on the common and in the tower. With each passing day she expects her to make a move, force her demands. Each morning Ettie wakes hoping, expecting...she'll be at the cottage with the sun streaming from the common...but it's the bare walls and the beamed ceiling of the back room. Each night she concentrates so hard her head feels it might crack open. So close to the cottage and yet so far in time...if only she can reconnect, find what brought her here and make it happen again...but it doesn't come. Something is missing, something not happening in that other time just as it did happen in this time to shift her so suddenly.

They see little of Thomas during the day as he flits between meetings, only increasing Martha's anxiety.

"He's still covering up what he really feels."

Afraid she'll be drawn into a discussion about the immediate future and forced to reveal herself, Ettie tries not to comment, but this becomes increasingly difficult as more and more disturbing news piles up. Jack Straw, John Kirkby and Alan Threder, leaders in Essex have been executed. The Norfolk rebels under Geoffrey Litster are routed at North Walsham by the forces of the Bishop of Peterborough. Then, even worse the Essex rebels are defeated at Billericay on 28th June. By Wednesday morning Martha is very nervous. Thomas has been out since very early.

"Running about stirring things up," she says, "but running around makes him conspicuous. If the king comes those that watch him now will remember and he'll be fingered," then looking with reproving and appealing eyes to Ettie, "*If* the king moves against us."

Ettie resists the implied question, but Martha's continuing stare is intimidating. Should she tell Martha of the voices that come to her – hers and her husband's? Maybe there's the making of an agreement between them. If she tells Martha a little of the future, will Martha tell what she and Thomas want of her? Do they know about the common and the tower, or are those disembodied voices as mysterious to them as they are to Ettie? No. Deals can't be done with the past. It's too dangerous. She can't dribble out bits of their futures like crumbs from the table. Play the past that way it becomes uncontrollable. Besides Martha doesn't just want to *know*, she wants to *change*.

"What do you think?" Martha says.

"I think Thomas should be careful," Ettie says, "he could be..."

"I don't mean about Thomas, least not him alone. I mean everything, everyone, what's to become of us?"

Ettie won't get away with a denial. Whatever Martha doesn't know, she does know Ettie knows. She keeps staring with taught determination, demanding to be answered. Is this the crunch point, must there be an exchange? She starts to work out a limited response, a best formulation, when a sharp rap at the door distracts Martha and gives Ettie a welcome reprieve. It's one of Martha's neighbours.

"Will's brother has left for Essex," the woman says.

"Dick Grindcobb? Why, we need him here?" Martha says tetchily.

"He goes to the king to plead for his brother."

"Then it really is worse than I'd hoped. What does Will say?"

"Nothing. He neither encourages nor discourages Dick. 'Where I go I am meant to be,' he says."

"Does Thomas know?"

"It was him told me?"

"Doesn't he come home?"

"He stays at the meeting."

The woman goes, spreading the news into further streets.

Martha is silent for a while and then says, "I won't stay in this town tonight. Come, we will go to my brother's in Hempston."

"But you said he would be here."

"No matter, Joan will be there. Come, we go."

Joan. As Martha busies herself preparing for the journey, the name reverberates with Ettie, conjoining with the news of the king in Essex and of Grindcobb's brother going there. This has to be another Joan, not the Joan with Alan, the couple from Essex she met in London, enmeshed together with her and Thomas with so many others that night before Smithfield. Essex...Joan...Alan...Thomas...the night before...

"Are you ready?"

Martha is at the door with a pack around her shoulder and another at the floor for Ettie.

"Will we be gone long?" Ettie asks.

"As long as needs..." Martha says, then as she opens the door, "but not later than Saturday before Will returns."

They see Thomas in the town, engrossed in quiet, but intense discussion. At first he takes little notice until Martha shouts 'I'm going' and he steps away from his companions.

"To Hempston, to Paul's."

"But Paul is here."

"But Joan is not."

Then she leaves, promising to return before Saturday. He stands forlorn, watching her go, but understands and returns as the others recall him to the debate. Ettie and Martha tramp most of the afternoon, taking frequent rests under the trees. Ettie is unused to such walking, but manages to keep up with Martha, for whom such journeys are not unusual. Many are on the move to St. Albans from the villages, anxious to hear the latest. Have the hard won charters been returned, have our people yielded to the abbot? When told the people are wavering, they nod their heads in silent acceptance, but their eyes light up again when told the charters remain in their hands. They pause on the ridge halfway between St. Albans and Hempston and Ettie looks across the valley to the north west.

"You can't see the village from here," Martha says, "and the people will come by a different road."

"What village?" Ettie says.

"Welstead."

So close? Ettie sits on the other side of the tree and stares into the distance, concentrating, willing...there has to be a way...if she can summon enough strength she can get back. In her own time they must hear her, feel her, if only she can...

"Come, we must go," Martha calls, "We've rested enough."

They reach Hempston in the late afternoon and Martha slows as they pass the houses. Too late before she realises, Ettie walks on ahead and instinctively stops at Martha's brother's house. She stares in amazement at the door as Martha comes up. This is the house destroyed by the Waintree developers.

"You know this place?" Martha says.

Ettie turns to her.

"Know it...no...no, I thought it must be...it's almost the last house."

Martha stares with the same accusatory understanding, but says nothing. For an instant Ettie feels back in her own time, desperate to speak to someone, but it passes. She has to look away.

"Martha."

A woman about Martha's age stands at the opened door. Ettie is introduced as a 'friend from Middlesex' and they go in. Martha and Joan have not seen each other for several weeks and there's much to talk about. Martha describes the fluctuating fortunes of the people and her fears for the future. Joan is pleased to see her, but wonders why she left the town, fearing for the safety of her husband.

"Paul is well," Martha says, "Thomas told me. He will be back with you soon."

"If he keeps out of trouble."

"He will, I know my brother."

"At least in town you have Thomas."

"Out all day arguing, plotting, conspiring, for what purpose? He can't keep away from the heart of the action. He's been much troubled since he came back from London."

"Will Grindcobb and the others will be safe," Joan says reassuringly, "these threats by the squires, it's only talk."

Martha shakes her head. Joan is either naïve or in denial. Martha is neither.

"It's serious. Thomas was lucky to get out of London when he did. Five days after Smithfield some of our men remaining in London were recognised by Richard Perrers, one of the abbot's squires. He had them arrested and dragged off to prison, intending to get them executed the next day. They got a message back to St. Albans and our people approached the abbot demanding their release."

"This can't be so," Joan says, very shocked.

Martha looks to Ettie saying, "You were in London, isn't this so?"

Ettie is perplexed. She wasn't in London after 15th June, but she nods and grunts "Yes, you're right."

"What happened?" Joan says.

"Next day, 21st June was the feast of St. Alban. The abbot sent a monk to London to get them released."

"So this is not the first time these squires have acted on their own."

Martha smirks.

"If you believe the squires really act on their own authority."

"But then the abbot got the men released, as at Hertford?"

"Didn't he so, the same pattern of events?"

"Are you saying the abbot was behind the squires all along?"

Martha shrugs and rolls her eyes in mock innocence.

"I only say it might suit the abbot to get rid of those who consistently oppose him. Will Grindcobb's been a thorn in his side for years."

"No wonder you fear for Thomas."

Martha's eyes dull and her mouth sets firm. She glances to Ettie. Is she silently asking her to intervene to secure Thomas's future? The talk moves onto other events, less close, less personal. Ettie listens, hoping she'll not be asked to comment and Martha and Joan get more engrossed, hardly noticing her. So passes the evening until tiredness overwhelms Ettie and she retires to a bed at the rear of the house. In the morning she wakes to find the indefatigable Martha already up and ready to leave, her misgivings about staying in St. Albans seemingly blown away in the night. She and Joan exchange goods and then they're away to Joan's cries of 'get that brother of yours back here soon.' By late morning they're back in town and home where Thomas is waiting. Now at last he speaks to Ettie.

Jenner waits for the fierce row between Charley and Chris to blow itself out. It takes some time. He finds most of it utterly meaningless, only increasing his frustration at being unable to talk to Chris. Two words persistently monopolise what little of the conversation he understands – rehanging and authenticity – Charley's obsession with the 'rehanging' scenes contrasting with Chris's equally violent opposition. He keeps repeating 'it's not relevant' while she says 'without it nothing else is.' As they reach deadlock, Jenner's ready to intervene, but then Charley opens up her second front, lambasting him because he's not been 'authentic.'

"It's a movie, not a treatise," he shouts.

"That doesn't mean it can't be true."

"Within reason, we should..."

"No, not within reason or within anything else, it's got to be as it was!"

"How can we be sure what's *authentic* after six hundred years? Even if the accounts are based on those that were really there, memories fade, witnesses get things confused."

Jenner can sympathise with this sentiment. It doesn't need six hundred years. Witnesses get things wrong after six days, even six hours.

"We know enough – you just want to leave out these important events."

So it goes on. Jenner turns away. They are preparing for another scene, the arrival of the king into St. Albans on 12th July 1381. Jenner has a faint recollection the scene has been shot before. Perhaps it was unsatisfactory. These film people never seem to be satisfied. An actor with a handkerchief hanging out of his pocket, one of the extras shuffling when he shouldn't have done or someone has a pained expression and the director shouts 'Cut!' Jenner wouldn't be surprised by a pained expression. They've probably been standing around for hours. He knows how they feel. There's an odd atmosphere in the studio, a lot of activity, much movement and apparent action, yet none of it very effective. He's reminded of the office juniors with not enough to do. Wandering around with a piece of paper, always on the way to somewhere else in case they're asked what they're doing. Except here they're all office juniors, all seemingly on the move, doing nothing. Now Chris is waving the script at Charley.

"*You've* not produced anything authentic for some time! This stuff is almost identical with Warren Grover's book. You might as well have got him to write the damn thing!"

"We can hardly do that can we?" she says.

Chris grimaces, puts the script down and glances shiftily at the detective. Charley walks away and Chris is ready to follow, but this is Jenner's chance and he bars his way.

"Mind now telling me exactly where you've been Mr. Pleasant?"

"Yes I do mind. I've enough problems as it is. What business is it of yours?"

Jenner looks at him stiffly.

"I need hardly remind you..."

"Yes, yes, alright, I just had to get away."

"Without telling anybody?"

"You've seen how it is, how could I tell anybody here. They were part of the problem."

"Problem?"

"This place, the film, the set, the cast, couldn't take it anymore, had to get away."

"A breakdown?"

"Thank you, chief inspector for being so understanding."

"And now you're alright?"

Chris looks at him and shakes his head.

"As alright as I'm ever likely to be with a cast who won't play the parts they're supposed to be playing, preferring to be guided by a writer who insists on scenes set out by a dead man. Yes I'm alright."

"It's about that dead man..."

"I didn't mean it like that."

"Even so, would you tell me where you've been?"

"I was away, alright? I had to get away, where I went isn't important."

"Let me be the judge of that."

"I was with a friend."

"Called?"

"John Butler."

"And where does this John Butler live?"

"Does it really matter?"

Jenner sighs.

"Okay, okay, Essex."

Jenner sighs again.

"I'll give you the address. It's near Chelmsford, but I still can't see the need. I told you before I had nothing whatsoever to do with Warren Grover."

"That's not quite true, is it?"

"Yes, as I said I've had no contact."

"But you knew him, didn't you?"

"I'd heard of him."

"Bit more than that. You were at school together."

"Have you heard of Robert Tresilian?" Thomas says.

What does Ettie say? How does she answer without divulging how she knows?

"I've heard the name, but I'm not sure what..."

"An accursed lawyer. He's been appointed chief justice and instructed by the king to enforce their so called *justice* here and in Essex."

"That's not good news," Ettie says.

"So you do know him?"

"No... no... I mean appointing anyone to such a position in these difficult times...it's not good news."

"No, it's not."

Ettie glances at Martha, who returns with her knowing, unspoken questioning.

"That slug Walworth, the mayor of London and his lawyers," Thomas continues, "arresting and charging honest folk. They swear twelve jurors to indict them. I hear they've even accused one man of being a spy in the pay of the French. What wild invention!"

Thomas goes out, only to return with more bad news. That same Thursday afternoon Dick, Grindcobb's brother returns from Chelmsford where he'd tried to see the king to plead for Will. There he heard the earl of Warwick and Sir Thomas Percy were coming to St. Albans with a thousand armed men to support the abbot and put many of the rebels on trial. Thomas and some companions meet that night, endlessly discussing their options until exhaustion finally overcomes them.

Friday 5th July is bright and warm. A larger meeting is arranged in the centre of town. Thomas is eager to attend and is full of energy despite having had at most only a couple of hours sleep. He waits at the door and beckons to Martha.

"You must come too, this conference must include everyone."

"It's not for me," she says.

"If you are affected, which you will be, then it's for you."

He stands waiting. Still she hesitates, looking again to Ettie, who knows her reluctance is not false modesty, but deep apprehension for the future.

"If we make the wrong decision...?" she says.

"All the more reason for you to be there."

She steps over to the door. Ettie hangs back.

"You too," Thomas says, "Everyone."

The meeting is long and rambling, issues tossed back and forth, the peoples' hearts and minds veering between confidence and fear.

"If we return the charters we are lost," Thomas says.

"If we don't return the charters we are lost anyway," his old friend Ned says, "we have to be realistic."

So the argument ensues, hour after hour. Are the stories true? Is a great army really coming to St. Albans to vanquish them? They look to Will Grindcobb.

"It may be my brother was deliberately told this story to frighten us into submission," he says, "We should ignore it and proceed as we always intended, as if he'd never heard it."

"But if it's true?" Ned says.

"If it's true there could be much slaughter. The charters guarantee our freedom. Possession of them ignites the fires of liberty. My hands would not grasp, my feet would not move if it meant returning them to the abbey, but I could not advise against it if their possession meant further destruction."

"But the charters are our protection," Abel says, "they will also protect you. Without them they'll take you back to Hertford."

"Don't trouble yourselves on my account. They will take me back to Hertford anyway. Last night I dreamed. There was a door. I knocked on it, knowing death was beyond. The door opened. I looked through and saw death. I fear it no longer. I have been there. I will open the door myself and go in. I'll not let them open it for me and thrust me through."

"No! No!" everyone cries.

Grindcobb raises his hand.

"Friends, I cannot advise a course which may lead to greater suffering."

"We will wait to see if the soldiers come," Abel says.

"If we wait till the soldiers come, there'll be nothing to wait for." Ned says.

The discussion goes on into the afternoon and early evening, but those for returning the charters and those for retaining them are evenly divided. One of the staunchest advocating they stand firm is Thomas.

"I'll not be a coward in the face of Will Grindcobb's courage. If he's unafraid of the outcome, then so am I."

"But he fears for us all," Martha says, "He said he couldn't advise a course..."

"We don't need to take his advice," Thomas snaps.

The others are silent. Grindcobb is not present. Realising he's unwisely spoken in haste Thomas tries to explain.

"I meant no disrespect...indeed we should be inspired and follow his lead."

"He'll not lead us into destruction," Ned says.

"I'll not let..."

Martha, who up to this time has taken little part in the discussions, flings herself at his feet. He tries to lift her from the ground, but she pulls at his legs and refuses to budge.

"Please, please, Thomas, you can't fight anymore. There must be an accommodation with the abbot or we are all destroyed."

Thomas lifts her up, sobbing into him.

"Very well. The charters will be returned."

It's enough. Many waverers follow Thomas, but they resolve to take no action until the next day. Thomas walks home with Martha and Ettie, accepting, but sullenly angry and very low. When they retire and leave her alone, Ettie ventures into the street. The moon casts a thin blade of light over the houses, leaving a narrow space between the shadows. She walks a short way, but stops at the corner. To go further could be dangerous. She doesn't want to explain herself especially to the Watch or desperate, ruthless men on either side. The town murmurs with distant dull drones of the day's deliberations. Knowing the immediate future makes her fearful and she identifies with the people's anxieties as if they really do affect her. But if she stays, it *will* affect her and she'll be unable to escape it.

She recognises the street names. So close in space, but not in time. If she'd had more time on the ridge she might have made the contact. It's quieter now. She closes her eyes and concentrates. After a few moments she senses a connection as if many people are trying to find her. She opens her eyes. The street is deserted. She closes her eyes again and the feeling returns. Then she hears footsteps. Someone is close. She opens her eyes. Two men stand at the corner, leering at her. These are not the ones with which she wants to make contact! They walk towards her. She turns quickly and runs back to the house, full of deepening presentiments, not just of the immediate future, but for those around her. Does Martha sense what is to come and craves Ettie's help to forestall what she dreads? She has to get back and soon! At the house she lies down but it's a long time before she sleeps, finally wearied of trying to find her escape route.

News of Will Grindcobb's return to Hertford, early on Saturday morning, while not surprising, still shocks. Nervous of their own positions and anxious to redeem their pledges, those that stood surety for him the previous Monday are quick to get him back in the early light. There he will remain until his trial. The day passes quietly, a subdued acquiescence permeating the whole town. Thomas remains in deep depression, muttering how he feels a betrayer and fearing the imminent arrival of the earl of Warwick. Martha confides her fears to Ettie.

"His spirits are not lifting. His mood deepens. On his shoulders he takes on the trials of others."

"I thought that was what Will Grindcobb is doing," Ettie says.

"Yes and Thomas would do the same if I didn't..."

With that Thomas comes into the room, morose and downcast. Martha breaks off immediately and turns to him.

"You've not eaten. You need to eat."

"I need to feel I have not been the betrayer. In the meantime I need fresh air."

"You've never betrayed anyone in your life."

"More reason not to do so now. I'm going out."

As he opens the door Martha looks to Ettie with that imploring, accusing stare she cannot bear. Ettie also moves to the door.

"I could do with a walk myself," she says, "may I join you, Thomas?"

Two days ago Ettie wouldn't have dared do this, but if she's to get away to her own time, she must tie up unresolved issues. There are still difficult questions he may put to her, but her nervousness with Martha increases and she's delayed facing him for too long. Before Martha can object she's out the door. Thomas walks quickly. Catching him up she makes an uncompromising frontal attack.

"You're still troubled by what happened in London?"

"I ran away in London," he says, stepping even quicker.

"What would have been gained by staying?"

He stops and turns to her.

"I would have seen it through to the end."

"To fight and be killed?"

"Maybe."

"And then where would your comrades be here?"

He walks on, confused and disturbed, contradictory passions hurtling through him with increasing intensity.

"You sound like Martha."

"She's very afraid for you."

"I'm afraid for myself...and her...for everybody...what about you?"

"What about me?"

"How will you get home?"

"Home...why..."

"Where is it you said you were from?"

"Oh...anywhere in England now...in London you talked of two Englands..."

He looks at her sceptically. It was a foolish thing to say, clearly an attempt to cover up where she's really from.

He'll challenge her, refuse to be sidetracked, question her integrity, even accuse her of being a spy of the authorities, ask her to leave the house...then his expression changes. He'll not challenge her.

"Through long ages the people sleep and it appears our England is dead or never was...but when the people awake then that second England reappears."

"Then don't be disheartened. If you still believe..."

"Of course I believe!" he shouts angrily.

She steps back, a little afraid. He apologises.

"It's not just believing. We know what we want, but how best to achieve it? At the outset our enemies were clear. Destroy or neutralise them and all will be well. It seemed that way in London. That night before Smithfield when we last spoke...then we were sure, but now...with so much gone wrong, what's best to be done? Looking back...so many things we ought to have done differently, so many things we ought not have done at all. If only we could change the past... (he looks at her questioningly)...or determine the future..."

He pauses. Is he like Martha, wanting her to stop the future she knows must be? He continues.

"I spoke to Will Grindcobb last night.

'I have made mistakes,' he said.

'We all have,' I said, 'We've been too lenient with our enemies. We were foolish to trust the knight. We could have taken Walter at Lee when the men of Barnet came with their archers, when we had the chance, when he first appeared outside the town. He acted so arrogantly towards the town and its people. We should have stuck his head on the pillory. That would have terrified all the judges and false justices throughout the land. That would have sent a message they'd understand.'"

Ettie shudders at the passion in his voice as he reaches a final crescendo of rage.

"What did Grindcobb say?"

"Nothing at first. He seemed resigned. You know, last year both his best friend and his wife died.

'I go to them,' he said and then, 'but I regret now not allowing the people of the town to act more ruthlessly when they were at their strongest.'"

'And now he's back in Hertford and I can think only of what should have been and what I might have prevented."

"Whatever happens, good, bad, wisely or unwisely, you're not solely responsible. You can't take everyone's liability on your own shoulders."

"Why not? Grindcobb assumes all our fates within himself. I wish I had his courage."

"Surely it's not about courage."

"What then?"

"Forces beyond your control."

"Then there's nothing we can do."

Seeing his sudden, grim, hopeless expression, the down curling mouth and sad eyes, Ettie immediately regrets this.

"I only meant...if the earl of Warwick's soldiers come..."

He's not placated and walks on. She follows in silence for some time and then says, "It will come, believe me."

"What will come?"

"The other England, *your* England."

Thomas goes to the house of his friend Abel. Ettie passes an hour wandering around the vibrant town, listening to the debates, trying not to get involved. She now knows it very well with certain landmarks impressed on her – the place of the debates coinciding with the development enquiry in her own time, the Moot Hall and the street where in twenty years to come the curfew tower will rise. The bubbling, fermenting town, alive with oscillating confidence and anxiety, its people veering between wild shouting and a withdrawn, uneasy sullenness. It oppresses her. In the enclosing streets the overhanging buildings bear down as if they might scoop her up! If only they could and thrust her back home! Fearing now both Martha and Thomas she must escape as soon as an opportunity arises, but how?

In the afternoon a meeting is held at the abbey. The abbot doesn't see them, but sends representatives. The townsmen return a little confused and another fiery meeting is held with the people. Ettie and Martha stand at the edge, listening to the discussion. 'Compensation' and 'recompense' and 'conciliatory gesture' are mentioned. Thomas takes no active part, but at the conclusion he's appointed to join the small band deputed to meet the abbot that evening. This he does, trudging disconsolately with his colleagues towards the abbey. Ettie and Martha go back to the house.

Despite them sending messages, the abbot doesn't appear, sending instead his brother, William Killingworth, prior of Wymondham to receive them. Annoyed at the abbot's absence, Thomas, asks why the abbot won't see them.

"I am here as his representative," is William's non-answer.

Thomas challenges William, but the others restrain him. With the impending arrival of the earl they're not in a strong position and now isn't the right time to argue. They present a book containing a record of old court pleas held between the abbey and the people. William takes it, but refuses to take back the charters and the two hundred pounds they offer in compensation for all 'the troubles.' Thomas hadn't been happy for them to make such an offer, but accepted it as a possible guarantee of closure. Now his suspicions return and the others feel the same. The charters are being returned in good faith together with a reasonable recompense for any ill feeling. If the abbot accepted them how could he later plead for action by the king?

"It's a ruse," Thomas says, "I don't like it."

"The abbot will see you at prime in the morning," William says.

Thomas is still unimpressed.

"More playing for time," he says to others as they leave.

Thomas returns just after nine and goes to bed tired and dispirited, but early on the Sunday morning before they are due to go back to the abbey there's a dramatic change of fortune. The revolt has spread well beyond the south east and the earl of Warwick, commissioned to arrest and punish rebels in Hertfordshire now hears of trouble in his own domains and is forced to return to Warwickshire. Knights arrive at the abbey advising of the delay.

"Don't be downhearted," they tell the abbot.

But the news quickly spreads around the town and Thomas' friends Ned and Abel are soon at the house.

"There's nothing to worry about," Ned says, "the earl's not coming!"

"He's only delayed," Thomas says doubtfully.

"But for how long and will he come at all with our comrades in Warwick to keep him busy?"

"I hear it's a hotbed up there," Abel says, "they say John Ball fled that way."

"Why were we so afraid?" Ned says, "We must have been fools to believe in such an army, put together at the abbot's request."

"We'll still have to return the charters," Thomas says.

"Not necessarily. The earl may never come."

"It's all lies," Abel says, "and we were fools to believe them!"

Thomas isn't so sure. Not because he has any better view of the abbot's integrity, but the last week has sapped his energy and memories of Smithfield are too recent to be discounted. This surprises and disappoints his friends.

"A week ago you were so excited and confident," Ned says, "now you seem hesitant and defensive."

Ned is right. While Thomas' conviction is as strong, if not stronger, it's now tempered with a pessimism he finds difficult to shake off. He's picked up Martha's cautiousness. Already their fortunes have been too buffeted around and he's less willing to jump at the first piece of contrary news, knowing in a few hours it may change again. But in his scepticism he's virtually alone. The proposed meeting with the abbot goes by and no one shows. Instead groups gather saying how wrong they've been to be taken in.

"We stupidly believed just as we stupidly served."

"Never offer money again or return the charters."

"Returning the charters will set a dangerous precedent."

"If the charters have to be returned let the abbot ask for them. He didn't want them back last night!"

"Don't be timid, brothers and sisters. Taking back the charters would be dishonourable."

Thomas, Martha and Ettie listen at the edge of these meetings. Martha hopes they're right to celebrate, but Thomas's mood troubles her.

"If only Grindocbb was here," he says, "He'd know what to do, he'd advise us. I can't help feeling this boldness is too late. Will said he regretted not letting the people loose earlier. Then we had the initiative. Then was the time to set their precedent – making the abbot, the lords, the lawyers and the king listen to us and take heed. We should have sliced the snakes in the grass when we had time, not let them get away and multiply!"

Chris is shouting at everybody, but the more he shouts the less effect it has. Having temporarily lost the fight to get the scene she wants included, Charley has wandered off to sulk. Though truculent, Chris appears in control as he barks his instructions and admonitions.

"Can't anybody get in the right place! It's surely not that difficult to line up. You're the king's party, the king's soldiers. You're entering a town for God's sake, to be met by the abbot, not slithering around like a Friday night boozing party in a bear garden!"

Jenner watches, not fooled by Chris's blustering aggression. Inside the man is quivering, taking out his trembling frustration on the others. Eventually he'd admitted knowing Warren at school, though 'not well.'

"If you don't know someone, there's not much you can disagree about, can you?"

"What about Melvyn Strange?" Jenner said.

"Didn't know him either."

"You must have been upset by his disappearance?"

"Why should I be, people go missing all the time."

"So I've noticed."

"Odd business, but there it is, these things happen."

"No talk at the time about why he might have gone?"

"Not that I recall – it's a long time ago."

"Quite so, but things like that when you're young, they're not easily forgotten. Problem with girls for instance?"

"No more than normal so far as I know. Look, what has this got to do with Warren Grover?"

"That remains to be seen."

Chris is pushing and shoving the cast into position.

"Can you try not to look so dishevelled? Jeremy, for God's sake stand still while they're getting behind you! You are the king, not a bloody sergeant major!"

Lawrence Bullock isn't here and for now Jenner's got as much out of Chris as he's likely to get. Yet he stays. It may be chaotic, but chaos like jest sometimes reveals hidden gems. Besides that earlier uncanny inability to move has returned. If only Ettie was here, she might have some ideas...where is she? Despite Chris's drilling and dragooning, the actors and extras are unable to keep in an orderly line. They keep drifting off and reforming other 'unofficial' groups as if they're looking for something or someone. Charley, recovering a little from her sulk comes up beside Jenner.

"Aren't you needed?" he says.

"It's his scene, I've done my bit, let him get on with it."

They sit silently watching the mayhem for a few moments. Then Charley shivers, though with all the bright lights it's far from cold. She keeps shivering and pulls her arms around her shoulders.

"Something wrong?" Jenner says.

"Nothing...it's just...don't you feel it...there must be a door open somewhere."

Jenner looks around. There's nothing to see.

"Oh no," Charley says, standing up, looking round anxiously and then putting her hands over her ears.

"Stop! Stop!"

"What is it?"

She calms, puts her hands down and shakes her head.

"Nothing, it's just...no...it was as if someone was talking to me...I'm alright, take no notice."

She sits down. Jenner looks around again, but there's no one near them. She glances at him nervously and then at the others. Now she's mentioned it, he too can't settle and keeps scanning around furtively and listening, trying to hear something, anything beyond the din of the studio.

"Come on, come on, get in line!"

Chris gets angrier as his frustration mounts. Rather than a disciplined line of soldiers, the extras are straggling and snaking around like an unruly queue at a pop concert.

"There's no point," Jeremy Lowther says with uncharacteristic assertiveness, "getting everybody lined up, all this pomp and formality, the king entering the town..."

"Exactly, Jeremy, got it in one, but nobody is..."

"But what's the point of the king coming into the town if there's nobody to meet him?"

"What do you mean?"

"The abbot, he's not here, where is Lawrence?"

Concentrating so intensely on the king's party, Chris hasn't bothered with the group at the other end of the studio. Now he strides over.

"Lawrence, show yourself! Jeremy can't see you!"

No one replies. Chris pushes into the gaggle of 'monks,' calling 'Lawrence, where is Lawrence?' There's much shaking of heads as he pushes on until he reaches the back of the group. Then he returns, stamps his feet and lifts his arms high.

"Where is Lawrence? Where the hell is Lawrence?"

Thomas returns home, weighed down with foreboding, for the rest of the day. So begin the five long days to Friday 12th July, as Thomas feared dominated by conflicting rumours, bold assertions and violently swinging events. Martha urges caution at every turn, though she's more fearful for Thomas than the general safety. She watches the developing situation with her own particular worries. Each day she gets more desperate. Any sudden change might present an opportunity for escape so she hovers around every meeting, listening to every discussion, trying to be in every place.

On Monday the abbot sends messages asking why the charters haven't been returned and saying the abbey is suffering now the customary duties have ceased. The crowd laughs and shouts at the clerks and abbey servants.

"The abbot won't go short. Tell him to salt the meat of the animals he's slaughtered to prevent it going bad. Tell him to sell the beer he's brewed to prevent it turning sour. Tell him to sell the loaves he's baked to prevent them becoming hard or mouldy or being eaten by mice!"

With increasing confidence the people are further emboldened and the taunting of abbey servants continues on Tuesday.

"Nothing good will come of this," Martha grumbles.

That afternoon some fool even insults one of the abbey squires, one of those who tried to get Grindcobb and the others condemned at Hertford.

"How stupid," Thomas says when he hears, "It's a bad move."

That evening, it's rumoured the same squire has gone to the king to complain and sure enough on Wednesday morning messengers from the abbey interrupt a meeting in town.

"The king is very angry. He wants to know why the charters have not been returned."

The debate erupts again and different answers are proposed to this difficult question. The hardliners are unmoved. This is yet another manoeuvre by the abbot. Ignore it and don't return the charters. A larger group is rattled. The charters should be returned immediately in the hope it will placate both the abbot and the king. The discussion goes on into the evening, neither side willing to give way. Then Thomas puts forward a compromise proposal.

"If we return the charters we should try to retrieve some of our former strength."

"That's impossible," he's told, "We can't go back. A week ago..."

"A week ago we gained our breath of freedom as Will Grindcobb told us. Now we're going even further back to the days of oppression. The least we can do is to free our comrades. We make it a condition of returning the charters that Grindcobb, Cadindon and Barbintsor are freed."

"That's outside the abbot's control."

"But not outside the king's."

"We can't dictate to the king!"

"Why not, isn't that what all this has been about or have you learnt nothing?"

To frightened people Thomas' suggestion is even more fearful, but the debate grinds on. He's sowed the seed and it germinates, but not in the way he expects or desires. Instead they return to the hardliners and resolve not to return the charters at all. Thomas has mixed feelings. Martha groans.

"This is folly," she says and turns to Ettie, "Is there any way this can be avoided?"

Ettie looks away from Martha's incisive, pleading eyes and curled accusatory lips, muttering almost inaudibly, "What will be has to be."

She hopes Martha may not have heard, but she has and is about to speak, but then the discussion is brought to a sudden conclusion.

"We should refuse to return the charters and say we've been putting it off because we are afraid of the men of Barnet and Watford."

After a short pause others join in, enthusiastically endorsing the proposal.

"We can say the other towns have threatened to set fire to St. Albans and kill us all if we take the initiative and return the charters first!"

"Yes! Yes!" the cry goes up.

"No! No!" Thomas shouts, "I've heard the Barnet men are already returning their charters."

But he's drowned out in the clamour

"Have the Barnet men really returned the charters?" Martha says to him.

Thomas shakes his head. He's confused, pleased they are standing fast and not returning the charters, but it's a volatile world they live in now. What if their fortunes change, what if the earl returns, or worse still the king? If the men of Barnet have returned their charters (and it's only something he's heard along with all the other wild and exaggerated stories) the abbot will see through their pathetic deception.

"Is there any way they can be made to accept my proposal?" he says to Ettie.

Is he asking her to intervene or asking advice on how best to prolong the debate? Maybe it's just a despairing cry of helplessness that expects no answer. He and Martha are like two birds, forever pecking, demanding release from an inevitable future she cannot stop.

"They seem determined," she says and hurries back to the house.

Thomas gets no comfort when Thursday morning's news vindicates his fears. The king is coming to conduct trials in person. Ned says he's heard the abbot is troubled.

"What is there to trouble *him?*" Thomas snaps.

"Because he's afraid the whole district will be devastated."

"We've more to fear than his woods and fields."

"If there are trials..."

"If the king comes there *will* be trials and swift ones too."

"Last night the abbot sent one of the monks to his friends in London, asking them to try and prevent the king coming."

"The king is the king somebody said yesterday," Thomas says with a rueful smirk, "If he wants to come nothing will stop him."

"He's really only a boy, fourteen."

"Aye and he was a boy at Smithfield when they cut down Wat Tyler."

By midday the monk returns. The king is not willing to change his mind and will be soon arriving.

"Two days at the most," Ned says.

"From last night, that means tomorrow," Thomas says, "So the abbot's pleading failed."

"If he pleaded. Some say the abbot paid the king a thousand pounds to hasten our destruction."

"Some say, some say! If what *they* say is right they'll need to do some pleading of their own!"

"That's already in hand. We've hired a knight, Sir William Crosier to intercede on our behalf. He's a justice of the peace for the county and..."

"Aye, I've heard of him."

"We are meeting with the abbot this afternoon. You must come."

"Have we not had enough of knights?"

"He is working for us, speaking for us. We need our best men with him. Come to the abbey."

Martha overhears the conversation and urges Thomas not to go.

"Another time to be recognised, another time to be remembered. They don't need you there. They have this knight. Don't go!"

Ned urges him, saying sensible men like Thomas must be there with the knight.

"There's no danger in meeting the abbot," Thomas says to Martha, though he's a little reluctant.

"The danger is in being seen," she says, "afterwards when the king comes they'll talk about who was there, who spoke. You're not needed."

This embarrasses him in front of Ned.

"I'm not afraid," he says finally.

A few hours later Thomas stands with a few others beside the knight in the abbot's chamber. Crosier argues for the men, saying they acted in goodwill, but may have been carried away by the whirlwind of events, perhaps occasionally overstepping themselves. Thomas cringes while the abbot raises an eyebrow at the word 'occasionally.' He listens politely and agrees to speak to the king as much as he's able on their behalf as long as they repair the damage to the abbey church.

"Damage?" Thomas says.

"The millstones removed from the pavement outside the parlour. There's also a house in the town which was damaged."

The house is owned by the abbey, the tenant a well known opponent of the people who has wronged many citizens in the past. It was unoccupied when attacked in the first heady days. Reluctantly they agree.

"One more thing," the abbot says, realising his strength and careful to extract every last morsel from the negotiations, "I require compensation to myself and my successors for damage and personal harm."

Crosier looks to the men, who shuffle uneasily. The abbot clasps and unclasps his hands and smiles derisively.

"Shall we say...two hundred pounds..."

The men breathe in sharply.

"...to be paid...by the next feast of St. Michael."

Despite the apparently successful outcome, Thomas returns from the abbey more downhearted than earlier.

"We can't be sure he'll keep his word. We've no control over what the abbot actually says to the king."

"He's given an assurance following the knight's mediation," Abel says, "he won't go back on what he's said to one of the gentry."

Thomas blows out disdainfully.

"Like the knight we met at Derfold Wood!"

At last Chris manages to get his soldiers, archers and courtiers lined up behind Jeremy. Though sitting on his horse, the 'king' looks decidedly unkingly. Chris constantly shouts for him to show 'confidence' and 'bearing' and 'act like a bloody king,' but his efforts are unsuccessful. Far from acting like a king, Jeremy is nervous and disoriented. It's not just the lack of the 'abbot,' Lawrence having still not appeared. He knows it's possible to shoot the scene in part with the arrival of the abbot's party tacked on later, but his earlier fears have returned and he finds the atmosphere in the studio oppressive. Many other actors and extras feel the same.

As the cast gets progressively disturbed and restless Chris feverishly rings every number he can think of in a vain attempt to locate Lawrence. Jenner watches with uneasy fascination. Lawrence's absence also perturbs him and he's not immune to the general disquiet, with a disturbing sense of an imminent happening. He's sure Chris also feels it, though he continues to disguise his agitation with blustering truculence. There's much toing and froing on the set, constant indeterminate swirling of people like a huge bowl of cake mix, slowly stirred in no obvious direction. But not everyone is on the move. Despite Chris's admonitions to 'keep in line' and not 'swan about,' people gather at the edge of the set like lost and frightened tourists.

Every time Chris barks an order Jeremy says "Where's Lawrence?"

"Stop saying that," Chris bellows.

"But we need the abbot."

"Of course we need the damned abbot! Where the hell are you Lawrence? Whatever scheming business you're up to, get away! We need you here!"

But his imprecations are not answered and with a shrug Jeremy gets off his horse.

"Where do you think you're going?" Chris shouts.

"You said yourself we need the abbot. We need Lawrence so if he's not..."

Chris throws up his hands. He won't be beaten.

"Alright, alright, everybody, get back in line. We'll put it together later. This scene is about the king, so that doesn't mean Lawrence, it means you! We go ahead with or without the bloody abbot. With or without Lawrence, but we go ahead!"

Friday 12ᵗʰ July dawns with Thomas in his lowest spirits since he slipped away from Smithfield a month before. Martha too is dejected and full of foreboding.

"Something is coming...soon...something disastrous. The king comes today. What then? We're on the edge. What will next week bring? In these few days...it's close...like before a storm, deceptively quiet, but we can't stop the storm coming."

Is it statement or question, acceptance or a plea for help? What does she want Ettie to do? Then she frightens Ettie even more.

"But we will be avenged...only then will we be free."

The same words Martha spoke on the common. In their desolation Martha and Thomas hardly speak to each other, shuffling around like two strangers. The atmosphere is too heavy for Ettie. She goes out...into the town...anywhere, wandering towards the abbey, drawn inexorably...to somewhere she may escape.

That afternoon the millstones are brought back to the abbey in accordance with the agreement. Repairs also start on the house. Concerned there may be difficulty in the two hundred pounds being paid in time, some of the more important people in the town make pledges for double the sum. Ettie sees Thomas near the abbey.

"I came to help move the millstones, though I'm not sure what good it will do," he says and then gesturing outwards with both hands, "The abbot says he'll not make any claim for injuries, but what if we are charged by the king? They say the abbot will make every effort to secure our acquittal and pardon. 'So he's promised?' I said. They said, 'Well...no, not exactly. He's willing to intercede as best he can, but can't make any promises for pardons are a matter for the king alone."

"So this has been accepted?" Ettie says.

Thomas shrugs and gestures again with his hands.

"Around vespers we will place the millstones in the floor. The charters will also to be returned and many are saying they'll bind themselves over against the compensation."

"Will you be here?"

He grimaces and looks away.

"I've helped get the millstones, but have a bad feeling about it. Grindcobb and the others remain in Hertford prison. If the abbot can't make promises, why should I? Nor will I witness the charters return. I can't trust myself not to say something I may later regret – not for myself, but for others."

"Martha will be pleased if you are at home."

Someone calls him from the abbey.

"I must go back, they need help with the last stones."

Ettie watches him walking towards the abbey. His diminishing figure saddens her. If she escapes she may not see him again. She should be relieved, but wants to help and even if she had the power it would be wrong to intervene. Should she spare him what's to come, tell him not to be in certain places at certain times? She walks back into town, roaming aimlessly, not wanting to go to the house. Martha's unease grows and Ettie prefers to avoid her. By now she knows every street, almost every house, memories she'll retain for long to come. She recognises faces as she passes, as they must recognise her. A few look at her askance. Who is this woman who walks around without purpose? It nears six o'clock. Vespers. By now they'll be placing the six millstones in the floor. All will be as it had been before. Except everything will be changed. Nothing will be the same.

A loud clanging of bells and then she hears singing. People stop and listen. Some move off towards the abbey and drawn by the sounds, Ettie joins them. She waits at the corner. A solemn procession is walking towards the west gate of the monastery led by the abbot. The singing gets louder. There's a solemn joyful triumphancy in this cortege, but the people are silent, watching with grim and anxious acceptance.

"The king," someone says, "the king is come."

Ettie looks to where the column is moving. Will she see the boy king she last saw in Smithfield? As the monks pass with their clangorous chanting she strains to see towards the gate. Then the king comes at the head of his party, riding alone except for a few soldiers. The monks see him too and lift up their voices. The abbot slows as he gets nearer. Keen to get a better view Ettie walks beside the column, but as she gets closer some soldiers bar her way. Then she sees the vast troop – hundreds of soldiers and archers, marching in solemn order – and at their front a hard faced, severe man riding near the king.

"Tresilian," someone says, "It's Tresilian."

Ettie knows the name. Robert Tresilian, chief justice, recently appointed. The cavalcade draws near. If it's meant to produce fear in the hearts of the people it's probably succeeded. Tresilian. What other name is a greater harbinger of vicious repression? Ettie feels the anger welling within her. The king is near. So is Tresilian, close enough for her to see his face, the deep, dark eyes, the large, pugnacious nose, the sharp mouth, the high cheekbones. She edges forward to get even closer. Suddenly in her mind's eye she sees Martha and Thomas, pleading, demanding. Now, when he's so close, they can't be denied. She must intervene, save them from the destruction to come. She looks round. She's alone. Even the soldiers have moved on. Not yet too late, she must stop him! She steps forward. His horse rears. She turns and faces him, raises her arms and shouts.

"Stop! You should not be here! Go away!"

Chris is relatively pleased. Jeremy has at last got a grip and leads with something approaching regal decorum while his party keeps together as they move up towards the gate. All cameras face one way as there's no welcoming party from the monastery. It means much of the scene will have to be re-shot, but for the moment Chris can do without Lawrence. The cast act professionally, no one plays up. He's almost beginning to believe this is a normal film studio with normal people. Not quite normal though. In the corner of his eye he sees the detective, making himself at home. Chris has answered all his damned questions while Lawrence isn't here to answer any. Why doesn't he go, what possible reason has he for staying?

Then, just as his mood reaches a kind of equilibrium, things start to go wrong. There's a disturbance in the crowd behind Jeremy. Some of the 'soldiers' are breaking ranks. Oh no, here we go again! Why won't they keep in line? Someone is shouting. Chris can't make it out. Something about 'what do we do?' How many times must he tell them? Surely it's not too much to ask them to proceed in an orderly file in a straight line from A to B? What a shambles, more wasted time!

"What the hell is going on?" he shouts, forgetting the cameras are still rolling.

No one answers and the flurry gets worse. Chris pushes his way through the 'crowd,' shouting for people to get out of his way, but the extras take no notice. Everyone is moving in the same direction, anxious to find out what is happening and creating a bottleneck. Chris strains to see. It's all around 'Tresilian.' He pushes on. Somebody says 'Where's she come from?' another 'How did it happen?'

"Get out the bloody way!" Chris snaps as he elbows people aside.

Then he hears a woman shouting. The voice is familiar.

"You should not be here! Go away!"

Adam Welton, the actor playing Tresilian sits on his horse, awestruck and hesitant. In front of him a woman has stepped from the 'crowd' and is berating him continually.

"Get away! You'll only bring destruction on these people. Get out of this town!"

Jenner has got up and followed the noise and consternation. He can't see anything, but is determined to get closer. This is what he's been feeling. This is the happening. Chris stops and stares in disbelief.

"What are you doing here?" he shouts, "Where have you been?"

"Ettie!" Charley shouts as she comes up.

Ettie turns and looks at her, then back to 'Tresilian,' utterly mystified. Jenner quickens his step, but Jennifer bars his way.

"Why are you here sergeant?"

"I've come to get you, sir."

"Get me, what do you mean? Quickly now, I have to get..."

"It's Lawrence Bullock."

"You've found him?"

"He's dead."

9

IT'S the same street, the same houses, the same people...no, not the same people...not all of them. Tresilian, he's the same, yet he's not the same, sitting up there, staring with that look of incredulity, but with amazement rather than anger. Has she so quickly changed the fearsome judge, forced him to concede, will he turn around and leave, never enter St. Albans, never carry out his trials...changing history as Martha demanded? And will all this be down to Ettie, hindering, transforming, *interfering*, doing what so many times she's implored others not to do? How could she be so foolish, carried away by unthinking emotion when all she really wants is to escape and get back to her own time?

People are crowding round her. Tresilian is getting off his horse. Someone calls.

"What are you doing here?"

She turns to see Chris Pleasant in modern clothes. This is impossible, how can he be here...unless...?

"Where have you been?"

She looks at him, stupefied, unable to comprehend his question. Been? Here of course, but where has *he* been?

"It's Ettie Rodway," people are saying, "she's back."

Back? It can't be. She turns again. 'Tresilian' stands by his horse, except it's not Tresilian. She knows now, he's too soft, his eyes unthreatening, as if the mask has been lifted. He's an actor! She scans the crowd. They could be, but they aren't, no Thomas, no Martha, no Ned, no Abel. All these people are actors. She really is back. Suddenly she's grabbed from behind and spun round as Charley stares, wide eyed with wonder and relief.

"Ettie, it really is you! We were so worried. Where have you been, how did you get here?"

Ettie smiles nervously and looks round again, studying all the staring faces. Then with visions of that past where she stood a few minutes ago, she scowls and shakes. She may have escaped, but they haven't and an overwhelming terror grips her.

"The day, there's so little time," she mutters.

"What day?" Charley asks.

"What day, what date is this?" Ettie says, taking her hand.

"The second," Charley says, "It's the second."

"Oh no," Ettie wails, "too late, how can it be? The second of August!"

"No, of course not, it's the second of *July!*"

"July, the second of July, how long have I been away?"

"Four days."

Four days! It can't be, she's been in 1381 for two weeks! This has to be the 12th July. Now she's hustled through the milling crowd of actors and extras, Chris on one side, Charley on the other. How can she come through on this day when she'd failed on all others? It has to be the filming.

"Why are you shooting the arrival of the king again?"

"We had to," Charley says adamantly, "we just had to."

Ettie looks to Chris, but he doesn't contradict her.

"We had to be here," Charley continues, "I wanted to shoot a particular scene, but Chris...well we disagreed."

"But the king's scene, you wanted to do that again?"

"My idea," Chris says, "It wasn't right the first time, I felt..."

"We were drawn...pulled..." Charley says.

So it was her, but how? Ettie's unfocused attentions were ineffective. They could draw, but not delineate. Only on the 12th when the king was entering the town did her concentration and the film making coincide to bring her back. But now is not the 12th. How is it she's lived through two weeks in 1381 yet only four days have passed here?

"...but made all the more difficult without Lawrence," Chris is saying, "We needed the abbot, but I told them to go ahead without him. Yet nobody seemed coordinated. I was getting annoyed. As you...arrived...I was just about to..."

"Lawrence Bullock isn't here?" Ettie says, "was he expected?"

"Yes, like all the others, he should have been..."

Ettie shudders. Lawrence's non appearance is frightening. Whenever she 'has it on' her with heavy feelings of impending doom, usually something relatively unimportant happens and her premonition lifts, but not now. This is no trivial absence. Something has happened to Lawrence and on this specific day in 1381, except it isn't, not here, not in this time.

"...so we went ahead."

Still she sees that other time. The faces change, flickering between ages, the excited amazement of the present, the dull nervousness of the past, the surging expectancy of now, the regimented apprehension of then.

"But you had Tresilian in the wrong position," Ettie says suddenly.

"What do you mean?" Charley says.

"He should be further back, closer to the king."

Chris shakes his head, but Charley is intrigued.

"But how did you...?"

"Something has happened to Lawrence," Ettie says dolefully.

"You mean he's not...alright?" Chris says.

"I...I...it's hard to say..."

They get away from the group surrounding them.

"We've got so much to talk about," Charley says.

Jennifer sees Ettie and comes over, but this unnerves Chris.

"I have to go," he says and walks away. Ettie watches him.

"Ignore him," Charley says, "now, about Tresilian, how did you know...my God, you've been there, haven't you, you've been..."

"Ettie!" Jennifer says, "what has happened?"

"You'll never believe it," Ettie says.

"That's the problem, I probably will."

"Even now, I'm not sure."

"Not sure where you've been?"

"Oh, I'm sure about *that!* I'm still not sure where I am now."

Ettie is very pale and shakes slightly. Jennifer and Charley steer her across the set to a vacant table and chairs. With Chris gone the dislocated shoot finally disintegrates. Jeremy Lowther and Adam Welton lead the way and soon everyone is dispersing. A few bemused rubber neckers hover around Ettie, but Charley shoos them away.

"You can tell *me*," Charley says, glancing suspiciously at Jennifer.

"I can tell you both," Ettie says, "Jennifer understands very well. She and I..."

"We don't need to go into that now," Jennifer intervenes, unwilling to discuss previous investigations in front of Charley.

"You mean, this has happened before?" Charley says.

"No...not exactly."

"I'll tell what happened," Ettie says, "though even now... have I really only been away four days...it's not possible...it seemed so much longer, but if you say...no it was longer..."

Slowly, haltingly with many pauses and hesitations, Ettie recounts her two weeks in the past compressed into a mere four days in the present. Charley and Jennifer listen attentively without interruption, both taking notes. When Ettie finishes Charley, overwhelmed in wonder, scans through her notes and repeats several incidents.

"So much detail we didn't know, so much we can build into the script. This material is fantastic!"

"But haven't you already filmed...?"

"Not everything, besides some scenes can be done again. I have to find Chris!"

She gets up and with a parting 'don't go away, I'll be back' dives through the crowd in search of the director.

"Four days?" Ettie says to Jennifer.

"Definitely," Jennifer says, "but how is it possible?"

"A time distortion."

"Which means?"

"If only I knew," Ettie sighs disconsolately, "It's frightening. If the past is running faster than the present..."

"But the past...it's gone."

"If only it was that simple. When the past overlays the present, nothing has gone, everything is now."

"I'll never understand."

"What has happened to Lawrence Bullock?"

Jennifer starts at the name.

"He was meant to be here, they had to adjust the shooting and..." Ettie begins.

"He's dead."

Ettie pulls up sharply and jerks her hands over her mouth.

"Killed," she mutters.

"It looks like suicide," Jennifer says, "there's a note..."

"No, no, he's been killed."

"It's too early to..."

"I know, I know he's been killed."

Ettie shakes her head and Jennifer nods hers.

"You've felt something...you felt something...back there."

"The chief inspector, is he here?"

"Yes, I saw him as I came in. He was right behind..."

"I have to talk to him!"

Ettie gets up and runs towards the exit, pushing through the crowd. Jennifer follows and then leads her to where she saw Jenner, but they can't find him. Both he and Chris Pleasant have disappeared.

Desperate to get as far from the studio in the shortest possible time, Chris drives faster than he should. It's dangerous, but it's better. It stops him thinking and there's a limit to how much he can cope with. He'd got used to Jeremy's tantrums, but what on earth was wrong with Adam Welton? All that commotion, why did Adam suddenly become speechless, gibbering such nonsense? He'd already told them. It didn't matter about Lawrence. They could cope without him for a day.

The traumas and vagaries of the film command his whole attention without third parties creating further havoc. Cast and extras lolloping about worse than school kids, no Lawrence, then Ettie suddenly appearing in front of Adam. Where had she come from? Finally that damned policeman barging in, demanding to be seen, hovering as if his business is more important. It totally unnerved Chris even before the disruption on the set. Everybody was crowding around Ettie. It was too much. He had to get away, pushing his way out of the studio. It was then he heard Lawrence's name mentioned several times. Why were they still going on about it, surely by now everybody knew he wasn't there? Then that single word. Dead. How it rings with dull resonance when said so quietly. He took little notice. Whatever it was he wasn't where he ought to be. Then the men at the gate held him up, yacking constantly about Lawrence, wondering where he was, everybody must be really worried, how they missed him, always peeping the horn of that fantastic car and waving. Really? He didn't know. Always a gent was Mr. Bullock. Still they kept talking, recounting endless anecdotes. When will they stop! Chris isn't used to listening so much.

Then he catches sight of someone else also heading towards the gate. It's that damned policeman! He has to extricate himself and lose him! It must be unpredictable. Don't go where he expects you. He twists and turns through streets and lanes, not stopping until sure he's not followed. For a half hour he waits in a quiet industrial estate, seeing no one except a delivery lorry. Then he heads for the motorway, accelerating rapidly even though he'll have to get off at the next junction. His personal pointless contribution to the world fuel crisis. He almost misses the exit and has to swerve across other cars into the slow lane with much screeching brakes and shaking fists. He calms slightly on the road to Welstead. Soon be home. He drives slowly by the common as remembrances of the studio return. Lawrence is dead. That's what they said. Yes, it has to be. He turns into the drive and parks, not noticing the other car at the end of the lane. The house is in darkness. He's alone. In moments like this he feels most isolated. However many times he goes through the motions, those first few moments are always the same...cold, dark, sombre. He'll step to the door, turn the key, grope for the light, no one around, it will pass as the place brightens, warms and fills with the artificial company of radio and hi fi and television.

He sits in the car for some time, half hoping for a sign of life, but that would also be alarming. Even the cleaner shouldn't be here at this hour. It's the first time he's been at wakeful rest for days. So much chasing and charging around, barking and barracking, running and racing from the studio. Perpetual motion clouds the mind. Sitting still clears it. As the awful ramifications begin to register his spirits plunge even further. Lawrence, is he really dead? Yes, it has to be faced. The car is a secure cocoon. Perhaps he should stay here, untroubled for even the house is contaminated by the outside world. He'll see anyone who approaches. But a cocoon is very small and ultimately vulnerable. In the house there's space, his space, his own preserve. He gets out and goes to the door.

Even then he hovers with the key. He could return to the car, slink into the seat, go away, somewhere, anywhere. He feels like a stranger, entering someone else's house, an interloper who shouldn't cross the threshold without invitation. He slips the key and turns the lock, waits and lets the door slide on its hinges rather than push it aside. He steps into the hall, but doesn't shut the door, conscious of its telltale click, not wanting to disturb the eerie silence or perhaps alert anyone who might be here. He's himself again, entering his own domain, yet oddly nervous of what he might find. He walks through the hall to the lounge, but stops at the open door. One foot in and one foot out of the room, he's filled with an overwhelming desire to run, get out of the house, escape from whatever awaits him even if it's only the uncomfortable prompting of his own conscience. There's no escaping at home, nowhere to hide, not even for the mind.

His panic goes, but he's still reluctant to enter. Usually when he comes back to the house it's like a sepulchre, a place undisturbed since he left and for a few moments he's reminded of all the things that haven't moved, but most of all how no one has been there. He doesn't feel that now. He's not alone. The light switch is next to the door, but he makes no move, unwilling to leave the dubious security of his ignorance. What you don't know you don't grieve about. If you ignore what you suspect, it might not be. He could go straight to bed. Oblivious sleep might soon come. But he'll be no safer there for though he feels nothing, sees nothing, hears nothing he knows it's here. However much you run you can't go faster than your own thoughts. It has to be faced. He switches on the light.

"You've taken your time."

The voice, soft, relaxed, but slightly menacing is from the far end of the room. A man sits in a chair, his motionless form clearly silhouetted beside the window. Why had he not seen him? Chris takes a couple of steps forward.

"You must have made a detour."

Chris takes the nearest chair, as far from him as he can get without running away.

"I thought I'd lost you," he says.

"You did," Jenner says, "but I was sure you'd come here."

"How did you get in?"

"You left a door open."

"I did?" Chris says doubtfully.

"At the back...the kitchen."

Chris looks at Jenner suspiciously and half turns as if to go and check.

"I took the precaution of re-locking it for you," Jenner says, "You really need to be more careful. I'm surprised you've not got an alarm."

"I've been busy, not got round to it."

"Quite so. Why did you leave the studio so suddenly?"

Chris hesitates, then says obliquely "You could have waited outside for me."

"I didn't want to miss you and it's more comfortable in here. You do have an unfortunate habit of...disappearing."

"I'd had enough, all the shenanigans with Jeremy and the others and then..."

"Yes?"

"Ettie's...arrival."

"No other reason?"

"No. What is it you want?"

"I want to know where you've been."

"You know where I've been. You were there at the studio."

"No...earlier today. Around the time of Lawrence Bullock's death."

Chris catches his breath suddenly.

"It's true then. I heard...at the studio...everybody was talking about it."

"Were they?"

"Yes, even the men at the gate."

"They actually said he was dead."

"Yes...well, no not exactly...but they kept talking about him not being there."

"Not quite the same thing."

"But on the set, you were there. Wasn't it you that told everybody?"

"Can you tell me your movements today?"

"I told you before...I was with a friend."

"Yes...in Essex. What time did you leave?"

"It would have been around...eight thirty."

"So between then and when you arrived at the studio, you were on the road, travelling?"

"Yes."

"Another detour?"

"I needed to think."

"Stop anywhere?"

"Yes I stopped."

"See anyone at any particular time?"

"No, I don't recall."

"So, apart from the relatively short time it takes to drive from Chelmsford, you could have been anywhere?"

"I didn't see Lawrence Bullock?"

"You're sure about that?"

"Of course I am. If I'd seen him I'd've made damn sure he was on the set!"

"Quite so, very inconvenient."

"It certainly is. It's bad enough not having an abbot for one day's shooting, but to be told he's not going to be around for any days. That's too much. Just like Lawrence to get himself killed."

"Get *himself?*"

"Well, if he's dead...?"

"You don't seem too concerned."

"Of course I'm concerned, I've got a film to complete remember."

"Quite so."

Chris's confidence evaporates again. Jenner's empty acceptance is unconvincing, he's not satisfied. It's unnerving.

"Shouldn't you be somewhere else?" Chris says, "the scene of crime or whatever it's called?"

"What makes you believe a crime has been committed?"

"I didn't say there was...it was a figure of speech...it was you that said..."

"I didn't say anything."

"In any case you obviously think I was involved, so you ought to be poking around at his house rather than breaking into mine!"

"When I start telling you how to make films you can tell me how to conduct my investigation."

"Have you finished?"

"I may need to see you again."

After Jenner goes Chris tries to settle, wandering aimlessly reconnecting with the things he left undisturbed this morning. Then he becomes unsure everything has not been disturbed. Jenner knew he was coming home. He got here first and started snooping around, all very unofficial and irregular and deliberately spooking him. Perhaps he should make a complaint...maybe not...some stones are best left unturned. He did hear Lawrence was dead...didn't he... no matter he *knew* anyway and the police would hardly be questioning him if it was an accident. He knows it wasn't an accident.

It's a short journey to Lawrence's house where Jennifer is waiting. Jenner breezes in without any explanation.

"Where have you been?" she says.

"Upstairs is he?"

"Yes."

He bounds up the stairs and stands at the edge of the bathroom. Lawrence Bullock lies in the half filled bath, his head propped against a pillow, his arms in the pinky water. His eyes are open, staring at the wall, his mouth set firm, but relaxed, almost serene. A small, sharp, blood stained kitchen knife is on the ledge beside the bath.

"Who found him?"

"Mrs. Dennis, his cleaning woman.

"What time?"

"About five."

"Bit late for cleaning isn't it?"

"She came to say she wouldn't be in for a few days, her daughter is ill and she has to look after her grandchildren. She couldn't get an answer, but saw his car in the drive. She has a key, came in, called out, got concerned, started wandering about..."

"She's not touched anything?"

"No. Saw him through the open door, called us immediately."

"And he was last seen?"

"About eight this morning by the same woman. He was still here when she left around nine."

"Nine to five."

"We'll have a more accurate time later. Did you want to see Mrs. Dennis, she's downstairs?"

"Not if you've seen her. She can go home."

The pathologist is ready to move the body.

"All finished?" Jenner says.

"Yes."

"And the time...?"

"Between midday and two I'd say."

"Suicide?"

"Looks like it, prepared the bath, cut his wrists, plunged them in..."

"Looks like it," Jenner repeats thoughtfully.

"There's a note," Jennifer says, "he left it in the bedroom."

260

They move away onto the landing. She hands him a small piece of paper enclosed in a plastic bag, "It's been checked for prints."

He reads it aloud.

"It was a millstone of guilt that has always hung around my neck over the years. What we argued about in the fiery passions of youth assumed vast importance. They seem so insignificant now. Compromise has never come easily to me – in those days even less so – but what I did can never be excused. As the years go by, it gets harder, not easier to bear. Now I know what I must do. Facing up to the truth is the only way. I only hope my actions now will go some way to make up for my the evil in the past."

He reads it again silently and then scans the paper, turning it over before looking at the front once more.

"So it looks like suicide," Jennifer says, neutrally questioning.

"Doc says it *could* be," he says.

"You're not convinced?"

"Anything about this strike you as odd?"

"Rather a long note."

"And?"

"It's not signed."

"Goes to the trouble of writing such a long note, which he then doesn't bother to sign."

"Of course there's no room on the paper. He starts at the top left and finishes at the bottom right."

"Yes, another oddity."

"Bit cramped, but neatness on the paper is the last thing you're thinking about when…"

"I suppose it is his writing?"

"I got something for comparison from the studio. The handwriting matches with the note."

"If it is a note. The way it fits into the whole space, it's as if it's detached."

"Like a page from a letter."

"Exactly. Part of something even longer. It's got the feel of something coming before it and something coming after."

"Perhaps, but even unsigned, it's his writing and…"

"Look at it. Are these the last words of a man about to kill himself?"

"He mentions his guilt about a past evil, which he's finding more difficult to bear..."

"*I know what I must do*...he doesn't actually say he's going to top himself..."

"Even so..."

"*I only hope my action*...action, what action? Peculiar word to use. This isn't a suicide note. It's part of a letter, this page carefully extracted to give the impression that it is a suicide note, conveniently in the dead man's handwriting."

"So if we find who the letter was sent to..."

"We have the murderer. What's the evil he refers to?"

"*...the fiery passions of youth*...something in the past, my guess is it's connected to the disappearance of his school friend, Melvyn Strange."

"So Lawrence murdered him?"

"Could be, except we haven't got a body."

"But Melvyn's never been found."

"It could still be suicide. This letter may have been a draft, never sent. Lawrence destroys all but this page, which becomes his effective suicide note."

"If Lawrence killed Melvyn and has been consumed by guilt ever since, why does it become too much for him now? Why is now so unbearable he can literally no longer live with it? No, this letter probably shows Lawrence killed Melvyn, so it clears up that particular mystery – so far as it goes without a body – but it doesn't explain his own death. I'm not convinced it's suicide."

"If Lawrence killed Melvyn, what was the motive?"

"We'll probably never know. More important is why someone, the recipient of the letter, would want to kill Lawrence now."

"Unless it has nothing to do with it. We may have partly solved the mystery of Melvyn's disappearance, but the letter is irrelevant to Lawrence's own murder, giving the killer a convenient device to make it look like suicide."

"Perhaps, but I'm not wholly dismissing the Melvyn connection yet. Many of those around then are still around now. We've a few people to see."

"I couldn't find Chris Pleasant at the studio."

"I've already seen him at his house."

"So that's where you've been. Your phone was switched off. I couldn't get you. Why did he leave so suddenly?"

"You know these arty farty people. Says he was upset with everything at the studio. That's what he wants me to believe."

"By now he'll know about Lawrence."

"Oh, he knew about Lawrence."

"But he couldn't have done."

"Said everybody was talking about it – even the men at the gate – though when pressed he couldn't be sure they'd definitely said Lawrence was dead."

"There's no way they could have known, neither could he...unless..."

"...he was involved."

"Surely he wouldn't be so stupid. He could have picked it up from Ettie."

"Ettie, how could she ...?"

"She said certain things when she...appeared. I'm surprised you've not been to see her."

"I will...tomorrow...I had to follow up Pleasant."

He speaks to the scenes of crime officers and then returns to the ground floor. Jennifer follows. He pauses at the front door.

"How was Chris Pleasant?" she says.

"Peculiar. The friend in Chelmsford checks out, but why go there in the first place? Then he takes a very long time to get back, unexplained movement when he could have been anywhere. Anything else?"

"Just one thing. We found this ring on the window sill in the bathroom."

She holds up a signet ring.

"It's been checked for prints."

"These initials inside," Jenner says as he examines it, "MM."

"Margaret Morton?" she says.

He hands it back.

263

"We have to see them all. Go and see Monica Freeson in the morning. I'll see George Carter. We also have to renew the hunt for Melvyn Strange."

"But he..."

"The body, sergeant, we have to find his body."

Monica is very shocked to hear of Lawrence's death.

"Whatever could have induced him to do such a thing. He was so full of life, brimful of his own..."

"Importance?" Jennifer says.

"...confidence. He was a man of so many talents. He had everything to live for, I just can't believe it."

She's even more shocked when Jennifer asks about her movements the previous day.

"Why should you want to know my movements?"

"You knew Lawrence Bullock well."

"Not really. He was an acquaintance."

"You've known them all for over twenty five years, Lawrence, Warren, George, Maggie..."

"Yes but, even so...Oh my God, it's not suicide is it, you think he's been murdered. No, not another one! Just like Warren. It can't be."

Just before she leaves Jennifer asks one last question.

"Your maiden name, Mrs. Freeson, was it Martin?"

"Yes."

"So your initials were then MM."

The preliminary post mortem results confirm Lawrence bled to death in the bath, but there are traces in his body indicating he may not have been a willing participant in his own demise.

"He was drugged," the pathologist says

"So that was what killed him?" Jenner says.

"No, but it was enough to render him unconscious."

"Making it easy to get him into the bath and slash his wrists."

"Precisely. Trying to make it look like suicide."

"So it's definitely murder."

As yet no forensic evidence has been found. Someone has been very careful to hide his or her presence, but what was the motive? The mysterious disappearance of Melvyn Strange is Jenner's only apparent connection, but that was twenty five years ago. It's a long shot, even if it's relevant. Jennifer could be right. Lawrence's murder may be totally unconnected to Melvyn's disappearance and possible murder. If they had a body they might have something to go on.

"Got to find Melvyn," he says to Jennifer.

"But where?"

"The common," he says vaguely, "start digging up the common."

"But we've got no..."

"Got to start somewhere, sergeant, can't sit around, got to find that bloody body."

Jennifer could point out the absurdity of it. The common is a big place. Apart from the disruption to the community (she shudders at how many institutions might need to be consulted) they have no indication of where to begin. The press will have a field day, asking innumerable unanswerable questions. But she's more worried about her boss's odd and erratic behaviour, leaving the studio so suddenly, going to see Chris Pleasant before visiting the crime scene and now issuing utterly impossible instructions. If she didn't know better she'd say he was stressed out and unreliable, but she knows he battles with internal conflicts, which will work through eventually. Meantime, what to do about digging up the common? Someone may remember the areas Melvyn frequented. She'll check again the original investigation reports.

Ettie might be able to indicate Melvyn's whereabouts. Jenner ought to see Ettie, at least as a friend, but he puts it off. She may talk of things he can't handle and in any case Jennifer may have already spoken to her. That'll assist her searches. George Carter is of more immediate importance, but he's not at the newspaper office and they've not heard from him for two days. Neither is he at home. George has disappeared.

After Jennifer dropped her off at the cottage, Ettie slumped into a chair and slept until next morning. She wakes with shock waves of all that's happened flushing through her. She sits for a long time, staring at the common, the one continuing, unchanging connection with the past. The concentrated horizon where grass and gorse meet the sky blanks out coherent thoughts. Then, slowly, jutting images pierce the green, blue and yellow overlay. She sees Martha and then Thomas as their words cut through... *"they need help with the stones...we will be avenged...then we will be free"*...only to leave as suddenly as they appear. She lets them go. They can't get any closer, can't touch her. Can they? How close do they need to be? She can't escape her own mind.

The images are gone. The only sounds the sighing wind in the garden and the gentle heaving of the roof and walls in this old house. She's no longer anxious, but isn't relieved. Relief needs a burden lifted, a danger removed, yet there's no menace, not even by those from the past, though she has no desire to go back. Neither relieved to be here nor comfortable with the prospect of return for she now inhabits a world where time expands and contracts bewilderingly, long in the past, short in the present. Four days become two weeks and then revert to four days again. Continually stretching and compressing, a coiling uncoiling spring, always nearly at the point of full recoil, yet never quite flying back as she bounces between past and present.

Those days in 1381 – six hundred years, a few hours ago, so immediate, so distant. Charley says she's seen and heard the *authentic* past, but her reality is sieved through partial observation, picked and poked through jumbled remembrance that so rapidly fades. How does she view those she met? Has she the right to judge them? If she's wrong, how will *they* react? Do they watch her now as she watched them then? Maybe she only really understood in those last few minutes as she tried to stop Tresilian coming into town, forestalling him, intervening, *changing* the past. She shudders at her foolishness. How could she have transgressed all the guidance she's so long given others? The past frightens her, but she resisted Martha and not interfered. No damage had been done. Martha is unseen and mainly unheard, yet is still with her, in the fields and the trees, above all in her head! She's escaped, but is still bound, still connected to 1381.

Then Martha is standing silently at the door with that elusive stare, half pleading, half demanding. Ettie stares back, frozenly waiting. Then she's gone. Ettie continues to stare at the blank wall as if Martha might suddenly reappear, but then doubts she was really there at all, a mental shard sliced from troubled recollections. She may have misread Martha. The connections to the past are no longer aberrations, but a time linked pattern, an arch of opportunity to be harnessed. If she can get back, reclaim the contact, it will be for a definite purpose and not as a freak!

She shudders. Going back. However much she might now rationalise the benefits, it can't be contemplated lightly. The contact is not a revolving door, easily pushed to get through or pushed to get back. She only managed it by the fortuitous oscillations of the filmmaking, artificial events coinciding with real ones. Such dovetailing of ages may not recur, leaving her bound and powerless in another time. But what if she's as helpless in this time, for the past's interventions may now be out of control, unrelated to the filmmaking with an unpredictable life of their own. She's still wary of Thomas and fearful of the interference of others. What if Tresilian, Thomas, the abbot have 'creatures' in the present to do their bidding? It makes her distrust almost everyone. Chris Pleasant's erratic film direction may have unwittingly helped Charley. What is she really up to? Is he really frustrated by vague threats from the past and the unreliability of his cast in the present? Even if they don't deliberately interfere, does their conflict invoke the past? Their endless arguments may be trivial, but in the 14th century they were crucial matters of freedom and destruction. Is the film the vehicle of transference? What if their artistic squabbles allow those desperate folk in 1381 to break free and drag their battles into the present?

Why is Chris so uncooperative, what is it he or his past alter ego wants to hide? Is the argumentative film director who mysteriously left the studio and just as abruptly reappeared, only to flee again today involved in Lawrence's death? His obsession with the Revolt and long cherished ambition of making the film seemed so admirable. A lifetime dream realised at last. Now she's not so sure. Eager to talk about his project, he chased Vicky to her friend's house in Kent during her vulnerable days, frightening the young nurse and further destabilising her unsettled state. Ettie dismissed Vicky's nervousness and when the London disturbances were over it seemed only natural to cooperate with his researches.

"...if the king comes..."

Martha's words...but there's no one at the door...it's in her head. Should she leave the free play of the past or try to block the dangerous forces it may unleash?

"...something coming...soon...something disastrous..."

Ettie looks up again. No one, but Martha's voice was so distinct. That something coming may not have been in Martha's own time. She may have meant Ettie's time. She may have meant Ettie.

"...we can't stop the storm coming..."

This time Ettie doesn't look up, but screws her eyes as Martha's image fills her mind. Is Martha telling her she should stay for by returning from the past has Ettie intervened? Is she responsible for Lawrence's death? No, that's crazy, but the film is the connection. By coming back through the film has she brought past's revenge?

"...we will be avenged...then we will be free..."

But revenge on whom and why here, why now?

"...what's to become of us...?"

She mustn't be afraid. Martha is no threat. She's afraid herself and needs help. The answer lies in the past, so, she must encourage the past, not resist it. But the right past, the right people, the right forces for in 1381 there are those doing great harm who might wreak damage here too. Hadn't she tried to stop Tresilian? That was wrong. The past must take its own course, but if Ettie can come through could they also come through? If the film released her from the past, could it also release sinister forces to exact their misguided vengeance? If she helps Martha will it stop such a menace? Is that why Martha tries to make contact? Ettie must concentrate all her energies, restore the connection and get back to her. She opens her eyes briefly, half expecting to see that familiar figure, but there's no one. She closes her eyes again, locking her mind on the meetings, the discussions, the determination, the fear, the desperation...

The telephone rings. The past is gone. It rings again. She opens her eyes. Maybe it will stop. It doesn't. She picks it up.

"Hello."

"Ettie, it's Charley. You must come back to the studio."

Digging up land without an 'owner' fills Jennifer with foreboding. It doesn't feel 'right.' Its very *public* ownership gives it a sanctity no *private* land could ever have. Excavating a village green would be bad enough, but this expanse exudes inviolability. When the first spade strikes the ground, the first sod turned, will the grass and trees cry in pain and defiance? Will that scrap of brown in the swathe of green widen and swallow those that dare lacerate its skin? Will the ground shake in rage, tossing them away like an elephant flicking flies off its back? Will the untold generations of folk who gathered their winter fuel and tramped the land howl in fury?

One part of the common is already a prescribed crime scene. Extending it a little further is not so difficult. With two murders still unresolved anything smacking of 'progress' is sanctioned surprisingly quickly and Jenner only needs a vague description to approve the excavation. He leaves Jennifer a note with a large area circled on a map, too large for an effective excavation – unless he intends digging up the common for six months. Jenner may have left notes and maps, but precious little else to guide her and he's not around for consultation. She feels very alone. Where is Jenner, why doesn't he make contact?

The reports on Melvyn's disappearance have yielded only patchy information. Melvyn and his friends may have had favourite places, but it doesn't mean he was killed in one of them. It would help if some of those old friends could be more specific. George Carter went to school with Melvyn, but he's not at the newspaper office and no one has seen him. Warren also knew Melvyn. She goes to see Kathleeen. She's reticent, unwilling to acknowledge the connection.

"The boy who went missing," Jennifer persists, "Melvyn Strange."

Kathleen repeats the name quietly, almost reverently, or is it fear, apprehension, then says, "Yes, I remember...Warren knew him."

"Do you remember where they...he...hung out?"

"Hung out?"

"Favourite haunts, meeting places."

"Well in town..."

"On the common."

"I've got a photograph," she says, going to the sideboard.

She rummages through the drawers, eventually producing a dog eared old snap of four young boys. She points them out.

"Warren, Lawrence, George and...that's Melvyn."

"Did you take this?"

"No, not me. I don't know, it was Warren's."

Then she reminisces more productively after some prodding, finally referring to a possible place.

"Lock's Spinney, some of the boys used to go there."

She describes the location.

"Did you mention this when Melvyn disappeared?"

"Nobody asked me."

"Did anyone else mention it?"

Kathleen shrugs. All the way back to the station Jennifer wonders about her. How she keeps things bottled up, is oddly uncommunicative and then suddenly opens up. Her concerns increase when she discovers Lock's Spinney is only a short distance from where Warren's body was found. She tries to locate Jenner again, but there's no reply from his mobile. She rings his mother.

"He didn't come in last night, but he said he might stay with a friend."

Friend, what friend? Jenner has connections here. An old friend in the old place of his youth.

Kathleen's information could be a total shot in the dark, but it's all they have. At least digging can begin, but where might it end? They are close, but not close enough. The longer she stays at the common her discomfort increases. They are not just disturbing the earth, but boring into the collective past. She wanders off, towards where Warren's body was found, but stops about halfway. The land may know, but it's unable or unwilling to reveal. Ettie would sense it. She must talk to her later. Then she feels it. One...no two people. Still sensing their presence she looks round and as she stares into the distance sees two men, one taller than the other, dark, stooping slightly...then they are gone. No one can be seen. She turns back towards the digging, then stops again, turns round, but sees no one. But they were there. They could not have run away without being seen nor is there any cover. They didn't go...they disappeared.

Charley is desperate. Since Ettie returned she's lost the energy for prolonged fights with Chris and the latest fierce rows have worn her out. Yet her determination remains. The copious notes she scribbled as Ettie described her experiences will long provide rich and comprehensive source material. She's already sketched out major amendments to several scenes, leaving them at the studio in Chris's room. At first she discounts Ettie journeying into the past as the outcome of an extremely fertile imagination, probably brought on during her four day 'drop out.' The result, not the process is crucial, but studying the notes later she wonders how such intricate information could be acquired. If a 'vision' it was unbelievably precise and thorough. Ettie may be used to dealing with extraordinary elements, but she's practical and reliable. Her integrity is beyond question. She doesn't make things up.

Like pressured water behind a dam, ready to burst through wherever the breach might appear, Charley's agitation tightens and strengthens as snippets of what Ettie said cut into her sleep. She may see without Ettie's vividness and hear without her clarity, but the diffuse and shapeless past connections are no less powerful. The people, fearful, but with a simmering anger and resolution are still unbowed, whatever the consequences. It frightens her. Immersed in the events, unquestioningly soaking up Warren Grover's *A Little Liberty* has she lost touch with what she's about as a screenwriter, detached from her own time, fatally exposed to forces she can neither understand nor control?

Now the *process* is even more important than the result and the notes seem tainted, even dangerous like precious stones as the haul from some frightful robbery. How can such material be used if it's been obtained by hazardous means threaten to return and harry the perpetrator like the victim of the robbery bent on revenge? Her new scenes with their fresh found realism could be the Greek horse of menacing authenticity thrust into the Troy of artifice, destabilising the whole project. How dare she use them?

Her head aching through over concentration and wearied by incessant worrying she longs for rest, but then remembers the notes she left for Chris and panics. He may do precisely what she originally wanted and go for those scenes. If he does it'll be a first – doing what she wants – but that's not now what she wants! She can't take the risk. Those scenes are too raw, too close, too real. She must get in early and retrieve them. The king's arrival scene, now compromised by Lawrence's death, has become the threshold. The period immediately before – 30th June to 12th July 1381 – subsumed within Ettie's sojourn and now contaminated by its dangerous authenticity has to be avoided. Everything must be either *before* 30th June or *after* 12th July. Safer to move on, beyond the king's arrival, but the abbot, previously played by Lawrence can't be written out of the story? Can they rely on already shot material and ignore him after the 12th July or must they re- shoot everything involving the abbot with a new actor?

If all else fails she'll have to deflect Chris's attention with entirely new material which is definitely *after* the arrival of the king. She pores over her battered and worn copy of *A Little Liberty* for inspiration. As she reads her head nods and her eyelids droop, but she perseveres, finally latching onto the arrest and trial of John Ball, the charismatic religious leader of the Revolt. He doesn't appear in the Hertfordshire events until 12th July, making him an apparently safe option. She puts together the scene of his trial, but is beset with a constant feeling of not being alone and has to stop frequently, looking anxiously around the empty room.

"Who are you, what do you want?" she calls, then reaching out as if it's her duty to assist, as if the past is beckoning, "How can I help you?"

The vigil of the unseen, unheard essence remains, ensuring she works on. As she studies her notes recurrent words and phrases jangle...*admit your involvement...will not deny...stand by the others...admit only to the truth...*

She gets up and stalks the room as if chairs and shelves, carpets and curtains are the inanimate accessories, hiding, protecting the undetectable, but unmistakable presence. Exhaustion permeates every fibre of her mind and body, but she has to complete the scene. She's driven, summoned and can't refuse. They call and she'll not let them down. *Only the truth...we only fought for the truth.* At last she completes the scene and slumps into a deep and restorative sleep. She wakes at seven thirty and jumps up anxiously. Chris may be already at the studio and have found the notes. She dresses quickly, grabs her new material and dashes out, but hesitates at the door. If her misgivings are justified, she really may need help and of a more practical nature than dissociated presences in the past! She rings Ettie.

"I may need your help, please come!"

Ettie says she's tired, but Charley knows it's more than that. Who can blame her for not wanting to return to the studio. It must be like going to the bank of the river from which you've just emerged after nearly drowning. Maybe she's afraid she'll be sucked back into the past especially if she believes they'll be working on scenes directly connected to her recent...journey.

"I've had second thoughts about...what we talked about yesterday..." Charley begins reassuringly, but Ettie cuts her off.

"You shouldn't put too much reliance on what I said."

"Oh I don't...no, I mean I do...that is I believe you... everything, but..."

"There could be some..."

"Danger?"

Ettie is silent, then they both speak together.

"Why do you say that?"

"No, I didn't mean..."

Silence again. Charley takes the initiative.

"I've written up an entirely new scene. I'm hoping...no I'm going to insist...Chris only shoots scenes that occur after the arrival of the king. That's after you...after 12th July when you..."

"Will he agree?"

"Without Lawrence Bullock he'll have to do something... different."

Ettie agrees, but the bigger battle with Chris is yet to come. Better be prepared. She rings Darren Slade, the actor who played John Ball in earlier scenes and tells him to get to the studio.

"You may be needed today."

"But I thought..."

"Change of plan, Chris is very insistent."

Darren is also reluctant, but he'll come. At the studio she gives him a copy of the new scene and then goes to Chris's room, but she can't find her notes of the previous day. She finds him leafing through them on the set and approaches apprehensively.

"They're just ideas," she says wearily, without warmth, "they need a lot..."

His response surprises her.

"It's so fresh, so different from your other stuff, all that obsession with...well, never mind. This could be our lifeline, more intimate, more closely observed. It's got great potential and it gets us away from the abbot. He hardly ever appears and with Lawrence..."

"We can't ignore the abbot altogether."

"Of course not, but at the moment...we can worry about that later. I like these discussion scenes with the townspeople chewing over their options and the scene in Hertford with that knight...what's his name...?"

"Walter at Lee."

"Yes and the squires and the peasants bursting in..."

"But we can't use it."

"Why not?"

"Because...because it's...before ..."

"Before what?"

"Before the king's arrival and yesterday we..."

"That's not important, without Lawrence this is ideal."

The Trojan horse wheeled in with the sinister forces about to be unleashed. Charley's desperation mounts.

"We should move on, get closer to the final scene. I've written something new with John Ball."

"John Ball? The Blackheath speech, we've done that."

"Yes, but he reappears after his arrest. The trial is important."

She hands over the new material. Chris grunts derisively as he skims through.

"We'll have to get Darren Slade to..."

"He's here and he already has the script."

"That's very presumptuous!"

"I wanted to save time."

Chris is unconvinced and wants to explore the other scenes. Another row is coming, but she persists, pushing the John Ball scene, saying it follows on naturally from the king's entry. He doesn't agree. What's so important with the arrival of the king anyway? She says it's important to get on with events *after* rather than before the king's arrival. She struggles when he challenges this, spluttering haltingly, afraid she might say that's the point of Ettie's return. Then Chris reacts, remembering her continuing concerns.

"You want to move on to that damned rehanging! That's what this is all about. Nothing to do with Lawrence. You want to do that and nothing else. Charley, you're obsessed. Give it up!"

Pummelling and countering, the row erupts again, the same sterile arguments hammered even more strongly, though at first in reversed roles, he on the initiative, promoting new scenes with her resisting. Then to break the deadlock she switches to her promotion of the John Ball trial. As she describes the scene, she sees people standing solemnly in a large room and Chris's pugnacious face is intermittently pushed aside by others, but the wide grey eyes and brown hair of one persists. She no longer cares about Chris's opposition, now determined to advance the cause of this man and of the thousands he represents.

The others gather round, no longer bystanders to some petty bickering, but drawn by Charley's witness to an old, yet ageless drama, Chris's interjections increasingly unheard through Charley's stream, though she's only the mouthpiece, the words come from another. Eventually, her task done, she stops, leaving Chris to argue impotently with himself as the small crowd erupts in spontaneous applause. Charley is amazed, but not triumphant. This is John Ball's victory not hers. Chris looks at the faces. Almost the whole cast surrounds him. He's not easily swayed by numbers, but shrugs and walks away.

"Will we do it?" Charley shouts after him.

"What about the other scenes?" he says, without turning round.

"We can still do them...later."

"If we shoot John Ball's trial, what about Grindcobb, we'll need Wesley Greville on set. I've not seen him."

"Yes, later too," she says, suddenly aware that she's not seen Wesley Greville either.

"Do what you like," he says, waving his arm, "where is Darren?"

Depressed and morose, Chris may be temporarily subdued, but the fight is not over. She has to find Darren quickly before he changes his mind again, but once Darren reads the lines, even Chris will be inspired. She finds Darren skulking in a corner. Like the others, he's been listening, but without enthusiasm. When he sees Charley approach, he moves away.

"I won't do it," he says when she catches up with him.

"You don't know..."

"You want me to play John Ball again. I won't..."

"Course you will," Chris shouts, "You've played him before, you'll play him now."

"I'm not ready, I've only just seen the script."

"So? Since when has that been a problem? You've just got to read it through and then..."

"I'm still not ready."

"What the hell do you mean?" Chris fumes, now standing directly in front of Darren, then turning to Charley, "You gave him the script, he's had plenty of time?"

She nods.

"Not ready," Darren mumbles.

"This is ridic..."

"Not ready...John Ball's not ready...needs more time... archbishop said...needs time...not ready..."

Chris and Charley stare at him stupefied.

"John Ball's not ready?" Chris repeats incredulously.

"He's been questioned enough!"

Chris stalks off, shouting, "You can all go home! First one scene, then another, so I agree because everybody wants to do it that way, but no, not everybody, somebody won't do it... okay, okay, have it your own way...forget it, forget the whole damned picture!"

Charley turns angrily to Darren.

"What are you playing at, it's your fault, if we..."

A firm hand is on her shoulder and she's spun round.

"Don't waste time with him, go after Chris!"

"Ettie! You're here!"

"Go after Chris, whatever happens he mustn't stop the film. It has to go on!"

Charley hesitates.

"Believe me," Ettie insists, "It's the real lesson from the past. I've been told."

"Told...?"

"Go after him. He's agreed. John Ball's trial is crucial!"

A moment's hesitation, a searching, unanswered glance and then Charley runs after Chris. Ettie turns to Darren.

"Sit down and don't move!"

He obeys immediately while she follows Charley. Everyone is on the set or almost everybody. She can't see Wesley Greville, the new actor assigned to play Grindcobb. The set momentarily dissolves, replaced by that old street she walked with Martha, filled again with people. It's been the same ever since she arrived at the studio, flickering visions ramming her mind. The past has not let go its hold. She's not escaped. The film is the chain and the links have been forged. It has to be seen through. Charley is right. *There* it's the 12th July. The king has arrived and so has John Ball. The trial must proceed.

They find Chris in his room, subdued, utterly dejected, all his confidence and vigour gone.

"I've had enough. The project is finished. I'll call the producers. They may insist, but they'll get nothing more out of me. If they can find another director..."

"You're not giving up," Ettie says, "The process can't be stopped now. You must shoot the scene of John Ball's trial and..."

"Oh yes and what about Darren? You heard him. 'John Ball's not ready!' What am I supposed to do?"

"...John Ball is ready...we are all ready...and we will be avenged..."

Ettie knows who speaks in her head.

"You have to go on," she says, "Don't worry about Darren, he..."

"Never mind about Darren, what about me? How am I supposed to work through this chaos!"

"...we will be avenged...then we will be free..."

"You have to begin the scene, there's no time to lose!"

Chris shakes his head, sinking lower in his chair. A figure in coarse brown cloth appears behind him. At first indistinct, the shape solidifies and she recognises Thomas.

"...I have seen him again...the tall man with the long hair...it is him..."

He points towards Chris, but only Ettie sees and only she hears. The realisation is immediate. She has to act quickly. She has to talk to Jenner!

10

ETTIE stands at the door, unable to move. The longer she stays the greater the danger. Staying at home means inactivity and inactivity means danger. Not to her, but to everything else for she has a role to perform, which can't be completed here, for she's drawn away in both time and place. She has her coat and hat. It may be cold and she needs protection. Purely physical covering isn't enough, but it's reassuring. A coat to a psychic is like armour to a soldier. Without it she doesn't *feel* right, while her hat exudes a particular intangible strength. She still doesn't know where to go. Once out of the house it'll become clear. She must trust her instincts. She will be guided. She goes back and stares at the common from the window. It draws, but not strongly enough, but then where else? Several police cars are in the distance. They weren't here yesterday. There's a knock at the door. She glances through the window. It's Jennifer.

"I don't suppose you've seen the boss?" She says.

Ettie shakes her head, then nods towards the window.

"Why are there so many police cars on the common?"

Jennifer explains about the 'dig.'

"We've started at a place called Lock's Spinney. It was where Melvyn Strange and the others used to hang out. I'm not sure it's going to get us anywhere, except…"

Ettie senses her unease.

"You've seen something?"

Jennifer mentions the two men she saw on the common.

"So it might be significant after all?"

"Funny Kathleen never mentioned it before. Ettie, I don't suppose you could come out with me this morning. Out on the common where we're digging, you might feel something that helps me."

Ettie is apprehensive as they drive to Lock's Spinney, suddenly fearful of the common. Jennifer is still anxious to find Jenner.

"The boss went to see George Carter, but he seems to have disappeared too."

Jennifer watches Ettie at the 'dig,' several times asking if she 'feels' anything.

Ettie shakes her head, saying "I can't help you with this... excavation. I've no idea where Melvyn Strange will be found if he can be found at all."

Jennifer is called by one of the officers and needing to be alone, Ettie takes the opportunity to walk further away. It's not that she doesn't feel, but that she feels too much. The air is dense and her feet thump dully on the leaden earth. She has to commune with whatever or whoever is close. She stops by a low hedge, out of sight and out of hearing of the police. She feels confined by a charged heaviness like being surrounded by hundreds of threatening, but silent birds. Everywhere buzzes with concentrated presences, but their meaning or purpose is shrouded and she struggles to understand. She wanders further, but the compression of the air and weightiness in the ground continues. She walks faster, hoping the speed and lightness in her feet may lift the oppressive solidity.

Suddenly she really is alone, to one side a short line of small, but close packed trees, while on the other the grassland falls away to open fields. The air is not only heavy, but utterly still and silent, the grass and the trees unchanged, as they have been over hundreds of years. She may have crossed some unseen boundary as she entered this grove. With no one around how can she know whether this is the present or the past? Yet her loneness is illusory, for in the past no one is alone. She feels vulnerable near the trees, so walks towards the slope and open country, but stops after only a few steps. She senses someone behind her. Unwilling, but unable to resist she twists round as different visions flood her mind. She closes her eyes as she turns fully, then slowly opens them again. Martha stands by the trees, her lips twitching in half smiled acknowledgement as she walks forward. Half fearful, half intrigued, Ettie knows this is no flitting appearance and is determined to take the initiative.

"You're a long way from home, even Hempston is..."

"My home may be everywhere just as Thomas...after the great calamity...he may be anywhere."

"The great calamity," Ettie repeats.

"He is an outlaw," Martha says in a wavering voice, shaking her head and smoothing the backs of her fingers as if thrusting water from them.

"Is he here?" Ettie says.

"I knew the guilt would consume him. I told him these things are beyond our powers and our wits. He couldn't blame himself. None of us could be blamed, but he wouldn't accept it. *Our wits are constrained only by the truth or we have no wit at all*, he said. After the terrible calamity..."

The phrase resounds and jars, confounding Ettie even more.

"...*the axe was sharp, the stroke was hard in the fourth year of King Richard*...those were his last words before he left. It means the return of the repressed, but he hasn't returned. He must come back, soon it could be too late."

"Is he here?"

"In the woods and fields as the birds fly in the autumn, but return in the spring."

Ettie reels in confusion. Today it's 3rd July, but Ettie was two weeks in 1381 and if Thomas is an outlaw, it must be *later* than 15th July, at least three days after Ettie left. That's ridiculous, this is not *any* date in 1381. That's the past, it's gone. But if Martha talks of events after 15th June then it can't be 3rd July, it must be...

"You must help me."

"But I don't know where he..."

"If he's to come back, you must…"

"No, I don't *know!*"

Ettie backs away a few paces. Martha walks slowly towards her.

"They have John Ball," she says.

"When was he taken?" Ettie says, confused again by Martha's switchback in her own time, now talking about events *before* the 15th.

Martha shakes her head, as if she too is confused and says, "Why, today of course, not yesterday."

"The 12th?" Ettie says.

"When the king came."

"And that was yesterday?" Ettie says, hoping, unsuccessfully, to fix Martha at some definite date

"They says he's confessed – *confessed* – confessed to what?"

John Ball's trial? Just like the film. Is this the present in the past or the past in the present? It's too much. This is a mistake. This is not the place she ought to be. She turns and runs, at first towards Jennifer and her 'diggers,' but then veering to the north, careering purposelessly towards the town. Someone runs behind and so she runs even faster. Surely soon she'll see someone who can help? If she gets to the town she'll be safe. She gets to the cricket ground. It's a bright morning. There should be plenty of people around. There's no one. She runs on, but losing energy and a developing pain in her side she stops.

She turns round apprehensively, but there's no one to be seen. Gradually she calms and turns away from town, making for the cottage. She crosses the road, glancing not just at the traffic, but also back towards the common, anxiously scanning for a woman in very old costume. Again she senses Martha speaking to her, asking her to act, to stop something happening, the past bent on changing itself! She wants Ettie to intervene for Thomas, but what does she expect her to do, *unmake* him as an outlaw? How can she intercede between right and wrong? The law is still the law even in 1381, but who's law? She'd seen *their* law in London, the unequal, repressive law that ground down the people. But their law is their past.

She resisted interference a year ago and must resist it now. If the past is rerun it can only be as it was lived then, not as it might be *meant* to be. What was must be what is.

When and where is Martha? Is she still there at the king's arrival when Ettie left or is she at another undisclosed aftertime? Is she at home in St. Albans or doe she stand beside the trees, then running through the grass and accosting Ettie on the common? The film is a chronological template, pulling past and present together. That's how she was brought back. Now they've stopped filming, allowing Martha to waver around in time and place and all for Thomas, the threatening outlaw. They must start filming again, but is it really possible to hold back let alone control the past? Now she realises. The location of John Ball's trial has been drawing her since this morning. In the cottage she gets out *A Little Liberty*, checking on the trial, reading on to the last few pages in which Warren set out the crucial events after 15ᵗʰ July. Then she understands what Martha wants her to do. It has to be and she gets ready to go.

Jenner eyes the staff of the *Mid Herts Herald* sceptically.

"You have no idea of the editor's whereabouts?"

"Not seen him for days," one reporter says.

"What was he working on?"

More blank looks.

"Is everybody here?"

They all nod.

"It's like interviewing a herd of bloody sheep," he thinks and says, "Alright, if he's not here, how will you get the paper out?"

"All the advertising's sorted," a woman says, "All the usual columns are completed."

"You're the deputy editor?"

She nods reluctantly, "All the items are on schedule, so..."

"...you don't really need an editor at all?"

"I didn't say that."

"It's implied. If you don't know what he was working on..."

"With George leaving so suddenly…"

Jenner glares pugnaciously around the group.

"This is a murder enquiry."

They all look nervously towards the deputy editor.

"You must have some idea of his projects. He must have spoken to somebody?"

The deputy editor squirms under his accusatory gaze.

"The last thing he mentioned was a dispute over a footpath. He talked about an interview."

"Who with, where?"

"A woman – a walker activist he called her – contacted him, saying she'd discovered an old map. Apparently she was very excited. It was over two hundred years old and the right of way was clearly marked. She'd been in dispute with the landowner and…"

"Where is this?"

"He was very vague."

"It had to be within your circulation area?"

"Despite its name our paper circulates in three counties."

"Where did he go?"

"We've already told you, he didn't say he was going anywhere."

"I'm not satisfied with your answers. I remind you that withholding information, particularly in an enquiry of this importance, is a criminal offence."

The threat produces no response. The deputy editor sits with her arms folded, impassive and rigid, the other staff taking their cue from her.

"Is he usually this secretive?" Jenner asks.

"No…not usually," the deputy editor says.

Then one of the others says, "But he has been lately."

"Where's his office?"

Jenner is directed to a small, cluttered room at the rear of the building, saying "and don't anybody leave."

He sits in the chair with the door open so he can see everyone in the front office. They can't say or won't say. Why would George be deliberately vague? The desk is very untidy, the drawers crammed with rubbish. He rummages through them, scattering unwanted material on the floor. The staff watches him apprehensively. What are they afraid he'll find? At last, stuffed into the back of a drawer he finds what he's looking for, a working diary. Had Carter deliberately shoved it out of sight before making his getaway? Jenner flicks through. Like the room, the desk and the drawers, it's very untidy. Not every page has entries and where there are the majority refer to routine meetings. On every page there are scribbled jottings, doodles, even little pictures, noughts and crosses and peculiar symbols at different angles. It resembles a young child's exercise book, having only just learnt to write. The days before his disappearance are crammed with this farrago of nonsense. Finding nothing of value Jenner is ready to give up until he sees a scrawled note on the page for today.

'Watling Street – the secret may lie there.'

A proposed interview at a place near Watling Street – the A5? It's too vague. He could search for a month and never find it. He skims back a few pages before closing the diary. Then, a week ago there's another note.

'In the old days they never cleaned the front windows.'

A pointless idle scribble from some idiotic reverie? Jenner turns the book round as if from another direction it might make more sense. He flicks back to the other page. The entries are around a week apart. What if the first note was made when the woman rang him and the interview was arranged for today? Watling Street and cleaning – or rather not cleaning – windows, what is the connection? He stares at the first note dumbfounded. The rest of the page is littered with more scribbled garbage. Then, right at the bottom below the last line – a name, Annabel Levins – is this the woman he went to see? There's no address or phone number. It could be anywhere, if only he knew where to look. All he has is that odd statement – *they never cleaned their front windows.* Something jars. He's heard the phrase before. Before the M1 was built the A5 was a very busy road and the villages had no bypasses. Then he remembers.

'It was so busy with the heavy lorries, the fumes and the narrow pavements, the women could never clean their front windows.'

Jenner's father, he can see him now, ruminating at the table, chuckling to himself. He was talking about the old A5. What was the place he meant? Jenner needs a reminder, a local map. There's a large scale map of the area in the outer office. The staff watches him with mounting anxiety as he studies it.

"Aha, got it!" he shouts as he finds the place and marches to the door, "Most helpful!"

He leaves a message on Jennifer's mobile for her to check back with the newspaper in case George returns. Then he gets in the car and heads for the A5, leaving the newspaper staff vigorously scrutinising the map. It's a short journey to Markyate, the village 'where they never cleaned their windows.' He's not been here for over twenty years. Now there is a bypass. He stops just outside and scans his own map. It has to be a hamlet very close to the village. There are two possibilities. He opts for the nearest – Dirringstead. It's a tiny place, only a few houses. Surely it won't be difficult to find Annabel Levins – if she's the one. He stops at the pub.

"Last house on the left," the landlord says, "Are you another one of those walkers? We don't want no trouble, she's already upset one of the farmers..."

Jenner is reluctant to divulge his identity. There are enough hares running across the landscape without adding to them. He's 'an old friend' and feigns ignorance of her 'campaign' to reopen the disused footpath, which the landlord is only too pleased to talk about at length.

"Has she had any other visitors recently?" Jenner says.

The landlord shrugs.

"No more than usual, plenty of the rambling lot beat a path to her door."

"Anyone specifically asked for her, perhaps from the newspapers?"

"No. Hey, you're not a reporter are you?"

Dutifully reassuring the landlord of his lack of journalistic credentials, Jenner leaves. He feels a fleeting nervousness as he walks down the lane to the house. Poking about in the past – even a *different* past – is not 'healthy.' The houses are old labourers' cottages, spruced up and gentrified with their neat hedges and pretty window boxes, but exuding another age. It's not difficult to imagine the original inhabitants, the men returning from the fields, the women plaiting straw for the hat trade. With each step he encroaches another decade on someone else's time. Or is it his own time or that of his father's father? It seems an alien, yet also oddly familiar place where so much is different, but where he's expected to know the rules. He reminds himself of the purpose of his visit. Why was he so diffident about his intentions at the pub as if he's afraid of being conspicuous?

There's a car parked at the side entrance, but no answer to his knock. He glances in the front window. Two people sit at a table in the rear of a long, dark room. A woman has her back to him while a man faces the window. The man returns Jenner's stare. They recognise each other simultaneously. George Carter says something and then gets up. The woman turns and looks to the window. Jenner returns to the door, pushes it open and steps into the room as George scuttles out the back. The woman is taller than she appeared, in her late forties, casually dressed, heavy, with a swinging gait as she approaches.

"What is the meaning of this intrusion...?"

Jenner tries to get past, but she blocks his way.

"You are Annabel Levins?"

"What do you want?"

"That man is George Carter?"

"Yes he is, but I don't understand..."

"I'm a police officer, madam, I need to speak to him."

George runs down the garden. Jenner manages to get past the startled Annabel and reaches the back door.

"Where's he going?"

"He's a reporter. He came to see me about the old path. He's very interested in all the old roads...or that's what he said...you see I have this map..."

"Can he get out of the garden?"

"Yes, there's a side alley..."

"Where does it go?"

"Back to the road."

"So he can't escape?"

"I don't know what this is all about, but…"

George is no longer in the garden. Jenner moves towards the front door, trying to get past Annabel again. She's even larger than he first realised and wedged between the wall and the table is a formidable obstacle.

"Madam, if you'd kindly…"

Then he hears the car in the side entrance.

"Your car…?"

"I don't own a car."

Too late, it accelerates up the lane. Jenner races out the front door to see it passing the pub. The stunned Annabel watches him run back to his own car and then drive away in pursuit. George is not in sight, but on the single road through the hamlet there's no chance for a deviation. If Jenner drives fast enough he can catch him, but George knows the road well and risks blind corners with ease. When he reaches the main road Jenner has lost him. At the A5 he turns north, sure he'll find George. He's not disappointed. On the straight road George's advantage of local knowledge disappears and after a half mile Jenner spies the familiar car. But why is he running? He recognised Jenner and doesn't want to be questioned. What is he hiding?

Then, as they approach Dunstable Downs and Jenner is sure he'll draw level and force him to pull over, the car suddenly swerves right, across the road and stops on the grass. George jumps out and runs into some trees. The traffic is against him and Jenner has to wait for it to clear, then pulls over and gets quickly through the trees, but George has gone, slipped into the emptiness of the Downs as if wafted in air. Jenner even looks up, half expecting to see George aloft. It reminds him of kite flying in his childhood. His father had a passion for kites and model aeroplanes, which he made himself. They would come here because the old man said they could get 'better lift.' Young Jenner didn't entirely share his father's enthusiasm, but it was a good day out. He's not been back for years.

He runs up the hill, looking from side to side in case he might spot George, but soon slows to a rhythmic trudge, his shoes springing on the hard dry grass to the regular intakes of his breath. It's a place of his past, but there's a more immediate, less personal past – the Waintree development and how its entanglements could lie at the heart of his investigation. Even the elusive newspaper editor could be involved, now seemingly evaporating into the Chiltern escarpment. He walks back towards the road. The past – all the pasts – pulls and repels. His own intrudes again, kites and planes and fathers, the magnetism of memory, the sadness of regrets. No point wandering around aimlessly reminiscing when work's to be done. He'll go back to Dirringstead, question Annabel Levins, find out what she knows of George, get some indication where he might have gone.

At the clump of trees he's about to walk to the car when a man approaches...

There's a plaque on the outer wall of W.H. Smith on the corner of Upper Dagnall Street. This was the site of the Moot Hall, where John Ball and the leaders of the St. Albans citizenry were tried after the great Revolt in 1381. Ettie glances at the passing shoppers. They've probably passed this place a thousand times and never even stopped to read the brief inscription. While of those that have, few will have realised its real significance. She doesn't blame them. A few weeks ago she was no wiser. Ignorance may not just be bliss, it may be safe, but not knowing your past might make it impossible to understand your present. If this is the site of the Moot Hall then it's probably the best place to make contact.

The shop is not busy. The counter assistant smiles as she enters. Ettie is tempted to say something.

"Excuse me, I'm not actually here to buy...in fact not even look at anything, but I do need to stay awhile. I have urgent business in 1381, which cannot be avoided, so I may need to stay for an hour or so. I won't get in the way because I won't really be here...at least not in the normal..."

An hour? Will she need that long? Surely if this is the place the effect will be immediate? She wanders around, expecting to pick up a presence, but feels nothing. Yet there is a pull and it is close. She keeps moving, stopping intermittently. Her senses remain drawn, but indeterminate. One of the assistants watches her. In a moment she'll ask if she can help. This is the fifth time Ettie has returned to the magazines! She moves back to the entrance. Either she's lost her gift of contact with the past or...this is not the place! Whatever the plaque may say this is not the site of the Moot Hall.

She returns to the street and stands forlornly, looking around vacantly, feeling distinctly foolish. What if this is the place? If she can't make contact at the site of the Moot Hall where those tragic men were tried then there can be no contact, no hope at all! She walks up and down the pavement in her frustration. Is this how Maggie Morton felt? Did this impotence drive her to distraction, even madness?

She's still drawn and wanders into the middle of the street where it gets even stronger as she reaches the other side. She walks along the side of the old town hall and it strengthens further. She goes to the tourist office, located in the old building, her legs carried by a burning impulse while her rational senses tell her it's ridiculous and vainly try to apply the brakes. Yet this has to be the place. Never mind about the plaque. She can't be wrong. The plaque is on the wrong side of the street. This is the site of the old Moot Hall! Inside she naively expects a vast open space, unchanged except for a few modern fittings in six hundred years! Instead she finds a narrow entrance leading to a small empty room except for a solitary woman behind the counter. She hovers a few moments beside the books and leaflets, unsure what to do hoping some extrasensory power might provide guidance. Then she realises she's left both her coat and hat in the car and they might act as both receptors and defenders in any perilous venture.

"Can I help you?" the woman says.

Only now does Ettie realise she's been nervously rearranging the leaflets.

"Are you looking for anything in particular?"

"I...er...looking?" Ettie says, trying to find an appropriate response and then unthinkingly, "Yes...of course...the court."

Before even finishing the word she's ready to take it back, but it's too late.

"The old courtroom? It's just there."

Ettie freezes as the woman points to a door, slightly ajar beside the leaflets.

"Just go in."

Old courtroom? Surely this can't be...?

"Yes, that door, you're right next to it."

Ettie nods and smiles as she reluctantly steps into an intact courtroom, around two hundred years old. She shuffles a few paces and sits down in one of the benches in the small public gallery. She's close to the dock and facing the high bench where the judge must have sat. It's very compact and she's alone, the emptiness enhancing her foreboding. She hears a click and turns to see the door has closed behind her. It probably means nothing, but it increases her agitation. She could get up, but the pull is at its strongest now and despite her fear she must remain. She glances around. Though not as old as the place she seeks, the atmosphere is heavy with the accumulated memories of two centuries and as she scans the empty benches the wigged lawyers, the noisy public and the wretched 19th century petty criminals people the desolate court. But this is not *the* time, so why does she feel other presences? Because this is *the* place, the site of that other, older...

...the walls and ceiling are suddenly less distinct, less firm, almost as if they move. Then after a brief waver like a flag caught in a breeze, the walls to each side disappear and she is at one side of a larger room with a high vaulted ceiling. Conscious of her modern clothes she steps quickly towards a large number of people. Despite her fears they seem not to notice her and she's able to find a vantage point next to the wall, relatively unseen, but from which she can see everything in the hall.

All trace of the old wood lined 19th century room is gone and the large hall is set out as a court. To her front is a long, stout table, with several clerks sitting at one end. There are also soldiers, armed with swords and what appear to be long spears with broad, fearsome ends. There's a large, ornately carved chair at the centre of the table, facing the body of the hall, flanked by another chair on each side. All three are unoccupied. The rest of the hall is crammed with people except for a wide passage down the centre, guarded at several points by more soldiers. Judging by their clothes the crowd is composed of a broad spectrum of the town's population, from wealthy burghers to the humblest citizens, dressed in little better than rags. They are sombre and generally quiet except for a few muted conversations. Quite close to Ettie, two women are speaking. She can hear, but not see them.

"They say he was taken in Coventry."

"No doubt by the same treacherous townsmen we have here."

"He was lucky to have got that far."

"He's a good man, he's done no one any harm, only preached God's word."

"Maybe that's what will condemn him. In a world where God's truth is trampled down, what justice can be expected for those that proclaim it?"

"There are those who…"

"Quiet, they are coming in!"

Like the rest of the crowd, they turn to see a man entering from a side door. The clerks stand and the soldiers come to a stiff attention. The man moves quickly to the table, glances arrogantly at the crowd and confers with the clerks.

"Is that him?" one of the women whispers.

"Yes, the new chief justice."

The man turns from the clerks and sits in the grand middle chair. It's the same man Ettie accosted as he rode into the town. Robert Tresilian. When was that? Today or yesterday, if today only a few hours ago by the reckoning of these times. Will he recognise her, demand an explanation, make her face him in the centre of the room?

"Bring in the prisoner!"

She looks up slowly. He glances in her direction, but seems not to notice. Either he doesn't recognise or…he cannot see her. There's a movement at the side of the room and two soldiers emerge with a bedraggled looking man.

"John Ball," the woman whispers, a little too loudly.

The words are taken up by others in the crowd and soon the clarion call 'John Ball! John Ball! John Ball!' resounds around the throng, increasing in volume until, almost becoming a chant, Tresilian intervenes.

"Silence!"

The soldiers in the central aisle brace themselves and point their weapons at the crowd and the noise dies down. John Ball is brought to the middle of the room. He makes no immediate acknowledgement of Tresilian and looks down at the floor.

"Face me," Tresilian snaps

A soldier prods John Ball and he looks up at the judge.

"You are John Ball, at sometime you were St. Mary priest of York?"

"I am, I was."

"You are charged with high treason."

John Ball says nothing for a few moments, staring at Tresilian as if to discern the true worth of the man, then says, "I am guilty only of..."

"Silence! This is not the time. You will be tried tomorrow and then sentenced."

"If I am guilty."

Tresilian leers down as if to deny the remote possibility of him not being found guilty, saying nothing for a few moments and then with a perfunctory, "Take him away."

John Ball is pulled from the table and hurriedly dragged back through the door. The clerks gather up their papers and Tresilian turns towards the crowd where growls and grumbles have resumed.

"The court is adjourned. If there is a repetition of this unseemly rumbling tomorrow I shall deal with it most severely. Clear the court!"

The soldiers bark at the people and hustle them towards the back of the room. Those around Ettie start to move off. She hesitates to join them, suddenly aware again of her appearance and reluctant to be seen as different, but if she waits she'll be isolated and appear even more conspicuous. As she juggles the alternatives a woman emerges from the crowd on the opposite side. She ignores the soldiers and walks over, looking directly at Ettie, who is ignored by everyone else, including Tresilian. Ettie sees that familiar pleading, demanding expression. What will Martha say, here in the court? She knows Ettie has already challenged Tresilian, will she want her to do it again? Ettie looks to the soldiers. They seem not to have noticed the woman striding across the room and are busily herding other people from the hall. Ettie has her back to the wall. No one is near and Martha is almost upon her. This has been a terrible mistake. Why did she interfere again with the past when she could have left it alone? She has to get back to her own time!

"Your quest has only just begun, while mine is almost at an end."

Jenner turns towards the road, intent on getting back to the car, wasting no more time, finding George Carter, but the road is different and very quiet. So quiet in fact it's utterly silent! Jenner has to blink to be sure, but now it's much narrower, more like a track with stony patches, though heavily potholed. An old Watling Street.

"I have been taken."

The man stands in a long, dark brown, coarse woollen gown, tied at his waist by a cord, from which hang some beads like a rosary and a bag, from which the top of a book protrudes. Big boned, with a large nose and wide nostrils, a ring of dark hair surrounding a large bald patch in the centre of his head, his wide, grey eyes stare with deep, open concentration.

"It's a dream," Jenner mutters, faintly aware of the man's identity, but unwilling to acknowledge it.

"I am a dream to you as you are to me," the man says, "for you can tell me of your days as I can tell you of mine."

"You are..." Jenner begins.

"John Ball, priest of God."

"No," Jenner says, turning and looking around him again, hoping for reassurance this really is a dream from which he'll soon awake.

But there's no metalled road, no cars, no hubbub, no people, only him and this man from...where...and when?

"I have not long to talk to you," John says.

Jenner refuses to believe his eyes and ears. This place

with its seductive memories ensnares him in a particularly vivid reverie. Yet this is no memory of his, no long buried recollection suddenly unearthed from its dormant sleep. More a fabrication from someone else's musings, snatches of conversation repackaged in his unconscious, episodes he's taken more notice of than he realised. He's absorbed the seeds of Ettie's talk, nurtured in this remembering place, now bursting forth with this fascinating, but ridiculous apparition. But this is no freeze framed daydream. This is real and this man should be challenged, questioned on his movements, where he's from, where he's going, what he's up to...but Jenner is oddly constrained and can only watch and listen.

"Be careful in your vigilance..."

Does John Ball know he's a policeman? He seems to know as much about Jenner as Jenner knows about him.

"I am always vigilant," Jenner says laconically.

"Then do not forsake your vigilance. For they will use it against you, for their truth is not your truth."

"They?"

John Ball looks around apprehensively.

"They will return shortly. They say I am to be taken to St. Albans to the king. I always wanted to see the king."

"You saw him at Smithfield."

"I left after Wat was so foully betrayed. Then I too was betrayed in Coventry."

"You will..."

"No," John says, putting up his hand, "What has to be will be. It need not be said."

"Yet, it will..."

But Jenner stops. He can't believe he's doing this. If this is no dream, how can he play the 14th century game, tinker with past and look into another man's future through the frosty glass of his present knowledge? Yet John Ball won't let him. Is it because he too knows?

"Where are your guards?"

John Ball opens his hands and nods to his side, "They are close, it's a long journey from Coventry."

"You could..."

"Escape? As you may...escape...to wherever...Try it."

But Jenner hasn't considered 'escape.' He's too stupefied at being in his own schoolbook past. Now as he turns to John's outstretched arms and waving gestures he sees no hills, no track, all lost in a distant haze.

"Where...when?" Jenner begins.

John smiles softly.

"Fleeting thoughts as we tramp through some soft sandbank of separated time, seeing and hearing each other in our dreams as we stop to rest. I shall remember you as you will remember me when you come to measure your truth against those of your rulers."

"I'm beholden to no man."

"Then you are lucky indeed or that really is your dream."

"My values are my own, not delusions," Jenner says angrily.

"When the great tread down the little they do not always do it with their own feet."

"Truth is important to my investigation, not others' narrow interests."

"If you only serve truth, then we are as one, but in this life there is no middle ground between those that live to till the field and those that live from its fruits."

"It's not so simple in my..."

"...in your time?"

"The investigation must fit the conditions," Jenner says irritably and tiring of where this 'game' is leading, "You won't understand."

"I understand eternal values. They have not changed since the beginning of the world and never will."

"We talk at cross purposes, there's no parallel, each person...."

"...makes up his own values to fit the circumstances irrespective of the people? I am of the people, I cannot go against..."

Jenner is fearful of being drawn too far and divulging what John Ball cannot know. Yet he must be warned.

"Yours is a troubled time. Being of the people makes you vulnerable. What you have spoken to the thousands will be used against you. For yourself..."

"Self, self...self lies at the core of the world's rottenness."

"We are all individuals."

"Can the one sailor sail the ship without the other sailors? Each is part of the host, willingly or unwillingly, strong or weak, we are as wise or as misguided as the host we choose... or are forced to belong."

Jenner is uncomfortable. John Ball speaks of his own time, but his six hundred year old values may be more transferable than he realises.

"Did you choose your calling?" John says.

Jenner doesn't immediately respond, though there can be only one answer.

"Yes."

"If you undertake the work of the rulers, you cannot escape their values."

Jenner turns away. Now John talks of clerks and lawyers, soldiers, bailiffs and stewards. Even 'escheators,' responsible for reverting property back to a feudal lord, disinheriting a tenant's family. What is this medieval nonsense? Who is this man to challenge his fundamental beliefs? He's only a projection, an animated sliver of history, prised from a book, a debilitating vision plucked out of a dream.

"They are coming for me," John says, "but you can escape no more than I."

"Of course I can. I've not been arrested, I'm not being held."

"Some of the stoutest shackles are not made of iron, but forged in folk's hearts and minds. So too are the keys that release them."

"No, no!" Jenner shouts, "I'll not be browbeaten by a hedge priest from the past!"

He runs towards the trees. Will the haze disperse? Will he see the road, cars or more rolling country bereft of those signatures of his own time? He is pulled as much as he runs, propelled on, further, deeper. He reaches the trees. There's no haze and he can see the grass beyond, but it's too far to the road. He looks back to a bare hillside. John Ball is gone. Perhaps taken by his guards to continue the journey south. Only a few miles now to St. Albans and the king's court.

Jenner stares unbelievingly into the distance. The further he runs away, the further he gets back to where he began, not in space, but in time. Beyond the trees should be the road and two cars, but there's no road and no cars. Still he's pulled as if he's lifted from the ground, as if he's being carried away.

Voices beyond the wall. Someone is asking for directions. The tourist office. Has Ettie really only been away a few seconds? She screws her eyes, hoping, willing Martha to be gone. Yet it's her not Martha expelled from the moot hall and no longer conspicuous in the crowd, but alone and back in the old courtroom. The high bench, the wooden walls close in. This is no place to be, neither 14th nor 21st century! She should get up, run to the door and wrench it open, but it opens without her and a couple enter.

"What an amazing place!" the woman declaims as if addressing the whole court and moves towards Ettie.

She's almost upon her! Get back to your stately homes and your day out leaflets! I don't want you here! This is the place of the moot hall and though it's unclear and she fears it, her purpose is unfinished. She has to go on and...She shuts her eyes in desperation, no more wishing to be in this courtroom than back there facing Martha...but where and when...it's unfinished...there remains...she won't be confronted... detained...she'll go...

"When was it last used as a court?"

Eyes tight shut as the question is repeated, but the voice fades. Just as she got away from Martha, surely she can get away from these people? Wooden benches are like vaulted ceilings and rough plastered walls, peripheral enclosures that can be willed into or out of time in place. She only has to concentrate long enough...hold it...and...the shuddering talk, at first soft, gradually increasing breaks through...the couple must have gone. Louder now, she opens her eyes and is back in the moot hall. Is it still today or already tomorrow? When was John Ball's trial, the 12th or the 13th? She struggles to remember the passages in *A Little Liberty*, but is unable to concentrate as the court is assembling again. Everyone stands as the grim faced Tresilian enters.

"Bring in the prisoners."

The people loudly grumble their disapproval.

"Silence!" Tresilian booms and the hubbub gradually subsides.

Ettie glances nervously into the crowd. She can't see Martha or at first anyone she knows, then as the men are brought in and all faces turn together, she sees Thomas sitting alone. If he is to be an outlaw, it has not yet happened. Fifteen men enter under heavy guard, led by Grindcobb, Cadindon and Barbintsor. They look drawn and nervous, except for Grindcobb who stares defiantly at Tresilian and smiles to the crowd as if they rather than him need reassurance and invigoration. They respond with something close to a cheer and Tresilian is forced to demand silence again. But Thomas remains quiet and serious, never taking his eyes from Grindcobb, perhaps sensing the outcome of events better than most.

"You have been brought here from Hertford to answer charges to be laid against you," Tresilian barks, "Have you anything to say?"

"We'll answer when we are charged," Grindcobb says quietly, "Until then..."

"...until then you will be held in custody," Tresilian interrupts him, "until Monday 15th July. Take them away!"

The soldiers shuffle the men out. This time the nascent cheer breaks out.

"Be silent or I will clear the court!" Tresilian shouts, thumping the table, his cheeks flushed, his eyes livid.

This time Thomas cheers with the others, but Ettie sees the despondency and wonders again what coming event Martha wants her to prevent. Does she expect Ettie to stop him running away and becoming an outlaw?

"Bring forward Ball," Tresilian says as the tumult abates once more, "There will be absolute silence when I deal with this prisoner or I'll not hesitate to arrest those disturbing it."

John Ball is brought in. As he looks kindly from side to side at the hushed assembly most gaze with curious and respectful reverence on the surviving leader of the great Revolt for the first time. Tresilian's imposed silence on the crowd will make the resulting interchange even more charged and awesome. His simple coarse brown gown contrasts with Tresilian's colourful and elaborate coat. They stare at each other in silence for a few moments. Tresilian stiff and inflexible, resolutely determined to carry out his terrible 'duty.' Ball eyes him with a serene, but fateful confidence, lacking in hate, but realistically wary. The clerk hands some papers to Tresilian, which he then waves at Ball.

"We have letters found in the sleeve of a rebel before he was hanged. They were intended for the Essex leaders, this communicant..."

"A messenger of the Great Society," Ball says quietly.

"Aha!" Tresilian shouts gleefully, "You admit you sent this letter."

Ettie shivers, remembering Alan, the 'messenger' she'd met in London. Surely he's not this man who was hanged, but safe in his Essex village. In her reverie she misses the next interchange, but is brought back as Tresilian thunders at Ball.

"You told the mob they were oppressed and preached to them the equality of all men?"

"It is true I told them all mankind are equal. We come into the world as helpless infants, why then these meaningless distinctions?"

"All men's positions are ordained by God."

"God did not make the lord and the serf. Sir judge, you are clad in furs and your cellar is stored with fine wines, your larder hung with dainties, while your vassal, as virtuous by nature as yourself..."

"...his deprivations are..."

"...the result of your tyranny, shivering in his rags, starving amidst the plenty he creates."

"You stir up men to evil and rebellion."

"I have said these things are wrong and I repeat it. Christ redeemed us all without exception, the lowly as well as the great. Surely it is therefore His will that all should be free. There will come a time when this great truth will be felt by all mankind and be confessed..."

"Confess? Now, do you confess?"

"I confess to the truth."

Tresilian doesn't immediately reply. No one speaks or moves and for a few moments the intense and charged silence permeates the room. Like the others, Ettie is transfixed, but unlike them she doesn't stare at Ball and Tresilian, but into the crowd, which she scans desperately, searching for familiar, though not reassuring faces. She should be relieved not to see Martha with her accusing, desolate eyes, but instead her unease increases. The suffused silence is broken as Tresilian speaks, but she doesn't hear him and edges along the wall towards the back. John Ball speaks and a rippling defiance rumbles through the room, quickly curtailed by Tresilian's call for 'silence' and a further warning. Ettie turns back. She fancies she sees a familiar face nearby, but this is lost as she catches sight of Thomas again, now also easing away from his group and heading towards the back of the room. He stares directly at her. She wants to look away, but can't. Tresilian is talking again, reading from a paper. The crowd is hushed and attentive. John Ball is nodding. Thomas is closer. He looks at her again and speaks, but it's impossible to make out any words. She squeezes past people and eases into the central aisle. She glances back. He's there too, coming towards her! She has to get away. She turns. There are no guards at the back of the hall. She runs towards the open rear door and as she leaps into the street, sees another familiar face, which she hears say 'He must be saved.'

Jenner glances around, startled by the unfamiliar clothes, the even less familiar speech, the bare room with its high ceiling. From his vantage about halfway up the central aisle he recognises the man facing the judge, the same man he encountered on the road. It seems just seconds ago. So where is this place? All eyes are on John Ball as Tresilian berates him.

*"John Sheep, sometime St. Mary priest of York and now of Colchester...*that is you, is it not?"

"I was in York, "when I..."

"...greets well John Nameless and John Miller and John Carter,

bids them to beware of guile in borough and stand together in God's name.

301

Bid Piers Ploughman go to his work, chastise well Hobb the robber,

take with you John Trewman and all his fellows and no more

*and look sharp you keep united and no more...*These are your accomplices, this John Miller and John Nameless and John Carter. What are their real names?"

"The names of no one and everyone, of one man and everyman, they are the people."

"Yes! You admit you wrote this letter?"

"I am familiar with it."

"*...beware of guile in borough...*you speak of London... stand together in God's name...a clear call to insurrection... *chastise well Hobb the Robber...*this refers to the late Sir Robert Hales, vilely cut down by the rebels and here you..."

"England has many robbers, not all have yet been chastised by the people."

"The people who must...*look sharp...keep united?*"

Ball says nothing.

"Your silence condemns you as much as your words. Confess! You sent this letter!"

Jenner is afraid to make the slightest sound, fearful of those around him and the august judge, but most of all of the stillness of the room, pervasive and dreadful. Tresilian's bullying irritates him. He's impressed by Ball's refusal to be ensnared in his trap, but puzzled by his ambiguous replies. Why doesn't he just deny any connection with the wretched letter? Unless of course he really did send it, even so...a slight noise distracts and he turns to the back of the room. A woman is running towards the door. There's something very familiar about her.

Tresilian is irritated and wearied by John Ball's 'intransigence.' He spends more futile minutes trying to dislodge Ball, who constantly repeats he 'only speaks the truth.'

"Your truth."

"There is only one truth."

"Which you have denied for a generation past. You've preached continuously in different places, speaking ill of both ecclesiastics and secular lords."

"If the lords deny the true intentions of God..."

"No! No!" Tresilian thunders angrily, "Earning the goodwill of common folk, not merit in the sight of God. You instructed people not to pay tithes unless the giver was richer than the rector or vicar and that tithes should be withheld if the parishioner were a better man than his priest."

"I have."

"You enticed the people by pleasing words and slandering the prelates. Oftentimes on Sundays after mass, when the people were leaving the churches you went into the cloister to preach. For your foolish words you have been held three times for several months in the Archbishop of Canterbury's prison for chastisement. Despite this you continued to preach your evil. When denied Holy Church you went into the market places and the fields, preaching your mischief to folk where they murmured amongst themselves and by your words were incited to revolt. As you refused to desist, you were excommunicated, arrested yet again and put back into prison. Indeed you were held until released by the rebels during the recent disturbances."

"If it is wrong to release a man so he can continue to preach the truth, then my brothers did wrong."

"You predicted you would be released by thousands of rebels."

"I did not predict, I hoped."

"You have spread your pernicious talk for twenty years, egging common rustics to believe all men were created equal by nature and that servitude had been introduced by unjust oppression against the will of God."

"I did. If it had pleased Him to create serfs, he would have appointed at the beginning of the world, those to be serfs and those to be lords."

"You told common folk to kill the great lords of the realm, slay the lawyers, justices and jurors so they could maintain themselves in liberty, nobility, dignity and power."

"I preached no killing."

"You preached at Blackheath a month ago and it was there the leaders of the revolt planned to meet the king, capture him and take him to the common folk to make it seem he approved of your actions. After killing the knights and squires who came with him, you would have killed the king, the lords and all bishops, monks, cannons and rectors."

In his excitement and fury, Tresilian's voice gets gradually louder and vociferous, but John Ball replies quietly and calmly

"I did not say these things. Why kill only to create more rulers of the same kind?"

"We have proof," Tresilian shouts, waving his hand impatiently to one of the clerks and then when a document is handed to him, "Here, the confession of Jack Straw, one of the leaders of the revolt. You knew this man?"

"I did."

"He admitted to all these things before he was..."

"...summarily captured and executed by the mayor of London."

"That does not matter."

"It matters much. These may not be Jack's true words, anymore than the lies that have been circulated about Wat Tyler reflect the truth of his death at Smithfield."

"You were not there."

"Neither were you."

"But we have Jack Straw's confession."

"Even if it is genuine, it has nothing to do with me."

"You deny you were a party to these evil plans?"

"I do."

Tresilian grimaces in frustration, grunts dismissively and then waves his hand again to the clerks. He grabs the letters and then turns malevolently,

"You'll not wriggle from these, John Ball. The names in these letters, you know who these men are."

"I have already said they are no one and every..."

"You refuse to divulge the true identities of *Jack Trueman, Jack Carter, Jack Miller?*"

"You are not familiar with rhymes, sir judge..."

"It is not my knowledge that is on trial here, but yours."

"If you knew them as..."

"You know them as you know these rhymes."

"As all people know these rhymes..."

"What *people?*"

"*The* people, they all know these rhymes. Do you intend to try the whole people of England, for it is they that stand accused."

"*The people* as you call them, villeins and ruffians, are no more important than if they were to stand in this court. *Men*, not people are accused and you are the chief of those men, you are not the people."

John Ball turns to the crowed and gently waves his arm.

"I am of them, we are all one," then, turning back to Tresilian, "There will come days when it is the people that will decide and in those days they will remember these days when they first rose..."

"And *spoke* I suppose?"

"Indeed, sir judge, but much more than that, when they were first *listened* to. For that these days will be remembered."

"I am listening to you John Ball and out of your own mouth you stand condemned. You are *John Sheep* or *John Shepherd*. He is John Ball. You wrote these rhymes and these names..."

"I have said these names are of us all."

"So you say."

Tresilian nods to one of the clerks, who passes further papers over.

"Names of you all," Tresilian says, first perusing and then pushing the papers towards John Ball, "Read!"

John Ball leans over and reads the papers. Then Tresilian snatches them back.

"John Ball greets you well and does you to understand he has rung your bell," he reads one of the papers before casting it aside and picking up another, *"John Ball, St. Mary priest of York, greets well all manner of men..."*

"...in the name of the of the Trinity, Father and Son and Holy Ghost stand together in truth," John Ball intones, *"Help truth and truth shall help you."*

Then Tresilian continues, *"...Now reigns pride in price and coveting is held wise and lechery without shame and gluttony without blame..."*

"...Envy reigns with treason and sloth is taken in great season. God sustains, for now is time. Amen."

"Amen indeed, for the author is clear, is it not? With what name do the lines begin?"

"John Ball," John says quietly.

"What? I didn't hear?"

"John Ball."

"John Ball! So you confess. You wrote these lines and sent these letters?"

Jenner feels the silent, massed concentration of everyone in the room bearing down as if a huge weight is suspended from the ceiling, close enough to touch the hair on his head. John Ball says nothing.

"Don't give in," Jenner thinks, "Deny it, they can't prove anything. Even if your name is on the letter, it could be a forgery, maybe it is..."

"Answer!" Tresilian booms.

John Ball nods.

"No, no, no!" Jenner shouts silently to the vast hall, the words resounding sepulchrally in the equally vast space of his mind, "Deny it, save yourself!"

"Say it!" Tresilian shouts, thumping the table with his fist.

"I preached the truth," John Ball says quietly, lifting his head and facing the judge squarely, "Those letters are the truth, so I..."

"No, no, no," Jenner mouths silently, almost but not quite audibly.

John Ball hesitates, then turns away from Tresilian for a moment, his wide grey eyes staring directly into the crowd, exploring the faces until he finds the one he seeks. Jenner speaks loudly, resolutely, though it seems only John Ball hears him.

"Your life is worth more than mere words, your truth is greater than semantics. Manipulate your words, they're always repeatable, but you only have one life."

John Ball shakes his head, smiling kindly, but firmly.

"Truth is in everything, deny it only once and it begins to die."

"But it's only a word," Jenner persists.

"As sir judge reminds me, I've spent my life preaching to the people. So my life has only been in words. If I deny the truth only in words, then I deny the people...even if it is only in words."

Jenner is ready to protest again, but hesitates, suddenly feeling very conspicuous in his modern clothes and speaking so openly in the large hall, though no one has moved or looked to him. John Ball turns back to Tresilian, who's remained impassive, seemingly unaware of his interchange with Jenner.

"...so I am a messenger of the truth."

"You were not alone?"

"There are many messengers."

"You will not name them?"

"I'll not provide you with the weapons to strike down innocent men."

"Then you alone must bear the responsibility. You admit you sent the letters."

"I admit I preached the truth."

"*Your truth* as in the letters?"

"The truth is not partial, it's everywhere."

"Including the letters?"

"The letters contains the truth."

"Then you as good as sent the letters."

John Ball remains silent.

"It is not so," Jenner shouts. John Ball alone hears him, turns and shakes his head and then looks back towards Tresilian.

"Your silence condemns you," the judge says, "You do not contradict me. It is a confession. All here have witnessed it. You have confessed to sending these treasonable letters, stirring up simple folk against the established order to cause rebellion and destruction."

"No, no!" Jenner shouts, "this is a travesty, this man has not confessed."

But no one, save John Ball hears him.

"Set it down," Tresilian says gravely as the clerk scribbles quickly, "John Ball, I find you guilty of treason against his gracious majesty King Richard. The sentence of this court is that you be taken to be hanged, drawn, disembowelled and quartered."

A tremendous surge of horrified revulsion convulses the crowd. Some women scream, many hold their hands to their faces in disbelief.

"It cannot be!" Jenner shouts, again heard only by John Ball, who turns, saying quietly, "It will be."

Heedless of the people's detestation, Tresilian shouts, "Sentence to be carried out immediately!"

"No, my lord, I must intervene!"

Everyone turns to the back of the hall where a man in church robes stands at the door.

"My lord bishop," Tresilian begins questioningly, partly with reverence, partly with impatient irritation, "I have a commission from the king, this court..."

"I don't seek to challenge your authority or your sentence."

William Courtney, bishop of London strides down the central aisle and stands, a little to the side of John Ball, facing Tresilian.

"For all his crimes, he is still a man and though misguided, has been a priest of God. He must have time to repent before meeting his maker."

Tresilian hesitates, shuffles his papers, then says, "We must act speedily..."

Courtney puckers his lips and is immovable.

"Perhaps tomorrow," Tresilian says guardedly.

"Tomorrow is the sabbath," Courtney says.

"This is most..." Tresilian begins, then reading the determination in Courtney's eyes, "Very well, Monday, the 15th, sentence is delayed until Monday."

He looks to Courtney, who nods approvingly before walking back up the aisle and out of the hall. Tresilian watches him and then says, "And now to the local insurgents."

He converses with one of the clerks and seeing John Ball still standing at the table, barks to the soldiers, "Take him away."

John Ball is shuffled aside, but not out of the room, remaining by the side door and very close to where Jenner is sitting. He's flanked by two soldiers, but neither appears to notice as he leans over and addresses a man in the crowd.

"Remember not to compromise. There is only one truth and it can never be forsworn...whatever the circumstances."

Jenner is tempted to plead with him again, but John's kindly, accepting yet intransigent eyes, tell him he would be unsuccessful. Besides, sentence has been passed. His opportunity to save himself has gone, even if it ever really existed.

As if reading Jenner's thoughts, John Ball says, "It is done and was meant to be. My role is completed, but yours is yet to begin."

Unnerved and intrigued, Jenner wants to ask what it means, but Tresilian shouts 'clear the court' and John is led away by the soldiers. People around Jenner are dispersing, but he's unwilling to leave, his feet immured to the floor as if encased by incredibly heavy boots. No one takes any notice of him though in his modern clothes he must be alarmingly visible, unless...they can't see him. The hall is almost cleared now. Tresilian and the clerks are at the table. A few soldiers are shepherding the last of the crowd from the room. Yet not everyone has left. A small group of men remain around the table. Jenner watches mystified. Then, to his surprise and consternation, one of the clerks approaches and speaks to him.

"Why do you stand here? You are required with the others."

Jenner stares at the clerk nervously, unable to move or speak. Why, unlike all others does this man pay him any heed? Jenner says nothing. How do you respond to a snatched image from your own imagination? The clerk continues to stare, waiting for Jenner to obey the instruction or explain his non compliance. Now Jenner realises this is no dream. Should he run as the woman did from the hall, but too late he hears Tresilian shouting.

"Bring him here, we've tarried long enough in this business!"

Jenner reluctantly follows the clerk and stands at the back of the little group as Tresilian speaks.

"I charged you yesterday as jurors, to present for indictment those who acted criminally and disturbed the king's peace."

The men remain silent.

"What is your answer?"

Still no one speaks.

"You are men of the town, you know who was responsible."

After some hesitation one man speaks.

"We know of no such men and therefore could not indict anyone for all are loyal and obedient to the king and have always been so."

"All of them?" Tresilian thunders irritably, "Every man in this town has been totally loyal to the king during all the disturbances?"

The man says nothing.

"I asked you a question, sir?" Tresilian says.

"Every one, my lord."

"I remind you sirs, all you citizens set out in humility to meet the king, requesting mercy and pardon. You will recall the words spoken on the king's behalf that you would receive pardon and forgiveness only on condition that you handed over the men who instigated and organised the troubles in the kingdom. Furthermore that if you failed to do so you would suffer the same punishment as the criminals when they are caught."

He pauses to let the gravity of his words sink in. Jenner looks from man to man, reading the fear, but also resolution on their faces. No one speaks.

"Now go home and think on what I have said."

Tresilian nods to the clerks and soldiers, waves his hand towards the door and the men shamble away. Jenner is careful to join the group in the middle, neither at the head nor the rear, where he's less likely to be seen, but no one heeds him. He hesitates at the door, uncertain whether to follow or remain. As the last man goes out he glances back. Tresilian and the clerks are leaving by the side door and two of the soldiers are walking towards him. He turns back to the door, wondering whether he'll step into a street in the present or the past.

11

IT'S three in the morning. The door opens creakily, a narrow sliver of light creeping around its edge. Inside there's no movement from the frozen apprehensive form. Keep still, keep silent, it's safer that way. The incisive beam of the security guard's torch picks out the studio's unkempt clutter. In the half light half finished equipment and materials assume roles their creators never envisaged. Ropes are strands of unfinished webs of huge spiders. Poles are lances to spear the unwary. Unpainted screens are fearful barriers hiding unspeakable horrors to the unheeding. Briefly the pathetic torchlight pulls away the skin of darkness, but once passed night enfolds the light, digesting the innocent jumble into a living mass, slightly retreating before the whitened streaks, but ready to return and surround like a cloying viscous malevolence.

The security guard is well used to the studio. He's anxious to get to his next clocking point and a welcome break from his rounds. Seeing nothing untoward and sensing no movement or presence in the darkness he carves a path to the exit with his torch. The door closes with a baleful, metallic clang that hammers and bounces its juddering echo for several seconds. The studio's sealed box is blackened again. The hundred shapes and patterns, the stuff from which the dreams of films are made, sleep soundlessly until wakened in the morning.

Yet no light to illuminate, no witness to see doesn't mean no sound or movement, only that they cannot be seen, cannot be heard. But what if within this treasure chest of artifice something moves, something stirs, something speaks if only to itself or within someone's mind?

"...work quickly and complete your work before the dawn...take down what should never have been put up and then take flight..."

Chris doesn't immediately switch on the light he switched off when he heard the door opening. Perhaps he should have spoken, not cowered like an intruder, but in the middle of the night he is an intruder. There would have to be explanations. Why hadn't he reported his presence to security, how had he got in without being seen? Better to keep quiet and unseen. Though now if he's discovered his behaviour will be at the least odd, at worst highly suspicious. But he's the director, he has every right to be here...at three in the morning when no shooting is scheduled? Definitely a lot of explaining to do.

He can't remember when he arrived. He's been here two, three or is it four hours? Time moves differently in the dark. Coalescing and fragmenting thoughts are the only triggers, circling and prowling, immeasurably elastic, truncating and expanding minutes and hours. In his hurry to get out of the house he's left his watch. The dawn, creeping through the cracks is the only clock he needs. A phrase from Charley's script keeps recurring.

"...work quickly and complete your work before the dawn..."

How quickly will he be able to work before his dawn? Should he have gone home earlier before all these terrible thoughts gripped him? He'd come to collect something from his room, though really an excuse to keep out of the house. Hanging about the studio was preferable to futile hours waiting for sleep that wouldn't come. Alone in a large space that normally buzzes with febrile activity is peculiarly invigorating. The vast emptiness makes him feel powerful, something he's not felt for a long time, but it doesn't last. The imaginings gradually take over and confidence, let alone power soon evaporates. He's used now to forms in the dimness.

More powerful light might pick out a different shape from the others, one that steals between, searching, stopping, going on, stopping again, just as he occasionally hears a reaching up and a taking down. But if no one is around and there's no light, how can he see, how can he hear? Anything's possible in a place where dreams become reality, but what about nightmares? He's even started believing what the others have been hinting, the real past has taken over the film. Dreams of historical revelation become a nightmare resuscitation, a time box of unknowns. Once opened it can't be closed and out of control where will it lead?

He hears the strange noises again. Should he switch on the lights? No, he mustn't attract attention and the dark allows him to reflect. The problem is Charley. Her dangerous obsessions have jinxed the film. One demand after another, an extending remit until there's no end. First irritating suggestions, then impositions, now commands. A screenwriter should never be allowed to wield such influence. He should never have given way. She might even be the instrument through which the past interferes. Yet he doubts if she alone can formulate, let alone dictate such a campaign. That's what it is, a campaign with him or his project as the opponent. The film was virtually finished including the dramatic climax at Smithfield. The 1381Hertfordshire events only got started after the turbulence in London had ended. There was never a sensible flow between the two. They were separate, distinct and should remain that way now. There he goes, expressing the past as *now* as if it really does live on. It's insidious, this incursion of the past. The mistake was agreeing to the loyalty scene. That was the thin end of a very wide and long wedge. With hindsight the tactic is evident. As soon as the king re-enters the story must move on. Now we have the trial of John Ball to contend with and her sinister obsession with the rehangings. He'll say it's too gruesome for the audience. Besides it's beyond the main sequence of even the Hertfordshire revolt. Including it loses the little tightness that remains in the damned movie! Worst of all, it brings in that local leader William Grindcobb she persists in calling *WG* and her suggestion, to which he should never have agreed, of bringing in Wesley Greville for the part. Odd guy, then he disappears.

He hears the noise again and peers into the empty studio nervously. He should have been aware of the dangers even earlier, taken seriously the fears of the cast and linked them to Charley's strange behaviour. It was wrong to involve Ettie. She's done nothing to curb the problems with the cast and even sides with Charley. She's probably made the situation worse though he can really only blame himself. Following last year's peculiar events in London he approached her and Vicky, but dismissed their more lurid accounts. That was a mistake. You can't play with the past, picking it up and setting it down at will. It's unforgiving. He made sure the press knew he'd contacted them, ensuring free publicity for the forthcoming film. Rather than the PR he might have taken them more seriously. He'd thought Vicky a neurotic idiot and Ettie a harmless nutter. Now he's not so sure. If only he'd left things alone, got on with making the film according to the original plan. Then he might have avoided outside interference, past or present.

How could he have predicted Charley as an adversary? Working with her before there'd been no problems, but she'd been different with this one from the start. He dismissed her odd remarks. Another mistake. Never underestimate those you don't understand. Now his concerns go way beyond the intricacies, serious as they are, with the film. What inexplicable powers does Charley possess, linking up with terrible forces in the past or even more serious, those in the present? *Lawrence is dead.* How much does she know about Chris and his past? He's left it long enough, no more skirmishing. She has to be confronted, settled once and for all. The security guard may return. He must be prepared, either to remain concealed or leave.

Only a few steps out of the Moot Hall and the oppressive, unjust past is gone. The sounds of the present are the first to return, the low, continuous hum, the rumbling drone of the modern town that never really subsides even in the night. Having lost it in the past, she'll never be able to ignore it again in the present. It'll always be there, just as memories of that other time can never fade. It gets louder and then the image changes too. Only a short way and she's back with the glass, the pavement, the cars. Then the smells. Even if she hadn't heard, hadn't seen, her nose would have told her. Only when it's gone is she aware of that fragrant medieval cocktail. Nothing in this time comes close to it. She looks back to make sure, but there's no doubt. It's as if it never happened. But it did. So far, yet so close, it was here. She touches the wall, half expecting it to crumble or slither through time. Nothing moves. Nothing changes. Gone. Yet not so, for she can still see and hear. It was only...minutes...or centuries and it goes on. The trial continues. What will happen to John Ball? She knows yet she doesn't know. She knows what the books say, what the chronicles record, what historians like Jessica interpret, but she doesn't really *know* at all. No one does. For no one now was there...yet she was...at least until she ran away. Now she'll never know what happened afterwards in those minutes...these minutes...as they are *then*. For while she stands and wonders, it happens. If she'd stayed...if she'd remained...now she'll not know...unless someone tells her... someone who was...*is* there. She shudders.

Martha will try again. Then Ettie will know. And what about Thomas? He followed her into the street. Which street, then or now? She looks around, half expecting...he's not here...yet how can she be sure? The time link is unpredictable and volatile. He's no longer wholly in the past just as she's no longer wholly in the present. He could appear at any time. Perhaps he went back when he couldn't find her in his street, *that* street, not *this* street. But if he did he can't now be here. Is that a comforting thought? How else then will she know? She shudders again, though this time for a different reason.

There was someone else she knew in the Moot Hall, not Martha, not Thomas, someone from...she dismisses it. Is he still there...should she go back...can she go back...how is it she came away? She makes her way along the side of the building to the entrance. This is crazy, though no more crazy than when she stepped inside before...how long ago was that... two days, two hours, two minutes? She hesitates, then steps inside. The same modern doors, the same modern emptiness. It's happening again! She'll turn into the courtroom again and escape as before. Get back to the trial, find out what happened! But what if it's not *like* the same, what if it *is* the same. All time is simultaneous she told Jessica. Everything happens continuously. What if this is some monstrous time loop that plays and plays and plays? What if she enters the courtroom into not just *the* past, but her own immediate past, becoming her perpetual present, to constantly relive that part trial, listen to Tresilian's malevolent questions and John Ball's spirited defence, see Martha and Thomas and run away, step back into the street, her street, only to go back again and again and again because she can no longer cut through the cycle?

The woman behind the counter looks at her questioningly. She freezes, unable to go on, unable to go back. If he was in the crowd he too may be marooned in a continually repeating past. Should she go back and get Jenner away? But what if the trial is over now? What if he recognised her as she recognised him? What if he ran away too? Is he waiting at the end of the street? She turns to the courtroom, takes two steps and then stops. No, she'll not go back. She'll get out! She runs to the door, out onto the pavement and then away, stumbling and crashing into people in a headlong dash to the car. If Jenner is there, he must look to himself. If he got there, he can get back! But how, he knows nothing of these things? She should help him. But then did she *really* see him? She stops, looks around, hoping perhaps he really did run after her from the Moot Hall and is waiting patiently in that matter of fact way beside her car. The alternative is too dangerous. She gets to the car. He's not there. What to do?

She sits for a long time. If she goes back, she can't be sure the Moot Hall is the best place to make the link. As time endlessly repeats itself it also moves on. There's no guarantee the trial is there or even if the Moot Hall is in 1381 at all. All is in flux, yet it's also moving inexorably towards 15th July and the 'great calamity' Martha dreads. In that at least she's right and can't be ignored. If they reach the 15th without resolution...what then? Jenner trapped in the past. Thomas flung forward into an uncontrollable present. Martha swinging dangerously between the two. Then only Ettie can avoid the past's uncertainties. There has to be something stable they can all grasp, linking them, yet also standing apart, detached enough not to be compromised. For all its flaws the film is the only hope. She must get to the studio!

She accelerates away quickly, but the car, seemingly with a mind of its own goes another way. Try as she might it turns right when it should turn left, turning around when it should go straight on. It's very frightening, like sitting on top of a runaway elephant, impossible to control and just as impossible to get off! Instead of south west towards the studio she heads north east along the Welstead Road. With the direction, if not the ultimate destination clear, her helplessness subsides. At last the car appears to respond, though as she slows, intending to turn round, it stalls and the wheel locks. She may be in charge, but only if she follows the assigned route! No matter how much she presses the accelerator the car picks up speed only when she catches the first glimpses of the common. She'd like to go back to the cottage, but senses that won't be possible. It responds as she eases her foot off the accelerator, but she knows it won't be possible to turn left. The car won't let her. Instead it slows and nudges into the centre of the road. She presses the pedal, but nothing happens until the road clears. Her hands are on the wheel but it's as if the steering is *super*powered, obeying some unseen force, turning right across the road and onto the opposite verge. Then it stops. Does she drive the car or does it drive her? How can an inanimate object possess such independent energy?

Once out she stares unbelievingly at the car in the same way she might look ridiculously at a telephone when someone has suddenly rung off as if the instrument itself is responsible. The car is no more responsible for its movements than a telephone is for someone ringing off. It's only a vehicle after all. She walks away, forgetting both her hat and her coat. She stands at the side of the road waiting for a gap in the traffic so she can go down to the cottage. Two minutes, three, five, ten or more. It seems every car and lorry in England is heading into or out of Welstead! She gives up and turns towards the common. She'll walk for a while and cross the road further down near the cricket ground.

But she doesn't reach the cricket ground. A sudden mist envelopes her and she's forced to walk further away from the road. Thick, impenetrable and utterly disorienting it lasts only a few seconds, but when it clears she can neither see nor hear the road. A hundred metres or a hundred miles, it makes little difference. Believing she walks away from both the road and the town she turns direction. Then, wondering whether she might have been right the first time, turns a third way, oscillating around the compass until stopping to survey the familiar, yet puzzling landscape. She stares confusedly at bushes, trees, gorse and grass. She's walked here so many times she should know every path and hedge and if she keeps going she must reach the road or the ponds or the cricket ground...somewhere...but it's as if she's here for the first time, rotating around the same place. Like driving the car she appears to lose control of her legs, but endlessly circling, they obey unheard commands, irrespective of the direction she points them. The more she walks the less she progresses, the more she tries to keep in a straight line the more she deviates. Is this what happened to Warren, decades of pacing the common, then suddenly losing all sense of place, leaving him vulnerable to surprise attack?

She sits on a tuft of grass and stares into the empty country wearied, but not bowed. Has she escaped the claustrophobic tyranny of the Moot Hall only to be imprisoned by the invisible walls of open country? Getting away was an illusion. The past has not yet done with her. Who has brought her here and for what reason? Having encouraged them too much, is she already compromised? Or is the real mistake that she's not yet truly engaged? After London Thomas must have recognised her in the Moot Hall. Is he misguided or very shrewd, chasing to attack or to warn? Is his interest the same as Martha? Can she trust anyone from those times? In the past she must guard against false friends, distinguish artifice from reality.

The film began as a re-enactment, yet now the past is a living presence, not a resuscitated corpse, but surely it can never be 'real?' Is Ettie the real danger, infiltrating then 'returning' from the past, influencing Chris and Charley, inadvertently setting the agenda for the film, making the past happen? Yet how can she make something she doesn't understand?

'Every age rewrites the past in its own image.'

How much worse Jessica, when someone meddles without proof, counterfeits the past? Stopping the film is irrelevant if the past has broken through to make the car force her into the mist and creating a subverted non time turning present into past. Can she make her own contact and regain some control? That means trusting *someone*. There can only be one choice, unpredictable and hazardous as that is. This must be near where she first heard Martha. She must concentrate on her and the places they were together, the house in St. Albans, the streets where the people gathered, the abbey grounds, the gatehouse, the cloister, the road to Hempston, Martha's sister in law's house, even the Moot Hall. The images flit and flutter and it's difficult to retain one more than a few seconds. Then she's more successful, holding them maybe a minute, but Martha won't appear. Yet the past gets stronger, its power growing, sucking her back into its realm! The more she resists, the weaker she gets. Nothing changes around her, yet she knows time is racing backwards, decades, centuries flying by.

Buffeted by whirling and circling ages, through which nothing moves and nothing changes, she's gripped by a sudden new terror. Is what little power she ever possessed now gone? Are these events flashing by in jumbled confusion only in her mind? She's back in the Moot Hall hears Tresilian's dreadful sentence, sees John Ball led away, then the town's rebel leaders are brought in...Grindcobb placidly defiant, Cadindon deftly, but vainly arguing with the judge... then they too are gone. Yet not so, they reappear with John Ball, walking slowly through a hushed and almost crushed crowd...

Now comes another crippling fear. Not that she's lost her powers, but they are too strong. She directs this jerking parade, the catalyst between past and present, so what might she make happen? To steady herself she grabs the twigs of a bush though the only movement is inside, earth, grass, trees and sky remain still. She slips to the ground and stares towards the empty common. It seems familiar, but has changed, the open country no longer open. Another trick of her over extended mind or the past further tightening its grip? It's a distortion of the warm air rising from the grass, but it's too clear, too firm and it's moving towards her! Now it's close, solid, impenetrable, no contortion of the light. Like a wall. But that's what it is, the back room wall in Martha's house, looming before her, yet the grass and the gorse...now the door opens. She sees no one, yet she passes through. Is it her that opens the door? She looks down. Her hand hasn't moved. Now a large, empty room with a vaulted ceiling...she's back in the Moot Hall...it cannot be! Then it's the side wall door through which came Tresilian...it opens and she passes through. It's gone and she's back in Martha's house, but the image turns again and she sees another wall, another door. The whole common is surrounded by walls! She runs her hand on the ground, feeling what should be the reassuring texture of grass and earth, but how can she be reassured on a timber lined common!

She gets up, shakes herself, determined not to be completely absorbed. Stand firm and it must pass. You've been in greater danger before, sheer will must win through! Hold on to what you *know*. Where you are and when it is. The 'walls' recede and waver. They are gone. Now she's back, having regained the familiar country. The constant movement passes, some control restored, but absolute return is impossible. Images of the past are too vivid and too frequent. It's not easy to break away. She walks, hoping to escape in space if not immediately in time and find the road, but it's a delusion and she's imprisoned by the same circular roving. She's there, in 1381, but not there. On the edge, uninvolved, unable to completely break free, a limbo between past and present. Get back to the studio, that repository of dreams and fabrications, let the *real* past confront the artificial one and restore the balance in the present. But there are dangers even there. Charley's obsession with certain aspects of the past, real or imaginary, may make her act prematurely and fatally undermine what has to be done. Ettie must get to the film, but she can't get out!

David Farley is waiting when Jennifer gets to the station that morning.

"I need to talk to your boss."

"So do I," she says sharply.

"He needs to see this," he says, waving some papers at her, "It's a leaked announcement and accompanying reports from the public enquiry into the Waintree Development and it's not good news."

She leans across and glances at the papers.

"What's that got to do with us," she says, walking away.

"It could have a lot to do with Jenner's investigation," he says, chasing after her.

"It's a murder enquiry. This land dispute would have to show some connection with at least one of the victims."

"Precisely. It's in the small print."

She stops and takes the papers.

"Have they thrown it out, then?" she says, struggling to make sense of the heavy text, "isn't it going ahead?"

"Burton makes several recommendations regarding environmental issues and some minor proposals have been rejected, but..."

"He's approved the development," she says, reading the front of the main report, "So what has all this got to do with our investigation? I suppose the Waintree lot are cock a hoop."

"Where is Jenner? I need to show him this."

"I've not seen him for days," she says, thrusting the papers back.

"There'll be fall out, unfinished business, the development has immense political dimensions. I have to talk to him."

"You'll have to find him first."

He pushes the papers back to her.

"Keep them. It's all in the relationships. Even though they've won...it's what I've been saying to him...when he comes in show them to him."

After he leaves she skims through the papers, but can't see their relevance. Leak from a public enquiry, grist to the mill for a journalist, but to her...what does he mean by relationships? Jenner might know, but he's not here and no one has seen or heard of him. All she's had is the cryptic message on her mobile.

"Keep checking with the Mid Herts Herald for George Carter."

She has, but like Jenner he too has disappeared. Should she have talked more to Farley? Jenner might ask, but then he can contact Farley himself. She can't help feeling Farley wanted a pat on the back for getting the news twenty four hours early or cry on his old friend's shoulder about the enquiry decision. All this other stuff is just a smokescreen for him to put a brave face to her. The boss's absence is very frustrating. There are things they need to discuss.

Digging up the common isn't really to her taste. She's got little faith in its success and has spent more time finding more about Melvyn and his friends. It's not been easy. Those that really know don't talk. Those that do talk only know *a bit* or have *opinions*, but when put together the bits produce a picture. Jenner may not approve.

"It's not what you *think* sergeant, it's what you *know*."

But if you don't know, you have to rely on what other people think. Welstead's not a big place, but even twenty five years ago not everybody knew everybody else. First there's George Carter, the newspaper editor who went away and then came back. He knew Maggie rather well in those days. Or in alternative versions, he would have *liked* to know her well. The fly in the ointment was Melvyn. Nice little unresolved triangle there. Then there's the unfortunate Lawrence. He and Melvyn were supposed to be mates, but Jennifer found a woman who'd been in the same class at school. Aged around thirteen there'd been a fight in a storeroom at the back of the art class. Lawrence had come off the worst. They were pretty cool with each other after that though she felt it was more on Lawrence's side. Her *opinion* was Lawrence never forgot being 'pushed around' by Melvyn and he also had a short fuse, which in certain circumstances could easily ignite. Though they knocked around together later, it was more because of mutual friends in the same group, rather than actually liking each other.

So, assuming Melvyn *was* murdered, both George and Lawrence had youthful motives. Lawrence is no longer around. If he killed Melvyn, who killed him? George could have killed them both, but there's nothing to connect him to Lawrence's murder and what would be the motive? It must be assumed they are two wholly separate murders. If Lawrence killed Melvyn as some sort of post adolescent revenge attack, perhaps following an argument, there's little to be gained in following it up even assuming they can find his body. His murderer is no more. Case closed. It also leaves Warren Grover's murder as wide open as ever. The only alternative is that Lawrence had nothing to do with Melvyn's murder. George may not have killed Lawrence, but he may have killed Melvyn or did a third person kill them both? He could also have killed Warren or is that a fourth person? Are there three murderers? She has to talk it through with Jenner, wherever he is.

George Carter is waiting at reception in David's hotel.

"Did you get it?" he says nervously as David comes over.

"Yes, I got it. Thanks for that. How did you..."

"It doesn't matter."

"Where the hell have you been?"

"There were things I had to do."

"There are telephones, you know. Why didn't you keep in touch?"

"Sorry, I've been a bit preoccupied."

"So have I. You feed me information – very useful I might say – then you bugger off from the enquiry and now this."

"I know more than that bloody enquiry whitewash."

"Don't we all. It's one thing knowing it, it's quite another proving it."

"You sound like the police."

"That's because when it comes to investigative work, we sometimes have to be like the police."

"That copper's been after me, you know, the detective, what's his name...?"

"Jenner."

"That's the one."

"Have you seen him?"

"Not since I got away from him near Dunstable."

"What's this all about?"

"I've found out things about the Waintree Development."

"Too bloody late now with the report out."

"Not necessarily."

"It'll have to be good."

"Could be."

"Okay, but can you prove it?"

Jennifer returns to the 'diggings.' There's a tenuous chance Jenner might be there. At the edge of the common, close to the as yet unproductive excavation at Lock's Spinney she sees Ettie's abandoned car. Why leave it here and so close to the cottage? Jennifer walks on, but she's uneasy. It's a warm day, the sun is bright and she feels no breeze yet she shivers slightly. The chill is sudden as if she's wafted by the cold air from the open door of a large freezer. It passes, but the air is heavy and very quiet even though she's still within earshot of the road. She looks round. To her surprise she can no longer see the road or any other familiar landmarks. She stops to reorient herself, but finds it difficult. She must have underestimated the distance.

She reaches the 'dig.' The officers have found nothing. She's tempted to mention if they've seen anything unusual, but thinks better of it. How could she explain what she feels? She drifts away. Not only is the road no longer visible, neither is anywhere else. A thick mist shrouds the light, making it hard to discern anything more than about fifty metres. On a bright summer's day she's immersed in a dense fog! She'll get back to the dig and familiar ground, but she can't find the way and wanders around aimlessly for several minutes before returning to the same spot. The earlier chill is now nothing to the greater shiver at being utterly alone in a place without any way of escape. But she's only a half mile from the town centre, even closer to houses and people. Her own officers must be even closer. She could shout, but what if they come running through a mist only she sees? She tramps around again, fruitlessly wandering back to the same place. Wherever she goes she can only keep turning and turning. Swallowing her pride she shouts out a plaintive 'hallo,' which with no response, she repeats, gradually louder.

"Bugger," she says angrily, "this is ridiculous!"

There's still no answer and though the mist remains she feels the intense heat of the sun, so much so that she has to take off her jacket. Pulling her coat over her arm a wad of papers falls from one of the pockets. She stoops down and picks up the public enquiry documents Farley gave her. After stuffing them back into the pocket she notices how much brighter it is. The mist still hangs to the west, over the road and the 'dig,' but north and east the air is clear, still and quiet. She can't see the town, but can see the open common and walks towards it. Yet it's not the same country she's used to. She walks on, apprehensive yet curious, fearful yet determined, pulled by something strong but inexplicable. It gets colder again and she puts her jacket on, but the horizon shimmers and wavers as if the air is hot. She feels the wad of papers in her pocket and takes them out, keeping them in her hand. Then the haze thickens again. She must break through the mist, whatever is happening it can't last. Then she hears the voice, quiet at first, muffled by the mist, but getting louder as if she's getting nearer.

"Got to get out...got to get it away."

The woman's voice is familiar, but only after the same phrase is repeated several times does Jennifer recognise it as Ettie's. The fog gets denser. She calls back.

"Jennifer? I'm over here."

Jennifer follows Ettie's voice, though as she gets closer the fog becomes so thick she can hardly see more than a metre in front of her. She puts out her arm as if to slice through something semi-solid, like a huge expanse of butter. She still holds the documents. Then the fog clears as if a curtain has been thrust aside and she sees Ettie huddled on the ground. Jennifer runs across, but has to pull off her jacket as the temperature leaps at least fifteen degrees in seconds. Seeing her, Ettie gets up.

"Ettie, what is it, what happened?"

"I'm alright, it's just...now you're here."

But Ettie is looking over Jennifer's shoulder in alarm. Jennifer turns to see the curtain wrenched back, the fog suddenly closing in again.

"You've cut through," Ettie says.

"Cut through what?"

"The enclosure of the past."

"But it's closed again."

"If you've come through, then it must be possible for us to get back out."

Jenner doesn't escape from the past. He steps into a street as unfamiliar as the Moot Hall courtroom or a traffic-less Watling street. Anxious to keep out of the judge's view he keeps behind but within sight of the townsmen, summoned as a jury by Tresilian. The judge's blatant threat angered him intensely. He wanted to shout out, but didn't want to do anything that might make matters worse. Yet from the odd snatches of conversation he picks up, they are not yet submissive.

"We know who he means."

"But they've only stood up for us all."

"They are honest and true men."

"Why should we do the judge's dirty work?"

"It's wrong for these men to be indicted, we should all stand together."

"Aye, if we can no longer achieve our ends by shouting them out, maybe we can at least save ourselves by our silence."

Then one whispers to the others and they continue in muffled tones that Jenner cannot hear. Have they seen him? Agitated men are unpredictable. He hangs back and steps into the shadows, increasing the distance, though keeping them in sight. They stop at the corner. He strains to hear, but only catches odd words.

"...later...at..."

Not much, but enough. They've arranged to meet again, but where? They disperse in different directions. He could follow one, but that might make him even more conspicuous and they might not all have been summoned. If he chooses the wrong one he'll miss the meeting. As he weighs up the possibilities, he hears soft footsteps behind. The tread is ominously familiar and he slinks even further into the shadows. All the men have gone and he curses his vacillation. Then he sees the man approach and realises how inadvertently he may have escaped something worse. Jenner's already acquainted with the gait and step and though he walks with a slight crouch as if to disguise his presence, the imposing figure of judge Tresilian is unmistakable. He pauses nearby and Jenner forces himself even further against the building, hoping the overhang of the floor above will be enough to shield him from sight. But Jenner isn't the object of the judge's scrutiny. Looking steadily ahead he walks on, passing Jenner without wavering. He's stalking the men!

Jenner follows, keeping close to the shadows. Tresilian reaches the corner and looks first one way and then the other. Then he strides to the left, seemingly sure where to go. Jenner follows at a discreet distance. Tresilian reaches a house in the middle of town. He knocks on the door, but immediately enters without being invited. He leaves the door ajar, allowing Jenner to slip across the street and look inside. Most of the twelve jurors are bunched around a table. Two are leaning at the fireplace and a third, the 'spokesman' who answered the judge at the Moot Hall stands next to Tresilian near the door. They have their backs to the street while those at the table are all concentrating on him so don't notice Jenner.

"How did you know where to come?" the spokesman says.

"This is your house, sir. I knew you would all meet here."

"And what do you want with us?"

'Whatever it is, do not trust him!'

Jenner hears the voice, but no one stirs. Do they hear as he hears? He knows the voice, yet it can't be...surely he's locked away in the abbot's gaol?

"I have something to show you," Tresilian says, pulling a roll from his sleeve and placing it on the table.

The men lean over and read the document. Jenner edges perilously into the doorway to get a better look. No one notices him. Some of the men sigh in disbelief.

"You know some of these names," Tresilian says, "and you are aware of the criminal acts laid out here."

"There are many names," the spokesman says.

"But some you know well," Tresilian says, pointing to various names on the list, "Look here and here and again and again here. Good men, who are loyal to their country have laid criminal charges against your neighbours. It is common knowledge, almost everybody knows about this."

Do not trust him," comes the voice again.

"Liar!" Jenner thinks, "Oldest trick in the book. He's got no evidence, no one has spoken."

"Do you think you can deceive us by your silence?" Tresilian continues, "Your intentions will not succeed, since we are in possession of both the names and the deeds of the very criminals whom you wish to present as just men."

"Don't listen to him. It's a trick!"

Riled and furious, Jenner mouths silently as no sound comes forth. After a short pause, the gravity of Tresilian's words sink in and he continues.

"So do what is best for you, save your own lives, lest while trying to protect your neighbours to no purpose, you stir up danger for yourselves."

"Do not trust him!"

John Ball speaks in Jenner's head yet again.

"Don't tell me, tell them!" Jenner answers silently, "He's a snake. Don't be intimidated!"

But the men look to each other, scan the names again and shudder.

"Others have already spoken?" one says.

Tresilian nods gravely, "So if you do not assist me it will not go well for you."

Agitated and alarmed, the men confer anxiously amongst themselves. Tresilian watches them, a satisfied sneer stealing across his mouth as he might watch insects running vainly in every direction from some sudden attack. His anger at boiling point, Jenner has stepped into the room and stands facing Tresilian who, intent on the distressed men, doesn't see him.

"Draw up the names now and be sensible," he says.

The hapless jurors, reluctant, but terrified, do as they are bidden, scribbling out an indictment of several men known to them, some from the country around and some from the town. Tresilian snatches it and is about to leave, but Jenner stands in his path.

"Take that back! This is a travesty of justice. Tear it up!"

Suddenly realising he's in the middle of the room and for the first time speaking aloud, he turns to see all the men and Tresilian gazing at him.

"I still don't understand, are we in the past or the present?"

Jennifer wants a straight answer, but doesn't really expect one so Ettie's response, while disappointing, is no surprise.

"Neither...and both. I know it's not helpful, but it's...you've seen... haven't you?"

Jennifer nods. She's seen and she's heard. As soon she arrived at this isolated and unfamiliar place in the middle of the common fluttering sounds and sights of the past flashed around her and Ettie. Short, sharp, three minutes, two minutes, one minute or were they just seconds, but so vivid she'll remember the images and noises for a very long time. Slivers from the great Revolt of 1381 Ettie told her. Then they were gone, coming again after a five minute lull, shorter, sharper. Then they stopped again. That was twenty minutes ago, since when it's been calm and quiet.

"Why here?" Jennifer says.

"Virtually unchanged over hundreds, maybe even thousands of years, the common is a time chest of all periods. What with this..."

Ettie breaks off. The mist has disappeared.

"It's you, Jennifer, you broke through, stopped the snaps from the past and now you've lifted the fog."

"But how? You're the one with the power to connect with the past."

"I may have some power, but it's erratic and I lost control. Your coming stabilised the connections."

"It could come back."

"No, not now, it's been too long. With the fog lifted, I'm sure. We are in the present. You brought your own time and saved me."

"But it's your time too."

"It is, but there had to be something more, something you used, something you brought."

Jennifer is puzzled and shrugs.

"What have you got?" Ettie persists.

Jennifer opens her jacket wide and wiggles about, then plunges her hand in her pocket.

"There's only this," she says, bringing out the wad of papers Farley gave her, "it's the Waintree enquiry report, it's not..."

Ettie takes it from her.

"When was it issued?"

"Last night, I think, no it might have been early this morning. David Farley brought it to show..."

"That recent, that's good."

"Is that it, something very new, is that enough?"

Ettie studies the papers quickly.

"It's also about the land. That's what makes it powerful. Linked with the land, the common, close to make the connection, but separate enough to break whatever enclosure the past was staking around me. We'll be alright now. We can walk away. We are free!"

They reach Ettie's car and are soon back to the cottage, but their euphoria as they stride across the common, open and bright and filled with welcome intrusive sounds of the 21st century soon dissipates. Ettie's thoughts quickly return to the past while Jennifer broods on the investigation and Jenner's continuing absence.

"The boss has been acting very strangely ever since they started shooting John ball's trial at the studio."

Ettie shudders, not just another reminder of the past, but also of the date, 14th July. Tomorrow is the 15th. The fluttering visions return, now as memories, but no less unnerving. Just a day to go as it was then, but her fear is not just of 1381, but of the present and Charley with her perilous obsession.

Filming the 15th on the 15$^{th.}$ Actual events on the actual day is dangerous enough, but with so much remaining unresolved what if they film beyond that date? She gets her things, this time deliberately bringing her coat and hat out of the car so they won't be forgotten.

"We can't delay, we have to get to the studio."

Jennifer picks up *A Little Liberty*.

"Any feelings about Warren Grover's murder? George Carter and Monica Freeson could be the culprits. The aggro between them, I wonder if they protest too much. The boss thinks it's tied up with the past, though I'm not sure we'll get anywhere digging up the common. Could Melvyn's disappearance be the lynchpin between past and present?"

Ettie considers it for a few moments.

"If it is, Warren had to be involved with his disappearance. The answer might lie even further back than Melvyn Strange, Warren himself thought so."

Then she remembers Charley and rings her.

"I've been trying to contact you," Charley says, "but your phone…"

Ettie fumbles in her pocket for her mobile. It's been switched off.

"…anyway, you must come to the studio. I've just finished a longish call with Chris. I think he might be finally coming round. He said there are matters to be sorted out, but was sure we could work through them. Isn't that great? I told him we have to plough on and get the rehanging scene completed today. He didn't object."

"Are you sure that's such a good idea?" Ettie says.

"You know how important it is and with Chris not objecting…strike while the iron's hot as they say."

"Even so, I don't think it's wise."

"Oh Ettie…"

"I mean it Charley, don't do it!"

"There's been enough prevaricating on this…"

"Don't do it, at least not today. It can wait for…"

"Ettie, I thought you of all people would understand. I'm not going to be put off. I'm on my way now. If you don't want to be there, that's up to."

"Charley, it's not often I..."
But Charley has already rung off.

Chris starts out confident and determined. He has a plan. He'll force Charley's submission. No more new scenes, just the ones essential to avoid the film ending too abruptly. He's already committed far too much of his own money. It was the only way to keep the other producers on board after the London scenes had been completed. Now they are getting restless again. He made excuses about turning the project into something resembling an old style 'mini epic,' but that hadn't gone down well. Old style epics sometimes don't make any money. If necessary some of the material already shot might have to be discarded. He even contemplated wiping out all the damned Hertfordshire scenes. He never really wanted them. Even in his weakest moments when he'd gone along with Charley, at the back of his mind was a nagging unease. They were too close to home. He'll brook no arguments. Her position isn't strong. Without Wesley Greville those final scenes with Grindcobb can't be completed. All this makes him feel better, but as he nears the studio the satisfaction at putting Charley in her place ebbs away. What does the woman know, who has she told?

He thought he'd put aside the memories of that night on the common, but in the last few days they've been coming back and won't go away. The mind frequently plays tricks with itself, slipping the worst phobias and anxieties under mental carpets, tucking them into the far recesses. But even that temporary respite has been getting more difficult. That night keeps forcing its way in. It's doing it now. Most memories lapse within days, a few last weeks, but when it gets to months with no fading they're bound to last for years, saving up the greatest damage to strike much later. Memories aren't like embarrassing books. You can't burn them in the backyard of the mind. The most contented man is the one who best destroys his memories. That's ultimate contentment, blissful annihilation, but so many memories are indestructible.

Warren's face haunts him. So long he'd known that face. How many times had he looked on Warren with contradictory feelings, juggling the irreconcilable? Now his strongest memory of Warren will be of him on the ground, cut down and lying in the dirt. Could it have been avoided? What had gone wrong all those years ago? So long he'd wondered, even wished for something like it. It seemed Warren had always been in his way. Why had she chosen Warren? She could never have been as close to Warren as she'd been to him. Nothing would shake that belief. Him and Kathleen, that was special. Nobody could take that away. Not even Warren.

He'd stayed too long. The gruesome sight was irresistible, almost hypnotic and he'd remained, transfixed, frozen, but it was unwise and as he hurried away he was sure someone else was there. Someone saw him. They've never said. Couldn't have done, otherwise the police would have mentioned it. He'd only caught a brief glimpse before breaking into a run, but he was sure it was a woman. Could it have been Charley?

At the studio he feels a complete stranger and staggers around like a little boy lost. He expects it bigger, brighter, noisier. Spending the night here has changed everything. Just like that night on the common, another night that changed everything. Now it's no longer so big, so bright. It's a place he revisits after a long absence, somewhere perhaps he last knew as a small boy. Young children's worlds are always so much bigger, higher, longer. They even stretch time. A few seconds waiting to cross the road become twenty minutes, a two hundred metre stroll through the village with the teacher a great distance. Coming back such places are always smaller, shorter. That's how it is with the studio even though it's only a few hours since he was last here. A little place, full of little people pursuing little ends. Except one. Her ends aren't little.

Charley is easily found. She's talking to a group of actors and handing out scripts.

"At it again, bloody interference," he thinks and then calls to her, "If there's any briefing of the cast it'll be done by me!"

To his surprise her face lights up and she trips over enthusiastically. An unconnected dialogue follows, she unhearing his stonewalling as he unhears her zippiness.

"You're here? Wonderful, we can talk!"

"We're proceeding no further with this business," he says gruffly.

Her expression drops slightly.

"But you don't know what I was talking about."

"Either way you don't talk directly to the cast, that's finished."

"Okay, okay, I respect your position as..."

"I'm the director. That means I do the directing."

"Of course."

"Now, about these scenes, there's to be an end..."

"Yes, I want to move onto the rehanging as soon as possible."

"What you want isn't important. This rehanging as you call it is not..."

"I agree, it might be too soon, which is why I've got a plan B – we can start on the intervening scenes."

Now his curiosity is too much.

"Intervening scenes?"

"The intervening events between Grindcobb's return to St. Albans from Hertford for appearance at the court on 12th July and the sentences being carried out on..."

"That man Grincobb again, I won't have it."

"But it's essential. After the trial, the jurors are sent away and..."

"No, no!"

No real communication, the unhearing replaced by the unlistening.

"I thought you wanted to talk," she says angrily, "What was it you wanted to sort out?"

"You," he says quietly, "I wanted to sort out you!"

She stands back aghast, suddenly realising he's in no mood for compromise.

"So you're not interested in proceeding with these scenes at all?"

"Not even with what we've shot already."

"You've never really wanted to film the Hertfordshire phase of the Revolt at all."

"Got it in one," he says with self satisfied firmness.

"And why is that, I wonder? What is it about those scenes you're afraid of?"

"Afraid, don't be ridiculous!"

"You've been lukewarm from the start."

"They lack dramatic content. It's an unknown story with no surviving contemporary records. Everything is based on feeling and concoction."

"That objection is wearing a bit thin, Chris. It's not what you really believe. The records show..."

"It's not the records, it's that damned book," he shouts, waving at *A Little Liberty* in her hand.

"We have enough besides this," she says quietly, putting Warren's book down, "and what we have is as dramatic as the..."

"It's not like the London material."

"That's the whole point. Here we can show the struggle closer to the heart of the people, get underneath the big issues and set pieces. It's got more depth. It's what we can *reveal*."

"That's exactly what he's afraid of!"

Neither has noticed George Carter standing near them. He's been listening for some time.

"What you want to do is a bit too close to home," he continues, "and by home I mean Welstead."

"How did you get in here?" Chris bellows, "We'd better call security."

"Same as when you stayed here all night. Nobody knew about that, did they? Take some explaining if..."

"How did you...?"

"Because I was here too."

"On the premises, you saw me come in?"

"Yes and saw you here."

All those twists and turns in the night. George was here!

"What do you mean *too close to home?*" Charley says, "What happened in Welstead?"

"Warren Grover was murdered in Welstead. Ask him where he was on that night. He knows a lot more than he's told anybody. He was..."

"Shut your filthy mouth!" Chris says, moving closer to him, "You don't know what you're talking about. I'll..."

"How is this connected to the new scenes?" Charley intervenes.

Chris tries to push her aside to get closer to George, but she stands her ground, her arms outstretched.

"Warren was killed on Welstead common, is that the connection? These scenes, especially the rehanging it's linked in some way, so..."

"So that's it," Chris roars, "You and him together, not just undermining the movie, but working to...there's not a shred of...I've had enough of this, I can't fight everybody!"

He leans back from her, turns and goes for the door.

"Run!" George shouts, "It's what you been doing for twenty years, running, always running, but I know more!"

His voice gets louder, the words spluttered with increasing intensity, but he makes no move to follow Chris and is finally answered by the distant banging of the door. Now Charley turns to George. He too tries to get round her, but she also bars his way.

"What did you mean?" she says aggressively.

Her intervention startles him, his anger suddenly melting away.

"It was...he...no, no, I don't have to tell you," he says, finally getting around her and edging away.

"If you have accusations to make, you can make them to me."

The woman's voice comes from the rear of the studio. George looks around nervously and pushes Charley aside as Jennifer comes up, Ettie at her side.

"First telling me where you've been."

"Been?" he says, "Where I always am, at the newspaper."

"Not when I've been there and not when chief inspector Jenner has been trying to find you."

"Is Jenner here?"

Jennifer notices George's relief when she says he's not.

"Have you seen Mr. Jenner?"

"No, it's nothing. I don't know anything about him."

"He's been watching Chris," Charley says, "he said so."

"Why would you want to do that?" Jennifer says.

"He said he was with Chris all night in the studio."

"No I didn't say that...it was him...not all night..."

"It was something about Welstead?" Charley persists, "Why were you watching him?"

George backs away from the three women.

"He said it was to do with Warren Grover."

"I was just...it was only..."

"To do with Warren?" Jennifer says, "when you were all younger? He and Chris were rivals, weren't they, for Kathleen?"

"Well...yes...Chris never forgave him. That was why he..."

"Bit of a lad wasn't he, Warren? It wasn't just Kathleen he was interested in when he was younger?"

"He got about."

"His interest in somebody else made you very jealous, didn't it?"

"I don't know what you're talking about," George says nervously, edging further away from them.

"Oh yes you do. It wasn't just Chris who was Warren's rival. You were both keen on Margaret Morton, weren't you?"

"Maggie?"

"But Warren had the edge, didn't he? It was him Margaret was going for. You didn't like that, you..."

Suddenly George turns and runs. Jennifer goes after him, but he's faster and reaches the rear door, banging it in her face. By the time she manages to wrench it open, he's half way to the main entrance.

"Did you resolve your differences with Chris?" Ettie says to Charley.

"Didn't get a chance," Charley says, still looking towards the open door, then turning back gloomily, "It's worse than ever. He won't consider any new material. He's even against what we've already done, but I'm not going to be defeated. I've written it up, we can at least rehearse the rehanging scene and then..."

"No, no," Ettie says pleadingly, "You mustn't do that, it's too dangerous."

"I've got everybody here. We have to..."

"What about the scenes with Tresilian, the trial, the jurors?"

"That would be after Grindcobb's return from Hertford."

"Yes."

"But we can't do that. We have no one to play Grindcobb. I was hoping..."

"You have Wesley Greville."

"We haven't, he's disappeared and no one knows where he is."

Ettie groans, "Then we are utterly lost!"

12

THE room is packed with the tension mounting. The press seats are full and David Farley has had to squeeze into the corner. He knows the gist of the announcement and has already made a minor scoop with the *Mercury* carrying the story yesterday. He's here today for the questions and to ensure his source got it right. It should be okay, there's been no comeback (other than the usual 'we never comment on leaks') and the documents looked authentic. That said, he's begun to have misgivings. His contacts with George Carter have been erratic to say the least and he always gets the impression he's holding something back. What does he expect to do, suddenly burst upon the world with additional titbits from his obscure provincial paper? It won't work. Surely he knows his best approach is to cooperate fully and openly with David and the *Mercury?*

There's a flurry of activity as David Burton enters. Then everyone settles down. Burton is a tall, wiry man, utterly conventional in his manner and speech, but prone to slight flamboyance in his dress, keen on flashy ties and gaudy shirts. Today it's a yellow tie and turquoise shirt. Bit like a Swedish flag, David wonders. His outfit oddly contrasts with his droning delivery, deliberately stretching out his introduction, repeating the terms of reference, listing all the sources of evidence and rounding it off with an exposition of the committee's methodology. David watches him with some amusement. He loves it, keeping them all on tenterhooks, wallowing in their agony of anticipation. Yet it's all somewhat artificial as the *Mercury* covered it yesterday and his only slight attempt at humour is a whimsical reference to 'those who may have gone before.'

Then, at last he gets to the enquiry's conclusions and recommendations. Except for minor variations of presentation, the final report much in line with George's leaked documents. The questions are predictable, the answers even more so. Burton's only slight hesitation is in reply to one by David himself.

"A development of this kind and the consequent opposition in the local community, has inevitably raised questions that go beyond purely local political involvement. To what extent did the enquiry take this into account both in its formal and informal work?"

Burton waffles for a time, eventually falling back on the age old defence of the 'restrictions of the terms of reference' and dodges David's supplementary question of direct political interference without actually denying it. He bats away most of the other questions, usually ending with his standard catch phrase.

"That is the verdict."

After hearing this eight times David's concentration flags. It's then he notices George is not in the room. This is a major local event and must be the lead for this week's paper. Having heard enough he gets up, turning at the door on hearing Burton's ninth 'That is the verdict' and notices someone familiar in the middle of the room. It's not George so he goes out to the comparative quietness of the corridor. He rings the newspaper and asks for the editor.

"He's not here."

"When will he be back?"

Hesitation. David explains who he is.

"We've not seen him for days, Mr. Farley. We don't know where he is."

Tresilian walks straight past Jenner, almost knocking him into the street. The men look open mouthed at the judge's advancing back, their eyes filled with distracted anxiety and an awful guilt.

"You're not to blame," Jenner says, "he fooled you, but that doesn't make you fools."

They turn to each other in silence, oblivious of him and unable to communicate other than in looks of mutual accusation and helplessness.

"There was no other way," the spokesman says, taking on himself the responsibility of voicing all their thoughts.

No one contradicts him. Though sympathetic to their plight Jenner is repelled by their apparent indifference. He turns to the door and with one last rueful glance steps back into the street. Is his judgement too harsh? What else could they do, simple men faced with the unyielding terror of the law? He feels a little ashamed. How can he judge the raw conflicts of 1381 faced with the comforting platitudes of his own time? Why didn't they challenge him, put him down, pitch such an arrogant stranger into the street? Yet he'd only tried to help them, fortify them against Tresilian's intimidation. They didn't want to know. Or they hadn't heard, hadn't seen. What is this world into which he's been thrown? They can't hear or see him while only he hears John Ball even when he's not present. Is John Ball now a free spirit of all times, belonging to none? Is Jenner's really here at all or locked in some endlessly repeating dream, tossed between past and present, constantly in someone else's future?

He has to deal with the here and the *now*. He quickens his step. Tresilian is ahead, walking very fast, retracing his steps to the Moot Hall. Jenner follows, no longer bothering with the shadows or staying close to buildings. Tresilian reaches the court where a number of men stand outside beside two of the soldiers. They all go in with the judge and before the soldiers can close the doors Jenner slips in, stepping to the side at the back of the room. These men are as apprehensive as the first group and stand nervously around the long table. Tresilian sits in the big chair with one of the clerks at the end. He spreads on the table the paper extracted from the first group.

"See here, I have summoned another jury and they have already supplied the names of these criminals in the indictment."

The men look down bewilderingly at the list.

"The cunning ba..." Jenner mutters to himself.

"Now answer me this," Tresilian booms, his arms flat on the table, his long spiky fingers spread out like the legs of some infernal spider, "How would you respond if you were held responsible as this first jury? Would you act in the same way so there could be no aspersions cast in your direction that might imply you were not true and honest men?"

The men are hesitant, but are trapped at the end of a blind alley from which there can be no escape.

"Come, come," Tresilian says, interrupting their unspoken conversation of knowing looks and slight nods, "We are all men of integrity, are we not? If these men had been known to you, would you not also have done the same as your neighbours?"

Still they hesitate.

"Come, I wouldn't wish to believe you were not honest and true. You would have done the same, wouldn't you?"

He glares at them threateningly and beckons the clerk.

"Is it ready?"

"Yes, my lord."

"Well?" Tresilian bellows and now each man responds with a nod or muffled affirmation, "So your verdict would have to be guilty?"

"Write it down," Tresilian instructs the clerk, "this honest jury, presented with such an indictment would convict and find these men guilty."

"But, my lord," one man says, "We have not been presented with..."

"No, no," Tresilian says impatiently, "but if you were, if you *were!*"

They all agree. Tresilian claps his hands.

"Good, good. Now, you men, the clerk will take you to the ante room and you will remain there awhile."

Some men protest, but Tresilian rebukes them forcefully and they are led away. After they've gone he nods to the soldiers at the back. This makes Jenner uneasy. Has he been seen, are they going to arrest him? But they ignore him, open the doors and lead in yet a third set of jurors.

"The cunning fox," Jenner whispers, "He's taking no chances."

"Come down, come down," Tresilian roars, now flushed with his success and desperate to finish the business quickly.

One soldier shepherds the men, but his companion holds back and seems to be counting. Noticing this, Jenner looks to the men and also counts. Then he starts. There are only eleven! He looks away and then sees the soldier coming towards him. Jenner glances around, but there's no one else. The soldier can see him and is getting closer!

"There's no need to be so concerned about an individual actor. The cause is greater than any one person."

Charley's sudden remark unsettles both Ettie and Jennifer.

"The *cause?*" Jennifer says.

"The project, the film," Charley says hurriedly, "We've more important things to worry about than the disappearance of Wesley Greville. I know he's good and we've already shot him in some scenes, but they can be redone and at least one scene involving the new material doesn't involve him at all."

"But you'll be shooting out of sequence," Ettie insists.

"Why is that so important, you don't shoot scenes in strict chronological order. It's not important, we've done it already."

"If only it was so simple," Ettie says, then turning to Jennifer, "She doesn't understand."

"I understand perfectly well," Charley says, "I've got a director who walked out – more accurately – *ran* out. You keep telling me how important it is for the film to be restarted and now when I want to go ahead, you try to hold me back!"

"But without Wesley Greville..."

"We can get a replacement."

"Not in time."

"We have all the time in..."

"We do not have time, today is the 15th! Everything must be accomplished today!"

"I've had enough of this, I'm going to..."

"Listen to what she says!" Jennifer says, taking Charley's arm.

"Let go of me! Who are you to order me about, you couldn't even stop Chris leaving and you've not got George Carter!"

Despite her remonstrations, Charley isn't prepared to defy Jennifer and sits down, mumbling irritably as she flicks through her script.

"Up to a point she's right," Jennifer says to Ettie, "I ought to be out there..."

"But your phone won't work and you felt constrained when you went outside, reluctant to leave the studio in case you were needed."

"How did you...yes, I felt compelled to stay, as if leaving would not only be unwise, but dangerous."

Ettie's confirmatory nods further unsettle Jennifer.

"You know something, what have you felt?"

Ettie draws her out of Charley's earshot.

"The interaction between past and present draws to its crisis. We have to identify who triggered it in the first place."

"Someone we know?"

"Could be."

"Someone under investigation."

"Though not necessarily an immediate suspect."

"Ted Skinner or perhaps Maggie?" Jennifer titters, but Ettie remains coldly serious.

"It's not just the present that concerns us. We are in real time in both past and present."

"Real time?"

"Today, the 15th July. Each hour now runs parallel with each hour then and there are uncontrolled individuals in both. What happens now happens then."

"Like Maggie?" Jennifer says, though now without amusement.

"Like Thomas. His redemption and his return have to be today. That imperative restrained you. Help me find Thomas. When we find him help me to help him."

She looks across to Charley, still engrossed in her script.

"She could be a problem," Jennifer says.

"She's essential. Everything has to be brought together today and to do that the filming has to start again."

"But what you were saying, surely the dangers...?"

Ettie grimaces and twists her hands in a gesture of resignation.

"Despite the dangers and they are many. I've wondered about Wesley Greville and Warren Grover. Whether Warren was somehow transmuted ..."

"...into someone in the past?"

"The past's involvement gets stronger. The key to your investigations lies in the past. We must crack it and to that we only have the film. Something has to happen...today!"

"You must join the others."

The soldier looks directly. There's no one else. It has to be Jenner.

"The jury...?" Jenner says.

"You are the twelfth man."

"No, no, there's a mistake. It's not possible, I can't..."

"Why not?"

"Well, it's just...you see..."

"You cannot refuse. Come, you must join the others."

Why now and not before? Why now do they see him, surely they must know he's not...? He should object, but how can he explain? He goes to the table and stands at the back of the group. The same paper drawn up by the first jury and shown to the second is spread out on the table and Tresilian is indicating the names.

"These men are known to you all and already one jury has written them down for indictment. As honest and true men would you not respond likewise?"

Jenner glances at the soldier behind him, but he seems not to be listening. Hardly surprising, he's heard this twice already. He turns back to the group at the table. If the soldier can see him and hear him, then these men, unlike the others will hear him, but will they heed him? He edges forward to speak. As he does the wall behind Tresilian changes, the vaulted ceiling replaced by something lower, smoother, almost modern. He looks round. For an instant there's no soldier and the room is packed with people, all dressed like him. Then it goes and he sees the bare floor again.

"Don't be intimidated like the others," he cries and then pointing to the judge, "That man is fooling you as he's fooled them. Don't betray your neighbours and friends. Screw up his paper. Tell him the truth!"

No one stirs except to engage in a separate faint conversation that Jenner hears only as an indistinct rumble.

"They *don't* see me!"

He runs around the group and stands next to the clerk (who looks straight through him at Tresilian) and hammers the table.

"Why don't you listen to me, listen to the truth!"

As he shouts the modern room, the comfortable chairs, the chatting lawyers, all impose.

"I'm not here, that's why they don't see me. That's why they can't hear the truth!"

"There is always a time for the truth."

The voice of the past and all time, comes from behind, near the side door, where the second jury were taken away and where...yes it is him...John Ball walks across the room. Yet like Jenner he's not in the room, but elsewhere. Where does he walk? Outside? He's not here at all, yet he is here.

"They can't see me or hear me. I'm not really here. This is an illusion, a dream."

"We are all part of each other's dreams and sometimes one dream is shared by us all."

John Ball reaches the back of the room and stops walking Yet it's not really the room at all for Jenner can see the street and the crowds.

"You're like me," Jenner shouts to him, "You're not here. Where are you going?"

"From where I can never return. Soon I shall be everywhere."

"Don't go yet, don't leave me here!"

John Ball's image is already fading as the walls of the room resume their shape and texture. Jenner turns back to the table and groans as he sees the third jury drawing up another paper, indicting the same men a second time.

"No, no," he shouts.

No one hears him and he turns away again. John Ball has gone and the room is now filled with people in modern dress. He turns back and there is Tresilian and the jury at the table. Is he in the past or the present? He looks to the side door and there is John Ball again, climbing up a wooden structure. Jenner calls out, but John Ball doesn't hear and his image fades once more. Jenner turns back to see the modern room again. Every time he turns he's in a different place and a different time. His head spins, pulled between three places – Tresilian and the jurors, the modern room and the last walk of John Ball. He tries to stand still, hoping he might stabilise in one place and one time, but he can't stop spinning round and round, though now he feels one place and one time drawing him closer, closer...

The actors listen spellbound as Charley runs through the next scene. They've not heard her like this before, with a mastery and command way beyond the needs of the writer, seemingly powered by one who has seen, heard and *been* there and can now infuse that insight within them. They'll not need to act, but retell as witnesses, mimic what they've just seen. Heard once is enough, locked and absorbed for instantaneous replay. She has the authority of the past as one who knows, one who can demand, vivid, pervasive, almost palpable, describing events as if they are actually happening. Her confidence and audacity transfixes them though for some it's too much and they draw away, hoping to dilute the impact of her words. Yet no one doubts her right to direct. Like the moon rising on an autumn night, Charley is in the ascendant. Ettie listens with admiration and anxiety, fearing the source of such power, its unpredictability disturbing her even more. But the film is the key.

"Surely there's someone with greater technical skills," Ettie wonders, looking towards the assistant director, the director of photography, the editor, but none show any sign of challenging Charley.

"So you're going ahead?" Ettie says, resignedly.

"These scenes must be done," Charley says.

"Must?"

"You said we had to work in sequence, especially today – the 15th – everything happens on this day and if we don't have enough time then..."

"Yes, yes," Ettie interrupts, but stops as suddenly

Charley waits impatiently. Ettie knows what she must say, but she's afraid. How can she be sure...if the forces can't be controlled...?

"I know it's gruesome," Charley says, glancing at the mind blown cast, "but surely the sentences imposed by Tresilian... they must be carried out?"

"Yes, they must," Ettie says almost inaudibly as if the quieter the acknowledgement the less she might be endorsing the inevitable, "but...today..."

"They happened today, the 15th, they cannot be avoided!"

"Alright, but the sequence..."

"...and if we film the sentences, then we have to do the rehangings."

"No, no," Ettie says in alarm, "That would be too late."

"If we go beyond today..."

"No, no, it would be out of sequence, it happened in August, long after the 15th."

"We can't stop, we've already started."

"You've started the rehanging scene?"

"We've already read through the script..."

"You mustn't do it yet, not until..."

"Until?"

Charley's pugnacious expression unsettles Ettie. The accusatory cast...it reminds her of Martha...she doesn't want to talk of Thomas, but that look can't be ignored.

"...until...until I've found..." but Ettie won't say, can't say, "no, no, never mind."

Charley thumbs through her now battered copy of *A Little Liberty*.

"Besides, Chris has already shot the king's fealty scene, which was on 20th July, so we've already moved beyond the sequence. That was in front of the king and the rehangings in August are also dependent on his proclamation. So...we can go ahead, there's nothing to stop us."

The spinning stops. This is the Moot Hall, where Jenner first arrived after his strange conversation with the hedge priest on Watling Street. It's the same crowd as on the day John Ball was tried and sentenced before judge Tresilian, but it is not Friday the 12th. Nor is it the Saturday or the Sunday when he listened with mounting anger to Tresilian's intimidation of the deluded townsmen. This is the end of the poor man's respite, giving him time to prepare. These people are gathered for a different purpose and the proceedings he's sure are about to begin fill him with dread. This is Monday 15th July 1381.

The side door opens and a solemn, dispiritedly serious group of twelve men troops into the room. Jenner recognises the second jury, bullied and tricked by the judge into saying they would convict on the indictment set down by the first and third juries. Two long forms at a right angle to the judge's table have been prepared for them. They are sworn and sit down forlornly. How can they now not convict their neighbours without appearing dishonest, going back on what they previously told Tresilian? Honesty, justice, truth, Jenner muses, three precious birds cooped ready for the slaughter by a wily fox.

The soldiers escort a line of prisoners from the back of the hall, bringing them before Tresilian in small groups. The first to be indicted is a group of fifteen men led by William Grindcobb, William Cadindon and John Barbintsor. They stand in silence. Some are clearly afraid and glance nervously to their friends in the crowd, but Grindcobb, holding himself erect and calm, stares only at Tresilian. Cadindon too is defiant and watches the judge unflinchingly as the clerk reads out the charges. Jenner listens carefully to the long and rambling indictment, essentially amounting to public order offences, no significant violence and no murders. Tresilian is about to turn to the jury when Cadindon speaks out.

"The abbot brought us to this position."

"I did not give the prisoners leave to speak," Tresilian says, "The time will..."

"But he must speak now, sir judge," Grindcobb says, "for if we are charged with disturbing the king's peace, then we can only plead our guilt at disturbing the ascendancy of repression."

A murmur of support ripples through the crowd. It temporarily unsettles Tresilian, but he recovers and is ready to admonish everyone. Grindcobb forestalls him, turning to Cadindon.

"Say what must be said, Will. We may not have long to speak."

Ignoring Tresilian, Cadindon turns to the crowd.

"The abbot is a hypocrite. (Low rumbling assent around the room) The semblance of holiness he shows outside the monastery has duped and deceived the lords and magnates. Sustained by their patronage he ill treats us with his tyranny. He has wickedly stolen the ancestral liberties of the citizens of this town with false documents. Heavy handedly he oppresses free men, not permitting them to erect a hand mill in their own homes, but like bondmen compelling them to grind their own corn at his mill."

"Silence!" Tresilian booms, "This is not relevant to the charges."

"It's the truth," someone shouts from the back of the room.

"Those that falsely accuse the abbot will be punished," Tresilian thunders, "the men will be hanged and the women burned!"

The crowd is suddenly silenced, but Tresilian is agitated and grabs some documents from the clerk, shuffling them nervously. Then he composes himself, confers quickly with the clerk, sweeps a threatening glare across the crowd and addresses the jury.

"You have heard the charges. Standing fast by your word and your honour, how say you? Do you find these men guilty of causing a disturbance to the king's peace?"

The jurors hesitate, then try to talk among themselves, but Tresilian is in no mood for prevarication.

"Come, what is your verdict?"

The men are silent. Then the foreman stands.

"Guilty."

The single word, sudden, stark and irreversible resonates across the room. No one speaks. Tresilian motions to the clerk, who starts to write.

"All fifteen?"

"Yes."

"Then I move to the sentence. You will be taken this day along with John Ball to be drawn and hanged."

An instant of stunned silence is followed by a long, low, despairing moan. Tresilian calls for silence again, repeating his earlier threat to punish individuals in the crowd. Jenner is shaken into a wakeful impotence, incredulously absorbing the fate of Grindcobb and his comrades, so shocked he's unable to protest. With a wave of the judge's hand the men are marched away and another group is brought in. Similar charades of legal process follow as further groups are brought before Tresilian to be tried and sentenced. As the litany of punishment mounts Jenner gradually recovers, seeing and hearing only Tresilian, the clerk, the soldiers, the accused, the crowd, the room itself all relegated to a hazy periphery of blurred images and muffled sounds. The savagery of the repression hammers at his unspoken, unquestioned tenets of 'rightness.' If this is justice there is no truth in it.

"The truth must ultimately prevail."

John Ball again, but only in the policeman's head.

"But truth concealed must ultimately be revealed," the policeman silently replies.

Much of the crowd disperses, but Jenner listens to the end, concentrating on Tresilian, his anger transforming into a burning determination to redress wrongs whatever the cost. There are no more capital sentences, but in all eighty men of the county, including some leading townsmen are sent to prison. The last group is about to be sentenced. Tresilian checks the indictments with the clerk.

"They are not all here...they are missing...escaped...then outlaws they must be."

Tresilian turns back to the group.

"That is my verdict..."

Jenner's concentration intensifies and the words of the clerk and the accused are lost, submerged beneath the judge's closing remarks, to which Jenner is forced to respond.

"Verdicts formulated with intimidated juries and fabricated indictments!"

Tresilian turns to him, accusatory and menacing.

"That is the verdict..."

Jenner stares back with equivalent vehemence, but now sees a different face and a different room.

Charley agrees. No scenes will be filmed beyond today, 15th July. Past and present are simultaneous so this temporary relief may give Ettie the time she needs, but real time is fraught time and so little of it is left. The respite also comes at a price as Charley busies herself with her preparations to recreate Tresilian's sentences with a creative ruthlessness equalled only by the brutality of the originals. Ettie watches apprehensively as do the cast, especially those who are to play major parts. The sets are constructed, the extras form up, the principals step forward, all rigged as in 1381, artifice and reality shuddering and converging, past and present merging and melding. Ettie wants to speak, but the words won't form and for the first time there's no clash between her and Charley. Jennifer has watched their interchanges with increasing bewilderment. Her mind is elsewhere, although also in the past.

She tries again to get Jenner on her phone, saying, "If we knew who killed Melvyn Strange we might be able to wrap up the whole case. As yet we haven't even got a body."

"Maybe not," Ettie says, "but I know who killed him."

The same phrase is repeated endlessly, faster and faster until the words are merged into an undulating white noise.

"That is the verdict"

Then it slows, the separate syllables gradually pulled apart as the whirling images also stabilise. Jenner no longer faces Tresilian, though a superficial similarity keeps the visage of the 14th century judge alive for some minutes. The words are the same, even the tone with its hectoring pronouncements, but instead of powerless peasants in a grim crowd, this man faces a phalanx of reporters and a more sophisticated audience. But appearances can be deceptive. Reality often lies beneath not on the surface.

He struggles to adjust, acclimatising to the modern room, his own time, his own...no not his own people, for his mind though stabilised keeps its hold on the world of Tresilian and John Ball. He looks around. It's not surprising he's unrecognised and unacknowledged with everyone dressed like him, talking like him. The man in the high chair speaks again. Something about the verdict again and 'I need say no more, gentlemen' whatever that means. This man is too gaunt to be the repressive judge. Besides he has no finery, no outward trappings of office and station, all very 21st century uniformity, hierarchy and power more subtly drawn. Jenner's unsure which he prefers, medieval finery and ostentation or concealed modern distinctions. He feels as uncomfortable and conspicuous as he was in the past, a discomfort now of what he is rather than what he may seem to be. The effect's the same. He might as well be dressed in 14th century clothes. Shouldn't they notice if he's just transferred through six hundred years? He shudders at the ridiculous thought, even now wondering if it's been a dream, a delusion. That's it, a daydream. He's been drifting off, musing on Ettie and Jennifer's idle talk. But then, where did he drift off *from?* He must have been here, listening to this announcement, this *verdict*, but he has no recollection of ever having been here.

He can't stay. This is not the right place. He gets up, shuffles to the aisle and slinks to the door as quietly and unobtrusively as possible. No one notices. They're too busy putting questions, which the man in the high chair is successfully parrying. It's almost deserted outside, only a man with his back to him, speaking on a mobile at the far end of the corridor. Jenner finds a vacant chair by the wall. The parallels are unnerving. The room, Tresilian, this man, the *verdict*, but he has to concentrate on essentials. A mind buffeted between past and present is a mind lost and that's not good for his enquiries. He keeps getting flashbacks. He must drive them out, concentrate on the now, the immediate both in time and place. After a few moments he feels surer, calmer, though far from better. He may dismiss images of the past, but how easy is it to ignore the message? Forget those trails and conflicts, they belong to another time.

"There is always a time for the truth."

He can't reject John Ball's words. The forms of the process may change, but not its essence. Nor can he get Tresilian out of his mind. The hectoring, the deception, the blatant intimidation, so unbalanced, so wrong, so *medieval*. Or is it? Like truth injustice belongs to all time. But those times are not these times. If there'd been an unbiased professional investigation, would events have taken a different turn or was the system so weighted and prejudiced there would be no other outcome, no other *verdict*? What is the point of a policeman doing his job thoroughly and honestly if the judicial process is flawed? Tresilian was into proving guilt when there was none, but now it might be just as easily the other way round. How many times has he been convinced of someone's guilt but couldn't prove it? In this investigation nothing is as it seems, no one reliable, not even those who seem to be helping.

The man stops speaking on his phone, turns and walks slowly up the corridor. Jenner mulls over the possibilities. Plenty of suspects, not much evidence. Three names recur, all knowing more about Warren Grover than they prefer to admit. Chris Pleasant, the decidedly *un*pleasant filmmaker, mining into the past, as long as it's never his own. Monica Freeson, anxious to be seen in the local community, but what of the things she prefers not to be seen? Things Warren knew? George Carter, now you see him, now you don't, the newspaper man who runs from rather than chases the story. Perhaps it's a story he prefers not to talk about.

"Derek!"

Jenner turns as David Farley almost reaches him.

"I didn't know you were coming. I thought I saw a familiar face, but then I was thinking of other things. Did your sergeant tell you about the enquiry?"

"Er, I've been away...not in the station. Are you going back in?"

"No, I've heard enough, unless...I don't suppose you saw George Carter in there?"

"No, I didn't, but then..."

"Neither did I. He's like the scarlet bloody pimpernel!"

"He has some information?"

"Yes, but it's all very …(he taps his nose and winks)…like a ruddy amateur, must think I've got nothing better to do than run round provincial hacks with more time than sense."

"Something to do with the enquiry?"

"Don't talk to me about that. Bloody debacle, that's what it is, bloody debacle! Come on, sun's over the yard arm, I'll buy you a drink. Unless that is, with you on duty…"

In the conventional sense Jenner is not on duty.

"Lead the way."

They retire to a nearby hostelry, Jenner recognising it from his youth.

"Used to be a rough place. Gone upmarket since then."

"Let's hope not too upmarket," David says, glancing at the lunch menu.

Despite repeatedly saying he 'doesn't want to talk about it' David won't stop dissecting the enquiry and lamenting the report.

"The leak was right, bloody whitewash, skimming over the real issues, refusing to explore unresolved matters."

"It was leaked?"

"George Carter, gave it me yesterday. Now when I need to follow up local information, he's buggered off! Thought you might know where he is."

"Me?"

"He said he gave you the slip near Dunstable. Seems to think you were following him."

"He must be mistaken."

"Hmm…anyway, even though Burton's enquiry gives the green light to the next phase of the Waintree development, all the political connections are bound to bounce back."

Jenner looks puzzled. David sighs impatiently.

"There could be significant political fallout if things are exposed rather than concealed."

"I've not been following politics very closely."

"You never did," David says resignedly, "All along I've believed the Waintree development was involved with the national political situation. You see the real significance…"

"That was last year," Jenner says dismissively.

"And a year ago we had the tension, the intrigue, the seismic movement of allegiances, why it was largely your work that led to the fall of..."

"...that's all resolved, got nothing to do with my investigation here. I've never been fazed by 'wider implications."

"Alright, where have you got to? The motive for Warren Grover's murder has to be connected to fiddles with the Waintree Development."

"What sort of fiddles?"

"Hard to say. I have my suspicions, but..."

"No evidence. Something George Carter knew about?"

"Perhaps or..."

"He was himself involved."

David shrugs.

"Whatever it was and whoever it was, Warren found out. With her political machinations, my guess would be Monica Freeson ...crowing about Burton's enquiry...it's obscene. It's just a matter of the evidence. Don't you agree?"

Jenner grimaces dubiously.

"You may be right about Warren, but what about Lawrence. If the same person was responsible for both murders Lawrence must have been killed for the same reason – what he knew about the development."

At first David hesitates, then says, "There you have it – Monica!"

Jenner is doubtful.

"We can't prove a link."

"What about your sergeant, she was...?" David says.

Jenner takes out his phone and tries to ring Jennifer, but gets a peculiar noise and can't make a connection. The problem may not be at her end. Who knows what all this lurching into the past does to modern technology? He puts the instrument back in his pocket.

"Even if such a three way link can be proved between someone and Lawrence and Warren based on the development," he goes on dolefully, "it doesn't necessarily mean they are the murderer."

"But you said..."

"...it's a question of evidence..."

There is always a time for the truth

"...if only we could *provide* clear evidence. It's a dead end. We can't even prove there's any fiddling with the development. It's all suspicion and innuendo."

He turns despondently to David who puckers his lips in a gesture of sympathetic solidarity.

Then Jenner says, "But I know who did it."

Monica's house is crammed with people. Judging they're all sufficiently fed and watered she moves to the centre of the large rear room and taps her glass. The guests, some great, a few good, most neither, gather around expectantly, their own chattering and chortling gradually damping down. The French doors are packed with those from the garden while many in the other room are straining to listen. Resplendent in a long cerise gown, her eyes garner attention and scan the party for any who might dare to continue speaking, her mouth quivering in a half smile of anticipatory pleasure. This is her victory, her day, her time. Within a few moments her imposed silence prevails and she beams imperiously.

"Friends, colleagues, supporters, above all fellow campaigners in the journey of rejuvenation, for that is surely the venture on which we have been travelling. (Grunting approvals, a few rumble 'hear hear') It has not been without its problems (suppressed laughter) nor at times its conflicts and I know some of you were privately dreading this day, fearful the enquiry would endorse our opponents rather than ourselves, but I never entertained such doubts. Not out of conceit, but from an unshakeable belief in the rightness of what we are doing. Our opponents talk about the land and how they fight to preserve our collective heritage as if we don't care about such things. We care as much, if not more, but we are also concerned our children and grandchildren will have something to inherit. They say we are tenants on this land, this country and have no rights of exploitation, of plunder (cries of 'shame') and the struggles of our ancestors should not be forgotten. Rightly so, but while we must respect the past, we must also provide for the future. The land isn't a museum to be cased up, labelled and left untouched. It lives

357

and we are a living part of it. Like everything else it has to be adapted to the times. Unchanged, undeveloped, it loses its value. After all, who can live in a museum? So, I ask you to raise your glasses..."

"...and toast the plunderers' victory!"

Heads move left and right, depending on position to George Carter who's suddenly pushed his way from the door and stands in the small arc of space in front of Monica. People stand back as he points his finger.

"You have it all now and I wonder how you got it. David Burton is just the latest puppet. What did you do to...?"

"How did you get in here?" she shrieks.

"The usual way," he says, waving his press card.

"You abuse your position."

"You abuse yours."

"What do you want?"

"To record the claptrap I've just heard. Make no mistake, I'll report it in the context of this bun party celebration."

"You've been reporting nothing else lately. Where have you been, people are looking for you? Up to no good, I'll be bound, but now you're here..."

He laughs.

"What people? Your empty threats don't frighten me."

"The police."

He laughs again, though now a little hollow and then points his finger again, this time around the room and the guests.

"Make the most of it while you can. What you do destroys what we hold in trust for those that follow. But what if you could be held account in the future now? What if the twentieth generation hence, say six hundred years, could appear now? You think you've won, but the good times won't last. It'll come out and it won't just be about this damned development either!"

Monica nods and mouths to someone at the back of the room, turning her right forefinger against her left hand. If George notices the telephone gesture he makes no comment, but backs away slightly.

"Get out!" she shouts, "I'm not going to let..."

"You're not going to silence me," George shouts back, though edging closer to the door, "You know a lot more!"

"I don't know what you're talking about."

"No? Do you want me to spell it out in front of all these people?"

"The police will be here shortly. You can spell it out to them."

"Warren Grover!" he shouts, now very close to the door, but unable to get through as some of the men close around him.

"Ridiculous. I hardly knew the man."

"Yes you did and so did the others!" a woman shouts.

She's pushed her way through from the garden and now stands, legs slightly bent forward, arms outstretched as she balances with her head and chest pulled back.

"My God!" Monica laughs, turning to her, "First tragedy now farce, from the scoundrel to the buffoon, the outlaw to the clown!"

Maggie is dressed in a long green frock, her long hair, usually in a bun is loose and falls across her face and neck as she screeches at Monica.

"You know what Lawrence did!"

"I'm not in the habit of speaking ill of the dead."

"You might have to when the police get here."

"There's nothing to tell. I've had no dealings with Lawrence Bullock."

"You knew him, you knew them all."

So far, Monica has remained still, hardly moving during the clashes. Now she steps towards Maggie, who straightens up both her legs and her back, ready to retreat.

"So did you, pathetic, vicious bitch!" Monica screams.

This caustic reaction, countering Maggie's attack with equal force shocks some of her party, but she's not finished yet.

"Get out of my house you miserable cow and get back to the gutter where you belong!"

She raises her hand to strike. Maggie steps back, then comes forward again, pushing her hands to her front, ready to parry a blow or deliver her own. Monica raises her hand again, but one of her friends restrains her.

"Get her out, get her out!" Monica says, turning away.

Meanwhile, during the excitement, George has slipped away.

The prisoner and his small escort make their way slowly towards the scaffold. The crowd is silent. A weighty, charged silence full of sorrow and suppressed anger, the still air broken only by the sweet plaintive call of a very distant bird as if it too feels the heaviness of the morning. Ettie doesn't question the sound of a bird in a studio, nor the open landscape beyond the immediate buildings. If she had she would have noticed the country was no set, the bird no sound effect. While the look in the eyes of the crowd, the roughness of their clothes, the wrinkles in their faces seem beyond the skills of make up and the transient artistry of the actor. Theirs is the presence of the past as if like the lines and parts Charley has given them they've been crudely ripped from another age.

'John Ball' stands calmly as the instruments of his execution are prepared. He looks to the crowd. No words are exchanged, yet his very weakness is his strength, the injustice of the sentence, the dignified helplessness of his position imparting an influence transcending the day, reaching out to...another time. He turns from the crowd and glances at those behind him, other prisoners, also waiting quietly. It's then Ettie realises. Charley is going ahead. The scene will include them all, but how can it be? She looks across the faces, Cadindon, Barbintsor and the others, fourteen in all. Fourteen? That's not right. There should be fifteen! Grindcobb is not there because there's no Wesley Greville to play him, but the scene can't go beyond John Ball without Grindcobb. It would be distorting history. Dedicated to the authentic events and clutching *A Little Liberty* like a pilgrim with her holy book, surely Charley can't consider it? That would be giving no time for *truth*. There's already been too much interference, but how will the interfered react to such distortion? If our time is their time and both in real time...yet if distorted how can it be resolved? Those that were then are now...waiting for resolution...how can they live now, how can they wait in this...living fiction?

Ettie sees two familiar faces in the crowd. Now there's no point in finding Charley, nothing to be gained from accosting her, for she no more controls events than Ettie does. The past is in control, this day, 15th July 1381 moves on inevitably. But are they any more real...if she blinks, they'll go away. She does, but they don't. They are as real as everything else, yet what will be the outcome with Grindcobb missing and no one to play him? Alone in the crowd, Thomas and Martha look not at John Ball, but at her. Ettie hears Martha's words clearly, though no one else turns to her.

"The guilt comes from him...make it happen!"

Then Thomas speaks without disturbing the silence for only Ettie hears him.

"The two Englands, they come together today."

Ettie shudders. Suddenly she's back in London, is it one year ago or six hundred, the night before Smithfield? He speaks again.

"The axe was sharp, the stroke was hard in the fourth year of King Richard."

Whose axe and wielded for whom? A lament for John Ball, soon to pay the ultimate price for speaking too much and too often for the truth? There is always a time for the truth. No, it's not the hardness of the stroke for John Ball he cries, but for others...for himself...the hardness of redemption, the sharpness of revenge. Martha speaks again with that accusatory pleading Ettie finds so hard to resist, so difficult to understand.

"...make it happen...the land endures...but free him from the land..."

Still Ettie doesn't understand, but for the first time feels Martha asking her to do rather than stop something. *Make it happen* rather than *stop it happening*. But that is still interfering and already there's been too much interference. Even if she dared, what must she do? The land *endures* yet he must be *freed* from the land. Is the land the continuing element that resolves past and present, is that what Martha is saying? Ettie must know more, but when she turns she and Thomas cannot be seen in the crowd. They are gone. To the land? He because he cannot escape and she because she must try to release him? It's a message Ettie can't ignore. The land, she must get to the land!

"You're right," she mutters.

"Who's right?"

She's forgotten Jennifer standing beside her.

"We have to get out, we have to get away!"

She grabs Jennifer's hand and runs to the back door of the studio. No one notices and filming continues.

"But the film," Jennifer protests, "You said it was important...?"

"We have to get out, we have to find the chief inspector!"

Ettie's desperation increases as she knocks over chairs and scenery in her rush to get to the exit.

"Try him again on your phone!"

"There's no signal, it must be this place."

"Nonsense! It's worked before. Try again. We have to speak to him, there may not be enough time!"

"But you said to stay here and..."

Ettie gets to the doors, but they won't open. She wrenches and pulls, but they won't budge. Jennifer helps her, tearing and writhing at the handles, but there's no movement.

"They're locked," Ettie says, "I'll get the others."

David Farley makes no immediate reply, avoiding the temptation to demand an answer. Then Jenner speaks, though tantalisingly at first still doesn't name his suspect.

"Someone knows who killed Warren Grover."

"If they did it, they're hardly likely to tell you."

"Or even if they have suspicions?"

"They're all so interrelated, afraid if anyone points the finger at another, it might be turned back on themselves."

Jenner nods.

"Nest of vipers all of them, George Carter, Monica Freeson, Chris Pleasant, even Maggie Morton and..."

"But she's only..."

"Mad? That's what they call her and she's certainly eccentric, but while eccentricity doesn't necessarily make you a murderer, it doesn't exclude you either."

"I can't believe she..."

"Then we have Rick Tranter, smooth, shadowy, but he knew them all and..."

"You don't believe it's him?"

"I've always included him. From the start you said he was involved in the development."

"Yes, but there's no..."

"Evidence? Quite so and that's my failure. I've been unable to pin him down to either Warren or Lawrence's murder. Assuming dubious land development is the motive, your 'wider implications'...though that might also..."

"Apply to Monica?"

"Quite. The circumstantial evidence is there, but could as easily apply to others."

"So you don't think it's him?" David posits tentatively, unsure where Jenner is going.

"Oh yes, it's him, but...it's so frustrating...the lack of evidence...if only..."

Now David understands Jenner's direction if not his ultimate objective. At first he hesitates, but then says, "If I didn't know you better, Derek I'd say you were seriously considering fitting him up."

The phrase judders, forcing an embarrassing silence except for Jenner muttering 'more time.' *There is always a time for the truth.* John Ball's words resound and in his mind's eye the detective even sees his kindly, but serious face emerging from the cowl of his coarse brown gown.

"I have so little time left, do not disappoint me before I go."

"No, I won't," Jenner mutters.

"What's that?" David says.

"Nothing, nothing."

"They will come for me soon. I must face the supremacy of the truth and so must you."

"You're right," Jenner mutters.

"That gives me no pleasure," David says.

"What, what do you mean?" Jenner turns to him, flustered, still seeing John Ball, now on his knees, praying perhaps.

"Very soon," Jenner mutters.

"I meant about being right," David says, "about you...being so sure... about Tranter."

"But he's right."

"Who's right?"

"I mean, *I'm* right. Right not to do it."

David looks in bewildered disbelief, wondering what new twist he's about to turn, not knowing Jenner is guided by another, seen and heard only by him. For John Ball, condemned to the end by his own unwavering belief and admission of the truth, can't be ignored. *There is always a time for truth.*

"If it can't be proved, then it can't be him," Jenner says.

"Can't be Tranter?"

"Of course not."

"But you said..."

"I've been too influenced by you," Jenner says sharply.

"I was only..."

Jenner takes his arms gently.

"It's not your fault. I've been too focused on these development issues..."

"You've always said you weren't interested, that you were conducting a murder enquiry."

"Quite so, but I was still persuaded the development was the key to the murders," he turns away, in his mind seeing John Ball's shadowy figure getting up, "The *truth* lies elsewhere."

"Don't be too quick to dismiss Tranter," David says trenchantly, unbalanced by yet another sudden and unexpected turn, "He's the real brains behind Waintree. George Carter always included him from the start and then..."

"George Carter, George bloody Carter, about as reliable as a wisp of Scotch mist! You can't prove anything!"

"No, but we have to..."

"...and neither can I! We can't keep confusing the two issues. Even if Tranter is behind all the development fiddles it doesn't make him a murderer."

"Okay, but if it's not him, who is it?"

Charley and the cast are utterly absorbed in the new filming.

"You must come," Ettie shouts at her, "You have to help. We have to get the doors unlocked!"

Charley waves her aside. Ettie approaches others, but they hardly acknowledge her. Then she realises. They won't help, they have to continue and even if they stopped they couldn't help. This is the past. It's too powerful and they've lost control. There's no point wasting more time here. She runs back. At least she can try and help Jennifer. It's a short run, but it seems endless as if time is suddenly stretched almost to stasis. They are filming the past, they are in the past and it won't let them go.

She gets to the door, but there's no Jennifer. She calls, but gets no answer. They are still filming. If that is what it is...more likely 15th July 1381 holding them, enfolding them. She can't get out. She can't *make things happen*. She could be marooned, unable to stop the film while it distorts that same past!

13

THIS time he won't lose him. This isn't Bedfordshire, not Dunstable Downs, but Jenner's own country. This time the editor of the *Mid Herts Herald* won't elude him. They skirt the southern edge of town and head out along the Hempston road. This was where his enquiry began when he first heard of Warren Grover's mysterious death and the Waintree development. George Carter doesn't stop in the village, but takes the St. Albans road. Jenner pulls up slightly. He's getting too close and doesn't want to alert his quarry, can't risk losing him now! George suddenly stops at the edge of Southstead Common and Jenner has to pull back even more to avoid being seen. Almost stationary, he gets a couple of annoying beeps from irritated drivers as they slow down to avoid him. George gets out his car. He doesn't notice Jenner, but soon will if he stays where he is and attracts further unwelcome attention from more passing motorists. Keeping an eye on the mirror to keep him in sight he accelerates quickly to pass George's car and parks off the road, further along the common.

He gets out and hovers near the car, away from George, who he can just see walking up the hill away from the road. Jenner follows at a distance when he's a fair way ahead. He stops at the brow of the hill. George is moving rapidly down the other side. Jenner sits down in case he turns round, but

George doesn't look back. From here Jenner can see most of the common. George is walking towards the hamlet of Dearswell. Jenner will have to be careful not to be spotted, but in the open country he can let George get well ahead without losing sight of him. After a few moments he gets up and then notices another figure, further ahead, also moving quickly towards Dearswell. At the bottom of the hill there's more cover. Jenner quickens his pace slightly to close the gap. He can see George clearly, beetling along, never deviating. There's no doubt now. George is following the other man.

They leave the common and get to Dearswell. Jenner is pretty sure now where George is going, but he has to keep up. They get to the end of the lane. The first man has already reached the Grover's bungalow. Then, unexpectedly George turns and looks back. Jenner jumps behind a tree, but it's too late, George has already seen him. He looks about, runs from the bungalows, climbs over the fence skirting the fields and heads back towards Southstead Common. Jenner could chase him, but his cover's blown. George knows he's being followed. He'll get to his car, leaving Jenner to follow him to the newspaper office in Welstead where he'll deny having been on any particular errand or being in pursuit of anyone. Jenner has to accept it. George Carter has given him the slip yet again!

He walks up the lane. The first man has gone. Jenner has recognised him and it reminds him of unfinished business. With so much else on his mind he's forgotten to follow up Annabel Levins in Dirringstead. Hardly surprising when you're accosted by a six hundred year old dead cleric, swept into the machinations of 14th century 'justice,' returning to be bombarded by journalistic hyperbole. He should have listened more to Rusk. Something George Carter had found out, perhaps from Annabel Levins in Dirringhstead. Is that why George was chasing this man? The lane ends at the last bungalow. Is he inside or has he legged it across the fields like George? He gets to the front door. It's slightly ajar. He goes in, expecting to find the man talking to Kathleen. But the only sound he hears is scurrying feet and a closing back door. He's wrong. This is like his earlier foray to Dirringstead and the house of Annabel Levins. As then the bird has flown. He goes through the kitchen and into the garden, but sees no one. It'll probably wait, but he ought to alert Jennifer. He rings, but gets no answer and leaves a message. He goes back inside. The living room door is open. Kathleen sits by the window.

"Why was Chris Pleasant here?" he says.

She doesn't turn from looking at the empty garden.

"There's no one here."

"*Was* here, why was he here?"

He sits in the opposite chair and also stares at the garden. She neither acknowledges nor challenges his presence.

"I don't know."

"What did he say?"

"Not much. He was disturbed."

"Has he been before?"

"No...not until Warren...he's been a few times since."

"Talking about old times?"

She turns to him. Her eyes are drawn as if she's not slept.

"Sometimes."

"You've a lot of old times to remember."

She doesn't answer.

"Why did he run away?"

"He didn't say."

"What's he got to hide?"

She looks at him with an expression part scorn, part resignation.

"No more than most when chased by a policeman."

"I wasn't chasing him, but someone else was."

For the first time she takes some notice.

"Why would George Carter follow him or were they both coming here?"

"Hardly."

"No? Because George has more obvious business with Pleasant than with you?"

"I've known them both a long time."

"Yes, but *knowing* Pleasant was very different interest, wasn't it?"

Her lips curl with the beginnings of a smile.

"You were very close when you were young?" he says.

She doesn't answer, her silence indicating assent, the half smile giving way to a wistful haze in her eyes.

"When we are young…"

"…Warren beat him to it."

She smiles again.

"You could put it that way."

"But the old feelings never entirely went away…at least not for him?"

She says nothing and he wonders whether such residual feelings were just one sided.

"Tell me about 1981?" he says.

She claps her hands and laughs, though more in relief than mirth, while her tone is almost disdainful.

"That really was Warren's year, the six hundredth anniversary of his great event. If you can't actually get into the past, then at least come as close as you can to reliving it."

"The re-enactment was his idea?"

"Very much so. He wrote everything, made all the arrangements."

"You were all involved."

"Not *me*," she says vehemently, even after a quarter century not wanting to be associated.

"But the others all had parts?"

"Oh yes, Chris Pleasant, George Carter, Ted Skinner, Rick Tranter…"

"Lawrence Bullock?"

"Yes," she says quietly.

"And Melvyn Strange?"

"Yes," quieter still.

"And the women…Monica…Maggie…"

She nods.

"But not you?"

She turns to the bookshelf and points to a copy of *A Little Liberty*.

"Later on, it all went in *that* book."

"Not quite everything."

She looks surprised.

"I mean events subsequent to 1981."

Surprise turns to concern. He can't know everything, otherwise he wouldn't ask, but enough to know there's more.

"About Warren?" she says tentatively.

"About Warren and George."

"Warren confided in George not long before...he was murdered."

"You know what he told him?"

"I can guess judging by George's reaction."

So she tells him, pausing several times, giving him the opportunity to interrupt, but he listens carefully, as if he's already guessed most of it. Then asks her to tell him the parts everybody played in 1981.

The tense scene reaches its height. Everyone concentrates on 'John Ball' as he waits on the platform. Charley is unaware of the studio, unaware of the actors as if they don't exist. This is 15th July 1381 and she is here. Then the noise intervenes. Fairly quiet at first, like a persistent mouse, but it gets louder, becoming an intrusive drumming, finally a heavy thumping like someone hammering on a door. It's no good. The power of the moment is lost. It's a studio again and a disturbed one at that. She stops the shoot. The hammering from the back continues. Then someone shouts.

"Help me! Help me get these doors open!"

Ettie is hammering with all her strength on the doors. Charley gets up. Others follow.

"We're locked in," Ettie says.

Several of the cast pull and tear the doors, but to no effect.

"Where's Jennifer?" Charley says.

"Gone."

"But she was here, how long have these doors been locked, did she lock them?"

"I came to get help, but you were all engrossed. She stayed at the doors, but when I got back she'd gone."

"She got out and then locked them again?"

"She wouldn't do that."

"You sure they were locked the first time?"

"Of course I'm sure," Ettie says angrily, "do you think the two of us would half kill ourselves trying to get out if they weren't?"

"So how did she get out?"

"She was alone then."

"I don't understand."

"While you were filming did you feel as if you were actually in the past and I don't just mean the realism of the set?"

"Yes, it was very powerful."

"I felt the same, but Jennifer was unmoved. That's why she got out when she was alone without my influence. While the rest of us were pulled into the past and subject to its powers she remained wholly in the present."

"The past is holding us, locking us in the studio?"

"It seems so," Ettie says resignedly, "We should be grateful at least she's got out."

"Oh great, that really helps us."

"She may not know what to do. I have to get to her."

Ettie walks from the doors. By now most of the cast, extras and technicians have arrived, gripped by a collective panic at the prospect of being unable to escape. Ettie looks doubtfully at the continued tugging and heaving around the doors. She'd desperately hoped their combined strength might have been enough. Now she's not so sure it will free them.

"Never mind about Jennifer," Charley screams, "Tell me what to do so I can help the others!"

"We have to find another way out," Ettie says, walking along the wall.

Charley trails after her, leading the others, as a kind of escapist's posse.

"Not you," Ettie says to Charley, "you have to carry on."

"What with?"

"The scene of course."

"But you stopped us, you wanted help, now you want us to start again. Make up your mind!"

"If only I could," Ettie mutters.

"What?" Charley barks.

Ettie hears the anguish in her voice. She too is afraid and must appear confident, but the words fail her.

"That was before I realised how weak we are..."

But this is no time for indecision. Charley's horrified expression galvanises her.

"We are in their time as well as ours. Never mind the doors, there are plenty of us to worry about them. You must go back and start the scene again. Take the people you need."

"But if the past is holding us, locking us, how can we be safe?"

"Nothing is safe," Ettie says, immediately regretting her frankness, "but if we don't recreate the events of the day, it will be even more dangerous," then with an apparent authority she doesn't feel, "It doesn't matter, carry on setting up the final scenes. Things will look after themselves."

Charley stands impassive with a blank, wearied expression, all energy drained from her.

"Go!" Ettie shouts, "Go now!"

Charley jumps, turns and runs back, quickly gathering the actors and technicians she needs. At the head of her little band her apprehension grows. She looks over to Ettie, who waves her on impatiently, then returns to the set. Everyone stands around like gangling schoolboys on the football field on a cold winter's morning, waiting to be told what to do, neither they nor the teacher really wanting to be there. What if they are still locked in at the end of this scene? Do they carry on to the final crisis with Grindcobb and the others? She picks up *A Little Liberty*, turning to the last pages for inspiration, but too agitated to read she puts it down again. What about Wesley Greville? Has Ettie forgotten her own misgivings about his absence? How do they shoot the scene without him? Ettie says it's dangerous, but not doing it is worse. She clutches *A Little Liberty* as a talisman. She wanted to bring the past truly alive, but can she live with that reality? Maybe someone else can play Grindcobb? She looks around, but no one seems suitable even if they could quickly assimilate the part. So find someone else! She feels better, then her heart sinks again. They're locked in, how can she approach anyone outside? How would they get into the studio? It can wait. But it can't wait. Ettie said everything has to be done today! Catch 22.

With her little group Ettie paces the walls of the studio. Already she's made two complete circuits. The others are a little way behind, thumping and crashing, emulating Joshua with their noises, hoping that alone might bring down the walls as he did in Jericho. By now her concern is not with any physical, but more *meta*physical means of escape. Her wandering not for hidden fissures to be prised open, but with places where connections might be stronger or blockages discovered, the one to be released, the other to be unblocked. It has to be a mixture of the two. A connection to the present, strengthened and accessible, a blockage from the past redeemed, fractured but not broken. She hears Charley in the distance but pays no attention other than assuring herself the vital task of shooting the scenes is going ahead. Even now she's unsure. Not engaging with the past is not an option, but how best to do it without risking...?

"...but we will be avenged...only then will we be free..."

Martha. Where is she now?

"...this may come as a shock, but it could require a total re-evaluation in 14th century terms..."

Jessica's words interpose with Martha's. Perhaps because they talked about the same thing, but Ettie failed to see it. She vaguely remembers her coming to the cottage and struggles to piece together the disparate discussion. How long ago, a few weeks, even less, it seems an age. If only she'd paid more attention. Too busy recalling events in London she'd only been half listening.

"...all periods are simultaneous rather than consecutive... past, present and future are like the walls between rooms..."

Now there's a real wall and they're desperately trying to break it down! Is it wise to remove the flimsy wall separating past and present? What if the past holds them here because of something that has to be done there?

"...renewal and revenge remain..."

Jessica again. If the wall and the locked doors separate renewal and revenge, what must she do?

"...15th July...I need your help to bring it alive...renewal and revenge..."

Charley's words, she too obsessed with renewal and revenge...while Ettie encouraged her, forced her almost, left her to recreate the vengeance of the past with no balancing forces from the present because the present is locked out! What will Charley unleash? Revenge, but whose revenge and how far must it be allowed to go? Is that what Martha wanted her to stop? No, Martha doesn't want her to stop anything. She wants her to make something happen. She wants Ettie to make it possible for Martha...or Thomas...to exact revenge. It cannot be, but she must not interfere. The studio is an enclave of the past in the present, from which they cannot escape because they are part of it! She can't stop it, anymore than she can stop Charley. This is the day, the past is happening!

"...things will look after themselves..."

Her own words of only a few moments ago come back to taunt her. Should she leave everything be or try to control... she looks to the set... much movement, much noise, but no words she can make out. Then nothing, only a blur and a dull muffled rumble. The past is shutting her out! She must get back to Charley. If they are imprisoned here, 15th July 1381 then the day must be seen through. *Seen* through? How when she sees nothing, hears nothing? She must get back. In its entirety, it must be endured. But she can't move. No, it's not she can't move, she *won't* move. Something stops her. Something close is trying to get to her. Suddenly John Ball is on the scaffold. He turns and points. She follows his hand. He's pointing to the door. Someone is trying to get in! She starts to walk back, but stops after only a few steps. Someone is at the door, someone outside! She must get to the door. She turns to go, but then stops again. She looks back, but John Ball is gone.

Chris is unsure of his destination, but he has to leave. He can't go back to Essex. That's the first place the police will look. In between throwing underwear into a suitcase he stops to consider likely destinations. North or west, one or the other, Scotland or Cornwall, somewhere remote, but these days is anywhere really remote enough? Abroad perhaps, but they'll alert the ports and airports. Have to be a clandestine crossing from one of the smaller places on the south coast. For enough money there are always people willing to make the trip. Have to be quick though, if word gets out too soon, even no questions asked sailors get windy and coastal towns are always gossip ridden. France then? Okay, but that means moving south without delay. If only he had a false passport. No time for that now. Just have to lay low.

There's a noise outside. He's not been watching the drive. He's only half packed, but it may have to do. Better to get away now than risk being stopped. He looks out the bedroom window. There's no one in the drive and he hasn't heard a car. If anyone's around they're not here on a social call. He waits, hears nothing more and carries on packing, though more quickly than before. He gets his coat, checks his money and lugs the case to the stairs. Just get the car out and away. He's still unsure where to go, though he's thinking of Sussex. Used to know a guy in Wittering, could look him up, he might know...that noise again as if a chair is being moved in the lounge. There it is again. He stops about halfway down the stairs. Silence. He's nervous. He's imagining it.

"Scuttling away while you can!"

A woman's voice, strident yet also slightly plaintive. Maggie. He leans over the banister. She's sitting in an armchair in the lounge, facing the front door. She must have been watching him coming down the stairs.

"How the hell did you get in here?"

"You were in such a hurry you left the door open."

"Well you can get out the way you came in," he says, reaching the bottom of the stairs and pointing towards the front door.

"Where are you going?"

"That's none of your business."

"Like it was none of my business that night you were on the common?"

"What night?"

"The night Warren Grover was killed."

"You don't know what you're..."

"I saw you."

"You were there?"

"I saw enough to..."

"You were alone?"

"Yes."

"Then it's just between the two of us."

He strides into the lounge, almost reaching her, but then suddenly pulls up.

"That's far enough, Chris!"

George Carter steps out from behind the curtain.

"You too?" Chris says, edging back towards the door.

"Yes me too, so you can forget any ideas about any indeterminate holidays far far away."

"Where I go is..."

"None of my business either? Not really, you see like Maggie, I know things about you, things you'd prefer me not to know."

"What things?" Chris says, glancing out the window.

Only the two of them...if he could get to the car...maybe he should make a run for it.

"Things like the Waintree Development."

"Not that again," Chris says with some relief, "You've been banging on about that for months, scraping up all the local tittle tattle for that rag of yours."

"But now I've got more to put in it. Like who's really involved, who owns what, how it all fits together, things Warren found out."

"What did Warren know?"

"Enough to rattle some people. Is that why you went to see Kathleen, to try and wheedle out of her how much Warren had on you?"

"I wanted to see Kathleen before I left, I wanted to say...how did you know I went to Kathleen, were you following me?"

"That copper was following us both, though he doesn't know his way around. I think we gave him the slip."

"That's about as likely as a Bedford badger in Bucks."

George is alarmed by Jenner's sudden appearance, but Chris appears calm.

"Spoken like a true native of Hertfordshire, chief inspector, but..."

"Where I'm from is not for discussion whereas your destination is."

Chris tries to get out of the room, but Jenner blocks his way.

"Sit down, Mr. Pleasant. Then we can all hear Mr. Carter tell us exactly what he learnt from Annabel Levins in Dirringstead."

George hesitates, but Jenner prods him again. Annabel's campaign over the footpath uncovered 'interesting land deals and complex counter- ownerships.' Jenner asks him to elaborate. Chris looks uncomfortable. Three of them now…it won't be so easy to get out.

"People owning land on behalf of others," George says, "Very convenient if you're trying to cover your tracks. Chris has an interest in the Waintree development, at least the first phase and similar arrangements were entered into by some of those…"

"Not me!" Chris screeches, "I had nothing to do with that."

"Really?" Jenner says, "so you knew it was going on?"

Chris is silent.

"Not the only thing he's not told you," Maggie says, "he was on the common the night Warren was killed."

"Was he now and why didn't you tell me *that* earlier?"

"Because she was afraid she'd be implicated," George cuts in, "She's afraid now, but she can't stand it any longer. She has to speak out."

"Which is more than you've been prepared to do."

"What do you mean?"

"Things you knew you've not been divulging and you've been very…elusive lately…reluctant to talk to anyone, especially me. Why have you been running away?"

George says nothing. Chris intervenes, almost gleefully.

"He's not been straight from the start, busy accusing everybody else when…"

"Were you on the common the night Warren Grover was murdered?" Jenner says.

Chris is silent again.

"Answer the question."

"Yes," Chris says at last, very quietly, adding quickly, "But I didn't kill him."

"That puts two of you in the right place at the right time," Jenner says dryly.

"No! No! It wasn't me," Maggie screams, pointing to Chris, "It was him and *them!*"

"Them?"

"Them in the past."

"Quite so, but which past and *whose* past?"

"No! No," she screams before subsiding into her chair, shaking and whimpering.

George goes to her.

"Leave her alone, can't you see she's upset?"

"You've all been left alone far too long and have a lot of explaining to do. Let's start with you Mr. Carter. You've been making accusations against Monica Freeson..."

"I can prove it. Annabel found something interesting. Look at this!"

George thrusts a document at Jenner, who studies it quickly before ringing Jennifer again. He can't get through, but leaves a message.

"It's as we thought. Get over there quickly!"

Maggie whimpers, Chris looks even more uncomfortable, George relaxes, but Jenner hasn't done with him yet.

"Warren knew this?" he says.

"And a lot more."

"He told you other things not long before he died?"

"Many things."

George recounts further details of land ownership and the Waintree development, leaning back with grim satisfaction as Jenner listens and nods.

"Anything else?" Jenner says when he's finished.

George laughs.

"Poor old Warren. What he knew made him dangerous to a lot of people, but some things he talked about made him an even greater danger to himself."

"Such as?"

"Things he said he'd seen which...well pretty fantastic..."

Jenner lifts his eyebrows. George has started he'll have to go on.

"...he was obsessed with the leader of the local revolt in 1381...a day or two before he was...said he'd been transmuted across time, that he'd actually become William Grindcobb."

Chris laughs. Jenner is impassive.

"You see," Maggie says, "As I keep saying. It's in the past, they did it."

George consoles her.

"Yes, yes, Warren said things, but it doesn't mean..."

"It means he talked to many people," Jenner says, "Nobody in this business acted entirely alone, did they? Take yourself for example, Mr. Carter. You talked to others and you didn't always say the same things at different times."

"Like he talks to Monica," Chris says.

George is about to attack again, but Jenner stops him.

"Things you know and things you appear not to know."

Chris smirks smugly. Jenner ignores him and turns back to George.

"I want you to make a telephone call, including some of the information you've been telling me and then we'll all go down to the station."

George makes the call and Jenner ushers them towards the French doors.

"We'll go through the garden, it'll be quicker."

Outside it seems oddly cooler. The garden is unnaturally dark and long shadows are cast over the lawn. They take a few steps towards the front drive, but their way is barred. A strange figure emerges from the dimness and stands by the side gate.

The shooting of the last scenes has been interrupted yet again. Alerted by Ettie's helpers, almost everyone is writhing and wrenching at the doors,

"It's no use," Charley says, "there's no one there."

"Don't give up," Ettie shouts as she runs across, "Keep trying, there is someone, I know there is."

"We should get back to the set and..."

"Pull!" Ettie shouts again.

Everybody grabs whatever they can of the doors – a handle, a lever, or just each other. The doors remain solidly immovable, but beyond the steel Ettie feels *someone* outside, pushing as they pull.

"Heave, heave," she shouts, "It has to give!"

For a few seconds the collective puffing and panting, scraping of feet, grunting and groaning cuts the silence of the studio and now with each pull and jerk Ettie senses the present gaining strength. It's still the 15th, but of now, not then. The past is receding, though she's fearful of losing what little control they have over it. Then with a sudden whoosh of fresh air the doors burst open, slam into the walls and everyone falls back to the floor. As they get up many rush through the opening, eager to be outside as if they've been imprisoned for months. Ettie goes over to Jennifer, who has landed on top of the heap. Charley examines the doors.

"They're not locked."

"They never were," Ettie says, levering Jennifer up from the floor.

"But how...?"

"The locks on this studio are not made of steel, nor were they turned by human hands."

"So Jennifer didn't lock the door?"

"No I didn't!" Jennifer says, "it closed behind me and I couldn't get it open again."

"How did you get out?" Charley says.

"After Ettie went to get you all, I pulled the door and it flung aside, nearly knocking me over. Once I got outside it closed on me. I tried to open it again, but it wouldn't budge. I called, but no one answered. Then I saw someone running away. I figured she must have locked the door so I went after her."

"She?" Ettie says, "Did you recognise her?"

"It was Maggie Morton."

"How did she get in the studio?" Charley says.

Jennifer shrugs.

"I went after her, then I heard the hammering at the studio door. I stopped and turned. When I looked back, she'd disappeared."

380

"But what about the door, you couldn't get it open before?" Charley says.

"I just touched the handle and then, well I fell in!"

"But how?" Charley persists, "First you can't get out, then you can, then you can't get back in again, then you can!"

Ettie nods.

"Unlike the rest of us Jennifer never lost contact with the present. When I was with her, the force of the past was too strong. As soon as I left she was able to open the door."

"But once outside she couldn't get back in?"

"Which means there had to be an outside force also exerting pressure from the past."

"Maggie?" Charley says.

"You're sure you saw no one else?" Ettie says to Jennifer.

"No one I could see. Is it important?"

"It's just...I felt...I thought it was male."

"Past or present?" Jennifer says.

"Who's to say. Maggie..."

Still intrigued by the vagaries of the door, Charley cuts in.

"So how was she able to get back in again?"

"Because the outside force from the past was no longer strong enough."

"When Maggie ran away?" Jennifer says.

"Should you go after her?" Charley says.

Jennifer is unconcerned.

"No immediate hurry. I know where she's gone. Besides, once outside my phone started working again. There was a message from the boss. It was a bit garbled. He was in a hurry. He told me to proceed. I know what that means. I tried to ring back, but couldn't get through. It was odd, there was a noise like my phone made when I couldn't get it to work in the studio."

"Do you know where he is?" Ettie says.

"He's seen Kathleen Grover and followed up the link between her and Chris Pleasant."

"I'm concerned for his safety. We have to reach him."

"Not from Kathleen surely?"

Ettie shakes her head.

"From Chris?" Charley says incredulously.

Ettie shakes her head again, "Someone else," but won't elaborate.

"What now?" Charley says, "The final scenes..."

"Must go ahead, but I must go with Jennifer. We have to find the chief inspector."

"We still have no one to play Will Grindcobb."

"Another worry..." Ettie mutters, already concentrating on finding Jenner.

Charley flicks through *A Little Liberty*.

"When we've completed the John Ball scene..."

"It will...look after itself," Ettie says, looking at the book, "You see I'm wondering whether Warren Grover was transmuted into the past."

"Into Grindcobb?"

The three stand transfixed in silence. Everything hazily changes, but they're unable to comprehend more than vague shifting shapes, coalescing colours and darting shadows. Only the strange figure remains, his grim stare grinding into them as if his eyes are poleaxes, grasping them to this emptiness, devoid of time or place. Are the hours and minutes compressed into seconds, is it really only a few moments or an age? Gradually the cloudy walls of their prison stabilise, the misty background solidifies and something faintly familiar appears. Jenner is the first to move, breaking the hold of the strange man and glancing to his right. At first he's relieved, seeing the grass and believing he's still in the garden. It's a momentary lapse, a sudden weakness, probably brought on by the tension of the last few days. He'll look back, see Chris Pleasant and George Carter and no more. Unless of course they've already taken advantage of his sudden infirmity and got away!

He turns in alarm. Chris and George are there, having not moved, but so too is the other figure, his swarthy complexion, his rough, coarse clothes and that wild unyielding stare. He's seen it before in that high vaulted room where the villainous judge dispensed his special brand of 'justice.' It can't be. Not again, he's not gone back? Chris and George are here, so he must be where they are...in the present...in Chris's garden...

which means this figure is...But he sees now...this isn't Chris's garden. The grass is too long and it extends...the common, they're on the common! So close to Chris's garden, yet no one moved...it's not possible, yet they've been transported from a place without time or place...now he has place, but of what time? Chris and George are also stirring and turn towards Jenner, but their way is barred.

"My revenge will be satisfied. Already I have waited too long."

Jenner moves towards them.

"Be still!"

The clothes, the demeanour, the way he speaks, the man is unmistakable...he is from 1381! But have they been transported to his time or he to theirs? Chris and George are transfixed again, but Jenner won't be cowed. This is the common. He knows this place. He's known it all his life. The land may be timeless, but it changes and this is not changed into the past. It is his common, not the common of the 14th century. He won't be intimidated. There's already been too much of that in the past.

"I won't be still and I won't be silenced. The authorities..."

"Authorities," Thomas repeats, part in perplexity, part in repugnance, "those that rule, they..."

"If you wish to call them that," Jenner says.

"Those that rule cast us down, murdered my friends, forced me to flee."

"I know there are difficulties..."

"You know, how do you know? Are you part of them...?

Thomas moves towards Jenner. Maybe he should not have spoken so quickly, so unadvisedly about authority.

"I was unable to do everything I needed to do. I have left it late, but not too late, there must still be time. Those that rule..."

"Who are you?" George shouts, "What are you doing? How did we get here?"

Thomas now turns to him. George is ashen.

"He is from the past," Jenner says quietly, "He has come to exact revenge."

"Revenge from the past, what the bloody hell does it mean?"

George tries to get away, but his feet won't respond.

"God, I can't move, what's happening?"

"The power of the past," Jenner says.

"Past, which bloody past?"

"1381. I suspect this man is one of the insurgents."

George turns on Chris.

"Insurgents, 1381, revenge, it's your fault, you and that damned film!"

"Not me!" Chris shrieks, then pointing to Jenner, but directing his words at Thomas, "He's a policeman. He rules!"

Thomas stops and looks again to Jenner.

"Shut up, you bloody fool!" Jenner shouts.

Thomas looks from one to the other, first at Jenner, then at Chris, then at George, back to Jenner.

"He is authority," Chris persists, pointing again at Jenner, "He is your enemy."

"Shut up," George says nervously, "This isn't something we understand."

"But *you* can," Jenner says, stepping away from the menacing glare of Thomas, "Think back to what Warren told you."

"Warren...what do you mean?" George says as Thomas gets closer to Jenner, "He's coming for you."

"'Course he is," Chris shouts, "Go for him, go for him!"

Jenner ignores him, though he watches Thomas with mounting trepidation. It's misfired. None of his planning took account of the past. Now he's reaping the harvest of his shortsightedness. Perhaps it was the phone call. Did George get it mixed up?

"You did make the call?" he says nervously.

George looks away briefly from Thomas.

"Call?" he says, irritated.

"It was...?"

"Yes, yes, what did you mean about Warren?"

"Go for him!" Chris repeats.

Thomas stops moving on Jenner, but Chris still urges him, pushing his arms forward.

"Shut up!" George says, getting between him and Thomas, then turning back to Jenner, "What did you mean?"

"He talked about the past, didn't he?"

"Warren was always talking about the past."

"And you didn't take it seriously?"

"How can you take seriously a man who talked about going into the past?"

"Not so easy to dismiss now," Jenner says, nodding to Thomas.

"No," George says apprehensively.

"What if he really did," Jenner says, hardly believing his own words as soon as they're uttered, "what if he really did go back into the past?"

It's as if he's listening from afar, separate, unconnected, not responsible, but he's here and he is responsible.

"You mean he could be still alive?" George says, similarly unsure, almost but not quite unbelieving.

"Alive, but in the past," Jenner says.

"But you're here," Chris shouts, dodging around George, then pointing to Thomas, "and he's here...here to get you!"

Thomas has been looking between the three, stopping and starting, taking a few paces towards Jenner, then listening to Chris and George, confused and irresolute. Now seemingly sure he moves with grim determination towards Jenner, urged and encouraged by Chris's diabolical screeching.

"It's him, get him!"

George is first to realise the danger and grabs Chris, holding him back, trying to stop his mouth with his hand. But Chris keeps shouting and Thomas keeps coming. George grapples with Chris, pulling him to the ground, but it's too late. Thomas is fired up and doesn't need the fuel of Chris's wild appeals.

"Too long I've held back, too long unable to avenge my own, too long living with my guilt when I could have done more and saved the falling man."

"The falling man?" Jenner says quietly,

Now he understands, but understanding is no good without the freedom to act and Thomas is in no mood for talking. In his own time too much talking and too little action

385

cost them success. Chris and George writhe and struggle on the ground. Thomas is very close now and they are too far away to help, even if they are willing to do so. Jenner is alone, but he must try. If he can talk to him, explain...

"Now you see what comes of not listening to me! I told you *they* did it, but you wouldn't listen. Now he is here and come for you!"

Maggie has come from the mist, out of the land and stands beside Jenner, pointing to Thomas, who stops, but then walks on, ignoring her. He's resolved. No more enforced absence, no holding back, now he's sure of his target! Jenner steps back and looks around desperately. Perhaps Maggie...then she's not there and he only hears her running. George just sees her and flings himself free of Chris, but the haziness suddenly encloses the common and by the time he approaches she's gone. He stops short. No one else is around. Between Jenner and escape is a crazy man from 1381 bearing down on him! It seems nothing in the present can save him. His only hope may lie in the past.

Monica is taken aback when Jennifer arrives, marching into the house and straight into the lounge.

"I assume she's here."

"What is going on?" Monica says, unaccustomed to tripping behind anyone, let alone a police sergeant.

"Where is she?" Jennifer says, looking around the room as if she might be hiding behind a settee or cupboard.

"She?"

"Margaret Morton."

Monica laughs.

"Mad Maggie? Do you really think I'd allow that crazy woman in my house after the last time? She had to be virtually thrown out."

"She's not been here?"

"No she has not."

"You would know?"

"Of course I would know."

"You've not been out?"

"Not since yesterday. Sergeant, what is this all about?"

"There's been…an incident…involving Margaret Morton. She ran off. I assumed she would come here."

"Why would she come here?"

"You tell me, Mrs. Freeson. Why did she come the last time?"

Monica sits down, rearranges her skirt and shakes her head slightly as if suddenly rebuffed.

"We were having a little get together, nothing particularly ostentatious, just a few friends and colleagues…"

"A celebration after the enquiry decision?"

"I wouldn't quite put it like that."

"How would you put it?"

"It was an opportunity to thank everyone who helped and supported."

"Which didn't of course include Margaret."

"Certainly not! She came here to make trouble along with the editor of that scandal sheet."

"What did George Carter want?"

"To insult me."

"About the development?"

Monica shakes again, rebutting unspoken accusations.

"He insinuated without saying anything specific. It's always his way. It was most embarrassing. Then he threatened me."

"With what?"

Monica hesitates, then looks up and stares directly at Jennifer.

"With the police!"

Jennifer doesn't respond. Monica shakes her head again, this time more vigorously.

"I can't imagine what about. Has he been to you?"

"No."

"I thought not. All bluster and innuendo…always his way…and as for her, all that that woman could do was to say I knew Warren Grover and Lawrence Bullock. Of course I knew them. Everybody knew Warren and as for Lawrence… but that doesn't mean…"

"Neither mentioned anything about land ownership?"

Monica stops shaking her head and looks questioningly at Jennifer.

"George Carter's accusations about destroying the land have been rejected by the Burton enquiry. He can rant on as long as..."

"But the *ownership* of the land," Jennifer persists, "and its precise position, isn't that what's really important about the Waintree development?"

"The development is about many things, it will regenerate..."

"But your involvement, Mrs. Freeson, you've surely considered how it affects you...?"

"Are you now accusing...?"

"I'm talking about *your* land..." Jennifer points to the garden and the fields beyond, "...that is your property isn't it?"

"It is, but I don't see..."

"...and it adjoins where the final phase of the Waintree development takes effect."

"Adjoins? No, you're wrong, you see..."

"I don't mean what is formally included in the proposals. I mean the ownership of land which could *become* part of that development."

Trying to fully grasp import of what Jennifer is saying, Monica is momentarily silenced and stares into the garden and to the fields as if they might miraculously offer some guidance.

"Now," Jennifer says, "Can we talk about the real details of who owns what?"

The mystery intensifies. It's not just that Wesley Greville has disappeared without trace. The studio's enquiries produce blank responses from addresses, phone numbers, contacts, as if no one has really known him at all. This only increases Charley's apprehensions but despite all the disparate strands Ettie finally knows what she must do. As for the film, perhaps Warren will assist them from the past.

"Go ahead, it will look after itself," she keeps saying.

Eventually and with some reluctance Charley goes ahead, restarting the final scenes. Ettie still wonders about Warren, but they must concentrate on the greatest dangers and

Jenner is in the most peril. Instinctively she knows where he is and wills herself to be there. It has to be. The time is right. So when it happens, the speed and suddenness of the transformation no longer surprises her.

Yet the light, breadth and openness of the common unnerves her as if she's landed on some distant shore, staring into limitless sand along a mysterious beach. But this is no far off country, part of some strange voyage of ineffable discovery. She's come to know this land with the accuracy of a native's familiarity with every blade of grass, a quarry of ancient memories, which must be excavated if the injustices of the past and the riddles of the present are to be reconciled. She must get to the place quickly. For the time she has is not her time. It belongs to others. They or rather what is happening to them is in control and events must go on. Unlike the present, the past is unalterable. Yet somehow that immutable law cannot be. For if nothing is changed there can be no reconciliation, no resolution. Does Martha want her to *prevent* something or *make* it happen? The past cannot be stopped, but there can be different kinds of *making*. There's making what never happened, but also making what *should* have happened. That's what she must concentrate on.

They had a plan and Jenner was part of it. Where is that plan now? She must get to him, but must also get to the other place and she's near to being overwhelmed by her helplessness. She tries him on her phone, but gets only a high pitched bleep of non connection. She may be in the present, but the influence of the past emasculates modern technologies. She knows the common, but those familiar blades stretch endlessly to unreachable boundaries and it's not just his presence she senses. Another force is close and threatens him. It's also close to her. 'Outlaw' Thomas, consumed by guilt and revenge is capable of anything in his desperation. She strains to take in the rolling grassland and furze, willing herself to soak up its entirety as she wills Jenner to resist, but sees nothing beyond the blanketing green and yellow, enfolding, absorbing, blinding in its vastness. Then she hears a sound. She looks round, but sees only the common's empty immensity. She turns back. It comes again, footsteps, getting louder, closer. She turns again. Two figures emerge from the green sea like bobbing boats on the swelling waters of a storm. She freezes as dozens of agitated imaginings grip her mercilessly.

"Ettie!"

Relieved by the sight of a friendly face as if they've been parted for months rather than an hour, Jennifer's call shakes her free.

"I still don't see why I have to come here."

Ettie doesn't recognise the owner of the second voice. Jennifer obliges as they come closer, introducing Monica Freeson.

"Any sign of the boss?"

Ettie shakes her head. Jennifer reads the concern in her face.

"Never mind about him," Monica says irritably, "why am I...?"

"Corruption in high places," Jennifer says.

"I've already told you, I didn't know..."

"Maybe, maybe not, but what did others know?"

"I was not involved..."

"Others like Warren Grover."

The name stuns Monica into silence. It's not the name she was expecting and Jennifer notices. It also resonates with Ettie. Jennifer is following Jenner's plan, but it brings back her forebodings. Monica says something. Jennifer probes and there's another response, but Ettie doesn't listen to the interchange, her alarm increasing as her thoughts drift back to Charley at the studio. Wesley Greville has still not appeared and without him to play Grindcobb in the final scenes nothing will be resolved. Then Monica's voice stabs through her reveries.

"Warren said many things..."

Is Warren their salvation? Did he really die or transmute into Grindcobb? Was it *his* body they discovered on the common? Who recognised it...it's dangerous to speculate about such a transposition between past and present...it breaks all the rules...what rules...today 15th July when time runs on and time runs out there are no rules! They have no choice. That's what she told Charley. The final scenes have to go on regardless of there being no one to take the part of the main player. She shouldn't worry. It's not really a film at all, but the re-enactment, the constant re-playing of the past... on and on...forever, unchanging, so why should it matter if there's no actor...the past will provide. Which means it will be Grindcobb himself, but if Grindcobb was really the man killed on the common, then he can't be there...in the past...to play himself...that would have to be someone else, someone transposed...Warren Grover...

"Lawrence Bullock definitely didn't kill Melvyn Strange."

Monica's strident voice thrusts her back again to the present. Jennifer is probing again, but Ettie's attention wavers. The threat to Jenner is imminent. He must defend himself! She wills him to resist, but can he do it alone? If the past threatens how can it be counteracted without assistance *from* the past?

Now she sees what he sees, vengeful Thomas moving closer. Resist! Yet too much resistance may be as dangerous. Hold him back, but don't destroy him. Destroying the past destroys the present and it will never be resolved. Contain him only...at least until we can reach you! Out of control, Thomas is dangerous, but he can't be excluded. If we help him he may help us. He has to be there at the place. The power of the past has to be forestalled, but must also be harnessed. That final scene must be completed, but not too soon for they have to get to the place, but how to get there when one of them is in so much danger! Her mind whirls in confusion.

Jennifer is speaking again. No, it's Monica. She stops. Jennifer tells her to go on. Monica hesitates. Then, slowly, deliberately she begins. Jennifer turns to Ettie.

"This could be important. You need to listen to this."

14

THE light grey mist encloses, so thick, so dense, Jenner feels trapped as if he's inside an enormous golf ball, except the danger is not from being hammered from outside, but from the desperate figure in front. George stands close enough to be immured within the mist, but far enough back for Jenner to shield him from Thomas. Jenner can hear his breathing. Further behind, terrified and voiceless Chris pushes against the hazy prison, untouchable, yet impenetrable as iron. Thomas has stopped moving, but his outstretched arms block any advance. Jenner has tried moving sideways, but it has no effect. If he penetrates the mist one way, it immediately closes behind him, while Thomas remains in his path even though he appears not to move. He half turns to face George, but the muffled slither of Thomas's feet stops him turning further. He must be ready to forestall any sudden attack.

"Don't turn your back on him," George whispers.

"I'll bear that in mind," Jenner says through gritted teeth.

"You could rush him."

"We could rush him. How about coming up next to me?"

George doesn't move, doesn't speak.

"I though not," Jenner says, "any more advice?"

"You could..."

George's voice fades away as Thomas edges forward.

"I will be avenged on those that killed my comrades!"

"Not me..." Jenner begins.

"Don't think he's listening," George says nervously.

Jenner moves a half step back towards George. He needs to get both him and Chris to the place, but the wall of mist immediately encroaches and he's left with even less space. Thomas takes another step closer.

"There will be justice!"

"There will be truth," Jenner mutters half heartedly.

The words resonate and he repeats them again to himself. The image of the hedge priest comes to mind. Only John Ball can save him now, but an unbreakable thread stretching over six hundred years separates them. Yet this man is from the past. If *he* can appear, why not John Ball? There must be a way, but even if he could make contact, John Ball is not free. He stands condemned. If only Jenner had Ettie's skills he might be able to screw up that thread and summon his help.

Thomas raises his arm. He's a younger, fitter man and in his hand he wields a weapon. A small club, a knife, it's difficult to see. Jenner looks round. There's nothing. He and George are alone, coralled in a tightening fog with this madman. Yet he doesn't feel alone. Someone is close, spiritually if not physically and her strength speaks to his inner self, willing him to resist, telling him he can do it. He must call up the help he knows is there.

"John Ball!"

Thomas stops and stares incredulously as Jenner repeats the name, the two words invested with a powerful, almost magical invocation.

"But," Thomas says," John Ball he's..."

"He's not..." Jenner says, "He's not dead, he can't be...not yet...he must come. John Ball in the name of truth I summon you to help us!"

Thomas steps back mystified, a little fearful, a little angry.

"But he...he's not..."

"Who calls me?"

The mist recedes enough to reveal the familiar brown clad figure to the side of Jenner and Thomas.

"I call you," Jenner says, "this man, he says…"

John Ball lifts up his hand.

"You must be vigilant in the presence of the oppressor."

He speaks to all, setting his eyes on no one for long and on them all in turn. Thomas nods and grips his weapon tightly.

"But who is the oppressor today?" Jenner says.

Thomas shuffles towards him, lifting the club, ready to strike, but John Ball with his raised hand now steps between him and Jenner.

"And so Lawrence wasn't acting alone. He…"

Monica stops as a figure emerges from the undergrowth and stands at the edge of the group. The others also look over as Monica turns to face Rick Tranter. He looks from her to Ettie, then to Jennifer.

"I…was…I was expecting…where is George Carter?"

Ettie and Jennifer look to Monica. She opens her mouth, but immediately closes it.

"Where is George Carter?" Rick repeats.

Ettie and Jennifer wait again for Monica, but with a nervous glance at Rick, she shakes her head and turns away.

"You were to meet him here?" Ettie says.

Now Monica looks back and doesn't take her eyes off Rick.

"I…meet…well, yes…he…anyway, what's this all about?"

"He called you?" Jennifer says.

Rick hesitates, then less confused says, "Yes, he did."

"What about?"

"Does that matter? In any case, I don't see what business this is of…you must know something?"

"She knows!"

George Carter is suddenly beside Ettie, apparently appearing from nowhere and pointing aggressively at Monica. She glances at him quickly, then looks back to Rick.

"What's she got to do with…?" Rick says.

"You don't need to ask her, do you? Like me you already know." George says.

"I don't know what you're talking about."

"The Waintree development, you know…"

"I should like to say…" Monica begins.

394

"Shut up," George bellows.

Surprisingly, she doesn't react.

"If she has something to say, we should hear it," Jennifer says, getting between them and pulling Monica away.

Rick gets up closer to George and whisks him round.

"You didn't tell me she was going to be here," he says, nodding to Jennifer, "the police..."

"Not just her!"

Jenner is now also beside Ettie, along with Chris Pleasant, suddenly materialising from the empty space of the common.

"Is he...?" Ettie says quickly.

Jenner looks round anxiously, "No, but he was close."

"Then he remains close. He's not gone, you've only pulled yourselves out of his immediate orbit."

"We were surrounded by impenetrable mist," he says, looking round again, "but now it's gone."

"That was the hold of his past over your present. Your will pulled you from him. The mist was only as strong as you allowed it to be."

"Maybe, but I felt...I was helped."

"We have to work together," she says, taking him aside, "You were confined in a small area?"

"Yes."

"That was his limit. It shows the power of the past is diminishing."

"So that makes us safer, the past is less dangerous."

"No, the opposite. It's like a wounded animal, it's even more dangerous, particularly the closer we get to..."

"Never mind about her," George is saying to Rick, "we should be more concerned with the other."

"The other, what other?"

"The man on the common."

"Him?" Rick says, nodding to Chris, "Is this why you called me?"

"No, no, he's been with me all the time, but the other one...he's no longer here."

"You didn't say he was going to be here?" Rick says in exasperation.

"What the man?"

"Which man, the policeman?"

"No, not him, I meant…"

"Thank you, Mrs. Freeson," Jenner says, stepping into the middle of the group, and breaking up George and Rick's incomprehensible cross talk, "that puts everything about the Waintree development in context. It's clear there are other matters which cannot be discounted, but for now we have the evidence of corruption so high that…"

"Is that it?" George interrupts, "Is that what all this is about?"

"Isn't it enough?" Jenner says.

"But there's more, much more."

"Indeed there is, Mr. Carter. Isn't that why you went to see Annabel Levins in Dirringstead?"

"Yes, but…"

"You and Annabel were fishing in the same waters. The names you were interested in also cropped up during her campaign over the footpath. Now, how did that come about?"

"It was something Warren said, something he'd discovered."

"Not this again," Chris interrupts, "you keep dragging up Warren…"

"Why is it anything to do with Warren makes you uncomfortable? Something to do with you being seen on the common the night he was killed?"

"What by that lunatic Maggie?"

"She's as good a witness as anyone. I'm sure the police here will…"

"Stop squabbling you two!" Rick shouts, "It's not helping. None of us need to be reminded any more of that night."

"Oh but we do," Jenner says, "and not just that night and not just about Warren either. Isn't it interesting how you're all here as you were back in 1981 when another of your group disappeared, young Melvyn Strange?"

"That was down to Lawrence," Chris says, "that's why he…"

"I think not. Whatever happened to Lawrence Bullock, he most certainly was not responsible for the disappearance of Melvyn Strange."

"Melvyn's body has never been found," Chris says, "He may not be dead. He may have just gone away."

"Oh, he's dead alright," Jenner says gravely, "You can help us there, can't you George?"

George turns in some alarm.

"Me? How can I help?"

"Because it all hinges on what Warren told you."

"Warren told me about a conversation he'd had with..."

"No, no," Chris shouts, "We don't want to hear this! George will say anything!"

The actor playing John Ball has mysteriously disappeared during a break and can't be found. The scene has had to be abandoned.

You must keep shooting. Whatever happens, you must carry on. There's so little time.

Ettie's words resound. Charley is desperate. There can be no carry over. What has to be done must be completed before the end of today, 15th July. She'll have to shoot another scene and hope she can return to John Ball when she has someone to play the part. There's still no one to play Will Grindcobb. The loss of one actor is unfortunate, but to lose two...on the other hand, is the position really any worse than it was before? She'll go to the scene that's driven her for so long – the rehangings. It'll be out of sequence and irrationally reversed – putting up what has not yet been cut down – August before July, but is there any alternative?

Despite their lack of rehearsal, the actors glide with uglified elegance through the tragic events, directed by unseen hands and unheard voices. Charley also proceeds like an automaton, her movements and commands manipulated by unseen forces, clutching *A Little Liberty* like the child still hugging her teddy bear long after she knows it cannot really protect her. There's always a chance such a lucky charm might shelter them from hostile forces.

The shoot is completed. There have been no interruptions, nothing needing to be done again. No one has muffed a line, nothing to mar a perfect performance. Everyone relaxes. Charley sits alone for a few moments, still wondering how such a complex scene of charged rawness has been achieved without a hitch. It's as if they weren't acting and she wasn't directing, all merely floating as in a dream. Yet not a dream, no play, no representation, but reality itself, less the *making* of a film, more the *rerunning* of a newsreel, first filmed six hundred years before. What if those in the past are not dead, but merely asleep and one day will wake up and hold us to account? She shakes herself. The concept is preposterous. The day moves on its inexorable way. John Ball's scene still has to be shot. If only she had an actor. Then he appears, unbelievably nonchalant, damnably unperturbed.

"Where have you been?" she demands.

"Outside for a smoke," he says with defensive surprise.

"You've been gone an hour."

"Never, two or three minutes at the most."

"An hour!"

"No, I just slipped out. Look at the time."

He points to his watch. She stares in disbelief. Five minutes since the beginning of the first break. She must have been sitting here for at least five minutes let alone setting up, running through and filming a complicated scene. It's impossible. Five minutes infused and stretched to an hour... yet from where came that hour? From the past? What the past gives, can it also take away?

"Lawrence wasn't involved," Monica says, "he was only..."

"Of course he was," George cuts her off.

"I was going to say..."

"You've said enough, you've been *saying* too much for years, it's what you and he were *doing* that matters!"

They glare aggressively, the mutual loathing oozing from every pore of their skins, every fibre of their being.

"Lawrence was not involved in the development," she repeats vehemently.

"But he was buying up the land!" George shouts, "I've got the evidence. Warren told me."

"I'm sure he did and he probably told you a lot more."

"Shut up, both of you," Chris shouts.

"What are *you* afraid of?" George says, "That Warren implicated *you*?"

"This is ridiculous," Rick intervenes, looking across to Jenner, who is unmoved.

"She's right about one thing," George says, "Warren did talk to me about somebody. I thought that person was giving him the support he needed. Now I'm not so sure. Lawrence..."

"I've already told you," Monica says, "Lawrence *bought* the land, but not for himself. He was only the front man, he was buying it..."

"Yes, yes, yes and Warren was playing for time while they tried to buy him off."

"Buy him off? There was no one..."

"The relationship was getting distinctly heavy. I assumed it was because Warren was getting too persistent. His various cultural projects continued to need financial support. Warren was very good at that you know, tapping people. I didn't know then it was really about the development, but you knew, you always knew!"

"I don't know what you're talking about. He never *tapped* me."

Then they shriek at each other together.

"It might not have been..." George begins, cut short by Monica's "Don't talk to me like that!"

"You're both right and you're both wrong," Jenner says, frustratingly waving his arms at them, "If only you could..."

"I have come for the traitors, they will no longer escape me!"

No one has noticed the man who now slips into the rear of the group. Now they all turn to him.

"So long as I am here I will avenge my comrades."

The breadth and thickness of the common seems shrunk to this one place where everywhere is nowhere and nowhere is somewhere, allowing Thomas to creep past the hedges unseen and slip through the grass unheard. His eyes flit from one to the other, yet lingering on none as if he seeks one who

399

is not present. The conflict is forgotten as everyone waits for Thomas to speak again. Except for Jenner. The acrimonious interchange has been interrupted at its most interesting point

"Why are you here, why have you come back?" he says pugnaciously.

Thomas's eyes narrow on him, but Jenner is determined and unafraid even if Thomas tries to attack him again.

"Where is John Ball?"

"He has gone," Thomas says with an airy perplexity.

"Why have you not...returned...with him?"

"He must make his stand and keep his appointment with the will of the people and the will of God...as I must make mine...but first...there are the traitors..."

"There are no traitors here," Ettie says.

Trying to recall a distant memory, Thomas stares at Jenner before focusing his eyes on him sternly.

"John Ball stood between us...it may mean he is not a traitor," he says reluctantly.

But the policeman has turned his back and is questioning George and Monica.

"If you two would only work together..."

Thomas tries to listen, but Ettie pulls him away.

"You could not follow John Ball," she says, "You wanted to, but you were unable."

Thomas is confused. Ettie continues.

"What did you see that night, here on the common?"

"Wanted to go...back," he says, "but why was John Ball here? They took him and then I ran. How could he be here? And now..."

"If only you would put what you know together," Jenner is saying to Monica and George, "the development, the contact, Warren..."

His voice distracts Thomas. Ettie has to regain his attention.

"Tell me what you saw..."

"Stop talking to them. It's him you should be after!"

Maggie bursts from the bushes, rounding on Ettie and Jenner before diving at Chris, who jumps back, almost falling down.

"It was jealousy wasn't it?" she screams, "You wanted Kathleen, you always wanted her and there was Warren on the common, on his own and you went for him!"

Charley looks at her watch. A few hours at most. *You must keep shooting. Whatever happens, you must carry on. There's so little time.* Not even enough to think. That's probably a good thing. If she thinks *too* much she'll wonder how it's possible for an actor to take a five minute break that lasts an hour. She should be grateful for an hour that shrinks to three minutes. Oh for a day, *this* day, that does the same. Maybe then she can shoot *everything* in this one day, this crucial 15th July. Yet she hesitates. She stares at the set as she might look at a familiar painting in a gallery, absorbing the facets she's known so many times before, yet focusing all her attention, waiting for those new insights which she feels must come to her. Or is it fear, a deep sense of a venture unwise to begin and impossible to stop? The set is prepared, but different as if it's not really a set at all. Is the picture unfinished, by accident or design has the artist left out some vital element, some pivotal component? She's had such misgivings before. Her irrational imagination is invading her logical mind again. Dismiss it. She calls the cast together. They are soon in position and stand patiently for the command like racehorses waiting for the wire. She fumbles with the script, looks again at the assembled company, flicks through a few relevant pages of *A Little Liberty*, then turns to the set again. No more hesitation, she's ready. Then there are shouts from behind.

"Go and get him."

She turns and asks what is wrong. The actor playing John Ball is not on set. He's outside again. Someone has gone to get him. That can't be, she's just seen...she turns back to the set...yes, she's right...he's there...John Ball is on the set.

"When John Ball left I tried to follow him, but in the open country... there was a wall and I couldn't see...I was stopped and crashed into that wall."

Thomas looks around in his confusion, rubbing his head as if still in pain from his collision with the invisible wall.

"It was then I knew the traitors were here. At last I could avenge my comrades."

He looks to Ettie.

"There are no traitors here," she repeats fearfully, but sees there's no aggression in his eyes.

"But I have seen what the traitors did."

"Tell me what you have seen."

He doesn't answer, but suddenly turns and walks south to the higher end of the common, towards Lock's Spinney and the place of Warren's murder. As Ettie joins him, the others gradually follow – Jennifer and then Chris, accompanied by Maggie, scampering and whooping at him, then George and Monica, still berated by Jenner, with Rick at the rear. They amble along like a motley troupe of medieval pilgrims, each intent on their individual affairs. At least three separate conversations are pursued in competition, even defiance as each intrudes and interferes with the others. Jenner continues to question Monica and George, resisting their attempts to stifle each other while getting them to open up and 'cooperate' about Warren and the Waintree development. His efforts are constantly interrupted by Maggie's increasingly noisy castigation of Chris, whipped up by Monica and George's frequent interventions, the first to oppose, the second in support of her. While through all this cacophony Ettie tries to simultaneously reassure and question Thomas.

"I heard her," he says, "as Father Ball went away she came to me."

"You saw...?"

"Not seen, heard, I heard Martha. She said 'It's time for you to return.' 'I can't,' I told her. 'You can,' she said, 'you can with the help of the woman you saw in London.' But I couldn't remember. 'What woman?' I said. 'The one that came to our house before you went away.' Then I remembered you and knew I had to find you. 'She needs your help as you need hers,' she said, 'Accept it and all will be possible.' I told her what I'd seen, but she didn't answer. Her voice had gone just like the vision of John Ball and I was left alone. Then I remembered more, much more and I knew I could tell, I had to tell."

"Tell me."

"I saw a man falling."

"The falling man," she repeats.

"He was my comrade. You must help me find the traitor who struck him down. He must be brought to justice!"

This last word resounds over Maggie's admonitions, above Monica and George's bickering, striking the inner link with the past Jenner's been trying to suppress, pushing his frustrated questioning beyond endurance. He stops and turns to Ettie.

"I know all these 14th century connections are important to you, but I'm conducting a murder investigation and…"

Ettie ignores him and continues questioning Thomas.

"Do you know the place where you saw the falling man?"

"I can't allow this to get in the way of my enquiries…" Jenner says.

"Shut up!" Ettie shouts, "can't you see I'm in the middle of something here?"

"So am I," he says angrily, "I haven't time to waste with this man from the past. I need to…"

"Don't discount him. Don't discount the past. Ultimately Thomas will lead us to the murderer."

"No, no, I have it from these two…"

Ettie turns her back on him and speaks to Thomas again.

"Please try to remember. Where did you see the falling man and his attacker? Do you know the place?"

Thomas is confused and looks from her to Jenner, back again and glances at the others.

"Yes, I can show you, it's…"

Suddenly Ettie is pushed forward as Chris bounces into her back. She almost falls and is about to upbraid him when Maggie collides with her too. Ettie is winded, but otherwise unhurt. Chris sidesteps away from her, though he's really trying to get away from Maggie.

"Get away from me, you bloody crazy woman!"

He slips behind Ettie as Maggie lunges around her trying to get at him. Ettie bobs from side to side to avoid her and Chris runs back towards George and Monica. Ettie turns round. Chris weaves past Jenner, closely followed by Maggie.

He runs to a clump of trees and she follows. They hear her shouting for a few moments and expect to see them both re-emerge, but then there's silence. No one returns. Jenner and Jennifer run back, separating at the trees, then return, shaking their heads.

"They're gone," Jennifer says, "no sign of either of them."

Then Jenner stops, looks around.

"Tranter, where's Rick Tranter?"

"They must have all three run, we need to follow..."Jennifer says, stopping suddenly, "It's back," then shudders and turns to Ettie pleadingly, "Why, why is it back?"

The light grey mist rises and enfolds like the smoke emanating from a hundred fires on the common, growing, almost solidifying as it creeps rapidly towards Jenner, who quickly steps out to join Ettie and Jennifer.

"It has to be because..." Ettie begins, then with sudden realisation, turns round, " because..."

But it's already too late. Her fears justified. Thomas is also gone and it's impossible for them to follow.

An eerie silence descends, broken only by the frustrated shuffling of impatient cast and crew. All prepared, everyone in place, dressed up and ready to go, but lacking direction. Charley sits staring into the space above the actors, through and beyond the set into a peculiar emptiness where she's buffeted between competing imperatives. Ettie said to keep shooting, everything must be completed today 15th July. That means John Ball's execution. It can't be delayed, yet she can't begin. The actor playing John Ball has returned. He waits on set, but she dare not look at him for when she does another face appears which only she sees. The face she saw when that actor was outside, when everyone else said he wasn't there... the face of John Ball.

This is unbelievably foolish. She's swallowing up what little time she has left justifying why she's not shooting the events of this crucial day. Chris wouldn't waste valuable time and resources, diverted by ridiculous 'puffs of an overworked imagination.' As a professional he'd get on with it. After all he's a real director, not an ersatz charlatan, thrusting her way into a role for which she's neither qualified nor suited. That's the difference. But Chris isn't here and she is. Whether she *should* see John Ball, she *does* and can't wish him away

Is the real John Ball here to deliver a message from the past, that he and the others can wait, *must* wait until she's completed another task? Trust to your feelings Ettie said because they're invariably right and Charley has desperately *felt* the need for another scene. She fought Chris for its inclusion and he's not here to oppose her. She can discard John Ball and the 15th July. They can come back and shoot it quickly before the end of the day. Now they must move on to what she's always wanted, advance in time to early August and proceed with the rehangings. Yet still she hesitates. She needs guidance. She picks up the little book that's always by her side. She'll consult *A Little Liberty*.

"What now?" Jennifer says, staring bleakly into the shrouding greyness.

"We move on," Ettie says.

"But where with all this mist around us?"

"It's not around us, it's around Thomas."

"But he isn't here."

"Yes he is, we just can't see him."

Jennifer wants to ask more, but Jenner cuts her off.

"Just as I'd got somewhere with these two..."

He nods to Monica and George. They stand behind him, a little apart, ignoring each other, still antagonistic, but quiet, she from puzzlement, he from a growing alarm. Jenner has explained how their interests really converge and tried to get them to cooperate, but they can't cast off years of mutual loathing.

"...now I'm denied the opportunity to follow it through. We've lost everybody. Both Chris Pleasant and Rick Tranter..."

"You mean the development?" Jennifer says.

"Yes with Tranter...as for Pleasant..."

"Nobody is lost," Ettie says.

"They've got away," he says.

"Perhaps from us...for a time...but not from Thomas. They have not and cannot escape from him."

"He's also escaped."

"No, no, he's no more escaped from us than we have from him."

"You mean he's still here, on the common?" Jennifer says,

"He is...around...there's so little time, we must move on."

The others wait apprehensively as Ettie approaches the seemingly impenetrable wall of mist. It folds around her and Jenner steps smartly forward, catching her up. The others follow and as they get closer they see Ettie again, the mist apparently opening up before her.

"Thomas said it was a wall, but it's receding as we walk," Jennifer says.

"I suspected Thomas couldn't follow John Ball," Ettie says, "When he mentioned the 'wall' I was sure."

"But if he's from the past, why can't he return?"

"A wall doesn't transcend time. A fog might, but he's not yet completed his tasks in the present. In a sense, he's not from the past. He's been marooned in the link between past and present."

"How long has he been there?"

"Six hundred years."

Jennifer gasps.

"But you saw him in the past, in 1381."

"Yes, but that was then, this is now."

Still not understanding, Jennifer tries a different tack.

"What task, what must he do?"

"He must help us. Only then can he return. He may be out of sight, but he's not gone away, at least not very far so he can't yet return to his own time anymore than we can truly return to ours."

Now Jennifer really is horrified.

"What do you mean return to *ours?*"

"That's why it's a fog and not a wall. When he was with John Ball and the others, the past intervened. In a sense they were all in the past."

"But what now? What time are we in now, the present or 1381?"

"Or another past?" Jenner says, "the past of 1981?"

"It could be both or all three," Ettie says, "Now let's not waste any more time. We have to get there."

"Where?" Jennifer says.

Ettie doesn't answer, but strides on into the mist. The others must either follow or lose her. They follow – Jenner and Jennifer quickly, Monica and George more slowly. Jennifer keeps asking Ettie for a more precise indication of their destination, but she just keeps walking and doesn't answer.

"She doesn't know," Jenner says, "until she gets there, but I tell you this sergeant, if we are effectively in 1981 when we get there we can start digging again or rather you can, because you'll be in charge."

George catches them up.

"We should be going the other way. We can't leave Maggie with those reprobates."

"Which ones?" Jenner says dryly, "those in the past or those in the present."

"It's not funny. She could be in great danger, lost in this… this fog."

The two last words trail away as he looks around and sees the mist has cleared.

"They're not lost," Ettie says, suddenly stopping.

"But where is Maggie and Chris Pleasant and Rick Tranter, are they in limbo with…?"

"Thomas? Yes, probably. The mist has cleared. It means the stage over which past and present overlap has expanded. If they are in a limbo, it's a limbo of place as well as time. They must have moved further and faster than we could possibly follow them on foot. Thomas will try to return to Martha and the others will be carried along with him."

"She said you would help him," Jennifer says, "Wouldn't that have made him stay?"

"He was frightened. If Maggie hadn't…(George looks at her angrily) …it doesn't matter. He's gone."

"Where, where?" George pleads in his anguish.

"To where past and present are most likely…"

Ettie stops with sudden realisation.

"What is it?" Jenner says

"What fools we've been! We've known the link all along! It's the film. Thomas has gone to the film! It fits with Chris as well. The film is no longer just a link with the past, it is the past and I insisted Charley went ahead without delay!"

"Go ahead with – what did she call it – the rehanging scene," Jenner says.

"No, no!" She can't do that, she *won't* do that...will she?" Jenner shakes his head, then tries to reassure her.

"It's a film. It's not real. How can it actually be the past?" But Ettie gets more alarmed.

"Reality is what we believe it to be and for Thomas reality is the film. Charley mustn't change the order of events. The rehangings are in August. Today, 15th July, she has to film today *today*. How can Thomas return to a past that's not yet happened, a past he never knew?"

Jenner is bewildered.

"If we are in 1981, then..."

"No, no, no," she says impatiently, "Nothing will be resolved in 1381 and nothing will be resolved now."

But Jenner is in 1981 and he won't be deflected, saying as an aside to Jennifer, "We have to be prepared."

"Is there a connection between the rehanging and the murder of Melvyn Strange?" Jennifer says, "Chris Pleasant was always against the rehanging scene. What does he know?"

"Just get everybody up here with spades," he says quietly.

"Martha wants Thomas back," Ettie says, "With her help we can make it all happen."

Jenner looks at her incredulously. They are close to resolving a twenty five year old mystery, so instructs Jennifer and sends her away.

"We have to get there. There's much to do," he says to Ettie, steering her round gently.

After a short pause she moves on towards that unseeable destination, mumbling to herself, but then turns back to him.

"Martha is our contact in the past, but who is *her* contact in the present?"

"You," he says.

She shakes her head ruefully.

"No, no, I am the link, not the contact. That has to be someone else."

He tries to go, but she won't move.

"Kathleen Grover perhaps," he says, hoping some name, any name will suffice.

Ettie puckers her lips and shakes her head again.

"Charley," he says with sudden insight.

"Oh God! Charley, she doesn't know what she's doing! She could be pitching herself into the middle of times, between the contacts! She may be in great danger!"

One of the most gruesome, bestial and at the same time moving aspects of the Revolt in Hertforshire was what has become known as the 'Rehanging.' After the fifteen men were drawn and hanged on 15th July their bodies were left to rot and be consumed by the birds. On the same day, the king issued his commission, requiring all free and bonded tenants, to resume the duties they had previously done for the abbot. This was proclaimed throughout all the towns and villages of the county. Five days later on the 20th, conscious of the continuing simmering discontent in the county, he summoned all men between the ages of 15 and 60 to swear allegiance. Even by then some had fled into the countryside as outlaws.

Yet the population could not have been wholly intimidated by this 'oath of fealty.' Disgusted and horrified by the sight of their murdered comrades swinging on the gibbets, the people cut them down and gave them proper burial. Meanwhile the king had left St. Albans and went on to Berkhampstead and then into Buckinghamshire. When he heard what the people had done he was extremely angry and sent writs on 3rd August to the bailiffs of St. Albans ordering them to compel the citizens to dig them up and rehang them.

'See to it that iron chains be made and the bodies of those that were hanged, wherever they are found, be brought back to the gibbets and be hung on them again with those chains for as long as possible.'

So the citizens were forced to dig up their friends with their own hands and rehang them with the iron chains. The bodies were now oozing with decay, swarming with worms, putrid and stinking and exuding foul odours. The dogs were free because it was their chains that were used. The bodies then remained as originally intended for as long as it took for them to be turned into gaunt and frightful skeletons. That much we know, but one mystery has remained to this day. Where were the bodies originally buried? The writ says 'wherever they are found,' but no contemporary accounts indicate the location. They must have been interred in a secret place. Not too distant, otherwise it would have taken too long for the bodies to be taken away without immediate detection, but remote enough to evade any initial forage by the authorities. After the writs were issued the bailiffs must have scoured the town and surrounding country to find evidence of recently disturbed ground. The people had no monument to their lost leaders other than the scene of their burial before their foul rehanging. A special, revered place, their violent passing forever commemorated in the land. It must have been seared into the folk memory for a long time, remaining to this day.

Charley puts down *A Little Liberty*. She's read this poignant page many times, but only now have these final sentences hit her with such power and burning intensity. How can she truly convey such horrific courage and terrifying glory? To do them full justice such scenes must activate all the senses. The deliverers sneak to the gibbets. In the darkness they cut and heave the mutilated yet precious bodies, carrying them away to taste the bittersweet fervour of the secret burials. Then to smell the foulness of their disinterment, slithering the chains over the decaying corpses and hauling them up with as much respect such a grisly duty allows. Above all, get inside the people and feel what they felt. That is the impossible task, to divulge the unimaginable, depict the unbelievable and reveal what must become the unforgettable. How can she enliven that grand tragedy, grasp that heart rending boldness without having been there or at least heard it from one who was?

Yet such things may distract her from the *real* task. She's not in the business of revealing, but of portraying and what she must portray is a *representation* of those events. It's only a film. If only it was. What we are is our memories. The film is a collective memory. If we distort our past we distort ourselves. We become a fabrication, an illusion, unreal, ultimately ceasing to exist at all. If she could make 'contact' as Ettie does she might link up with the past and create an *authentic* picture. That's what Warren intended in his short preface to *A Little Liberty*. It would be a fitting memorial to him. Ettie talked about someone called Martha. She must be the prime contact in those far off days. If Ettie can contact her, why can't she? As the creator and deliverer of the film she must now be the prime mover in *these* times, making her Martha's contact. With everything in place, surely it's only a matter of concentrating long enough and hard enough? Then it will happen and she'll hear that voice from the past.

"I have come for the traitors. I will avenge my comrades!"

Not the voice she's been expecting. No gentle voice of entreaty, guiding her through the twists and turns of the past, but strident, demanding, desperate. The voice of someone at the end of his tether, to which he's been too long attached, but it is an *authentic* voice of the past! Thomas strides from the back of the studio and he's not alone. Two men and a woman follow with some trepidation, mystified by the place and glancing around nervously. At first no one takes especial notice of Thomas, assuming from his clothes he's yet another extra, but Charley knows better. Not his clothes, but his defiant stare and angry interjections tell her he's no player, no *representation*, but a true and fearful *representative* of that world she endeavours to portray.

"Show me, show me!" he shouts as he gets closer, "Show me the traitors!"

He's now in front of the set and can't get closer without becoming a part of it. No one answers, everyone watches him anxiously, a few slipping behind others in case he might suddenly lunge forward. His modern companions are tense. Even Maggie is silent. Chris is standing behind Rick as if he doesn't wish to be seen, but Charley sees him.

"Where did you come from?" she says.

"From the common," Maggie says, "Where are we now?"

'Film studio' forms in Charley's mind, but she can't mouth the words for as she follows the puzzled looks of the new arrivals she too sees more than a set. Beyond the platform and the gallows a wide expanse of green recedes to a distant horizon beyond any mere prop or falsely scenic view. This is no studio, no artificial fabrication, but real fields at the edge of a real town where train and car and plane have never been seen, never been heard.

"One moment we were there, the next here," Maggie says dreamily, staring like the others into the vastness.

"You *walked* from Welstead?" Charley says incredulously.

"Yes, but not very far. It only took a few minutes."

"But it's twelve miles!"

"Is it? No, it can't be."

"But it..."

Charley and Maggie turn suddenly. Chris and Rick have also turned and are trying to run back to what they think is the rear of the studio, but like the space beyond the set, their way is barred by a widening openness. There is no studio, only houses and streets and hundreds of closely packed people...and Thomas. He leaps around Maggie and jumps side to side with outstretched hands as Chris and Rick try to get round him.

"Traitors!" he says, "You cannot run!"

"No, no," Chris says, "we've been through this. Ettie said..."

Squeezing herself between them, Charley grabs Thomas's hand and pulls him back towards what had originally been the set. But now the platform and gibbets stand in stark and forlorn isolation, a terrible compressed cluster of oppression against the broad and beckoning freedom of the fields, yet surrounded by even more people than before.

"Come," she says, lugging him along, "You are of the time, this is your story, you must be part of it."

"But the traitors..." he splutters, surprisingly allowing himself to be dragged away.

"They are no traitors. The only traitors here are those that got these brave men and..."

"Traitors," he mutters and then staring into the fields, "I am imprisoned in the open, I must get away."

"No you must stay, this is where you belong."

He turns towards the town and shudders.

"I must redeem my guilt."

Chris tries again to get behind Rick. Charley laughs.

"I've already seen you and so has everybody else."

Chris looks anxiously towards the crowd, his eyes flitting haphazardly as he miserably tries to recognise actors and extras.

"Come and take your place," Charley says, "You're the director. This could be your crowning achievement. We have the country, we have the people and..."

He eyes her warily. Charley is utterly carried away by the moment, submerged in the 'reality' of the past. Is this a genuine offer of a great opportunity or a cruel mocking of his failings?

"...this film will be the ultimate accomplishment," she continues, "this man was actually there..."

"What is this?" Thomas says.

"It's August, these are the gibbets where the leaders of the Revolt were brought back, this is the rehangings."

"No, no!" he shouts, lifting his hands in front of his face and turning away, "This cannot be, I cannot stay, I am not... was not here!"

Maggie watches as Thomas turns away. He seems to be listening.

"Who do you hear?" she says.

"No one," he says, "No one speaks, but if only I could hear her!"

He turns back to Charley though without real purpose, then looks again to Maggie, not because he wants to talk to her, but there's no one else to assuage his agony. She's like the helpless attendant on the wounded man, full of sympathy, but unskilled to help. Their eyes meet with unspoken messages. Whether either really understands the other – she believing the past is implicated in the crimes of the present and he obsessed with treachery and guilt – really doesn't matter. It's enough that in this maelstrom they seem to understand.

Then in her eyes he senses what she is hearing though he cannot hear it himself.

"The time for running is over. The worst has passed. He must confront it."

Deep within, Maggie has always known this woman's voice even though it's not someone she knows. She's always been there, waiting for the right moment to speak, someone she ought to know.

"Who is coming? I feel their presence."

There's real alarm now in the voice. Then silence and Maggie knows she'll hear no more.

This is an uncomfortable place for Chris. Charley is ascendant and he is exposed, the withered and torn down filmmaker, but now he's seized by another greater fear.

"You've always been besotted with that foul rehanging scene," he shouts at her bitterly, "It will not, cannot be filmed, I tell you no, this must stop!"

"Don't tell me," she shouts back, "You left, you abandoned us!"

"You can't do this!"

"Why? What are you afraid of?"

He cannot answer. How to tell of that night on the common, of finding Warren? She wonders if he'll try to run away again, but he only turns his back, away from her, from Thomas, from the crowds, above all from those chained and lifeless bodies lying on the ground. Rick now comes forward and calls to Charley.

"Stop this nonsense now!"

He turns to Thomas and then waves at the gibbets, his voice rising to a whining squawk.

"He shouldn't be here, none of us should be here. Take away this...this obscenity...while there's still time...get rid of it...stop this...stop it now!"

"And why should that concern you both so much?"

Chris and Rick gaze dejectedly, then seeing Jenner and three others marching onto the set, dart around to get away. They have two slim chances of not being caught – run into the expansive green, hoping no one will follow or slipping into the crowd, hoping no one will give them up. At best the open country offers an illusory escape. They would be conspicuous in the landscape, easily picked off by the fleet footed. The crowd is no longer composed just of extras. There are other faces, swarthy, beaten down by sun and wind and injustice, suspicious and hostile, whose loyalty lies more with the sleeping cadavers at their feet than any wakeful authority. Such a horde may not give them up, but would they ever emerge again? In any case bounding into the country or slinking into the crowd is impossible. Charley bars their way to the first, Thomas to the second.

"Where have you come from?" Charley says to the new arrivals.

"Out of the air," Maggie says.

"From the common," Ettie says.

"I suppose you walked as well?"

"Not exactly."

Charley throws her hands up despairingly.

"First these three walk in a few minutes what should take half a day and then you arrive having…"

"No one has *walked* anywhere," Ettie says, glancing at her watch and irritatingly ignoring Charley's confusion, "At least not in the way you mean. Time and place are one, so…"

"How have you come immediately from the common?"

"We had…business there…still do…we were *summoned*."

"By that man?" Charley says quietly, nodding towards Thomas.

Ettie takes her aside, speaking very quietly.

"Thomas left us suddenly in great distress. We are all trapped in a distortion of past and present. Thomas is at the centre of that distortion. That is why he brought the others with him."

She nods to Maggie, Chris and Rick. Charley is very alarmed and speaks even more softly, unsure who can be trusted, anxious not to alert any of them.

"How do we get out of this?"

"Thomas needs to be released. That is why he is here. But we too are constrained. His release is crucial to any resolution. Until he is released we cannot be released, but he is constrained by…"

"Stop, stop, I'm so confused!"

Ettie takes her hand.

"I'm sorry. We are up against the deadline of today. There's so little time to explain. I'm sure you've been experiencing some peculiar things here..."

"You could say that."

"You see the film..."

"...is no longer just a film?" Charley says.

"I'm afraid not. The intervening centuries between us and 1381 have telescoped as has the country between here and the town and the common. We no longer move, we *transfer* just as time..."

"I knew it, I was right all along!"

Maggie jumps in front of them. She's been crouching nearby and has heard the whole of their conversation.

"He has to be released. I always said the answer lay in the past. We are in the past aren't we, we are there now?"

Ettie hesitates. Maggie raises her voice.

"Tell me! Tell me!"

The others listen with mounting alarm. Ettie must keep some control. Chris and Rick are moving away. Saying nothing will be more dangerous.

"Yes, in a way," Ettie says guardedly.

"I knew it, I knew it! It's what she said."

Thomas listens with the others, but what Maggie says frightens him and he edges away from everybody.

"*She* told me," Maggie shouts.

"Who are you talking about?" Charley says.

"Martha," Ettie says, "We have to..."

She's interrupted by a commotion as Chris and Rick rush away desperately from both the open country and the crowd, heading the way they came, which was then the rear of the 'studio,' but Monica bars their path, arms outstretched. Chris collides with her, knocking her over, but is then brought down in turn by George. Rick sidesteps her, but gets only a few paces, until Jenner brings him down.

"Hold him," Jenner says to George, "don't let him get away.

"He's not going anywhere," George, says as he sits on Chris, "but I have to see to Maggie, somebody help me."

416

Jenner beckons to the 'crowd' and some extras come over to help restrain Chris.

"Do it," Maggie shouts to Charley, "It's the only way. She can't stop it. Let the past take its course!"

George runs across, puts his arms around her and pulls her close as she snuggles in.

"It's the only way he can return," she mutters with a lumbering intensity as if she repeats someone else's words.

Then she turns back to Charley.

"Do it, start filming!"

Charley shouts to the cast. Ettie objects, but jostled by the lurching 'crowd' her protests are ignored as Charley's long cherished rehanging scene finally begins. All eyes are turned to the ground where the decaying bodies lie and then the crowd opens up as a group of men enter to begin their grisly work of returning what is left of the corpses to the gibbets. Ettie tries to force her way through, but can't penetrate the massed phalanx surrounding the gruesome scene. Charley watches in amazement as the action unfolds, unscripted, unrehearsed yet without hesitation or clumsiness. Even now she can't get used to it not being 'played' at all, for just as there's no real 'set,' there's no 'acting' either. What she sees is what was...what *is*.

Then as the men fumble with the chains, their hands smeared and their clothes soiled as they begin to haul up the bodies, she gasps in shock and awe, hearing nothing save her own breathing, which seems not only unduly loud, but irreverently intrusive on the horrid spectacle. The silence slows all movement, magnifying each twist of the chains, each jerk of the corpses into a monstrously beautiful ballet of horror. The crowd sways in crumpled congestion and noiseless clamour. Charley turns in every direction in a futile attempt to find the source of the silence, like looking for the space between the trees in a forest.

Chris and Rick, Maggie, George and Monica are subsumed in the crowd, as silent as the others. At the edge, Ettie and Jenner watch helplessly, frustrated and desperate to speak out though for different reasons. Then the silence is gone, suddenly invaded by the jangling of the chains, the wheezing and straining of the men and the bitter rumbling of the crowd. Yet even this is relegated as the bodies reach the gibbets. Decayed and repulsive, they were at least recognisable as once human even after the barbaric rituals of execution, but no one is prepared for the incredible forms they now see. An arm, a leg, even a head or a torso is missing, but only for a split second. Then they reappear, flashing and flickering, gashed and gory, limbs and eyes, ears and bellies, gorged and slashed in diabolic butchery. Then they are gone yet again, leaving frightful incomplete bodies until in a few seconds their misplaced parts reappear, conjured in some horrific fairground peep show. Charley stares in incredulous disgusted wonder.

"Is this a film again," she thinks, "has the real past been wiped away by the special effects of some unseen animator and obscene computation?"

"What have you done?" Ettie shouts, "Your meddling has not just distorted time, but mangled physical reality itself!"

She tries once more to push forward, but the crowd jeers, packing even tighter, unwilling to allow the interloper to speak, let alone get closer to the grotesque show. She looks from face to face, forward and back, side to side, but these are not the extras she's seen so many times. These are people of another age. This is their time and she interferes at her peril. She shouts again, this time trying to get above and beyond the crush and appeal to Charley directly. Again the solid human wall encloses, pushing and prodding, glaring with wide and hostile eyes. Who is this woman who dares disturb their repressed grief? Have they not suffered enough, already ground by the millstones of their rulers without this intrusion into their very public humiliation? The jabbing and shoving increases. Jenner takes her elbow and pulls her back for her own safety.

"It's no use. No one understands. Don't provoke them."

"But I have to stop this. Can't you see, bits and pieces of people, first they're there, then they're not? This isn't real. It's what I feared. Jumping around with events, rerunning them out of order. She still thinks she's making a film. You can't do this with the *real* past. I warned her. You can't shuffle the past like a pack of cards. It's dangerous to fiddle with time as if you're rearranging scenes in a film script."

"She doesn't think she's making a film anymore than you do. It's not her that's doing this. It's something else."

Ettie points to the horrible swinging corpses, their putrid and mutilated remnants still further mauled by these constantly changing shapes to their forms.

"What else could it be?"

"It may not be the destructive confusion you fear," he says, "but a symptom of other changes. Why else do you think we were brought here?"

"But we are in the past, not watching some pathetic re-enactment from a safe distance."

"If this is the past then it's meant to be and we are part of it. Look again, look at those bodies."

"I can't, it's enough to witness this obscenity without concentrating on the details. I feared this scene all along. I told Charley..."

"Look and consider. If this past and the newer past, 1381 and 1981 and the present are caught together on this day, then consider what it might mean."

Ettie forces herself and turns again towards the gibbets, now concentrating less on *what* she sees, but on *why* she sees it. Then, as the implications become clear, she turns back.

"Those bodies reflect what may be happening elsewhere," he says in response to her silent question, "think of the soil falling down and being scraped away..."

"Yes, yes, I see now. Part of the bodies would be seen and then not seen...the whole, then less of it as they are..."

"...pulled out of the ground."

There's a flurry of activity around the gibbets. Realisation is dawning, but there's now so much noise Ettie is finding it difficult to think. She turns away again. Jenner takes her arm.

"This can only mean..." she begins.

"This has to be done," Maggie is screaming, "I always said it was them. We have to do it!"

She writhes around the gibbets, in earnestness rather than pain, determined to prove not only she's right, but also ensure the scene is completed.

"You can't meddle with them!" Ettie shouts at her, "These people..."

"She doesn't mean the people," Jenner says, steering her further away from the crowd, "she never did. She means..."

"It has to be done. I always said he had to return."

The voice is no longer confined to her head, but comes from the crowd. She turns back and even through the massed hundreds sees Martha calling her.

"Don't delay! Get on with it!"

Maggie again.

"Two mad women," Ettie says angrily, "one in the past, one in the present, neither knowing what they're doing!"

"One in the past, one in the present," Jenner repeats, "think about it."

Ettie nods.

"It's the connection. Maggie and Martha, they *summoned* us here. Why couldn't I see it?"

"You were too concerned with everything having to be in sequence. August couldn't be before July, but what happened in August was so crucial."

She looks back into the crowd, but can't see Martha. Maggie is quieter now, breathless and exhausted by her passion and excitement. George has pulled her to the side.

"If Maggie doesn't mean the people, who does she mean?" Ettie says.

"Those responsible for the executions," Jenner says, "just as we need to be concerned with those responsible for the murders."

"So there's a parallel between..."

"...1381 and 1981."

"That means we have to get back!"

"And get him back as Martha said."

"Because he's an outlaw and there's a deadline."

She walks quickly into the open space away from the people. Jenner hovers for a few moments, making sure he's not in the crowd, then rejoins her.

"He's not here, where has he gone?" Ettie shouts, running in circles, flinging her arms in the air, "I've been so distracted and forgotten about Thomas. Where is he? You did look, he's not in the crowd?"

"That's the last place he'll be," Jenner says, "The rehanging was too much for him."

"No, not too much, but too close. It's pulled him back. Jennifer must have found something. He has to be there just as we have to be here."

15

FOR hundreds of years the verdant expanse has been a storehouse and a sanctuary. Each hard winter it gave up its precious hedged and tree filled treasure, succouring its folk from cold and darkness. They may no longer gather their fuel, but its soul sustaining peace remains, its tireless lung breathing deliverance and revival. The land supports and the land demands. It supports the people, nourishing within its wide green swathe their hopes and fears, absorbing within the soil the collective memories of the centuries, ready to germinate and sprout in the fateful spring of truth. It waits anxiously and demands allegiance. Each generation must protect its inheritance, remember the sacrifices of those that went before, maintain their achievements lest they lose them. The land is everything. Without it there can be no rebirth.

Men came before. They broke the soil with their cutting and scraping, but the land was not ready. It had been too recently defiled, so when they came with their sticks and shovels, it muddied and tangled, the grass shrouded and the roots enveloped and nothing was revealed. They tried to come again with their blades and their buckets, polluting the air with their noisome din, wounding the earth with their ugly 'improvements' and the earth cried out in silent screaming. For a quarter century the land has enclosed the past and locked out the present. For then blood was spilt too close to the inviolate time. How could the land betray such a secret exactly six centuries after the bitterly sacred remembrance?

Welstead common is a pleasant retreat, an unimposing background landscape to a dramatic painting. Yet no longer an accessory, the repository of past struggles, the main player. Its sinewy grass verges, like magnetic lines of force pull all towards the centrepiece. For the time has come for it to divulge some of its secrets and when the past gives to the present, the present can give to the past. Now, when the past has been disrupted and the grass has been reddened yet again, the time has come for the unearthing of memories and the revival of remembrance. Now the land will not cry against those that tear its surface, obstruct those that delve or choke those that probe. It will welcome the wound, open the soil and the earth will deliver up the truth.

Jenner had been adamant, but imprecise. Jennifer was to get every available officer and commence excavations.

"Dig until you find it."

"Find what?" she'd said.

"You'll know when you find it."

No doubt she will, but now he's gone and is it seems uncontactable. Once more a section of the common has been closed to the public and a large team assembled, but where do they begin? She's where she left Jenner and the others, but it has the uncanny feel of the wrong place. She feels she's invited her friends to the wrong party. Everyone watches her, waiting for instructions. Without any other indication of where to go she leads them in the direction she saw Ettie moving. They should still be on the common, but Jennifer senses they are not. The feeling gets stronger the nearer they get to Lock's Spinney, but she's not deterred. For as she walks a little ahead of the team another feeling grows. They are not alone. She's unaware of the destination, but knows she'll get there. Someone helps. Someone draws her. Wherever she looks a persistent image trips into her mind with increasing frequency. It won't go away, no matter how hard she tries. Everywhere she sees him, among the trees, over the stream, gliding through the grass, though she knows there's no one there...dancing, slithering, running...no, none of these things...he's falling. She keeps seeing a *falling* man.

She pauses when they reach Lock's Spinney. The place of death is no longer a crime scene, all evidence having been gathered and taken away, but a malign fascination still pervades the ground. She wonders what Warren Grover was really like as distinct from what his wife, his friends, his enemies say of him. She looks around almost expecting he might suddenly appear from behind the trees. His spirit haunts the place. What mysteries might he unravel if for only a few moments he could be retrieved before the earth repossesses him? So close to the clamouring dash, the bustling emptiness, this place is an oasis of calm, but it is seared and sullied. She listens for nowhere is ever totally silent, but hears no voice, only the sighing of the wind, the rustling leaves, the creaking branches. She waits, the spell continues, but then the other officers catch up, it's broken and she moves on.

There are several paths she could take, but she hesitates only a few moments before choosing the right one. All she needs do is turn slowly until the drawing power is strongest and the image of the falling man is firmest. For he is with her all times now, even when she closes her eyes, falling, always falling, but never fallen as if he's caught in some perpetual freeze frame, ever going down, never landing. The sky darkens and the path narrows as it meanders south towards St. Albans. With each step she feels they move not just away from the town, but further back in time. How far, a quarter century or six centuries? She shudders, fearing the return of the mist, wondering whether without Ettie she would ever find her way out. She might even be cut off from the other officers. She turns back nervously, but they are there, tramping patiently, impervious to her inner struggle.

Almost at its end where the common land gives way to that of the farms and where there once stood dense woodland, where men could hide and heath, where men could fight, the path too gives out, cut short as if reaching a wall or a fence. But there's no wall and no fence, only a depression in the grass, shrouded by a few bushes. This is a boundary path, hardly if ever used. She's been guided to a last stop, along a path to nowhere. A place from which there may be no escape! She looks around, half expecting the enclosing mist to have descended, truly cutting her off, but there's no fog and the country is as open as it was earlier. Yet suddenly she's cold. She looks up. The sky is deadeningly murky, the air gloom heavy, not threatening, but filled with melancholic expectancy as if something long concealed may be uncovered at last.

What if this path is not an end, but once went *somewhere* or *came* from somewhere? A boundary, but not a closed one, a place for outlaws, the long gone woodland and heath, places of escape and refuge. In a time when few were free, was this where those within the law met those outside the law? She looks into the depression and sees the falling man again, but now his fall is slower and he almost reaches the ground before his image is gone. This is a place cut short or cut down. Then he falls again, then up and down, almost at the ground. Up, down, up again, down...and so it goes on, faster and faster...a flickering image running into a merged mass...a man bent double with the strain of being pushed and one colour, brown, brown, always brown...brown like the earth.

"Dig!" Jennifer calls, "Start digging here!"

She grabs some tape and jumps into the depression, turning and turning, the vision of the falling man stabbing and chasing. Then she stops, twists a few times back and forth to make sure his image is at its fiercest and stakes out the tape over a small area.

"This is the place. It has to be here."

She steps back to allow the officers to get to work. The ground looks hard, but the spades bite surprisingly easily. Jennifer peers down from the edge of the gradually deepening hole, with each clod of removed soil expecting to hear the tell tale ring of steel on bone. As the hole gets larger, she's afraid in their impetuousness they might destroy the very evidence they are trying to find.

"Easier now," she says.

The officers look up with looks of 'make your mind up' and 'I know what I'm doing.' She feels even colder, yet the men seem unconcerned. It darkens suddenly. She expect to see the sun obscured by a black cloud, yet there is no cloud, nor sun either, but a low, grey hanging mist like a suspended ceiling. Yet it avoids the ground and she can still see the common and the fields.

Then she hears the unmistakable scrape and one of the officers says, "Got something," the others standing back as he gently clears the soil.

Jennifer is about to jump down beside them when the vision of the same man reappears. Like her he's on the edge of the hole. He leans forward, apparently involuntarily as if...he's pushed...or struck. He topples slowly as before and as before will stop in mid fall. Then he'll disappear or commence another balletic plunge, but no...he carries on...keeps falling until...he falls right into the hole, where his image remains, shrouded over where the officer has cleared away some soil.

"Get that soil away!" Jennifer calls anxiously, "Get it cleared. Now!"

One of the others helps him, but the ghostly figure remains. Gradually fragments of bone are uncovered and with each small exposure part of the vision is suddenly gone. Jennifer stares aghast and afraid at the horrible patchwork of corpse and bone. Only when the whole skeleton is revealed is the last vestige of the man gone. The stark and spiky whiteness stands out against the brown earth and grey stones. A shadow looms across the hole. Jennifer looks up. The sun has returned, the mist gone. Yet this is not the day it was before. Despite the bright sky and the warming breeze there's a cold darkness, but not the cold of the air or the darkness of the clouds. This is the cold of the heart, the darkness of the spirit and she knows their bare discovery can be no mere relic. How can it be, for she is now in that other day? So these are no degenerated, worm eaten remains, but someone recently cut down. *This* now is *that* now and twenty five years are rolled back. She shudders. The officers are brushing away the last of the soil. They haven't noticed the day has changed. Why should they? For them it hasn't, only for her and only from within. She asks if there's any identification.

"Nothing," one officer says as they prod around the bones.

Jennifer gets down. The skeleton lies face down, consistent with the vision of the falling man. Yet as she looks, the vision of the mini moment doesn't surprise her, for she's back in that other day, a generation gone with different clothes, different fashion. She sees the man again, but now the back of his blue-grey jacket prone over the skeleton. Then it's gone and only the skeleton can be seen. The rear of the skull is damaged.

"Hit from behind," she says, "We'll get the doc to have a look, but I'm pretty sure, this is..."

"It's as I said. It's him!"

Jennifer turns and suddenly looks up to yet a further day, not just this day or the day a generation gone, but a third day, stretched from an even longer thread of time. A man stands on the edge of the hole. He's unkempt, unshaven and dishevelled, his clothes archaic in their coarse brown simplicity, but in their wild, determined vigour his eyes betray the man of the past, the vengeful outlaw of 1381.

Jenner has finally cornered George near the platform beneath the gibbets and their terrible dangling relics. Maggie cowers beside him, exhausted from her exertions, all her energies expended on making the gruesome scene finally happen. The cadavers or what is left of them, no longer hideously quiver, one moment whole, another truncated or entirely expelled. The hideous jerking between whole and part is gone. Except for a slight, sad, almost peaceful swinging, they are still and hang again in wretched, frightful exhibition. George tries to get away, but Jenner gently, but firmly pushes him back against the platform.

"What do you want?" George says, still cradling Maggie, whimpering beside him.

"To finish what you began," Jenner says, settling himself in front of them, somewhat uncomfortable, but blocking their only means of escape, "before we were unfortunately interrupted by this...(he nods upwards, George shudders as he follows the indication)...repeat performance...you were telling me about your conversations with Warren Grover. I want you to tell me again and this time with nothing left out."

"Not here," George says, trying to get up again, "it's not... appropriate."

He glances at the crowd, which is gradually dispersing.

"Here is as good as anywhere," Jenner says grimly, "I'm not chasing you all over this damned studio."

"It's not suitable," George says, again trying to move, then waving his hands at the distant houses and fields, "Anyway, it's not a studio, it's..."

"Real? So is what happened twenty five years ago. Talk and be quick about it!"

George glances down at Maggie, who stares straight ahead, beyond Jenner to some unseen place, before turning back to his interrogator.

"He said so many things," George begins, then as if to deny any responsibility, "a lot of it didn't make any sense."

"I'll be the judge of that, " Jenner says flatly and then helpfully, "You can start with what anyone else was supposed to have said to him."

"Some guy spoke to him on the common."

"Who?"

"That's just it. It was supposed to be him here, in the film, the leader of the Revolt."

"William Grindcobb?"

"That's it. Warren had always been obsessed with 1381. He'd organised the re-enactment back in 1981, but this was ridiculous, a man six hundred years dead talking to him on the common! I couldn't take it seriously."

"But you take it seriously now?"

George shakes his head, more in bewilderment than denial, then carries on.

"Warren genuinely believed Grindcobb had spoken to him. He regarded it as a sacred trust. Afterwards he became very distressed because he felt he'd not done enough to...what did he call it...*process* what Grindcobb told him. '*We must avenge and you must avenge,*' Grindcobb said to him."

"Avenge," Jenner repeats solemnly.

"Warren interpreted that to mean he had to do everything he could to carry on the work of 1381 in the present."

Jenner screws his face in perplexity.

"Just what I thought," George says, anxious to join Jenner to his own befuddled state, "but there it is. Warren got even more into his book – that one she keeps close to her at all times (he waves towards Charley) and got another re-enactment going, but his main interest was in Chris's film. Warren must have known something about him that was more than the film. That's why Chris was after him. Maggie saw him that night on the common. That means he must have..."

"It may mean, it may not mean," Jenner intervenes, "I don't want your speculation, I want your evidence. Get back to Warren."

"He got worse after that. Absolutely obsessed with Grindcobb. Said he was getting so close to him it was like he and Grindcobb were becoming one. He was being *transmuted* into Grindcobb, that's the word he used, transmuted. How could I take...it was really difficult. At the same time he was talking to me about the Waintree development. He wanted me to support his anti development campaign more vigorously, but he was getting more and more way out so I wasn't sure I could take anything he said seriously. Even his wife was dismissing it as nonsense."

"So you ignored him?"

"I wish now I hadn't. He wanted to talk to Ettie Rodway about Grindcobb and the film. Now I know more about her work, but at the time, with all this off the wall stuff coming from Warren, I thought she was as way out as he was. So when she came to see me after his death, I'm afraid I gave her short shrift. Warren talked about 'the real revenge,' but by then I wasn't prepared to listen. I sent him away, but he was desperate to resolve what he called 'the vengeance continuing into the present.' He didn't trust Lawrence Bullock, so couldn't talk to him either. If only I'd listened to him. Some people have this uncanny ability to link up with the past. Warren was one of them. Maggie is another. So he went elsewhere...with disastrous results. I let him down. I won't let her down. She's the..."

"...link with the past," Ettie says, joining them.

"People think she's crazy," George says.

"That's because she doesn't understand her own strengths or those she's in contact with."

"I've always said it was them in the past," Maggie says quietly, "but nobody would listen."

"I'm listening. Tell me what they say."

"No one *says*, anything, but what I feel is like someone talking. *He has to come back* – that's what I feel – *the time for running is over. He has to come back before it's too late.*"

"A woman has been communicating with you. Her name is Martha. I have seen her and she has spoken to me, but I've not been listening...not properly...I realise that now. It's very important you two stay together," Ettie says, glancing knowingly at Jenner, "Thomas has to be reunited with Martha. You can help him because the two of you are the links, their parallels."

"All very well," Jenner says, "but I have to conclude my investigation. Your...contacts...with the past may be important, but these...events...have constantly beset my enquiries and this man has vital information. If progress is to be made I have to keep very much in the present."

"But they are one and the same thing! We've been working on what we thought were entirely different mysteries, but they are completely interlocked. The exhumation on the common finally fuses past and present in both time and place, so..."

"Exhumation? We don't know yet..."

"Of course we do! Jennifer has found something...it's the only explanation for Thomas' sudden disappearance...and that's where he is."

"But my concern is with the present, not the past."

"No, it's very much in the past for the present can only be resolved against the past and for that we have to have to keep this contact open."

"To 1381?"

"And also to 1981."

"Precisely, which is why I need to question this man very closely. Now, George, who did Warren talk to?"

Before George can reply there's a tremendous creaking and cracking in the timber holding up the gibbets, then the whole structure starts to sway menacingly. Under the great stresses, part of the platform rips upwards shooting lethal slivers of wood in all directions. Ettie pulls Maggie away, while Jenner grabs George. The four run back towards the crowd as the edifice lurches from side to side before finally plunging forward. The hideous corpses are rocked incessantly, increasing in speed like fairground swing boats. As the main timbers splinter and tear the crowd scatters, some tripping over others in their haste to get away, one man slightly trampled underfoot, though he soon gets up.

Charley and Monica sit together. Impervious to the surrounding hysteria, Charley has been watching the unfolding disturbance in awful fascination. Mesmerised by this unrehearsed 'special effect,' she still doesn't move, not even turning when the four get to her. They are now out of 'falling distance' and turn back to see the lumbering timbers, having passed the point of return, splayed and stretched in a grotesque explosive dance. They watch stupefied in these final lengthened seconds at the slowed destruction and wait for the imminent crash to the ground. But it doesn't come. Tottering uncontrollably it almost reaches the ground, but then is gone, no gibbets, no corpses, no chains, no struts or platform. Nothing. Most of the crowd has dispersed as if they were never there. Everything is gone, even the town and the fields, replaced by a wilder, uneven country – the common.

Ettie and Jenner, George, Maggie and Monica are alone.

"Where's Charley?" Jenner says.

Ettie picks Charley's battered copy of *A Little Liberty* from the ground.

"She's in the studio, with her film, her set and her August scene. She can't be with us now for this is 15th July."

"I don't understand."

"I fear it's the result of her insistence of filming out of sequence."

"But surely she wasn't filming...in the normal sense...it was...real."

"Perhaps, but still out of sequence."

"So now we are...in 1381?"

"I only know it's the 15th July."

Utterly bewildered, Jenner shrugs and looks around. All except two of the men holding Chris and Rick are gone and there's no sign of their charges. Jenner curses. While Ettie debates time and place he has lost two suspects! He hurries over. Their information might at least enable him to start a search. Like the other extras they are dressed in 14th century clothes, but as he gets closer and sees their faces more clearly he quickens his step. These are not extras, but Chris and Rick! He starts to run, afraid they will get away, but they too must have witnessed the frightful spectacle and its equally startling disappearance. Shocked and disorientated they make no move. They notice him, but are examining each other much more, standing back and feeling the garments, as surprised as he is by their costumes.

"How did we get these clothes?" Chris says incredulously.

"You tell me," Jenner says suspiciously, wondering what he will do if they make a run for it.

"It was after that...that thing came down," Rick says, "They just appeared."

Chris runs his finger along the seam of Rick's jacket and then along his own.

"There's something oddly familiar about them," he says.

Ettie is calling. She and the others are walking towards a clump of bushes where a number of people are gathered. Jenner sees what appear to be bobbing heads at ground level! He looks again. They must be lower down, in a hole. They are police officers. They are excavating! Other people are on the surface. One is talking and directing the others. It's Jennifer!

"Come on, you two," he says, nudging Chris and Rick and hurrying them along.

They walk in front of him, like two hapless soldiers, prodded and pushed over the top into an unpredictable nomansland. They look about the wide grassland and trees with the same incredulous stupefaction they examined their own clothes. Moments ago they were beside the gibbets in a town surrounded by houses and before that in a film studio, but not long before that in this same open country on the same common. Their minds tell them it can't be, but their eyes tell them it is. Jenner gives their outlandish clothes only scant consideration. Initially he assumed they'd picked them up on the set, ignoring how they'd done this without being seen, but now he's completely unconcerned. So many inexplicable things have happened he's almost past caring. He has to keep focused on his enquiries and it seems Jennifer has discovered something interesting.

"Keep a hold of those two," he says to a couple of officers, jabbing his finger towards Chris and Rick and then to Jennifer, "What have you got?"

She's looking down into the hole and he follows her gaze.

"Melvyn Strange, DNA results will confirm, but we know what he was wearing at the time of his disappearance – a blue grey jacket."

"And?" Jenner says as he bafflingly scans the skeleton for any signs of clothing.

Jennifer hesitates. He turns to her, reads the reason for her reticence, but says nothing.

"There were traces," she says, "very small, we've sent for analysis, but..."

"You are sure they will indicate a blue grey jacket," he says, looking down once more at the bare skeleton and then, turning to her, "because you saw the jacket?"

She keeps looking down, shudders slightly and nods her head.

"As I feared," he says, "and 1981 was the year he disappeared."

She looks up and then across to Chris and Rick.

"Why are they dressed like that?"

"Because," Jenner says with sudden realisation, "that is also the year of the re-enactment of the Revolt and I'd put money they are wearing the same clothes they wore then."

"But that must mean..."

"...we are now in 1981."

Standing next to Ettie and Thomas, George and Maggie are also jolted by their sudden acquisition of 14th century clothes. Maggie groans loudly and doubles up as if seared by unbearable pain.

"No, no, not again, not again."

"The 1981 events are happening?" Jennifer whispers.

"We must hope so," Jenner says.

Comforted by Ettie Maggie has quietened a little. George makes a puzzled inspection of their clothes, especially at Thomas, but says nothing. Jenner watches him with interest, but gets impatient

"Well now, George," he shouts, "what do you say to this?"

George glances around apprehensively and is about to speak, but Thomas has seen Chris and Rick in their 14th century clothes and cuts him off, striding aggressively towards them. This is not what Jenner expected and he follows quickly, as does Ettie.

Thomas stops and looks down into the hole, muttering tearfully, "my comrades, my comrades," before shouting, "It's him! It's him!"

"Don't let him near them!" Jenner shouts to the officers beside Chris and Rick.

"Why not?" Maggie suddenly shouts, lunging forward.

George restrains her gently, but she pulls away from him.

"He was there that night on the common. Chris Pleasant was with Warren and you saw him, didn't you, you saw him too?"

Thomas stops, looks back and shakes his head.

"You," he says to her, "You are like...no, it's the clothes, only the clothes."

"But you saw him!" she persists.

"No point keeping it to yourself," Rick says to Chris, "make a clean breast of it."

Chris looks at him mystified and disappointed.

"I thought you were my friend."

"I am, that's why I urge you to speak out," Rick says, stepping a little away from Chris, distancing himself from what might now be said.

"It's true I was on the common that night...when Warren was killed."

"You see, you see, he's admitting it, I told you, I told you," Maggie shrieks.

"Shut that bloody woman up," Jenner shouts.

"I'd seen Kathleen several times since I'd come back," Chris continues, "It was all very innocent. Nostalgic adventurism is always profoundly disappointing. Going back over your past is never satisfactory. What you've held dear for so long has utterly changed for everybody else. Memories never coincide when you talk over old times with a friend you've not seen for many years. What's memorable to them, isn't to you and vice versa. It's even worse for lovers. Or it should be. It wasn't for us. We kept having those silent conversations when you know exactly what the other is thinking and you're thinking the same yourself. All we could think about was why we'd let Warren ever come between us.

'Seeing Kathleen again, it was as if we'd never been apart. The life between – her life with Warren, my life in film – was a great black hole. Only the life before and the life since mattered, the life before Warren, the life after him. As I walked across the common that night I realised coming back had been a colossal mistake and a heart wrenching release. The film should have been finished with the Smithfield scenes. It was a fitting end, full of drama and pathos. What followed was never meant to be. Oh I knew about the Hertfordshire events, but I never wanted to film them. They belonged to Charley and that wretched book. It was his book – *A Little Liberty* – it belonged to Warren. The Hertfordshire scenes she insisted on were his scenes. It was *his* life, her life with him. But Charley persisted. She was so insistent and I was weak. Then she homed in on the rehangings (his voice wavers on the word and he shudders) and it was too much. It reminded me of that night. It reminded me of Warren. I wasn't to know he would be there. Then...then he was dead."

"I was right," Maggie shouts, "I told you I saw him that night on the common."

"No, no, listen to me," George says, moving forward, but he's cut short again by Thomas.

"It is him," he shouts, waving his arms, "He did it, he killed my comrades. I was here. I saw him do it."

"And you told someone, didn't you?" Ettie says, spinning him round away from the others, "You spoke to a man you saw on the common and you told him everything?"

"My God," George says, "it was you Warren was talking to. He thought it was Grindcobb, but it was you. That was what Warren wanted to tell me. It was what you'd told him, what you'd seen...back in 1981!"

"It's not me," Chris shouts in alarm.

"You've already said..." Jenner says.

"Not in 1981, not then. I was telling you what I saw the night Warren was killed, not the day Melvyn disappeared. It wasn't me. Ask her, she was there then, it must have been her."

He points to Monica. She glares and shakes her head, but remains silent. Thomas alternately stares at her and Maggie, then turns away, shaking his head. The rest remain around the hole and its grim contents. As he glances down Jenner fancies he sees not one skeleton, but many more. Then they are gone and only the single one remains. He's about to say something to Ettie, but he's distracted by Thomas, walking further away.

Ettie also watches Thomas. He is the pivot, balancing three time periods – their fragile present, which he has invaded, his own suspended past of 1381 and now Jennifer's dreadful discovery of a generation ago, which must be the cause of his and their sudden return to the common. Where is the film studio, somewhere in the firmament of other times outside this motley jumble of ages, three times in one and one in none? Even now she's unsure which time they occupy.

She follows Thomas tremulously, wondering how best he might be tackled. He turns to face her. Her mind and body freezes. He brought them to this shoal of compound time and she feels more vulnerable than ever. Unpredictable and angry he could easily send them away again...to where? Perhaps he's just as afraid, blaming her for beaching him on this sandbank, wrenched from his past and barred from his future? She knows he's confused, is he also weak?

He turns and holds up his arm. She is his adversary. He will strike her down. She wants to cry out, but the words won't come. It wasn't her. She's not responsible. She didn't bring him here. His eyes are questioning. He's remembering when they last spoke in the town or is it farther back, in London on that night before Smithfield? What was it he said?

There are two Englands.

He walks towards her, in his deranged fury blaming her for being marooned. This is not his time, he's desperate to get

436

back and she is barrier to his release. He will have to destroy her, cut her down! She steps back, slips on some pebbles and stumbles. He's almost upon her, his craggy frame and swarthy face, a mind wearied by excess worry and a body worn by excess labour, but a soul set for the fight, ready to pounce and clear away his last obstacle. Then he stops. His hands are firm and his eyes still piercing, but he looks beyond Ettie into the distance and shakes his head. She follows his studied concentration. Jenner is talking to George and the others look on. Except Maggie who is looking towards Thomas. He stares back. Ettie understands.

"It's not her," she says, "It's not Martha, it's just the clothes."

"You are sure?" he says, "They are very much alike."

"I am sure. Now tell me exactly what you saw here."

"He cut down my comrades."

"All of them or just one?"

He stops to think.

"Think carefully," she says, "it was two men you saw wasn't it?"

He hesitates, then nods his head.

"Yes...two men. One was my comrade."

"You are sure you saw his face? Tell me exactly what you saw."

"He was dressed like me, who else could it be?"

"What you saw, not what you assume."

He hesitates again.

"I couldn't see his face clearly. They were arguing. The other man was well dressed, not like us. He was one of the lords. He pushed my comrade and he went down. It was here. Then the lord ran away."

"So you believe this...lord...killed your friend?"

"No, no, he didn't kill him. My comrade was stunned, but he wasn't dead. I saw him move slowly. I was about to go to him when another lord, dressed in even more finery than the first came from the bushes. As my comrade tried to get up he kicked him down and hit him hard on the head with a large stone. Then he went down again and never got up.

The lord looked down, but did not try to revive him. It was deliberate murder. He must have been near and like me, saw the argument. He made sure my comrade was dead and then he too ran away. I went over, but...I get so confused...he was there, I saw the body, but then I saw him with these strange clothes...then he was gone, the ground was bare. I ran away into the woods and hid for a long time. I never saw the body again. They must have taken him away. I know others were brought here. They came from the town in the night to bury them and then they were dug up again. I know these things, though I did not see them, but I did see my comrade cut down, I did, I know I did."

"This man who cut him down, this lord, the second one, you've seen him today, haven't you?"

"Yes. I said it was him, it was Tresilian!"

Meanwhile there are further surprises. Finally extricating himself from Maggie, George is berating Chris and valiantly *defending* Monica.

"You're wrong, wrong, she had nothing to do with Warren's death!"

While Chris keeps blubbering 'it's not me, it's not me,' George gets angrier. Getting closer it looks like he might even strike Chris, but Jenner intervenes and pulls him away.

"Warren said he'd seen a man from the past," Jenner says, "and he talked of revenge."

"I got it wrong, I got everything wrong!" George wails.

He bows his head and flails with his arms until they almost touch the ground. Jenner is exasperated. He pulls George up again and spins him round.

"'Course you got it wrong, we all got it bloody wrong. What about revenge, what did he mean?"

"I realise now," George says, "Warren was wrong too. He was so obsessed with 1381, he thought *the vengeance continuing into the present* meant carrying on with his work on the Revolt, but it wasn't about that at all. It had to be taken literally. It was about avenging something in Warren's own time – in our time. But I could only hear his crazy talk. If only I'd really *listened*. (he glances at Maggie) That's why I can't reject anyone else who feels these things, someone in tune with the past. I made an enormous mistake with Warren. I – you, any of us – mustn't do that again."

"What did Warren do when you wouldn't listen to him? Who did he talk to?"

"Someone he thought was his friend, someone I thought was his friend, someone I believed was supporting him. I knew their relationship was on the wane, but I assumed that was because Warren was over playing his hand, tapping him too much for his cultural work. Warren could be very persistent. Now I know otherwise. All along and in our different ways Warren and I were pursuing the same person. Someone involved in the development."

"You see," Chris interrupts, pointing again to Monica, "I said it was her."

She ignores this, but is intrigued by what George has said.

"This...person...was involved in the development? (George nods) If only I too had known."

"Quite so," Jenner says, "If only you two had spent your time talking rather than lambasting each other."

"Lawrence was buying up land for the development," Monica says, "but it was not for himself. He was the front man, he was buying the land for someone else."

"I knew he was involved in the development," George says, "but we now know Melvyn was murdered. He could have been involved in that too. They were always rivals and..."

"Whoever killed Warren also killed Lawrence," Jenner says.

"Because of these land deals?" George says.

"Perhaps. You were sniffing about and getting very close to the truth. That would make Lawrence nervous, but he would be even more nervous because of what happened in 1981."

"I *knew* it! He was involved in Melvyn's murder. He left a suicide note."

"You're right, he was definitely *involved* and he certainly always *believed* he killed Melvyn. The real killer exploited that, manipulating Lawrence to help him in his nefarious activities. So for over twenty years they kept this apparent secret, that Lawrence really had killed Melvyn Strange. If Lawrence objected there was always the threat of reporting him, so he did as he was told. It wasn't a note he left, but part of a letter, put there by the person it was addressed to, the same person who killed him."

"But how can you be so sure?"Chris says truculently, "The killer hasn't confessed."

"Indeed," Jenner says, "and how would you know he hasn't confessed?"

"Well...it stands to reason, you wouldn't be talking like this...I mean it's obvious..."

"We know because we have a witness," Ettie intervenes, "someone who believes he saw one of his comrades cut down, but who really saw Melvyn being murdered."

"Him?" Chris says, pointing with sudden and superficial bravado at Thomas, "How could he have seen anything in 1981?"

"It was the day of the re-enactment," Jennifer says, "The players were all very excited and went onto the common still wearing their medieval clothes, just as you are doing now. But the camaraderie was false. Maggie and Monica detested each other, but there were other tensions. There'd always been a three sided relationship in which Lawrence and Melvyn were rivals. The party soon broke up and after the others left they were soon arguing."

"Thanks to Warren," Ettie continues, "the re-enactment was incredibly authentic and had reawakened the spirits of the past, always strong on the common. They were particularly powerful here, for unbeknown to Melvyn and Lawrence, not only was it the exact six hundredth anniversary of the terrible events on 15th July, they were haranguing each other on the very spot where Thomas's comrades had been secretly brought from the gibbets to be decently buried. Thrust from his suspended past and seeing how they were dressed, Thomas assumed Lawrence hitting Melvyn was one of his comrades being knocked down by a lord. Believing Melvyn was dead and panicking, Lawrence ran away. Melvyn was stunned, but not dead. Then Thomas saw someone else approach and deliver the fatal blow. This 'lord' was the third member of the triangle."

"Melvyn's attentions had developed beyond teenage hero worship to something much more serious and unwelcome," Jennifer says.

"He may have also been more than irritated by Melvyn," Jenner says, "In his desperation for attention Melvyn knew the object of his desires didn't fit the image of the clean cut young man he always fostered, though that only increased rather than diminished his passion. We found a signet ring at Lawrence's place inscribed MM."

"You see," Chris shouts, "It was her – Maggie Morton!"

Jenner shakes his head.

"No, not her, but another MM. Monica Martin as she was known then."

"Monica!" Chris shouts.

Jenner holds up the ring.

"Is this yours?"

"My God," Monica says, utterly stunned, "I've not seen that in..."

"Over twenty years? Yes, it was yours, probably stolen during one of the rehearsals. It was given to Lawrence as a present with the demand it should never be worn, a *special something between us*, a promise he kept to his dying day. Somehow Melvyn found out. He was hurt and angry. Jealousy compounded by humiliation. It was probably what they were arguing about. Unknown to the murderer, Lawrence left it at the place of his murder. It gave me an important pointer."

"For a generation the secret was safe," Ettie says, "Until now, Melvyn's body was never discovered, but ironically the killer's activities with the Waintree development led to his undoing. When the house was demolished in Hempston it unleashed the forces of the past, left sleeping since 1981. Believing his comrades had been cut down Thomas was fearful for his life and ran away. The house had been his resting place, but it was no more and he drifted back to the nearest thing unchanged from his own time, the edge of the common where the ancient woodland had been. Here he wandered aimlessly, but not for long. His anguished past was picked up by Warren's receptive spirit. Now he had someone to talk to though it was a confused and vague message of revenge and guilt."

"Warren was as confused as Thomas," Jenner says, "He thought he'd been communing with William Grindcobb, he'd even begun thinking he might *be* Grindcobb."

"He read about what had happened last year in London," Ettie says, "and so approached me. I agreed to meet him, but..."

"After failing to convince George," Jenner says, "Warren sought help from the only other person he thought would be sympathetic, who for years had helped him on his various projects. Frightened he'd be ridiculed he sought a quiet place for his appointment, here on the common, unknown to him an appointment with his killer. Warren couldn't understand the true significance of what Thomas had told him, but the confused and disparate ramblings with their constant references to revenge and guilt sent frightening signals to one who knew the truth. Convinced Warren had witnessed the tragic events, he decided he had to be silenced. Warren's death upset everyone, but particularly Lawrence, still harbouring his own guilt for a crime he'd never committed. Then there was the development and the land deals, the subterfuge, the corruption, the threats if he didn't keep his mouth shut. It was too much. Like Warren he made comments which were interpreted that he knew much more. He was no longer just embarrassing, but dangerous, so he too paid the price."

"In the 1981 re-enactment Melvyn Strange played the part of someone Thomas knew very well – one of the leaders, William Cadindon," Ettie says, "Not knowing precisely what had happened to his comrades he assumed he was witnessing *them* being cut down."

"He cut him down," Thomas suddenly shouts, "Tresilian!"

"Who played Tresilian in 1981?" Jennifer says.

The group is silent. Many glances, some knowing, some innocent, some enquiring are exchanged. Then someone moves away as if to run, but Jenner has already stationed two officers to bar any escape. At his signal the man is taken.

"Richard Tranter, I am arresting you for the murders of Warren Grover and Lawrence Bullock."

Rick struggles for a few moments, but the policemen hold him in a tight grip while Jennifer cautions him.

"You can't prove any of this. It's all hocus pocus, innuendo and how do you propose to call your main witness?"

George, Maggie, Monica and Chris – stare at him incredulously. Rick's question has already crossed his mind, but Jenner ignores it.

"The evidence will emerge," Ettie says reassuringly, "but there are more immediately pressing issues. Jennifer's exhumation brought Thomas into this time, but everything is out of sync. We have been at the rehangings in August. But the events of 15th July, that is today haven't happened and..."

"Haven't happened?" Jenner says.

"In the film it hasn't happened."

"This isn't a film."

"You were there. It wasn't a film studio, but what else do we call it? Then and now and both together, but the film is still the catalyst. The house that was demolished originally belonged to Martha's brother. Thomas disappeared as an outlaw, but he was neither a real outlaw nor really free. His guilt and yearning for revenge suspended him between times, but with Martha now living at the house, it became his place of stability. Now we must help him resolve his unfinished business."

"The house was demolished during the development," Jenner says bitterly.

"Contact with Warren forced him into the present, but when the house was demolished he was in limbo again, made worse when Warren was killed, severing his only link. So events have moved on. All the players in 1381 are being re-run in the film. It's no longer a film representing reality, accurately or otherwise, more reality aping the play. Real events and the film have fused...but it's not *right* for August to come before July!"

"He has to come back. He cannot stay here."

Maggie speaks slowly, carefully. This is no sensational eruption. As she talks the pitch and intonation of her voice

443

changes as if it's not really her speaking at all, but someone Ettie has heard before.

"He was not there on 15th July! He ran away."

Maggie speaks, but the voice gradually becomes that of Martha.

"Running away saved his life even if he became an outlaw, but he is consumed by guilt. He must come back for the deadline approaches and after it passes he will lose his chance to redeem himself peaceably. You must tell him *the time for running is over*."

Ettie wracks her brain. What deadline? Then she remembers and after checking with Charley's *A Little Liberty*, turns to Thomas.

"In November this year Parliament has issued a general amnesty to all those who sue for charters of pardon before the next Whitsuntide in 1382."

Thomas says nothing, but repeats several words quietly to himself – amnesty, pardon, Whitsuntide – though the only audible ones are 'Parliament,' which he pronounces with grim bitterness and 'Tresilian,' which he mutters slowly and deliberately. He looks at Rick, starts back, then clenching his fists at his side, walks resolutely towards him. Rick doesn't notice him until Thomas shouts 'Tresilian!' Rick turns with a disdainful leer. Thomas angrily repeats 'Tresilian' again, louder, demanding, threatening. Rick's expression changes, he's been recognised. Ettie watches incredulously, never believing she would see that face again. For now she also sees the hard faced chief justice, yet younger than he appeared before. Without the fine clothes he might even be a young man playing the part, one of an amateur group re-enacting the infamous prosecutor's activities in 1981, but to Thomas he is no actor, he *is* Tresilian.

"You struck down Will Cadindon, condemned him and the others, then viciously murdered him!"

Ettie wants to correct his error, but the uncanny resemblance to the awful man she'd seen entering St. Albans overpowers her and she's unable to speak. Rick looks between Thomas and Jenner, wondering which poses the greater threat and determined to escape from both wriggles between the two officers. Jenner tells them to "Hold the bugger." Ettie expects Maggie to speak again. She stays silent, but she too has changed. Like Rick her face has reverted to the player of her youth, yet it's also oddly different and the more she looks the more Ettie is sure. Like the voice it's the face of Martha.

"I will be avenged," Thomas says, edging nearer, though less threatening as if he expects a response from 'Tresilian.'

Rick says nothing and has even stopped struggling. Jenner is ready to stop him getting to his prisoner, but then Thomas turns back to Ettie.

"You talked of a pardon. You said I was an outlaw."

"Everyone who ran away is an outlaw."

"But the oppression. I have heard they have been cut down in Essex and in St.Albans men have been executed and imprisoned."

"It is over."

"But I am known. If I go back they will take me."

"Not if you return before the Whitsuntide deadline. You will no longer be an outlaw."

"No longer an outlaw," he repeats.

"The time for running is over."

Ettie turns in the direction of Maggie's voice, but the words are not hers. Thomas looks at her too and his eyes light up. Ettie looks back. There's no trace now of Martha in Maggie's face, but Thomas continues to stare at her. To him she is Martha and he is ready. In his mind he sees his house, his street, his friends, his own old world and longs to return.

"No longer an outlaw," he says again.

He and Maggie stare at each other, though he only sees Martha and his time where he is no longer an outlaw. He must go to her, speak to her. She stands by the recently excavated hole where his comrade was cut down. Now he too momentarily sees the skeletons Jenner saw earlier and suddenly he's back in that day, this day, 15th July, but now there is only one skeleton. They talk of 1981, not 1381. How can that be? Whenever it was he can't get that day out of his mind. Yet how could he have seen Cadindon cut down on 15th July? Wasn't that the day his comrades were executed in St. Albans? The dreadful scene sears his mind. But he wasn't there. With others he'd fled. For that he would always be guilty, for living when they died, for not even being there.

A man is getting out of the hole, like a ghost rising from the grave. Yet no ghost, no translucent image, but a real fleshy creature already up on the ground above while a second comes up behind, then a third and a fourth and a fifth. He knows the first man. It's Will Cadindon and he knows the others, he knows them all. He stands stupefied as more men get out of the hole, watching them, counting them. Cadindon stops a little distance away and the others gradually join him until the men stand in a line of desolate dignity. The last man appears and he alone turns as he gets up with a faint twitch of his lips, almost a smile. Thomas shudders. It is William Grindcobb and he is the fifteenth. They stand silent, gaunt, immovably soldier like, their eyes searching the horizon accusingly. As they watch they are watched for the others also see them now.

"It's them, isn't it?" Jennifer whispers, "The fifteen condemned men."

"They are returning," Ettie says, "To where they were on 15th July 1381."

Thomas drops to his knees, lowers his head and cries out.

"I am sorry I deserted you. I ran away to save myself."

"Did I get it right?" Jenner says quietly, slowly.

Ettie nods.

"We are really in 1381."

Grindcobb lifts his hands and turns to Thomas. They strain to discern his words clearly as he speaks in the distinctive intonation and strong accent of the late 14th century.

"There is no need to feel guilty. You cannot save us. You have done all you could. Why sacrifice yourself for nothing?"

Thomas replies in the same dialect

"But you will be avenged, I swear it!"

"You are still too hot and will remain so for some time," Grindcobb says, "The things we hold dear, which seem so far off one day will be achieved. In the distant future the people, cool and considered will wield the greatest vengeance."

Thomas shakes his head.

446

"I cannot wait that long. I see now *the time of running is over*. The only way to purge my guilt is to return, but I won't go back alone. I will take Tresilian with me."

He turns and walks back to Rick, but as he approaches with his ragged hair, fixed bright eyes and large dirty hands it's not just Rick that's uneasy.

"Keep him away," Jenner shouts, reading the alarm in his officers' faces.

Thomas stops, but leers malevolently at 'Tresilian.'

"It's not..." Rick begins, but is restrained by one of the officers as Jenner barks "Shut that bugger up!"

"You did this," Thomas says, shaking his fist at Rick, "these men can't hold you forever, I will have you then!"

He moves forward, but Ettie crosses his path.

"This is not Tresilian."

Jenner joins her saying, "Keep out of it, Ettie. Don't interfere."

She ignores him, saying, "The chief justice is in St. Albans, not here in the country. You are angry and rightly so, but this man is not Tresilian."

In his confusion, Thomas averts his eyes from Rick and looks from side to side repeatedly, saying "St. Albans, St. Albans."

"Yes," Ettie says, "He..."

"Ettie," Jenner tries again, "you must not..."

"...cannot be here. Tresilian is in St. Albans."

"Tresilian is in St. Albans," Thomas says, "Tresilian is in St. Albans...must get to Tresilian...must get to St.Albans."

Jenner tries one more time to intervene, but Ettie cuts him off again.

"Yes, in St. Albans. Tresilian is in St. Albans."

Thomas stops the lateral jerking of his head. Suddenly empowered with superhuman strength he wrenches Rick from the officers, the force of his attack shoving them back like contorted springs. Rick struggles, but a heavy blow to his head and shoulder from Thomas's elbow quietens him and he's dragged away.

"There are two Englands, even now," Thomas shouts to Ettie.

He hauls the inert Rick and runs towards the line of fifteen sentinels, awful reminders of anguish and courage. The two officers come after, their lumbering and furious boss, muttering 'don't let him get away' and 'bloody peasant.' Rick's feet slither along the ground like some disabled sledge. This slows Thomas, but he's still too fast for them and reaches his comrades, impassive, resolute, their determined innocence still accusing. He holds Rick in front of them like some trophy from the hunt. They say nothing. He is blameless. No one speaks or moves, everyone watches and then in a blink he and Rick are gone.

16

THE sentinels remain, but in the blustering, panic stricken search they go unnoticed. Jenner, Jennifer and the other officers scour and prod the ground as if it might suddenly open up and disgorge the two men like unearthed tubers from ripe potato plants. Ettie stares into the empty clear air into which the two escapees have evaporated, wondering if at any moment they might rematerialise. Then she too looks to the ground.

"The land gives up its secrets."

"You have your man," Maggie says coldly, but it's the voice of Martha, "but I do not have mine. He has to go back, you still have not helped."

"But we *don't* have our man," Jenner says, "They are both gone. Thomas dragged Tranter away, but how could he do it while the rest of us remain?

Ettie has no answer. If Thomas and Rick have returned to the 'real' 15th July, must they return too?

"Rick was changed, young again as he was in 1981," Monica says.

"So he is in his own time," Ettie says, "He and Thomas are the only ones who are."

"If Thomas was attracted when the skeleton was found," Jennifer says, "it must mean this is where the fifteen were originally interred after the people brought them from the gibbets. So does that put us in their time too? But I saw Melvyn's jacket which must put us in 1981."

"Maggie looked younger too," Monica says, "so she too is in..."

She stops suddenly. Maggie has gone.

"It can't be," George shouts, "Not with them!"

Panicked and distraught, he rampages in wide circles, flinging his arms impotently, successively blaming Ettie, Jenner, Monica, anybody until finally slumping to the ground.

"Are they gone to 1381?" he whimpers, "If we are also in the past we should be able to reach them!"

He turns to the others, but no one responds. While he's been shouting and abusing them, Ettie has taken Jenner aside.

"If only events remained in the correct order. Rehangings, executions, digging up bodies, two times, three times. If only I'd not talked about Tresilian in St. Albans."

"You were concerned that Thomas returned before the expiry of the amnesty in 1382."

"Because our situation can only resolved by him returning to the past, but it has to be today and this fateful day is over."

"It's not over," Jenner says firmly, "Think, what are the links?"

She considers this and then says, "Maggie with Martha."

"And George?" he says, nodding to the wretched man, now pawing the ground.

"He could be a link to Thomas, but we don't have Maggie... but we do have the continuing link, parallel to our own time... the film...but how do we get there and how do we get back?"

"We can only..."

Jenner stops. In the distance a familiar figure in coarse brown approaches. Ettie hasn't seen him. Neither has Jennifer or the officers. Monica is looking at George, while he grovels impotently on the ground. Jenner alone sees this man for to him he is special. He is speaking, but is too far ahead to be heard, but Jenner hears him in his head.

"Come and see me one last time, my friend."

"I can't," Jenner whispers, "I can't get to you."

"Come and see me for only you can save your friends."

Jenner sees the kind eyes, the care worn brow, the sad, but hopeful mouth. Then John Ball turns suddenly and is gone, walking in the same direction taken by Thomas. He has shown the way and breached the barriers of time and space. Jenner knows, they must follow.

"If we are quick we can do it, but we can't delay. Things have already started happening," he says to Ettie, taking her hand and waving to the others.

"It's too late," she says wearily.

"No, we can do it."

"Where are we going?"

He's about to say when a figure crosses their path and then another and another. So intent on their discussion they've ignored the fifteen. They have remained, but are no longer impassive. With the same rugged determination and hard relentless expressions, they walk one behind the other, Grindcobb at their head, heading straight towards them.

Even though she's surrounded by the cast and hundreds of extras and technicians Charley feels alone. She feels for Warren's book in her pocket. Bruised and tattered, it's become more than a reference aid. It's now a teddy bear, a comfort blanket and a talisman rolled into one, an indispensable companion. She pokes and prods, turns out her pocket, even takes off her jacket, but it's not there. She searches the ground, roughly pushing and pulling people away in her panic. She must have dropped it. She's lost *A Little Liberty!* She's even more alone, not just cut off from people she knows and trusts, but a terrifying loneliness of never again being able to *touch* her own world, an awful empty desolation.

Everyone mills around expectantly, gyrating in a slow centripetal mass. At its centre is a familiar structure she thought she'd never see again. The gibbets have mysteriously reappeared as if they never collapsed in the first place, as if what happened never was. They've returned to the studio. They never really left. This is the original set that inexplicably collapsed. They'll have to check it's safe. But it's not a film. It never was and the gibbets have reappeared because they've never fallen down. Not yet. For that was August and this is July. A figure suddenly appears on the scaffold. When she saw him before she was unsure if he was an actor...now she has no doubts. This is no player, but a real man. John Ball scans the crowd, his eyes lingering on Charley and when he turns to the crowd she feels he speaks particularly to her.

"The great tread down the little, the strong beat down the weak. The great robbers steal for greed. The little man may steal because he is desperate. The first is lauded and the second is hanged. But it will not always be so. Good people, what they do to me today may end my life on this earth, but it does not end our struggle for that is only just beginning. They can rip my body to pieces and leave it to be pecked by the birds and consumed by the beasts, but they cannot destroy us all. They can stop my tongue from speaking, but they cannot unsay what I have said and they cannot rip out what is in your hearts. In the dark winter days that lie ahead keep breathing life into our good fellowship so one day it will once more burst forth in the springtime of Truth."

Their eyes meet. Still he stares, still she stares back, locked together while the world waits, but the world cannot wait and she must end it. His eyes tell her. She knows what must follow. This awful day, 15th July has to unfold in all its brutal ingredients, but it is suspended and only she can release it.

"What now?" someone shouts.

"Shoot the scene," Charley shouts back, "Action!"

John Ball speaks for the last time.

"Our fellowship is our life, our true community. What we have done will live forever. Remember me, remember what we achieved and remember such days can and will come again."

Then they hang him, draw out his organs while he is still alive and finally cut him up into quarter parts. All this is done not for what he did, but for what he said. And this is no illusion, no special effects generated on a computer to be synchronised with his image later. This happens now and she sees it.

At the last moment the fifteen take a different path and with the same purposeful determination march into the distance. Suddenly they disappear and with them goes the relief Ettie and the others feel. For they have unswervingly followed Thomas and Rick.

"I thought they were coming for us," George says.

Ettie shakes her head.

"It's not us they seek, but we must follow."

"Never mind them," he says, "We should be looking for Maggie. Where is she?"

"The same place the men have gone, where Thomas and Rick..."

"Why are we wasting time? We have to get out of here. If they can get away, so can we. Do something!"

"It's not so eas..."

But before Ettie can finish George runs wildly in circles again, flinging his arms and shouting incoherently.

"I have to concentrate," Ettie says to Jenner, "There's not much time. Maggie and Charley could be in great danger. If I can fasten onto the past..."

George seizes her by the shoulders, shaking her violently.

"Maggie's in danger. For God's sake, woman, you have the power, you must get us out of here!"

Jenner grabs him, but George pushes him away, still shaking Ettie and shouting "Do something, do something!"

"Leave her alone," Jenner shouts, "Ettie needs to concentrate. Get away."

George keeps shaking, but Ettie is transfixed and limp like a rag doll in the hands of a peevish and violent child. At last Jenner manages to prise George away, hurtling him to the ground. Ettie stands motionless.

"Are you alright?" Jenner says, steering her gently away from George.

"Yes, yes," she mumbles.

"Blithering idiot, I ought to arrest him for assault," Jenner says, then calls to one of the officers, "Hold that bugger!"

"We haven't time for..."

Ettie stops as she sees the mist running like a tide up the common. They both turn the other way, but the mist is enclosing fast from that direction too.

"Too late," Ettie says, "If only I could have concentrated a little longer."

Within seconds the fog surrounds and intensifies. Bunched around the hole they can see only a short distance in any direction.

"We're marooned," George wails.

"We are in danger," Ettie says, "We cannot stay."

The gruesome, blood spattered scaffold is deserted except for two men crouching over John Ball's dismembered remains, unsure what should be the next grisly act in their horrid task. After a cursory examination they are still undecided and look up towards Charley. Are they actors, completing a tense and decisive scene or the brutal executioners gloating over their actual butchery? She stares back with a heady cocktail of emotions – disgusted, perplexed, irritated, exhilarated. Everything *looks* real, but she's learnt to trust her inner instincts rather than the superficial evidence of her eyes preserved in the artificial moment of a celluloid reality. That's no conclusion, no return to the safety of a *real* present. Where does the fabricated world end and the actual one begin? No studio was ever bounded by fields and sky. No 'actors' ever looked so menacing and at the same time so puzzled. Then she realises. They are asking her, pleading with her. But if this is 14th century reality why do they need to ask *her?* How can she know more than them? But she does know what must be on this day. The men wait, the crowd gathers, quietly, slowly, expectantly. The scene is not yet over. If only Ettie was here to advise...but she's not...it's up to her.

The fog is absolute. The common is not even dimly recognisable, no wraith like trees or ghostly bushes, nothing but impenetrable greyness, murky and impermeable as if they are enclosed in the solid rock of a claustrophobic cave. They huddle around the hole. It might offer escape into some unknown nether world but it's now a smooth bored grassless depression, colourless except for the pervading greyness that permeates the ground as much as the sky. No one speaks, but everyone looks to Ettie. It's not just the lack of any landmark or physical feature that heightens her anxiety. Before they couldn't be sure in which time period they were – far past, near past or present, even trapped in all three simultaneously. But the fog thrusts and imprisons them in a morass of *no time* and *no place*. It's very frightening and she looks back to the others in wretched impotence. Only Jenner is relatively calm.

"There has to be a way to get back," he mutters, his eyes, immovable and intent, locked onto something beyond the solid wall of mist.

His unflinching concentration restores some of Ettie's confidence.

"Tell me what you see?" she says.

"Like watching a film, fading as the scene ended. Except it's not ended and was no film...a scaffold, so vivid, so bestial... a man was about to..."

"Did John Ball speak to you?"

"We must follow the others to where we have been before. It's not yet completed, but it will be."

"You and John Ball have a special relationship. We have to be where he is. The film is the pivot. It's become past reality. It's not yet completed, but it will be."

"It doesn't matter," he says despondently, "Tranter is right. Even if we get back, I can't prove he did it."

"Getting back might itself provide the proof. If only we had something that linked us to the past, to the film."

"Or to someone who is there," he says, tapping the side of her coat.

"Warren's book?" she says, putting her hand in her pocket.

"No," he says, "Charley's book."

She pulls out *A Little Liberty*.

The scaffold is silent and empty. As the hideous moments unfolded thick black clouds obscured the sun and a baleful darkness descended over the scene. Now as the dreadful relics of what was once a man are taken away the sky brightens and the soul of John Ball moves through the crowd. His body may have been ripped apart, but his spirit is everywhere. In the fields and the forest, in town and country, wind and rain, above all in the hearts of men and women, his words spreading throughout the land to be reborn in future generations. Beyond the heaving and shuffling there's a drawing apart to make way for a peculiar procession. Plainly dressed men file through the throng accompanied by grim faced, yet oddly irresolute soldiers. They too feel the perverse passions of the day and though they will do their duty, it will be with heavy hearts and chilling memories that will grip and return for the rest of their lives.

The executioners return to the scaffold. The men are prepared below, waiting in turn to suffer the same fate as John Ball. Charley watches. She's given no instruction and no one has asked what to do. Standing a little way off more soldiers attend a small group. They have nothing to fear, the crowd, crushed and beaten down is quiescent. One man surveys the scene with concentrated intent. Charley doesn't know him. He's not the king, but must be important with his fine furs and colourful coat. The hard, merciless face frightens her. It has to Chief Justice Tresilian. She looks away. Events must proceed inevitably, yet this development doesn't seem right and his presence unnerves her. She's utterly unprepared and fumbles in her pocket. Then remembers with an ache of disappointment that's she lost *A Little Liberty*.

The first man is being prepared. She knows what must come. As a screenwriter this should be her greatest moment, filled with a tremendous sense of personal achievement, but how can she exult surrounded by so much barbarous misery? *It's only a film.* How often has she heard that phrase, it's banality even more hollow today? A second man is brought onto the scaffold. The sun is obscured by cloud again and wide orbs of ground are cast into dullness. It gets colder. She shudders, but not from the cold for where she stands the sun still shines. Perhaps it really is only a film for she feels an intruder, a player in her depiction *invading* the past. If it is a film it's one like no one has made or seen before. The film creates a distorted reality. The past is dead until revived by a Charley, each time recreated slightly differently like a succession of remakes, adding or subtracting from the one before until the original is lost in the mists of time. The past is only the present wound backwards. But what if the past is no longer seen through a glass very darkly in memories and inaccurate records? What if the film no longer becomes the past, but the past becomes the film?

A third man mounts the scaffold. No, this is the past, but there's discord, interference. Something taints it. In awestruck, terrified silence, the mass concentrates on the men on the scaffold, but like Charley one man stares at Tresilian. He's dressed simply like the others, but looks at the chief justice as an equal and with irritation rather than fear, as if they have recently been together only to be suddenly and forcibly parted. He edges through the crowd against the crush, away from the scaffold, gradually getting closer to Tresilian. She knows the face. Thomas, a man from the past she's seen in the present. She looks across to Tresilian and for a moment sees him in different, modern clothes. She blinks, rubs her eyes and now sees him in his long flowing robes. A trick of the dim sunlight, a disfigured image concocted out of her tiredness? No, whoever he is this is not the true Tresilian, but a man from the present masquerading as a man from the past. This interloper is causing the distortion. Is this the crucial time, 15th July 1381 or the present and they really are making the film?

A fourth man mounts the scaffold. The crowd is too many and too strong. Thomas is very close, pushing desperately but forced still like the fish swimming against the tide. Tresilian sees him and looks uneasy. He knows this man, but how can that be? Thomas was never brought before the chief justice. If only she had Warren's book. There are two others in the crowd, a man and a woman in modern clothes. Charley knows them. One waves a book. It's her copy of *A Little Liberty*. It's Ettie and Jenner! She tries to reach them, but the crush is too much and she climbs back to her perch so as not to miss them in the crowd. They are close to Thomas, but haven't seen him.

A fifth man is on the scaffold. Suddenly the mass surges forward and the quiet is broken as the throng jostle to get nearer. Ettie and Jenner are pulled closer to the front, but

Thomas holds his ground, leaving fewer people between him and Tresilian, who looks back anxiously. It's a tense moment and the soldiers jerk around nervously. Another man in modern clothes joins Ettie and Jenner. George is very agitated and constantly twists and turns, but not in fear because he pushes people away indiscriminately. He and Jenner are looking for someone.

"Not much time," Ettie shouts and then waving the book again, "It got us here. Past and present brought together!"

Charley can't hear, but lip reads. The crowd is so close to the remaining men at the base of the scaffold they might easily snatch them away. The soldiers push them back. Charley counts the men...nine...and five on the scaffold, making a total of...fourteen. Fourteen? It can't be, there should be fifteen! Someone is missing! How can this be real? They have no actor to play Grindcobb. Wesley Greville has disappeared so there cannot be fifteen. The present is distorting the past, the day cannot be! Now she sees no movement on the scaffold and hears no sound. Time is freeze framed. In the crowd only Ettie, Jenner and George are moving.

"Where is Wesley Greville?" Charley shouts.

She climbs down and makes her way through the static mass. It's like pushing through closely packed, but flexible bollards, secured at their bases, yet springing back and forth at the slightest touch. George hurtles in all directions like a child leaving a bent down trail in a cornfield. Jenner goes towards Tresilian. She can't see Thomas and her anxiety increases. By the time she reaches Ettie she is shaking violently.

"What's happening, is it me, is it the film, is it that man?" she says, pointing to Tresilian.

"You're safe!" Ettie says, "Now we must find Maggie."

"I thought we were living through the past, but it's still a film, or should be, but everything's at a standstill...if this is a film then how...fourteen, not fifteen...we have no actor, we have no Wesley Greville!"

"There is no Wesley Greville, there never was."

"I don't understand. You always said we had to keep shooting. We had to get through the whole of this day...this special day."

Then they see Tresilian, moving through the crowd away from Jenner.

"Why is he trying to get away?" Charley says.

"That's not Tresilian," Ettie says, "That's Rick Tranter, wanted for the murder of...never mind, we haven't time."

"He can move, but he's from the past like..."

"That's why he can move. He's not from the past, just like me and you, the chief inspector, George and..."

Then she sees Martha in the crowd, at first as still as a statue like the others. Then her lips move.

"He has returned."

But it's not Martha. Her modern clothes, her dishevelled hair, her eyes, her hands, everything different. It's Maggie. Then it's Martha again, then Maggie, then Martha.

"What is happening?" Charley says, "Is it the past or the present?"

"Both," Ettie says, "Soon if we find..."

"Over here!"

They turn towards Jenner's voice. He has caught up with Tranter/Tresilian and George is beside him. George's face and clothes change and distort, flicking between two times, two people.

"It's happening to him, just like her," Charley says, pointing back to Maggie.

Gradually the face from the past becomes clearer.

"This is impossible," Charley says, recognising Thomas again, "You always said he was never here on the 15th."

"Neither were we," Ettie says and then thrusts Warren's book into her hand, "Take it and hold it."

What was Martha becomes Maggie, what was George becomes Thomas and then back and forth again and again. Suddenly there are distinctly four and Ettie's fears are gone. Tresilian is no more and Thomas approaches where his form, now permanently changed to Tranter, has been. Jenner follows him and they reach Rick together

"You are the traitor," Thomas says.

Rick backs away.

"Who is this, is it George or...?"

Thomas gets closer. Jenner does nothing to stop him, but Ettie stands between them.

459

"You must return by Whitsuntide. You are no longer an outlaw."

"Keep him away!" Rick shouts, "For God's sake keep him away from me!"

"You admit to the murders of Melvyn Strange, Warren Grover and Lawrence Bullock?"

"Yes, yes, anything, just keep him away from me!"

Thomas leans forward menacingly.

"I have seen it, witnessed it. You did it. I will have my revenge!"

He has one hand outstretched towards Rick, while the other is about to push Jenner aside. Rick staggers back, holding his head, swaying from side to side.

"Okay I did it, I did it, but I didn't kill those others. Tell him I didn't kill those others. How could I? I wasn't there. I was on the common, not in St.Albans. I came on Melvyn and Warren and I killed Lawrence in his house. Yes, yes, I did for them, but not his people. Keep them away from me. God, I can see them, they are coming for me too! They're alive. They're not dead. Can't you see them? Keep them away, keep them away!"

Thomas elbows his way around Jenner and approaches Rick, but Ettie comes between them again.

"You must go back. The Whitsuntide amnesty deadline approaches. You have so little time."

"Go back...so little time?"

"You must go now!"

He turns around to where Martha stands. Everyone looks to her. She nods and then is gone. When they look back Thomas has also disappeared.

"Are we in past or present?" Charley whispers.

"The past," Ettie says, "Thomas is not here, he was never here on 15th July 1381. At last past and present are separated and resolved. He has returned and we have solved our mystery."

"Then we too can return?"

"Shortly, but first the past must unfold unhindered. The events of this day must continue to their resolution."

Then, no longer embedded like elasticated statues, the crowd murmurs and surges around them. There's activity too on the scaffold as they prepare the gruesome business of savage execution. Charley counts the men on the platform.

"There are fifteen now. Look, one is stepping forward. It's Wesley Greville, where has he been?"

"It's not Wesley Greville," Ettie says.

"But it *is* him. If he's not Wesley Greville, he must be..."

"William Grindcobb. He's been with us, from the beginning."

The crowd is silent now and Grindcobb speaks.

David Farley is proved right. Jenner's enquiries, the arrest of Rick Tranter and his confession to the three murders has wider repercussions. Nailing Tranter produces further contacts, opening up a financial scandal that broadens well beyond the Waintree development.

"You upset the dominoes and they're all falling over," David says, "We had all the pieces, but they were never going to fit together without somebody talking."

"It all unravelled from Tranter," Jenner says.

"At one stage you were ready to fit him up."

"Modern justice," Jenner says quietly, "taught to me by a man from the past."

"But you never said how you'd got him to confess."

Jenner doesn't reply. David goes on.

"I hear he's getting worse. Keeps talking about seeing men being cut to bits. Over and over again he says it. Then he raves about a bloke coming to get him, calling him Tresilian. I've done a lot of research, but I can't find a Tresilian with any connection."

"You won't," Jenner says mysteriously, "He's no longer around."

In the end there's so much material two films are released. *Hurling Time*, depicting the dramatic events in London is a major success, but the later 'sequel' called *A Little Liberty* stirs the public imagination even more. Many people come out of cinemas stunned by its 'realism' saying 'it wasn't like

461

a film at all,' feeling 'they'd actually been there.' It's almost seven years before Ettie returns to Welstead. Jessica Tennant arrives. They talk of many things, only peripherally touching on Jessica's great interest, the Revolt of 1381. Then Jessica asks if Ettie has stayed in the Old Fox Hotel before. Ettie is silent.

"My God!" Jessica says, "This is it, isn't it? This is the place you first stayed in...did you ever...hear or feel anything after Rick Tranter was arrested?"

Ettie looks from Jessica to the window and then back to Jessica.

"Only once, after that day..."

"...15th July, the same day John Ball, Grindcobb and the others were executed."

"I was preparing to leave the cottage and return home. I walked on the common one last time. Plenty of people were enjoying the brightness and warmth. It was as if nothing had happened, but then that's how it should have been. The land is unchanging. It had given up its secrets, why should anything have changed? I wandered up by Lock's Spinney. The air was suddenly very still and though no one was about I knew I wasn't alone."

"You saw someone?"

"I saw hundreds on the far horizon just as I'd seen them on the march those weeks before when I first arrived. Then I saw them no more, but I heard their marching getting closer and closer. I put my hands to my ears. Surely it was not starting again, but then I heard them marching away followed by a single woman's voice. The same voice I'd heard at the beginning. Martha. *He has returned before Whitsuntide. He is free.* Then nothing and I've seen nor heard anything since."

"They say Rick Tranter heard voices," Jessica says, "The vengeance of the past has finally taken him."

"Taken?"

"You've not heard? Died in prison, six years and seven months after his arrest, exactly the same time between the executions on 15th July and Robert Tresilian's death on 19th February 1388. He was executed for treason, you know. Amazing...uncanny coincidence, but then there are so many incredible aspects of the whole affair. I'll never know how you did it...naturally I can't expect you to divulge the secrets as it were of your professional arts...but your account of Grindcobb's final speech on 15th July. It can never be authenticated of course, but I have no doubt...let me see, I have it here somewhere..."

Jessica opens her bag.

"No need," Ettie says, "I can remember every word."

I go to my ancestors and my friends, for those I have known best have already gone. They wait for me. I only hope I am worthy of them. Like the sprits of our forefathers and foremothers, they move within us. They did not live to see our great events. They are gone. I can go to them. Did I not tell you it would come? Today they kill us, but they cannot destroy us. For whatever they say, whatever they do to you, your hearts are free just as we will be with you for all time. Where there is a love that transcends death there is no death. I have already embraced death so how can I fear this one? For as long as you hold fast to Truth there is always life. Do not weep today, for we only sleep, but if you forget what we have done our sleep will be forever. Always remember and wake us tomorrow into those truer, freer days I know must come.

Cross Cut

ISBN 978-0-9557928-0-9

"All darkness now. Silence, then the sounds again, scratching, voices. Someone is close, very close as if they're breaking through to him..."

Where is Bernard Weston? Is he dead or alive? How is his disappearance connected to the campaign to reopen the brooding and abandoned Cross Cut canal?

For Detective Chief Inspector Jenner a routine missing person enquiry quickly turns into something more sinister with the present dislocated against the turbulent background of 1840s Nottingham. Trusting his instincts as much to reason and logic and teaming up with Ettie Rodway with her psychic insight, he's forced to adopt unconventional methods. Combining their skills of intuition and deduction produces a powerful partnership, but this is stretched to breaking point as they try to avert disaster.

Looming ominously throughout this tense thriller is the foreboding atmosphere of the canal with its shrouded secrets and the fearful power of its tunnel to reach across time.

Can Jenner trust his gut feelings and take a path he's reluctant to go down? How much can Ettie risk her own safety to help him? Can they unravel the crime only in the present or must they step into the past?

Cross Cut is historical novel meets thriller, ricocheting through time, keeping the reader guessing to the end with its dark alleys, riots, foreboding tunnels and caves, gaslit docksides, terrifying train journeys and nerve racing pursuits across town and country, vividly recreating the desperate world of the past.

Out of Time

ISBN 978-0-9557928-1-6

"...a tall angular figure appears, dressed all in black with sharp penetrating eyes, a long nose and short black hair ... she flies around the whole circle, accompanied by the ear splitting clamour of the birds and the whoosh of her black cloak, pointing her finger in menacing jabs..."

International financier Sarah Layman wants to discuss a 'mystery' with freelance journalist Carla Diemer, which has nothing to do with finance. Carla arrives to find Sarah dead and is immediately embroiled in a murder investigation led by the dogged Chief Inspector Jenner.

Carla links up with psychic investigator Ettie Rodway, who has also been approached by Sarah. Joining them is a maverick historian, obsessed with a lost Anglo Saxon Chronicle and Carla's dubiously motivated father. Their perilous search of revenge, discovery and intrigue spans 1200 years, from the perilous wetlands of eastern England to the shrouded hills of the west and even to America, pitting them against forces of power, greed and deception.

From the 9th century they must find a ring, a sword, a brooch and a belt, which can solve the mystery, but also unlock immense unpredictable powers, sweeping them into the swirling currents of a distant age where fearsome warriors fight out their bloody inter family feud. Confronted by ruthless adversaries intent on the same discovery further deaths follow, the hunters become the hunted and they realise the Chronicle is much more than an obscure historical document.

A riveting quest, combining mystery, thriller, detection, historical drama and the interplay of past and present, Out of Time unravels against this tense atmosphere, penetrating to the heart of origins and identities in which friend and foe are difficult to disentangle. Once the past's magical powers are invoked, all the pieces have to be fitted together against a frightful deadline in which Time could itself be the ultimate victim.

...only those that dream can return from the far journey...